Time Tree

THE GUARDIAN

Lisa Rae Morris

AUTHOR ACADEMY elite

Library of Congress Cataloging-in-Publication Data available upon request.

ISBN 978-1-64746-188-1 (paperback)
ISBN 978-1-64746-189-8 (hardback)
ISBN 978-1-64746-190-4 (ebook)

Library of Congress Control Number (LCCN): 2020904656

This is a work of fiction. All of the characters, persons, organizations, and events portrayed in this novel, other than those in the public domain, are either products of the author's imagination or are used fictitiously.

Cover design: Elena Karoumpali, L1 Graphics
Back cover photo of Ford Mustang by Paul Raab,
courtesy of Vanguard Motor Sales
Author photos: Leslie Fairman Photography
Interior design: Chris O'Byrne

Printed in the United States of America

For Jennie...

Life giver, life changer, relentless advocate.
Thank you for shaping my life with stories.

Prologue
Sedona, Arizona ~ a.d. 1400

A murky vapor hovered in the dim desert air, listening. With lidless eyes, he fixated on a modest hut of red stone, which sat solitary amongst the junipers about a furlong's distance away. Its occupants had their lamps burning—unusual during the hours just before dawn.

A piercing cry broke the desert stillness. He grimaced. *Another one.* These creatures, the least worthy of all living beings crawling this planet, had increased again. That would explain the additional enemy that had reported for sentry duty nearly a year ago.

He slinked along the ground like a globulous sea creature, taking a circuitous route to an opposite vantage point, hoping to learn something further. It was a risk, drawing this close to the ancient, twisted juniper so jealously guarded by this lot. He could feel the tree's irritating vibration as he crept nearer.

He squinted into the distance. *Perhaps this offspring is only another useless female.* The walls of the little house were merely a thin barrier to his eyes. Behind them, he could see the Guardian tending to his wife. She held an infant to her breast... *a male, this time. The usual curses never work on these creatures!*

One of the enemy, the latest to arrive, stepped forward on the threshold of the house, directly in his line of sight to the newborn. *They know I'm here.*

"You have no business here, Skliros," the enemy called out casually. "You never shall." He rested his luminous hand on the hilt of his sword. "But you already knew that."

Skliros spat out some choice blasphemies, loud enough for the entire guard to enjoy, before he streaked away into the twilight. He finally slowed to a stop when he reached his own red stone structure, which rested against a sheer cliff face several miles away.

"What news, Red Ba'al?" asked the undulating shadow that had crept up beside him.

"It's male!" he snapped. "It seems the line must continue."

"Ever so," said the shadow.

"You needn't remind me, Vroma."

Vroma shrank back in fear of reproach, but something else had caught Skliros's attention.

"What is the strange stirring among my people here?" he demanded. "Their energies are restless."

"They are leaving, Great One," Vroma simpered. "It was decided only yesterday. They go to join their people on the plateaus."

"Their fealty is fragile," Skliros growled. "Have I not been good to them?"

"Always, when it suits you."

"And look at that!" He pointed to the cliff face above the uppermost wall. "A most devoted portrait of me in my radiance, holding up the moon and multiplying their herds. Have I not been a generous god?"

Vroma hesitated.

"Speak!"

"Perhaps, oh Great One, the recompense you exact has grown... *costly* of late."

"Costly?" he seethed.

"Human beings treasure their infants. They become uneasy when too many are taken."

"Good riddance to them, then!" Skliros let out a grumbling roar so loud that its waves pierced the veil into the physical world. A few of the closest humans stirred on their sleeping mats, suddenly awake, eyes wide with an awareness of some hidden horror.

Vroma, too, had backed away several paces. "So we shall not follow them?"

"This..." Skliros gestured around him. "This is my kingdom. *My* place. Shall I trail after a herd of faithless humans like a common vagabond?"

"The god of the plateaus is formidable, as well," Vroma added.

"I fear no one!" Skliros boomed.

Several humans jumped from their beds, suddenly motivated to get an early start on their packing.

"I could easily have the plateaus for my seat, and everyone upon them at my feet if I wished," Skliros continued. "But this is the choicest of dominions. I shall not relinquish such an advantage. Even the human creatures can sense its energy. More will come. When they do, they shall celebrate me in whichever way I choose."

"The Guardians of the Great Tree will not," Vroma cackled, backing away from Skliros once more. "Many times have you attempted to appropriate its power and failed."

"It is mine already," he smirked. "It cannot lie secret forever. I will reveal it to the world as a symbol of my mystical power."

"*Mystical* power?" Vroma mocked. "The mystics only worship The Three."

"Not if I can help it." A fiendish grin flickered across his shadowy face. "Perhaps I will spare their infants next time. Instead, I will draw the humans to worship at the energy portals among the rocks."

"Portals?" Vroma scoffed. "Merely the earth's natural magn—"

"They will believe!" Skliros guffawed. "I will bide my time until the moment presents itself."

"When more humans come, they will see that your people have abandoned this place. They may not worship you so easily."

"They can worship themselves, for all I care. After all, it is not merely human lives that The High Prince demands. It is eternities."

Chapter 1

Tucson, Arizona ~ 1965

E ugene Thomas clicked off the desk lamp over his work table and closed his notebook. He rubbed his forehead and squeezed his eyes shut, still seeing lines and letters floating across his vision. He glanced at his wristwatch. Almost a quarter to ten. He'd gotten more tree ring samples analyzed and catalogued in the last four hours than he'd been able to do all last week during regular hours. Having people around meant constant interruptions. Not to mention the distant thrum of heavy construction equipment banging away above his head all day. He could tune it out, of course. But it was annoying to have to. A waste of his mental energy.

At least these cramped quarters were temporary. The tree ring research lab, with its groundbreaking contributions to multiple scientific fields, deserved its own space… its own complex! Someday, he'd be running this place. He would bring it the prestige it deserved. They wouldn't be mapping out the history of the world from windowless rooms in the bowels of a football stadium for much longer. Once his thesis was published, funding would pour in.

He relished the stillness of the deserted lab. Being nocturnal had a certain appeal….being his own man, answering to no one. People can't criticize, complain, or comment if they're asleep. But even as glorious as the past hours had been, the grit of fatigue

1

had begun to gather in the corners of his eyes. He sighed and pushed back from the desk, idly wondering if Eva was awake.

I hope not.

She had been so… *off* lately. Sure, he'd been a little busy the past year. He was doing important work. It's not like he could spend every spare second talking to her. He couldn't remember most of their last conversation, just that it had mostly consisted of her rattling off a list of things he wasn't doing right, in that matter-of-fact tone that made his brain boil.

He lit a cigarette and took a few puffs to fortify himself. Then he donned his jacket and stuffed a few manila folders full of field notes, along with his notebook, into his satchel, and headed for the exit. As he emerged into the chilly March night, he zipped his jacket and glanced up at the sky. It had snowed in Tucson this time last year, and it felt like it might do it again.

The west side of Arizona Stadium was surrounded by scaffolding. A construction crane perched to one side, a giant sleeping bird guarding its concrete nest. The lab was tucked away in the dark below the ten thousand new stadium seats being piled on. Eugene rolled his eyes. *Over a million dollars of the university's money, just so more people can watch a bunch of knuckleheads toss a football. I could do with a million dollars.*

It was a fifteen minute walk home, not even three quarters of a mile west. Normally, he used the time to think. But tonight, he felt a fresh wave of annoyance as the wind bit into the back of his neck. If Eva didn't always insist on having the car, he might actually be warm right now.

Eugene cut across Highland Avenue and down Lowell, head bowed, muttering against the cold. He spent two cigarettes arguing with Eva in his head, but he knew what she'd say. And how she'd say it. And her mousey brown hair would probably be in those stupid rollers while she said it.

He crossed Park, making a beeline toward his usual shortcut between a couple of residence halls on his way off campus. Over on his left, he heard a small gasp followed by a curse. He glanced up and took in the strange sight of the person who had made the sound. It was a woman in a dark coat that was fitted and flared to match her long, full skirt. She also wore a plain knitted scarf and a strange antique hat. Her blonde hair was wound into a loose, messy bun underneath, and her exasperated face was smeared with dirt. She turned and kicked the gravel with a dainty buttoned boot.

Eugene stamped out his cigarette and approached. "Uhh… do you need some help there, Miss?"

She whirled around.

"Sorry if I startled you," he chuckled.

"Oh," she breathed. "I'm fine. It's just… the stupid strap on this bag keeps breaking, and it's… Ugh!" She huffed in frustration.

"I can see." Several books, a few articles of clothing, a makeup kit, and two lipsticks lay scattered in the landscaped bed just outside the entrance to the dormitory.

"Here…" He laid his satchel on the sidewalk and began to collect the items and stuff them back into the ruined bag.

"Oh, you don't have to," she objected.

"No, I'm…" He smiled up at her. "I'm happy to." He looked at her more intently. Even beneath the odd hat and the dirt on her cheeks, he could see that she was beautiful. Strands of blonde hair framed her large, blue eyes. The gratitude in her face warmed him. He returned to gathering her things, feeling her presence as she stooped to join him.

She reached for a lipstick that had rolled beneath a small prickly pear cactus, and snatched her hand away with another curse. "Sorry…" She looked sheepish.

"Mean old cactus," Eugene sympathized. "I'd have cussed him worse. Let's see." He offered her a hand.

Tentatively, she reached out. He took her hand gently in his, and examined it. It was soft and delicate, like a little bird.

Sure enough, a small cactus spine protruded a few millimeters out of the back of her hand.

"Oof. He got you. Okay if I pull it out?"

She squinted in anticipation, pressing her full lips together, and nodded. "Do it quick."

"I'm Gene, by the way," he said.

"Nice to meet you, I'm—"

He pinched the end of the spine and pulled.

She sucked her breath through her teeth. "I'm gonna set that cactus on fire!" she growled. A small drop of blood formed on her hand.

He held up the spine, chuckling. "That, I'd love to see. Maybe I'll help you. What did you say your name was?" He still held her hand.

"Kat." She smiled.

"Like Katherine, or like kitty-cat?"

"Like Kathleen," she corrected.

He held her hand up, tilting it in the dim light of the street lamps. "Well, Kat, it looks like you have glochids."

"Excuse me?"

"Those little prickly hairs off the cactus."

She pulled her hand back, peering at it. Tiny, almost translucent cactus spines glistened against her skin in the orange light. She cursed again. "I'll be up half the night pulling these out! Who in the heck plants cactus on purpose, anyway?"

"You must be new here, because the place is lousy with 'em. You a freshman or something?" he asked.

"Yeah. New here, *and* new to town. My parents and I just moved from L.A."

"My condolences."

"Yeah," she sighed.

"Still, it's a good school. That is, it will be if they ever finish it!"

"No kidding! Look at that dorm going up across the street. What a racket all day long!" She looked at her hand once more, and moved to rub it.

"Don't scratch it," he warned, giving her wrist a gentle squeeze. "Got any rubber cement?"

She frowned. "Maybe?"

"Put a nice thick layer of rubber cement on that hand. Let it dry, peel it off. The prickles will come right off with it. It'll be a cinch."

"Really? Gosh, thank you. I've never heard of that trick!"

"It's nothing. Glad I happened along." He used the toe of his brown loafer to slide her lipstick a safer distance from the offending plant, and popped it into her bag. "There now," he said, handing the bag to her. "That's a beach bag. No wonder it broke... you've put too much work and not enough fun in there. You need a serious college bag if you're going to make it as a coed."

"Thanks." She smiled up at him, eyes bright. "I'll have to go shopping soon."

He grinned at her, drinking in the pleasant feeling of having a civil conversation with a woman for a change.

She turned for the door, but he stopped her. "Can I ask..."

"Yeah?"

"Why are you dressed like a Victorian era beggar woman?"

Her white teeth sparkled as she let out a melodious laugh. "I'm not!"

Eugene raised an eyebrow.

"I'm dressed like an *Edwardian* era beggar woman," she teased. "It's far more modern."

"Silly me!"

She laughed again. "It's my costume. The College of Fine Arts is putting on *My Fair Lady* this week. We just had our last dress rehearsal. Tomorrow is opening night! Surely, you've at least seen the posters around campus."

"Sorry, no…" He shook his head. "I stay pretty busy with my graduate work…"

"Oh, how groovy! With like, a thesis and everything?"

He gave her a sideways grin. She was… what was the word? *Adorable.*

"Yes, with a thesis and everything."

"I'm a theater major," she stated proudly. "When I graduate, I'm going back to L.A., maybe even New York."

"You'll be a smash!"

"You bet I will!"

They laughed together.

"Listen," she said. "One of my castmates has an extra complimentary ticket for tomorrow night. I'd love for you to have it… y'know, as a thank you. For rescuing me from that dreaded cactus."

Eugene cocked his head. "*My Fair Lady,* huh?" he mused. "Audrey Hepburn, right?"

"Uh-huh! Did you see the movie?"

"Yeah, in December. I took my w—" He stopped short, not totally sure why. "I took my mother. She absolutely insisted I see it. She says I need to get out of the lab and get some culture once in a while."

"She's right!" Kat flashed him a winning smile. "So you'll come?"

"Well, I…" He wracked his brain. *What did Eva say she was doing tomorrow night? Tupperware party? Book club? Composing a poem about my faults?*

"Oh c'mon! It'll be fun! Pretty please?" Kat had gone from adorable to irresistible.

"All right. I'd love to."

"Fab! It'll be a gas, you'll see. I'll leave your ticket at will-call, okay? Gene what-again?"

"Thomas."

"Okay, Gene Thomas. I'll see you mañana."

He waved.

She disappeared into the building with a giggle.

His stomach jumped. *Nothing wrong with accepting a thank-you.* He lit another cigarette.

Five minutes later, he rounded the corner of his own street and headed up the front walk to the tiny flat roofed Spanish style house he shared with Eva. The house was nearing its fortieth birthday, and had certainly seen better days. One arched window glowed, leaving a stretched yellow rectangle on the sidewalk.

Eva was curled up in the armchair reading *Vogue* when he walked in. She was wrapped in her fuzzy pink bathrobe, with her toes splayed apart at grotesque angles, held apart by cotton balls. The living room reeked of nail polish.

Eugene grimaced as he shut the front door behind him. "Man, that stuff is nasty." He opened a window.

"Hello to you, too," Eva retorted, not looking up from her magazine.

A woman with a ridiculously huge, puffy bow enveloping her head gazed blithely at him from the magazine cover, likely without an intelligent thought in her brain. Eva wore an almost identical expression.

"I think you should quit smoking," she said, as though they were somehow already in the middle of a conversation. "It says here that 'the smoking picture is not so hot' these days, and that we are 'consumers too soon.'"

"What the heck is that even supposed to mean?" Eugene dropped his bag on the floor and kicked off his shoes.

"I always trip on those when you leave them by the door," she said, still not looking up.

He picked them up and dumped them into his matching armchair. "Happy?"

She ignored the gesture. "It means that people started smoking before any big questions were raised about whether it's a healthful practice. I don't think it is."

"I'm twenty-eight years old, Eva. I'm not a child, and you're not my mother. Just leave it alone, okay?"

"Fine. Die of lung disease, then."

"I'm not dying of lung disease. On the contrary, smoking relaxes me so I can listen to you complain."

She glared at him and slapped her magazine down on the footstool, revealing the article she'd been reading, opposite a full-page ad of a woman wearing only nail polish. Its caption read, *Basic Pink goes with absolutely nothing.*

He noticed that Eva, too, was wearing Basic Pink.

"What is that smut you're reading, anyway?" He reached down and flipped the magazine closed. "And if you want to talk about healthful practices, how about the way you fill the house with that toxic stench and then make us both breathe it?"

"Fine, I suppose I'll just sit outside in the freezing cold while I dry, so you can light up another one, Marlboro Man!" She stood and penguin-walked toward the door, calling over her shoulder, "And don't think for one second that I don't know about the smut *you* read!"

Eugene gritted his teeth, holding back a few choice expletives.

"Go ahead, if you want the neighbors seeing you like that."

"Oh, who cares what anyone thinks?" she snapped. "My own husband doesn't care, so why should I?"

"Maybe you don't," he agreed. "You barely have a waistline anymore, sitting around the house all day. Nail polish isn't gonna fix that!"

Eva's face went red. "Yeah? Well maybe it's because I'm p—" She stopped herself.

"You're what?"

"Nothing. Just… never mind." Her shoulders sagged. "I feel queasy."

"Then go to bed," he replied without feeling. *What a surprise. I might as well get her some jewelry engraved with the words 'Not tonight, Dear.'*

Eva stared at the shag carpet, unmoving. "I should have listened to my mother when she told me to finish my nursing degree."

"Hey, you didn't have to quit school and get married," Eugene shot back. "Nobody had a gun to your head."

"Yeah, well…" She looked up, her eyes beginning to moisten. "You were a lot nicer back then."

When Eugene opened his eyes the next morning, he had the feeling that he'd spent the night thinking rather than sleeping. He must have slept, he reasoned, because he'd woken up. Yet somehow, he could remember his brain chewing away at ideas the entire time… the volume of work to be done for his thesis, the freezing walk home. Eva, looking for all the world like she couldn't stand the sight of him. Then there was that blonde freshman. *Kat. Oh, to be eighteen again.* He'd almost forgotten that life wasn't all work and research and bills.

That's right. I'm still in my twenties, for crying out loud! I should be having more fun!

He sat up. Eva was still asleep beside him. He crept out of bed and headed for the shower, careful to step over the floorboards that he knew would creak. It wasn't so much a concern for her sleep as a desire to avoid another conversation.

As the hot water pounded his back, he thought about how much things had changed in five years. Eva used to hang on his every word, having him describe all the details of his scientific research to her. When he'd explained how much they could learn about the past from tree rings and underground mineral deposits, she'd been so interested. *Acted* interested. She'd been

9

so proud to marry a future professor. *Or just eager to live off a good income and impress her parents?*

He scoffed. *I was completely fooled. As if Eva ever gave a rat's behind about applied geophysics, geochronology, or dendroarchaeology. Or my career. Or me.*

He tried to remember what he had loved about her five years ago. She was... *what was she?* Suddenly, Kat's face flashed into his mind, looking up at him with those big blue eyes. *No... Eva, what was Eva like when I met her?* All he could picture was his wife's face glaring up at him from behind her fashion magazine.

He shut off the water and pressed the towel into his face. *She hates me.* He searched his mind for a reason. *Maybe I'm not raking in the cash fast enough for her? Not my problem. She knew what it would be like before she said "I do."*

Towel around his waist, he lit a cigarette and wiped the fog off the mirror with his fist. Halfway through, he remembered: *She hates it when I do this.* He could hear her voice in his head: *"It leaves streaks all over the mirror!"* He shrugged and completed the task, then lathered his face with shaving cream. *So don't look in the mirror so much. Problem solved.*

As he shaved, he returned his mind to the task of remembering something, anything, appealing about his wife. Her cooking was... okay. She did her household duties, but she always seemed to find reasons to harass him about it. She spent his money just fine, too, though she never thanked him for it. Kat's face reappeared in his mind. She had shown him gratitude, even for something as small as helping her out for a minute. *How hard it is to say "thank you" once in a while?*

He dabbed styling cream into his hands, smoothed it through his dark brown hair, and combed it to perfection. Nice straight part. Not too Elvis, not too Cary Grant. Something right in between. He winked at his reflection.

Finally, it came to him. *Eva was smart in school.* He had liked that about her. *Good. There's one thing.* He tiptoed to the closet. *Evidently not smart enough to realize I'm out of clean shirts.* He sighed and pulled out yesterday's shirt and tie, dressed, and meandered to the kitchen. *Man, she sure sleeps a lot. Gotta rest up for another hard day sitting around the house, I guess.*

He checked the cupboards for coffee, only to find a jar of instant coffee crystals. *Can't even be bothered to percolate coffee anymore either, I see.* He left it on the counter. His visions of sitting down to a nice cup of coffee and making some progress on his thesis had evaporated, so he shoved his loafers on, grabbed his bag and jacket, and headed outside.

A gust of cold, dry wind smacked him in the face, setting his teeth on edge. He glanced at the blue Beetle parked in the driveway, and briefly considered jumping in. But he didn't want to deal with the phone call he'd get from Eva later about how trapped she felt at home.

He headed into the wind. As he trudged by Arizona Hall, he chuckled to himself when he saw the Dreaded Cactus. He thought about Kat's soft hand. *I wonder if she got the rest of the spines out. Did I really say I would go to her play tonight? It'd be nice if I didn't have to walk there in the dark.*

The morning sunlight glinted off of something on the ground near where he'd stood with Kat last night. He jogged over to take a look. It was a rhinestone earring. *Must've fallen out of her bag, too. It would have been easy to miss in the dark.* He pocketed it, making a mental note to return it to her tonight.

Twelve minutes into his fifteen minute walk to the lab, he had made a decision. All this walking in the cold was for the birds. He wasn't some high school kid. He would just have to get his own car. He was only teaching two classes today. If he cut his office hours short, he could get out by three. It would be a bonus to avoid dealing with undergrads anyway. It was always the same inane questions, especially from those silly coeds. It was like they were making up excuses to see him. *Maybe they are.* He smirked.

By five o'clock, Eugene Thomas was seated behind the wheel of a brand new Mustang convertible. The burgundy color of it was like a racy red that had been toned down for sophisticated adults. The white stripe down each side and the red-banded tires asked for just the right amount of attention, he thought. He relished the feeling of the cushy black bucket seat and the easy motion of the four-speed manual gear shift. And even though one of his main reasons for buying it was to get out of the cold, he couldn't help but take a really long route home with the top down and the heater blasting.

He cranked the radio to KTKT just in time to hear Frank Kalil promise Tucson a full hour of top Billboard hits. He spun the volume knob even louder when the Righteous Brothers came on. He sang along at the top of his lungs. "You've lost that lovin' feelin'! Whoaaa, that lovin' feelin'… You've lost that lovin' feelin'! Now it's gone, gone, gone…"

Suddenly, he realized that the person next to him at the stop light was staring. He stared right back, smiled, and kept singing. This moment was too glorious to give away even one second of his happiness.

Eugene rolled up to his house almost euphoric. He cut the rumbling engine and took the front walk with a lighter step than he could remember having in years.

Eva opened the door before he reached it. Her eyes glanced over the car, her husband's face, and back to the car again.

"Well? What do you think?" Eugene beamed. "Two eighty-nine cubic inch V-8, rally-pac, power convertible top, air conditioning…"

"We're never buying a house, are we?" she snapped. "We're going to be renting this dump for the next twenty years because you just blew our savings on… *that*."

Eugene was dumbfounded at her reaction, yet he knew it shouldn't surprise him. Eva could ruin just about anything.

"How much was it?"

"I didn't blow our savings," he said, annoyed. "I got a great deal! This was the only one like it on the lot! I put ninety-nine down, and we can afford the payments."

"Payments?" She eyed him suspiciously. "How much?"

"I don't know the exact number... about fifty-three dollars a month."

She turned and walked back into the house.

"What?" he demanded.

"Fifty-three dollars a month? Are you crazy? Are we just supposed to stop eating or something?"

"Well *I* don't eat that much!"

Her mouth fell open. "I don't know how much you think I eat, since you're never home for dinner! And anyway, that's not an actual plan. If you were any kind of provider, you'd have a plan."

"Well, maybe we could buy fewer magazines, for starters!"

"Fine, that'll save you the trouble of hiding *yours* under the bed!" she shot back.

He huffed through his nostrils. "*That...* is none of your business!"

"Right, I'm only your wife."

"Yes. My wife. The person who is supposed to honor and obey. And yet I get nothing but sarcasm and disdain from the second I walk in that door until I go to sleep at night!"

Eva seemed to be trying to make herself taller. "You didn't even consult me! You just went out and bought a brand new car?!"

Eugene growled and threw his hands in the air. "*Why* should I consult you? Did you earn even a penny of that money? No! I did! And I'm the one who's gotta walk everywhere, Princess. Because her royal highness must have transportation to the stores so she can spend the rest of my money!"

Eva rolled her eyes. "Well I'm glad you got such a souped-up set of wheels with a great big engine, so everyone else can see how much you're compensating!"

His eyes narrowed. He cursed at her.

She picked up a vase and hurled it at his head, eyes welling with tears.

He ducked, a look of shock on his face. His anger reached a level he'd never felt before. He walked slowly toward her, eyes locked on her face, and stopped a few inches short of their noses touching.

She shrank back an inch, but held her ground.

"Is that what we're doing now? Throwing junk at each other? You *dare* threaten me, in my own home? Did you see that on a soap opera or something?"

She kept her eyes on him, but began to cry.

"If I'd done that, you'd have the cops here." His voice was low and menacing. "And if I called the cops on you, I'd look like a pantywaist, so you know I won't. You think that because you're a woman, all your drama and all your tears, and now trying to put a *mark* on me, is going to teach me a lesson? Hm?"

She cried harder.

"Well here's the lesson, your majesty. This is life with me. This is as good as it gets. If you don't like it, there's the door. Go be happy somewhere else. It's a free country. Find a man who will put up with you. Just be glad we never had children. It'll make things a whole lot easier."

She crumpled to the sofa and sobbed.

He sneered. "What, don't have the stomach for a fight anymore? Run out of things to throw?" He roughly tilted her chin to face him. Mascara ran in inky streaks down her face. "I didn't think so."

Eugene headed for the door.

"Where are you going?" she whimpered.

"Out."

Chapter 2
Vancouver, Washington ~ Present day

I ris's first full day back at Rookwood Senior Home had been peaceful, in a way that only a day full of canary droppings, unfamiliar songs, flying raisins, and cleaning glitter glue off of wrinkly people could be.

She walked out to her car, considering her day... and how she felt about having hundreds more just like it in her future. Being here without Angus was going to be tough at first, she knew that. Perhaps, after a time, she'd get used to it. She still loved the feeling of making the days brighter for these people. She had come to think of them as friends. And knowing that Will was right downstairs made her heart skip.

But something had been different today. She'd been hoping to feel that same spark of fulfillment she'd felt before, when she'd finally started connecting with the people here. But as much as she enjoyed their smiles, her mind kept wandering to the six crimson roses lying where Irene's pillow had been. How many more friends could she stand to lose?

And it wasn't just that.

Meeting Angus had ignited her soul. What they had done together, been through together, had impacted more than just a handful of people like what she'd done today. It had changed history. It had changed *her*.

She had merely set out to reunite him with his family. Instead, she'd experienced a love that transcended everything she thought she knew about friendship—the kind of love that laid down its life, regardless of the cost, just for the sake of knowing another person would be safe. There was something so unexplainably *right* about that.

A whole new universe had emerged—more mysterious than Iris had ever imagined—its architecture framed on principles of physics beyond the understanding of the keenest human minds. An entire world of ancient spirit beings and Guardian families shared a responsibility to protect it, even though humanity remained oblivious to their existence.

Most stunning of all, it wasn't governed by random coincidence, as she'd first supposed. It was held by *Someone*. Angus had called Him friend. He had been sure that this Someone saw her, heard her... knew her... and was guiding her to a destiny she'd never imagined.

God, Angus said you'd show me what to do next. I know that helping these sweet people is a worthy calling... but is it mine?

She unlocked her car door and reached for the handle.

"Iris Jacobs?"

Iris whirled around.

In front of her stood Jason Reynolds, her old science teacher.

"Mr. Reynolds, hi!" she breathed. "You startled me!"

"Sorry..."

"How did you know I was here?"

"It's in the database." He gazed intently at her. "I've come to talk to you on behalf of the Council of Guardians."

Her stomach fell into her shoes. She was afraid to speak. If he was talking about something else, and she said too much...

Jason laughed, his eyes merry. "I've freaked you out, I can see that. Iris, it's okay! Yes, *that* Council of Guardians. Your name's come up more than once in the central database. We

16

find it interesting when someone gets a mention back in the nineteenth century, and then another one in the twenty-first."

Iris finally found her voice. "Uh... am I in trouble or something?"

He suppressed a smile. "Why would you be in trouble?"

"I cut the Great Hawthorn... with an ax?" She looked sheepish.

Jason shook his head. "Sounds like it was a good thing you did. We've all read the MacCrann diaries. Every detail's been recorded. According to them, you were the hero in that scenario. Iris, you *saved* the Great Hawthorn, and everyone within its reach... for all of time!" He searched her face. "Do you realize how many people that is?"

"A lot?"

"*Countless!* The Council is impressed with you. You're the first non-Guardian ever to stand in the midst of a massive time disturbance and not only live to tell about it, you can still remember it. Means you can keep a secret. That's valuable to us."

Iris processed his words in amazement. *Talk about secrets... this man has been a Guardian the whole time and never let on? He's good.*

"W-well..." she stammered, unable to decide on an appropriate response. "Tell them I said... thanks for the compliment?"

Jason chuckled. "They want to offer you a job."

Iris frowned, her mind pinging from one thought to the next, unable to land on anything logical. She turned her back to her car and leaned against the door. "A job? What... I mean, how is that..." She squinted, trying to form a better sentence, but failing.

Jason was still smiling at her, his blue eyes twinkling from behind his horn-rimmed glasses.

Iris began again. "Darrick never said much about the Council... only that they passed some kind of resolution giving his family permission to talk to Angus and me. But I don't even know who they are. I thought the Guardians were just a bunch of families all over the world. But now you're makin' 'em sound like a corporation with an H.R. department."

Jason laughed again. "The Guardians *are* a bunch of families all over the world," he agreed. "But the Council of Guardians is something else altogether. Not a corporation... just a well organized, well funded group."

"A group of what? I thought Guardians always stayed near their Trees. How do they have time to hobnob all over the world, offering jobs to people they've never met?"

Jason's smile was contagious as he studied her. "Iris, I forgot how fun you are. Even in high school, you questioned everything! And I love this slight Scottish accent you've picked up. Is that all the time now, or just when you've been back home?"

Iris smiled back. "Dinnae ken. Still tryin' to decide. Both accents feel pretty normal to me." She shivered slightly as a chill seeped through the sleeves of her jacket. It began to drizzle.

Jason pulled the collar of his wool pea coat up against the biting January breeze. "Maybe we could talk somewhere warmer?" he suggested.

"Aye, let's just... I dunno, want to hit a coffee shop or something?"

"Best not," Jason said, looking at her over his glasses.

Iris's eyes widened. "Oh my gosh, I can't believe I suggested something so careless!"

Jason shook his head and smiled, pulling out his wallet and thumbing through it. He drew out a card. "You'll develop better instincts soon, don't worry." He reached inside his coat for the pen in his pocket, and scribbled on the back of the card. "Here's my address. Can you meet me in a couple hours? Say... six o'clock?"

Iris took the card and examined it. "You want me to come to your house? Like... where you live?"

Jason chuckled. "Yes, Iris. Where I live. Safest place I know of to talk away from listening ears. Unless you'd like to meet in a cave. But I'd rather not. I'm cold."

Iris smiled, feeling a little awkward. "Sorry, it's just... you're my old science teacher! I just got used to you having a first name besides 'Mister.' Now you're telling me you don't even live at the school?"

"Oh, the mysteries are only beginning!"

"Hey, should we order pizza or something tonight?" Charlie called from the kitchen. Iris's roommate stood by the open refrigerator in their tiny shared kitchen, one hand on her hip.

Iris joined her and began rummaging through the cupboards. "Nah, I'm going out tonight. I just need a granola bar or something."

"It's looking a little bleak in here, now that I've finished your parents' Christmas party leftovers. It's so nice when they invite me to their parties and feed me."

"My parents!" Iris blurted. "I never called them back!"

Iris's mother had texted her last night, asking her to stop by after she got back from Scotland. Between her preoccupation with Will and her mysterious conversation with Jason, she'd already forgotten about it. *I'm a terrible daughter.*

"No judgment here," Charlie said, "but that makes you a terrible person."

"What? I am not!"

"That's true, so why were you were thinking it?" Charlie said with a sly expression. "That's your guilt face. I'm just giving you an early intervention before you start spiraling into a full blown guilt complex."

"I don't spiral!"

"You're right, you haven't done it all year."

"It's January third."

Charlie smiled.

"I dunno…" Iris continued. "I guess I worry about disappointing them. I'm their only child."

"You're not their only child anymore. They've adopted me, too, remember? I have the quiche to prove it. Well… *had* the quiche. But if the way they brag about you to their friends is any indication, you're not in any danger of disappointing them." Charlie gave up on the fridge and opened a bag of tortilla chips.

"Well, maybe we should consider grocery shopping," said Iris. "I still can't believe you ate that cheese log for breakfast. Gives the 'Twelve Days of Christmas' a whole new meaning."

"It was perfectly fine!" Charlie protested. "Twelve days isn't that old, when you're cheese."

"*You're* cheese."

"The date on the package said May."

"How many times must we go over this? The date on the package is only good until y'open it! I swear, someday I'm going to come home and find you dead of food poisoning."

"Well when you do," Charlie said with an air of grandeur, "kindly remember to have my headstone carved into the shape of a holiday cheese log."

"I'll do that." Iris finally located one lonely protein bar hiding in the back of the cupboard under the cereal and tore into it. "So where's Will taking you?"

"Hm?"

"Didn't you say you're going out tonight?"

"Oh yeah. I'm not going out with Will. I'm going to see Mr. Reynolds."

Charlie paused mid-chip. "Mr. Reynolds, like… science teacher Mr. Reynolds?"

"Yeah, remember? He was helping me research some stuff?" As soon as the words left her mouth, Iris regretted them. Jason's recent involvement in her life was something that only she and the Guardians could remember, since it had been wiped from history after the Great Hawthorn had been repaired.

"I'm pretty sure you never mentioned researching 'stuff' with Mr. Reynolds," Charlie said with a look of growing curiosity.

Iris could feel her face getting warm, so she turned and exited the kitchen.

Charlie and her bag of chips followed. "Oh, c'mon, Iris! There's no way you're getting off that easy! Sooo… what are you researching?"

Iris shrugged. "Just a… sort of a project."

"What for? You haven't done anything remotely academic since you left college."

"Well, I can't really talk about it. Jason's expecting me in half an hour, so…"

"Jason? You call him 'Jason' now? Wait, isn't he married?"

Iris stared at Charlie, who was still holding a half eaten chip. "I have no idea if he's married! What does it matter?"

Charlie dropped her chip. "Of course it matters! What about Will?"

"Wha— Charlie! I just started dating Will. I'm not going to cheat on him, especially not with someone my dad's age!"

"All right, geez. No need to go full Scottish on me. I'm just looking out for you," Charlie retrieved her chip from the floor, blew on it, and popped it into her mouth.

"I know. And I appreciate it. I'm sorry, it's just a really long explanation. I could've sworn I'd at least mentioned it to you before, but you're right, I never did." She smiled as a thought occurred to her. "You know I've been wanting to do something history related since I graduated, right?"

Charlie nodded, a lock of blue hair falling into her eyes.

"Well, I've been thinking more and more lately about how science and history relate to each other in a lot of ways. I emailed Mr. Reynolds some questions a while back, and… he thinks he can help me. Y'know, with… some career ideas. That's all."

"You don't like working at Old People Manor anymore?"

"Rookwood Senior Home, and yes, I do. It's not that. It's actually really rewarding. But I just… I guess I just want to make sure I'm doing something I'm really passionate about. I don't know if I've found that yet."

"Hmm, see? Now was that so hard, taking two seconds to fill in your best friend so she doesn't have to assume you're making bad life choices?" Charlie smirked.

Iris stole a chip. "Would it be so hard to quit assuming the worst all the time?"

"No, but definitely less fun."

The address on Jason's card took Iris along one of the main roads that headed north out of Vancouver. As she turned into his tree-lined driveway, she was unsurprised to find herself within walking distance of her old high school. But as she squinted through the winter darkness, trying to get the lay of the property, a memory flickered in her mind. *Wait, doesn't this land adjoin an old cemetery? Kids at school used to spread rumors that Mr. Reynolds lived in a graveyard. That was actually true?* She used to drive by this place every day, but had forgotten it was here. The yard itself was a proper half acre of neatly trimmed lawns, trees, and bushes. But to the south, over a broken hedgerow, she could see the pale glint of tall Victorian era headstones resting in crooked rows.

Darrick was right. Nobody would bother the trees in a place like this.

She knocked at the front door. When it swung open, Jason Reynolds was standing in front of her, holding a raw steak with a giant fork. His blue apron featured a cartoon portrait of Albert Einstein eating a slice of pie while standing in front of a chalkboard that read:

πr^2
(ACTUALLY, PIE ARE ROUND)

"Iris! Right on time! C'mon in." He stood aside and let her pass. "I hope you're not a vegetarian."

She laughed. "Gosh, no. Love me a hunk of cow."

"Good, good!"

She followed him through the simple, spacious living room into the kitchen, where another man stood with his back to her, wearing a matching blue apron and chopping colorful bell peppers. He turned to smile at her. He had a striking full beard, deep russet in color, with wavy auburn hair, and eyes that seemed to be both blue and green.

"Iris, this is my son Grayson. This is Iris Jacobs."

"Hey, welcome." Grayson shook her hand. "Call me Gray, if you like."

"Nice to meet you." Iris returned his smile. "So you must be... the Guardian Heir?"

Gray turned back to his cutting board. "I am indeed. Although, not so much anymore."

Iris looked at Jason. "You're retiring already? You can't even be fifty yet!"

Jason opened two more packages of steak and plated them. "Just turned, actually." He shook liberal amounts of garlic salt over the meat. "In this family, we have a philosophy that those who've paid their dues get to retire as soon as possible and have fun, before they get so decrepit that it's no fun to have fun."

Iris laughed. "I like that philosophy!"

"Well, I *am* twenty-seven," Gray admitted. "Can't party forever."

"Yeah, you biology teachers," Jason huffed in mock disapproval. "Buncha party animals."

"Oh, you're a teacher too?" Iris asked.

"Yeah, I teach at the same school as Dad. It's been fun watching the kids have to start calling him 'OLD Mr. Reynolds' in order to keep us straight."

"Maybe that's what they tell *you*," Jason chuckled. "They tell me I'm just Mr. Reynolds, and you're 'Wooly Reynolds.'"

Gray stroked his beard. "Is it possible they've just been telling us both what we want to hear?"

"Nahhh," Jason shook his head. "High schoolers would never do that."

"So your idea of retirement fun is teaching high school… while getting a PhD in particle physics, if I'm remembering your email correctly?" Iris asked Jason.

"Well yeah! What Guardian has time for that?" Jason lifted the lid on a bubbling pot and poked several potatoes with a fork. "I could never have gotten through all those classes without Gray keeping an eye on things. It's a little self-indulgent, I admit. A PhD doesn't get you much traction, nowadays. But I've always wanted one. And pretty soon, I'll get to travel again. Haven't done that since…" He got a faraway look. "Well, forget how long since. Long enough."

"Can I help with anything?" Iris asked, shedding her coat and draping it on a nearby chair.

"Thanks, but I think we've pretty much got 'er made here," Jason answered. "You can keep us company."

Iris took a stool.

"So Iris, you're Scottish?" Gray asked.

"Oh dear," she sighed. "I guess I didn't realize how much my accent had come back."

Gray chuckled. "Why 'oh dear'? You don't like it?"

Iris shrugged. "It's not that. I guess I'd rather people focus on my words more than on my vowels. It's why I worked so hard to get rid of my accent in the first place. I've had a few people tell me they think it's cool, but I feel like if I keep on with it, I'll have to begin every new relationship with, 'Hi, I'm Iris. I'm Scottish-American, so I might sound odd sometimes. Please ignore it.'"

Gray laughed. "I get weird questions about my beard all the time. I know it's not the quite same thing you're dealing with, but it gets old, too. I just want to tell people sometimes, 'You know most men's faces do this automatically, right?'"

Iris giggled. "So we understand each other!" She sighed. "Well, maybe I'll just match the accent of whoever I'm talking to. That seems simplest."

"Ah, excellent. Remind me to introduce you to this guy I know who's from Kentucky!"

"Ha!" She crossed her arms, but smiled at him. "So... Grayson and Jason. Do your names rhyme on purpose?"

"Kind of," Jason replied. He fished a large cast iron skillet out of the metal drawer below the oven with a deafening rattle and placed it on the cooktop. "My wife, Gina, wanted him to be Jason Junior, but I wasn't having it. I need variety in my life."

"So she did the next best thing..." Gray said.

"Yes, picked a rhyming name and asked me about it when I was half asleep!" Jason chuckled at the memory. "I think she was trying to get my goat a little bit, too. I'd just found my first gray hair that week, and she named our child 'son of the gray-haired one.'"

"Well, it's true enough, now!" Grayson teased.

"Your turn's coming, Wooly Reynolds!" Jason said, waving a pair of tongs in his direction.

"Gina sounds like fun," said Iris. "Will I get to meet her, too?"

Both men's faces became a little more serious.

"I'm sad to say you won't," Jason sighed. "Gina passed a few years ago."

"I'm so sorry," Iris murmured.

"Thank you, but... I'm okay. We spent our best years together. And I still have this guy around to give me a hard time." Jason lifted the steaming pot to the sink, dumped the boiled potatoes into a colander, then back into the pot, adding an absurd amount of butter. He looked around the kitchen, glasses completely fogged over with steam.

Iris giggled.

"Dad, what are you doing?"

"I'm looking for the spud contriturator!"

Gray rolled his eyes, with a sidelong smile at Iris, and handed Jason a potato masher.

Once they had settled into their meal, Jason spoke. "Iris, you're probably dying of curiosity by now. I'm sorry for just springing this job thing on you out of the blue—it probably came across a little weird at the time. But based on what I've read about you in the central database, you seem okay with weird."

She nodded. "It's getting easier all the time."

"You had some questions about the Council of Guardians. Shall we start there?"

"Yes, before you tell me what the job is, it'd be nice to know who's asking. You said they're a well-organized, well-funded group, right?"

"Accurate, but not the whole picture. They probably sound a little mysterious, but truth be told, it would be safe to think of the Council as a big group of grandfathers who give great advice."

"Grandfathers?"

"Yes, quite literally. Every Council member is a retired Guardian with a lifetime of experience. Membership is completely voluntary, but a Guardian only qualifies once his son has taken over."

"So these Guardians join the Council and then just… give great advice?" Iris asked. "Don't they make laws or something?"

"No, they don't make any laws." Jason shook a bottle of steak sauce. "When they pass a resolution, it's just a consensus about how to handle a given situation. They talk amongst themselves about a problem, sometimes for weeks, and then issue a formal recommendation. The reason people follow their advice is that most often, it really is the most sensible way to solve an issue."

Iris poked her salad. "Do people ever ignore their advice?"

"It happens," Gray answered. "But c'mon… if you could ask a panel of a thousand seasoned experts to help you solve a dilemma, and they pooled their wisdom just for you, why would you ignore it?"

"Makes sense." Iris nodded. "So what about the… well-funded part?"

"Ah, yes," Jason chuckled. "Well, that's just part of Guardian culture. Because of how we live, we've come to be a very forward-thinking people. It's a unique challenge, adapting to a shifting environment in order to stay in one place. Keeping our Trees protected today is only part of the job. It's also doing what needs to be done to keep them safe in the future. In some parts of the world, things haven't changed in thousands of years, and the Guardian job is pretty straightforward. But here, keeping a Great Tree undisturbed gets a little more complex. It can mean buying real estate, developing land, political lobbying… and it certainly means investing wisely so that if protecting a Tree becomes a more full-time occupation, we aren't stuck in a job with no way out."

He dunked a slice of bell pepper into his mashed potatoes, chewed thoughtfully, and continued. "So because we need that flexibility, we always set aside a good chunk of our income for our sons to inherit. Every Guardian benefits from the legacy put in place by the ones before him. After a family's been doing that for a couple millenia, it tends to add up." His eyes twinkled. "And when it comes to the Council, the members themselves donate from their surplus whenever there's a need."

"So... you're saying that most Guardians are rich?" Iris asked.

Grayson laughed. "Uh, they *tend* to be, but it's not part of our culture to act like it. Money attracts attention. And anyway, it's only money—a means to an end. Having money doesn't change who we are."

"But... neither of you actually *has* to teach?" Iris was still having a hard time processing their lifestyle.

"No, but I love it," Gray replied. "I can't imagine doing anything else!"

"Most of us work side jobs, just for the joy of it," Jason added. "Between the two of us, we actually have three salaries. Two for teaching, and another fifty grand a year for being federally funded cemetery caretakers. It's basically glorified yard work, since this is a historic site—no funerals here anymore. Because of our inheritance, we don't really need the money, except for steaks and the occasional PhD. But the more we live like everyone else, the less curious people are about us. Plus, if something around here were to change, we could build a museum around that tree outside if we wanted to. That's really the point."

"Besides, the alternative to our teaching careers would be sitting around all day, staring at each other," Gray added, eyeing his father. "Not a pretty sight."

Iris helped Gray clear away the dinner plates, while Jason put on a pot of coffee and dished up thick slices of his homemade apple pie.

"I'm not sure I can eat all this!" Iris laughed when Jason brought her plate.

"Well, if you remember that all the atoms in that pie are made up of ninety-nine percent empty space, I think you'll agree it's possible," he said.

"All right, if it's in the interest of science," Iris laughed. "So... I gotta say, this has all been pretty interesting so far, but my inner history nerd is still full of questions." She took a bite of her pie. "Oh my gosh, this is amazing, Jason."

"Aw, thanks. Baking is just one more science I love. What kind of questions?"

"Well, Gray said there were a thousand members in the Council, so I assume they communicate with each other over emails or discussion boards or something, right?"

"Yeah, about a thousand people at any given time, plus or minus a few," Jason nodded. "And yes, they do communicate online nowadays. There are hundreds of Guardians all over the world who maintain dedicated servers and encryption software for our central database. The Council have a discussion forum on there where they work through any problems that other Guardians bring to them."

"Okay, but what about before that? Like thousands of years ago? How could the Council possibly stay informed enough on what the Guardians were up to without the internet or even a post office?"

"Ah, great question," Jason nodded. "Originally, there weren't that many Guardian families. Maybe four or five in total, all centered around modern-day Turkey and Mesopotamia. So there wasn't that much to keep track of. They used to meet once or twice a year at Eridu, mostly because they enjoyed the camaraderie. That place is nothing but an archaeological dig, now. The group had to find different locations to meet as they grew. But they've always been fond of staying in touch. They still make a point of trekking in once a year to catch up, work out problems, and decide where to meet the following year. Not unlike family reunions, I suppose. Things got a lot more difficult once the languages changed and people had to scatter, but they worked through it."

"What do you mean the languages changed?" Iris raised an eyebrow. "Are you referring to the Genesis myth of the Tower of Babel, or something?"

"Myth?" It was Jason's turn to raise an eyebrow.

"C'mon, you're saying that's actually *true*? A king tries to unite people under one government, so God Almighty zaps their brains so they can't understand each other?"

"The fundamental question right now is whether *you* can believe it's true," Jason said with a slight smile. He sipped his coffee. "I'm merely telling you what's in the Histories. You can choose to disbelieve it, but I must tell you, linguists the world over have studied most modern languages back to their roots, and they've found a most unexpected result."

"Which was…"

"A lack of common ancestry. Languages with different vocabularies, grammatical structures, and sounds, all seemed to arise spontaneously at one point. If people came from a single origin, what would be the benefit of doing that to themselves?"

Iris shook her head. She couldn't think of one.

"You might say God 'zapped their brains.' But put another way, you could also say that by inventing hundreds of complex languages in the blink of an eye, He used His genius to give people new ways to understand their world, and the motivation they needed to go fulfill their destinies." Jason leaned back in his chair, smiling with satisfaction. "You've seen enough things you can't explain to know that what I'm saying is plausible… wouldn't you agree?"

Iris thought long and hard, staring at the wood grain in the table. She remembered the unbelievable feeling of standing beneath the Great Hawthorn as it hummed and sang, one century disappearing and another reappearing, right before her eyes. She thought of Angus's letter… an *impossible* letter, addressed to her from a man long dead before her birth, talking about pizza. And about how he missed her.

That letter is tangible proof of the impossible. How much harder would it really be to believe what Jason is saying?

"Listen, I respect academic skepticism as much as the next guy," said Gray. "There's a lot of stuff out there worth doubting." He refilled his cup, and then held up the pot to Iris in the form of a question.

She shoved her cup forward a few inches in response.

"But," he continued as he filled her cup, "you can't doubt everything. *Something* is true. At some point you'll have to make a decision about how you're going to look at reality. I respect that you want to live in a world based in fact. I think every sane person does. But I think you're starting to understand that there are a lot of unseen aspects to those facts... evidence that can't be explained any other way."

Iris looked up from the table. Both men looked serenely at her, in no rush for her to believe anything they said.

"This is a lot to digest," she said at last. "I thought I was good with weird, but... having to renegotiate my entire view of history is more than I expected in one night."

"That's understandable," Jason said in a fatherly tone. "Nobody expects you to. But I'm sure you can see how having this basic knowledge of how Guardians operate would be crucial to working with us. We can get to the specifics about that part later."

"So... is being a Guardian some kind of... religion you guys are part of?"

They chuckled.

"No..." Gray said, still smiling. "We find that religion quite often tends to confuse the simplest things. Guardians are just guys and their families, serving the Three, and living out what we know to be true. We love our Creator, we love each other, and we believe the Histories. Simple as that."

"Simple as that, huh?" Iris gave him a crooked smile.

"Like apple pie."

31

"Do you think I could get a copy of the Histories? Y'know, so I can maybe read through them for myself?" she asked.

Jason leaned back in his chair and reached toward the bookcase behind him, picking out a small, tattered, leather bound volume. "You might already have a copy at home, but here's one you can borrow in case you can't find yours."

"But… that's just a—"

"Yep." He winked. "Do yourself a favor and keep an open mind, okay? Compare what you read with what you've already seen. Then let me know where you end up. Deal?"

She took the book. "Deal."

"Still have that card I gave you?"

"Yeah?"

"My number's on there. Call me anytime you have questions."

"Oh boy, you may come to regret that offer. I'm the girl who questions everything, remember?"

Jason smiled. "I'm glad."

"So… this meeting is going to end up in the central database too, isn't it?"

"Of course!" said Jason cheerfully. "There's a whole discussion thread on there devoted just to you, Iris."

"Seriously?"

"Well, yeah!" Gray interjected. "You're kind of a big deal!"

Iris took another sip of coffee while she processed that idea.

Jason grew serious. "But I want to respect your privacy. If you want, I'll leave out the part about how much pie you ate."

Iris blew a raspberry.

Chapter 3

Tucson, Arizona ~ 1965

A wispy black shadow darted across the desert. Gaining distance was his only objective. There was no hiding. Not here. He glanced backward, wincing at the glare that met his eyes. His luminous pursuer stood atop the nearest outcropping of rocks, sword in hand, glowering.

He picked up speed.

Once out of sight beyond a distant hill, he slowed to a crawl, weaving aimlessly between scrubby mesquite and stands of cacti. Misery overtook him, more acute than he'd felt in a century. Inside was outside. Life was death. His entire being writhed, prickling at the intense sensation of exposure. It was as though his very essence was fracturing into the ether. He let out a guttural moan, a sound of pain and rage in equal measure. The grating echo of that strange woman's voice still rang in his mind. *She bore the Seal on her forehead! But that mark is invisible to humans... how did that female know she had the authority to send me away?*

He let out another bellow of indignation as his nagging torment deepened.

Roads, small buildings, and the occasional gas station began to zip past as he drew near civilization once more. He scanned the distant city, looking for shadows. Having to squint against the occasional flashes of light that dotted the landscape was a mere nuisance compared to his present affliction. There was a fair amount of danger in this place, but it would be worth the risk. It was his nearest and best hope of finding shelter.

He selected one of the smaller blobs of darkness in the distance and aimed for it at top speed. Just to hide among those akin to him would be welcome, even if he couldn't locate a host right away. He avoided the larger areas of darkness, fearing the ranking leaders he would find there. The brutish manner in which he'd just been ejected into the wilderness was a welt on his pride. In his miserable state, he preferred not to be mocked, or bullied into any assignments just now. Although almost anything would be better than wandering through dry places in agony.

The commanding brick theater was a magnificent structure with five consecutive archways across the front, gaping at him like open mouths. He approached with caution. He sensed only four other beings inside, and to his relief, very little commotion. If there were some sort of campaign underway, there would be a great deal more stirring and clamor, as well as the customary insults being hurled back and forth. He entered through a side wall and paused. He was chafing, but the darkness helped.

The other entities were immediately aware of him, but seemed content to ignore him. One sat perched on a balcony railing, gazing through the exterior wall at some distant goings-on. Another stared at him from inside the green room, wearing a blasé expression. He approached.

"What goes on here?" he asked the pulsing black mist.

"Woven sounds, woven words," it replied. "Thousands who gather to hear. So many tender minds. I shove the ones who need it—the ones who love to want to hate to *love* to be afraid." A hissing chuckle came from somewhere near its center where a throat would be.

"How long have you been here?"

"Just since I killed my host," it said, looking bored. "This is what she looked like..." It oscillated out of phase, bending the light, until a holographic image of a woman appeared. She wore a long, white dress and stared at him with a doleful expression. The white face widened into an eerie expression of horror as the creature snapped back to black with an echoing snicker. "But you're not used to it," it observed, sensing his discomfort. "It's annoying me. Go talk to Apateon. He's not used to it, either. I don't think he'll be with us long."

He could feel the one called Apateon turn his eyes on him at the mention of his name, so he drifted to the huge empty stage, where Apateon stood in the center.

"Thelo," he introduced himself.

Apateon merely waited.

Thelo could think of nothing to say that didn't reveal his acute disadvantage. Admitting his eviction, a monumental defeat, rankled him.

In a gesture rare among their kind, Apateon threw him a bone by speaking first. "You're a bit uncomfortable, aren't you?" he jeered. "What happened to your host?"

"I killed him," Thelo lied.

"Excellent. I sent mine to the abyss as well. Now, I'm just..." he inhaled slowly, "waiting for the right scent to come along."

"Same," Thelo agreed, mimicking Apateon's posture, trying to appear more at ease than he was.

"I specialize in females," Apateon boasted. "After all, someone must tell the poor dears of their own potential. There have been some particularly savory prospects flitting across this stage in the past few days. This is truly a field ripe for harvest."

Thelo settled in beside Apateon and focused his senses. He listened to voices, tones, and vibrations. He tuned out organized geometric waves, instead searching the atmosphere for chaotic frequencies. He sampled the air, sniffing out the energy emitted by electrical human hearts in turmoil.

"It's particularly appealing when two energy fields collide," Apateon whispered. "The synergy is delicious."

Thelo chuckled. He knew exactly what this being was talking about. His old host had had an energy field at least twenty feet in circumference, leaving everyone around him almost powerless to argue with him. When his partner, a witch, had joined him, the two of them had been unstoppable. And then it had gone so utterly, completely awry. Just one wrong person with one wrong idea came along, and Thelo was blown a mile into the stratosphere. He would have to be more careful.

The two of them waited, listening.

Eugene slid back into his new Mustang and slammed the door. He pounded the steering wheel with his fists, roaring in frustration. His left hand began to ache where his fingers had jammed together against his wedding band. He ripped the ring off of his finger and chucked it into the glove compartment, flipping it closed with a sharp snap. It was all he could do not to hurl the cursed thing into a storm drain.

One of his neighbors peeked at him through her curtains. He glowered at her, cranked his engine, and peeled out.

He headed for the theater on campus. The thought of sitting through three hours of singing and dancing wouldn't normally have appealed to him, but anything was better than spending one more second dealing with a marriage that was never going to get better. Plus, he still had Kat's rhinestone earring in the pocket of his jacket, and he wanted to make sure she got it back. *Or just see her again.*

He collected his ticket at will-call and slid into his seat just as the lights dimmed. Not a seat in the house was empty. He flipped through his program as the overture ended, but realized it had become too dark to read, so he settled in to watch. His brow was furrowed. His roiling thoughts kept bubbling to the surface, dark in comparison to the flowing music. He kept trying to imagine how things could ever get better with Eva. Was it even possible to go back after the things they'd said tonight? *Do I even want to?* His mind kept him preoccupied for most of the opening number, but he absorbed just enough of the action to keep up with the story.

Until *she* appeared on stage. Kat was wearing a slightly different costume than last night—same dress, but the coat, hat, and dirt were missing. She grinned and danced with expert steps as the actor playing Alfred P. Doolittle twirled her and sang, "The gentle sex was made for man to marry, to share his nest, and see his food is cooked. But... with a little bit o'luck, you can have it all and not get hooked!"

Eugene chuckled. *Ain't that the truth.*

Throughout the performance, Eugene made a game of seeing how quickly he could spot Kat in the chorus. She was stunning in her Ascot Races costume—a fitted gray sheath dress with black buttons down one hip and an impressive black hat topped with white ostrich plumes. He couldn't take his eyes from her. At last, she reappeared on stage looking exactly as she had when he'd met her, with messy hair, odd hat, and grubby cheeks. She pulled off the perfect cockney accent as she sold a small bouquet of violets to Eliza Doolittle.

He made his way to the side stage door as soon as the curtain call had ended. Kat's face lit with a radiant smile when she saw him. He suddenly felt a little foolish, and a little sad that he hadn't thought to bring flowers.

"Gene Thomas! My white knight!" she cried. "I'm so glad you made it! What did you think? Was I spectacular?"

"You were the best thing in the whole show!" he laughed.

"You're just saying that cause it's true," she giggled. "Come meet my friends!" She tugged his arm. He suddenly found himself backstage being shown to a dozen strangers in assorted costumes. "Everybody, this is Gene. Gene, this is… everybody!"

Gene waved. "Nice to meet you… everybody!"

"Give me ten seconds!" Kat said, and bounced away into a dressing room.

Eugene could only stand around awkwardly, but at least "Everybody" was ignoring him now.

It was longer than ten seconds, but eventually, Kat emerged wearing a light pink minidress and white boots that showed off her California tan. Her face was clean, and her hair taken down and brushed. It hung almost to her waist in luscious blonde waves.

Thelo, who had been watching from the shadows in the corner of the room, felt a ripple of energy come from this man. He pounced.

Eugene was overcome with intense longing. It filled the pit of his stomach so fiercely that it startled him. His mind flooded with ideas… ones far more interesting than those he'd entertained so far. *I've never felt like this before. Not even for Eva.*

"What, haven't you ever seen a pretty girl before?" Kat teased.

"Not this pretty!" Eugene replied with great feeling.

Kat did not blush, nor did she look away. She was searching his face. "Well then," she said. "You should take me out for coffee."

Eugene nodded. "I really should."

"Now's good."

"You're not busy?"

"I said now's good, didn't I?" Her lips curled into a sensuous smile.

Apateon appeared at her side. "I like this one," he breathed into her ear. "She's… driven."

Eugene managed to find words again. "I… I have something for you." He reached into his pocket and held up the sparkling earring.

"My earring!" Kat exclaimed. "I thought I'd lost it for good!"

"I found it under that mean old cactus as I walked by this morning."

"Then you've rescued me yet again." Her eyes held him captive. "It was my grandmother's. I was so bummed when I realized it was missing."

Eugene opened her hand, placed the earring in her palm, and closed her fingers around it. "Glad to be of service."

"On your marks..." Thelo snickered so only Apateon could hear.

"Yes," Apateon breathed. "Looks like we'll be working together."

Kat looked amazing in the passenger seat of Eugene's Mustang—as if she belonged there. She turned on the radio like she owned it, which Eugene found charming.

"I got sunshiiiiine on a cloudy day," she sang aloud. "When it's cold outside, I got the month of May..."

"You have a great voice!" Eugene said. "You could be on records!"

"That's the plan!" she beamed. "Y'know what? I've just decided I don't want coffee. Let's go to Bacchi's!"

"Oh, are you... twenty-one? I thought..."

"Of course not, silly! I'm eighteen! But I've got a wicked fake I.D., and that's practically the same thing! Plus, no one ever checks around here, anyway."

Eugene felt foolish again. *What am I doing? She's just a kid. Am I really going to take a teenager out for a drink?* Then his thoughts took a dark turn. *Am I really going to miss the only fun I've had in years and go home to someone who thinks I'm garbage?*

He grinned back at her. "Bacchi's it is!"

"How old are *you*, anyway?" Kat asked casually. "It's impossible to tell with men."

"Oh, who cares about that?" Eugene teased.

"I'll find out," she warned with mock severity. "I have ways!"

"I dare you."

"Hmmm…" She tapped one slender finger on her lips. "You said graduate studies, so you've gotta be at least twenty-two or three."

"I probably am," Eugene chuckled.

"Oh fine, be like that," she pouted. "There are easier ways to find out."

"What ways?"

"You better keep an eye on your wallet." She gave him a devious grin, which intoxicated him. He was almost willing to tell her anything she wanted to know. *Just about.*

They parked and walked in to the dimly lit tavern, where several couples were slow dancing in the center of the floor. The bar was crowded, but a few tables were open. They sat at the one farthest to the back. It was illuminated by a yellow and orange stained glass lamp overhead, which gave Kat's hair a warm glow.

"What'll it be?" said a bored waitress.

Kat spoke first. "Gordon's and Sprite on the rocks, please. Double."

Eugene's eyebrows went up. *That's a lot of gin for such a little girl.*

"Uh…" he wavered. He hadn't been out for a drink in years. *Eva never… Ugh, who cares.* "Same for me. Why not?" He smiled. "I'll try something different."

"So," Kat said, eyes sparkling. "Mystery Man, are you going to offer me a cigarette?"

Eugene smiled, pulled out his pack of Marlboros, and gave her a light. He pulled out a second one for himself.

"Man, these are way better than mine." She took a long draw. "I only smoke Newports because I bum them off my roommate." She blew a plume of smoke straight into the air, and then looked at Eugene with a serious expression. "This won't turn me into a cowboy, will it?"

He cracked up. "Geez, I hope not. Cowboys aren't really my type."

"Good to hear that." She leaned forward. "So what *is* your type?"

Eugene took a puff, contemplating the question. Finally, he said, "Kindness. That's my type."

"Kindness?"

"Yeah. Basic human decency. Respect. And gorgeous blonde hair doesn't hurt, either."

Kat smirked.

"There's a wedding band hidden in his car!" Thelo chuckled to Apateon.

"Poor, pathetic soul," Apateon replied. He leaned toward Kat and touched her temple with a misty black finger. "He's hurting. He needs you."

Kat studied Eugene's face. "Kindness and respect," she repeated. "Someone must've hurt you bad."

He grimaced. "I'd rather not think about it."

The waitress set their drinks down without a word and sauntered away.

Eugene picked up his drink. "This'll help."

Kat raised her glass. "To kindness."

The next two hours flew by in a blur. Their conversation flowed easily. There was never an awkward pause, never a sign of boredom. Kat seemed as keen to know him as Eugene was to know her. He had never felt so understood as he did right now. Plus, the gin had sanded off the edges of his pain and made Kat's face look even softer and more beautiful to him.

At some point, he couldn't remember exactly how or when, she'd left the table to go to the restroom and then slid in beside him when she returned. She was so close now, he'd had to rest his arm across the seat behind her. Her hair smelled like strawberries.

"How's your owie?" he asked.

"Almost all better." She showed him her hand, leaning into him. There was a tiny pink spot where the cactus spine had been.

"Aw," he said with a teasing pout. He lifted it and tenderly kissed the spot. "There, now it'll be all better."

Just as he let go, she caught his hand. "Dance with me."

He checked his watch. *Two o'clock in the morning?* "Geez, I didn't realize how late it was. I should probably get you home."

"It wasn't a question." She stood and tugged his hand.

Several couples still occupied the dance floor. As they left the table, Eugene felt something touch his backside. He turned just in time to see Kat opening his wallet. *The little pickpocket!*

"Twenty-eight!" she giggled.

He sagged. "Too old?"

"Just right," she said, wrapping her arms around him and returning his wallet to his back pocket. "Anyway, you said it yourself… who cares about that?"

Eugene was lightheaded.

"And how about me?" she murmured. "Was I born too late?"

He rested his cheek against hers and swayed her to the music. "I'm here, aren't I?"

After dropping Kat by her dorm, Eugene went straight to the lab. He couldn't sleep, even if he wanted to.

As he parked, a tiny sparkle caught his eye. There, on the passenger seat, lay the rhinestone earring he'd just returned to Kat several hours before. He chuckled, and put it back in his pocket. For some reason he couldn't put his finger on, he was almost glad to still have it.

The lab was deserted—his favorite working conditions—so he tried to busy himself with plotting data points on a survey map. He had a crudely drawn map with raw field data from his last geomagnetic survey. He'd been lucky enough to get his hands on a borrowed fluxgate gradiometer—a cutting edge instrument. The data was both exciting and encouraging, but it was unpublishable until he translated everything from his own shorthand into readable figures. Once he had isolated the sharpest deviations, he could pinpoint the strongest geomagnetic anomalies on the map, and plot the locations for his next research trip. This is where he would measure tree growth and take tree core samples. If the tree ring data showed correlations to everything else he'd measured, it would make a graph so gorgeous he might have to frame it and hang it over the fireplace.

Nobody else was studying this idea. Scientists had uncovered plenty about how birds and other animals responded to the earth's magnetic fields, but what about trees? Their growth habits, perhaps even their evolution, must be affected by such an environmental trigger. After all, trees could sense gravity, and the strength and duration of light waves. Why not EM fields? And if trees did experience unusual growth habits in the presence of strong geomagnetic anomalies, could it signal the presence of underground mineral deposits? The applications for mining, geology, and even archaeology were potentially staggering. He could imagine several profitable industries that might be interested in the time and money they could save by using abnormal tree growth as a neon sign saying, "try here!"

The very first time these questions had occurred to him was five years ago when he'd visited the little town of Sedona, about two hundred thirty miles north. He'd hiked several of the trails around Oak Creek Canyon and realized that the place was a geologist's paradise. What had most intrigued him, however, was the way the trees grew. One tree would have a completely straight trunk, while another of the same species would grow in a perfect spiral, like a candy cane. Even trees that were nowhere near cliff edges, and therefore minimally affected by wind, would grow like they were in the midst of an invisible tornado. *Why?*

Unable to focus on the maps, he switched to a task that was less mentally involved. He opened his metal desk drawer and took out a kit containing a bottle of oil, a piece of cork, and three small sharpening stones of varying sizes. He laid the items out on a towel, then reached into his satchel for a long tool that looked like a metal tube—an increment borer for taking core samples of trees. He disassembled the borer and mindlessly began sharpening the auger bit.

His work demanded perfection. Only the cleanest, most pristine samples would do. Therefore, only the sharpest borer would do. Those trees would give up their answers, he would make sure. It had become the bee in his bonnet, setting the trajectory for his entire thesis… a paper that could set him apart in his field, as long as his theory was provable.

That bee in his bonnet had annoyed Eva from the beginning. He should have seen the signs of doom back then. Granted, that trip to Sedona had been their honeymoon. Eva had picked the place because it was "romantic." And probably because it was where several of her favorite John Wayne and Burt Lancaster movies were made. She sure did have a thing for cowboys. *In that case, I don't know what she ever saw in me. John Wayne wouldn't be caught dead writing a thesis.* She'd complained the whole trip, accusing him of being distracted. *Scientific curiosity hits when it hits! How can I help it?*

And the passing of five years had only amplified the complaints, revealing to Eugene how little he and Eva truly had in common. Their house didn't even really feel like home anymore. It was her house, and she tolerated his presence there. The thought of going there now, and answering the inevitable

"Where have you been?" question made his skin crawl. He knew his face would give him away—he looked too happy. She'd immediately know something was up, and lock onto him like a guided missile. *Seek and destroy.*

He closed his eyes. This time, instead of pushing away thoughts of Kat, he savored them. She had given him a lingering kiss on the cheek when they parted, although he could sense they both wanted more. She had agreed to see him again the next day.

I don't even know her last name. Oh well, I can ask.

Eugene's thoughts wandered to his upcoming research trip back to Sedona. Although he would be there to work—hiking to his plotted points and taking core samples—the idea of spending time in the great outdoors was a welcome relief from hanging around the university. Or home. *I wonder what Kat's doing over the break next week...*

The vision of her seated next to him in his Mustang gave him butterflies. She seemed up for an adventure. *Should I ask?*

He examined his newly sharpened borer.

Would that be scandalous?

He found a piece of paper on the desk and gave it a feather-light tap with the auger. It punched a perfect hole.

He grinned. *It's already scandalous. Works for me.*

Chapter 4

Vancouver, Washington ~ Present day

As soon as she got home, Iris set to work devouring the little brown volume she'd borrowed from Jason. The first part seemed a little familiar. She'd definitely heard someone in clerical robes reading this aloud at some point—although most of her dim recollection involved her five year old self wondering when she could go outside and play.

What she didn't remember about it was this feeling it caused—awe. When she got to the part about the special trees in the garden, she couldn't help but wonder if those, too, might have been humming a little. She was struck by not only the genius of the One speaking, but by how much trust He seemed to put in humans. *Did He really create this giant planet and everything on it, only to hand the keys over to a couple of regular people?*

Iris contemplated the idea of this garden. If the planet was so perfect after being made, why plant a whole separate garden to live in? Unless… Her mind wandered to all of the ancient mythologies she'd read in school. It was actually a common idea for gods to rule from a paradise on earth—Mount Olympus, for example. That idea had to originate somewhere. But those gods didn't go for walks with commoners like this one did. This one wanted to live *with* the people He made and rule the planet together! If He made a paradise on earth, that must've been His ruling seat, where His home and creation were meant to overlap. Literally heaven on earth.

Iris was stunned at the enormity of such a gesture. That would have meant seeing the actual Creator face to face, and seeing all kinds of spirit beings walking around. *What a strange and interesting world it would have been. Not strange to them, I guess.*

She felt a little dismal at the rapid descent everything took after that. Lies… blame shifting… curses… death. The human rulers were banished from the presence of true power and given mortal limitations, forcing them to rule earth in direct competition with their immortal enemy. *How would that even work? There'd be no winning against those odds.* Iris felt herself frowning, and wondered how long her face had been doing that. Quite a while, by the feel of it. But something was niggling her.

Who was this enemy… this serpent character? How could it be allowed anywhere near the paradise of this God? Her inner researcher began tapping her foot. She couldn't stand it.

She flipped open her laptop and began a word search. Since this was a Hebrew text, she would have to start there. English was such a comparatively modern language, it would be useless to her if she was going to understand this properly.

"Okay, serpent, what's your actual name…" she muttered. *Nachash.* She located that word in an online Hebrew lexicon, and scanned several other references using the same word. Snakes, and more snakes. Poisonous ones, metaphorical ones, brass ones. *But why would a little snake be talking in the first place, much less care who's in charge? This wasn't Narnia!*

She clicked on one reference that led to a dissertation written by several Jewish scholars. It explained that there was a close connection between this word *nachash* and another word, *saraph*, or its plural, *saraphim*. One meant your basic "snake" or "serpent," and the other meant "burners" or "serpents that burn, as with venom." That word led to a bunch more references that changed the spelling to "seraphim."

Seraphim? Like the ones on Christmas cards? Or maybe she'd misunderstood that word all along? Seraphim seemed to be a lot of things… these references talked about some that crawled around biting people, and others that had more human characteristics like hands and feet. They flew near the high throne, guarding it with fire. Iris frowned again. The Jewish scholars seemed to be frowning along with her, yet they remained undeterred in their insistence that their culture supported this interpretation of the word.

She read: *"We must not assign our modern sensibilities to how YHWH chooses His household staff. If all of His creatures were good when He made them (as the serpent of the garden is complimented as being perceptive and clever), why should He not designate serpent-like angelic beings to attend Him at court, if that is His pleasure? Should we tell Him we disapprove of His choice? Is it not the venomous words and acts of a fallen saraph that have brought all future embodiments of this creature, the nachash, such ignominy in the eyes of men?"*

Iris pondered that idea. Again, her mind considered other cultures she'd studied. The concept of serpents surrounding the throne of a powerful king wasn't such an oddity, after all. It popped up in other places, too… like ancient Egypt. Perhaps this is where that symbolism had started, and it caught on from there.

So… maybe it wasn't an evil creature who infiltrated forbidden territory just to tempt these people. Maybe it was a disgruntled member of staff. She drummed her fingers on the table. *But clearly, one who thought his own ideas were better than the Boss's ideas. He wasn't just targeting innocent people. He was recruiting help to stage a coup.*

But why did they go along with it? They already had… everything! They had to be banished from the only home they'd ever known!

Even so, Iris could sense more sorrow than anger in the One who sent them away. He kept them from the garden and its tree of life because He didn't want them to live forever in that awful state. *That's actually pretty merciful.*

Then more murder, ambition, and chaos ensued. Iris became more and more absorbed. Was there really an invasion of supernatural beings—"sons of God"—who wanted human wives, giving rise to a race of real, actual giants? *Sons of God...* Iris knew from her previous historical research that "son" didn't always mean a biological child. Maybe these were the "Messengers of the Three" that Darrick had spoken about. *More beings who wanted something forbidden, just like the snake. And they just... took whatever women they liked the look of?* Iris was horrified. *But I thought the Messengers were good!*

She thought of the tall, cloaked figure who had stood beside her while Angus fought to keep her warm and alive in his lap. The figure of a man blowing on her, warming her, had seemed like a dream—yet there was no other explanation for her rapid healing.

"You saw your guardian," Darrick had said.

Well, there must be both good and bad ones.

And their sons, these giants, went on to become famous world leaders. Iris could think of several ancient civilizations whose mythologies boasted a supernatural founder who claimed to be half god, half man. This account of how it all began didn't really seem to conflict with anything she'd learned about ancient history. In fact, it kind of... made sense. *But why do I suddenly buy it?*

Her phone vibrated against the table, causing her to jump. It was a text from Will, containing only symbols: ♡😎📞 ?

Iris giggled. *That's new.* She punched in a response: 😄 ♡📞 👍

Five seconds later, the screen lit up with Will's name while the phone played his favorite song by Boston. She picked up.

"I'm glad you're awake," he said. She could tell he was smiling.

"Me too. Although, after that text exchange, I wasn't sure whether I'd be able to hear this conversation, or if it'd be all in pictures."

He laughed. "Which would you prefer?"

"Pictures," she teased.

There was a pause. Her phone let out a quiet little *boop-boop*, and then flashed a notification: *Will Donovan asked to change to video call.*

"I was kidding!" she cried, frantically trying to remember when was the last time she'd looked in a mirror. Will's face appeared, plastered with a goofy grin. After five more seconds of silence, he mimed impatiently checking his watch.

Oh well, he already saw me without makeup this morning. She pressed the "switch to video" button.

His smile grew with delight. He waved.

She waved back.

He held up a booklet in front of his nose. Its title was *Favourite Scottish Meat Recipes*. He wiggled his eyebrows.

She gaped with appropriate delight and gave a hearty thumbs-up.

He opened to the table of contents and held up the book once more, pointing to the words "Devilled Kidneys."

Iris scrunched her nose and stuck out her tongue.

He gave a perplexed frown and double checked what he'd pointed at. He snickered and shook his head, then moved his finger to the right spot: "Curried Lamb Shanks."

Iris put her hand over her heart and gazed at the ceiling with an enraptured sigh.

With an approving smile, he stood and walked to the kitchen of his small apartment, holding the phone aloft so she could see him. He held up a package of raw lamb meat, followed by a small spice jar labeled "saffron."

Iris knew exactly what this meant: Don't bring lunch to work tomorrow. On their three-hour drive from the Seattle airport last night, he'd told her how much culinary experimentation he'd been doing while she was away in Scotland for the holidays. He'd entirely given up on throwing lunches together from leftovers at work. Instead, he'd been upping his game by preparing his own ingredients at home and finishing them in the professional kitchen during his breaks. Both Candace, her boss, and James, the admin assistant, had raved to her today about how much they'd enjoyed eating the results. She was starting to feel jealous of what she'd missed!

Will turned the camera back to himself with an expectant grin.

She nodded a vigorous "yes" and bobbed her fists in a little happy dance.

He put his cheek in his hand, smiling in mock embarrassment. She giggled.

Then he gazed at her for several seconds, almost long enough to make her think the video had frozen. But then he pointed two fingers at his own eyes, then at her, and mimed the word "*WOW.*"

Her mouth hung open slightly before she scoffed and shook her head.

He raised one eyebrow and tilted his chin at her, as if to chide her, and then nodded slowly up and down.

Iris laughed. She hoped it didn't show on camera that her face had gone slightly pink. *What should I say back?* She felt butterflies, but took a risk. She pointed at him, then at her own cheeks where dimples would be, then pressed her hand over her heart.

She could tell by his face that she'd just given Will a dose of his own cooking. He laughed and seemed to be having a hard time facing the camera.

"Pssst!"

Will looked up at her.

She gave him her most confident smile and nodded slowly up and down.

He just continued to chuckle. He knew she'd beaten him at his own game. At last, he sighed and pretended to nod off, chin on chest. He snored like a cartoon character with a nice whistle at the end.

Iris gave him a nod of agreement and a wave goodbye.
He waved back, and with one last dimply smile, he signed off.
Goofy man.

As soon as her alarm went off at seven o'clock, Iris's brain put in a requisition for ten more years of sleep. She had to remind herself that she'd only been back in the country for two days. She'd read somewhere that the brain needs about a week to recover from an eight hour time change. *Staying up half the night reading probably wasn't the slickest move, Iris.*

But even as she fought to open her eyes, her mind went into gear, showing her flashes of last night's incredible conversation with Jason and Gray, and all the strange things she'd read. She sat up. *What is this job the Council wants me to do?* She grabbed her phone off the nightstand and debated. *Well, he said to call anytime.* She dialed.

Jason picked up his phone on the third ring.

Before he could even open his mouth, Iris spoke. "So what's the job?"

"Good morning, Iris," he chuckled. "Have you slept, or were you up all night reading?"

"Some of both," she admitted, padding to the kitchen in her fuzzy socks. She reached into the fridge for a giant cup of cold brew she'd made for herself last night in anticipation of this moment.

"How far did you get?" Jason asked.

"Over halfway."

"Overachiever."

"It's not my fault! I couldn't put it down!" Iris tried to sip her coffee without slurping in Jason's ear. "The real reason I'm calling so early is because I have to know what this job is. It's driving me crazy. I knew you'd be up getting ready for school, so I thought maybe you could tell me real quick? Please?"

"It's not real quick!" he laughed. "How about we get together again and finish our conversation tonight? I have parent meetings, but I could get home by five."

She gasped in mock annoyance. "You're telling me I have to work all day with this burning curiosity?"

"Yes. Deal with it."

Iris giggled, remembering how often Jason had employed that phrase in the classroom when she was in his high school physics class.

"All right," she sighed. "Five o'clock. I'll bring cupcakes."

"Oh, how dainty!" Jason said. "We don't eat many of those since Grayson grew a beard."

"Hmm, intriguing!"

"Ha. See you tonight."

Iris tossed her purse onto the passenger seat of her little white hatchback, mashed the clutch, and brought the engine to life with a low rumble. Daphne's previous owner had fitted her with an aftermarket muffler and wide chrome exhaust pipe—nothing even close to what Iris would have chosen, but she took a small kind of delight in the growl it produced anyway.

She was grateful to find nothing on her windshield this morning except a little condensation that was easily cleared away. She cranked the heater, kicked her shoes off, and released the parking brake. Iris had always preferred to drive barefoot.

She had only backed three feet out of her space when she remembered that she still hadn't called her parents back. She knew they'd be up by now. Finn and Heather Jacobs were early risers. If she waited much longer to get in touch, her mother would think she was avoiding them. She threw the car in neutral,

pawed through her purse for her earbuds, dialed her parents'
landline, and then continued backing out. She had a twenty
minute drive ahead of her—plenty of time to chat.

"Hello, Iris!" her mother answered. "I was starting to wonder
if you'd lost our number!"

Apparently, I waited too long.

"Hi, Mum! How are you?" Iris attempted to sound cheerful
despite the dig.

"Fine, since you're askin.' The Christmas Eve party wasnae
the same w'out you, of course." Unlike Iris, fourteen years in
the States hadn't dampened Heather's Scottish accent one iota.

"I was sad to miss it," Iris said truthfully. "I was thinking
about you guys that day. But Charlie told me she appreciated
you inviting her again."

"She's a delightful girl, but is she goin' to settle on a proper
hair color anytime soon?"

Iris sighed. "It's just hair, Mum." It began to rain. She turned
on her wipers.

"I left your father unsupervised, and he decorated the tree
lopsided. But we muddled through."

"I'm sure he did his best."

"Aye, and I'm keen to take it down. But he's insisting we
leave it up because there's still a present under it. You'll come
tonight for dinner, right? I'm doing a stew."

Iris cringed. She should have anticipated this. Since her job
had changed, her mother assumed that she had nothing else to do
besides work during the day, and sit around at home every night.

"I sort of… already have plans this evening."

There was a long pause.

"Oh? Have you met someone? A man?"

The only thing Heather seemed interested in more than Iris's
education was seeing that her daughter was properly married off.

"Yes, Mum. I've met someone. A man."

It was the truth. Even though she would be at the Reynolds' tonight, letting her mother think she was seeing Will was the easiest way out of a dinner invitation without anybody getting their feathers ruffled.

"Well, now!" Heather said, suddenly sounding more cheerful. "You should bring him along, in that case!"

Iris cringed again. *Should've seen that one coming, too.*

"I'd better not, just yet. I don't want him to feel rushed. But soon, okay?"

"Fine, then. When might your father and I make it into the queue for a spot on your social calendar?"

"I'm off tomorrow. Name the time."

"Your father is doing a guest lecture tomorrow. I'll have to let you know."

"Sounds good." *What else can I say?*

"Goodbye, dear."

"Bye, Mum."

Her mother had never been much for verbal niceties. Her affection always came in less obvious ways. Sometimes far less obvious.

Iris spent the rest of the rainy drive watching the sky grow lighter, but feeling broody. She pulled into her usual spot in the Rookwood parking lot, trying to regain some emotional buoyancy for the sake of the people inside. She gazed up at the creaking weathervane on the nearest rooftop spire, remembering the first day she'd walked up the castle steps. She'd just been hoping to make rent that month. She had no idea she was about to meet a time traveler. She smiled as she trudged up the path in the rain, thinking of Angus. He was no more than a historical figure to the people around her. His brief presence at Rookwood had become part of a time that never was—a secret of the Guardians. *But he sure gave great hugs.*

She clocked in, stuffed her purse into her locker, and wandered toward the stairs. The smell of coffee tempted her.

Despite the cold brew she'd had, a cup of warm coffee sounded delightful. Her watch read three minutes to eight. Even more tempting, Will was in the kitchen. And now she could smell bacon.

Iris paused outside the kitchen door and peeked in through the round window. Will was standing at the stove in his usual chef jacket and backwards baseball cap, flipping ingredients in a pan while barking out efficient orders to the three cooks who busied themselves around him. As if he could sense her eyes, he turned and looked directly through the window at her with a dimpled smile. She grinned back at him. He checked his watch, grabbed something off a nearby counter, and headed toward her. When he pushed the kitchen door open, he was holding a paper cup with a lid on it.

"Aren't you almost late?" he chuckled.

"Yes! I was just hoping to get some—"

He handed her the cup.

"...coffee," she finished. "That's for me?"

"Of course."

"Oh, you're good," she sighed, inhaling the aroma of the fresh beans.

He shrugged. "You're a creature of habit."

"Am I that predictable?"

"Yes."

"Can I keep you?"

"Perhaps." He looked down at her with tender amusement. "Lunch later?"

"I literally dreamed about it last night."

He laughed, and turned back toward the kitchen. "You're late!"

"No I'm not!" Iris shouted and ran for the stairs.

As Iris neared the Activities Office, Candace emerged with a look of focused determination and marched right toward her. Today she was wearing her turquoise velour tracksuit and paisley Converse high tops.

"Good morning, Candace!" Iris greeted her. "I was just—"

"No time for that now, kid!" Candace beamed. "I just got the best news… Zoo Day is back on!"

"Zoo Day?" Iris fell into step beside her.

"Twice a year, a group of volunteers bring their pets in, all of them certified therapy animals, and we put on a Zoo Day for the residents to come interact with them. They weren't going to be able to come again till summer, but the director called me this morning to say they'd had a last minute cancellation. They can come today! That is, if we can be ready in time. We don't have long."

"How long is 'not long'?"

"Less than an hour!" Candace flashed a broad grin.

"So what are we doing?" Iris asked as they entered the Activity Room.

"We're making space to host a dozen animals," Candace answered. "So let's stack most of the chairs and push back all but two of the tables. We want enough space for everyone to make a circuit around the room." She began dragging furniture. "Oh, Iris? Could you get the Zoo Day signs out and put one up in the lobby and one just outside the door here, too?"

"Storage closet?"

"Yep. No! They're in my office closet. I keep meaning to move them."

Iris headed for the door.

"Oh, and could you go down to the kitchen and tell Will it's a Zoo Day, Code Red?"

"Code Red?" Iris laughed.

"Yes! My gosh, what kind of hosts are we if we don't offer our guests a snack?"

"You're right. What was I thinking?"

"I don't know, this must be your first Zoo Day or something." Candace winked.

"Ok, I'm going... unless you can think of anything else..." Iris edged toward the door.

"Double time!" Candace shouted.

Iris giggled and speed-walked to the office, then located and placed the signs. She trotted, out of breath, down the stone steps to the kitchen.

"*You* again!" Will greeted her fondly, holding a tray laden with balls of cookie dough. "You finish that coffee already?"

"Not even close," she lamented. "Candace has sent me on a very important mission with the message, 'Zoo Day, Code Red.' You're supposed to know what that means."

"Oh, seriously? That's back on? How many?"

"How many what?"

"Animals."

"She said... a dozen?"

"All right," he said, shoving the cookie sheet into the oven. "Gimme a sec." He wiped his hands on the towel across his shoulder, twisted the dial on his timer, and disappeared into the walk-in refrigerator. He came back with a plastic-covered pan and a crate of produce, set them on the counter, and disappeared again. He returned with a box of dog treats.

"Joy?" he yelled.

"Chef?" replied a petite woman about Iris's age. She was dressed in pants and a jacket similar to Will's, but hers had no name or title embroidered on it.

"Coffee break for a dozen on the fly, please," he ordered.

"Yes, Chef!" Joy scooted off.

With expert efficiency, Will began to assemble a huge tray of fresh lettuce, carrot sticks, bunches of parsley, strips of bell pepper, chunks of apple and banana, a bowl of raw unsalted nuts, and a plate of cooked, shredded chicken. He set a tall water glass in the center of the tray and filled it with dog treats.

Just then, the cook named Joy returned pushing a two-tiered wheeled cart. It was loaded with a silver coffee urn, a dozen cups, cream and sugar, stir sticks, and a generous tray of muffins, doughnuts, and croissants.

"Love it. Thank you very much!" Will praised her. "You're on cookies until I get back, okay?"

"Yes, Chef." She blushed, glanced curiously at Iris, and returned to the large stand mixer to continue scooping cookie dough.

Will placed the tray he'd assembled on the cart below the pastries and pushed it toward the door. "C'mon, I'll walk you up," he said to Iris.

"How are you going to get that upstairs?" she wondered.

"Service elevator, silly goose!" he chuckled. "You didn't know we had one?"

"Nothing I steal from the kitchen is big enough require wheels, so it's never come up!" she answered.

"I guess we can consider ourselves lucky, then." Will pushed the elevator button.

"Joy seems… nice."

"She is, yeah. Nice kid."

"Kid?" Iris looked at him quizzically. "She looks about my age."

"No, what I mean is…" Will held the door as she boarded the elevator. "She does good work, but she doesn't seem real confident yet. Needs a lot of hand holding."

"*Needs* a lot of hand holding… or *wants* a lot of hand holding?"

Will gazed at her with a puzzled expression.

"Well, after all, she does have a very good-looking boss…" Iris hinted.

The elevator dinged and the doors slid open. Will gave her a strange look before pushing the cart into the corridor toward the Activity Room.

"I'll give that some thought," he said finally. "It would explain some things, actually."

"Dear me," Iris chuckled.

"Willy!" Candace crooned as they appeared with the treats. "You're my absolute favorite person right now!"

"Anything for you, Candy! You know you need only ask," he said with a bow. He winked at Iris and left.

"I'm just about set up in here," Candace told her. "People should arrive any moment."

"Helloooooo!" called a tall middle aged woman from the doorway.

"Speaking of," Candace said. "C'mon in, Denise! Iris, this is Denise, the director of the organization that puts on Zoo Day. Denise, this is Iris, my right arm, pretty much."

"Nice to meet you!" Denise replied. She entered the room, leading three dogs and a miniature horse, all wearing service animal vests. She unclipped the dogs' leashes and said, "Release!"

The dogs began to sniff around the room in a curious, unhurried manner.

"I let them off leash to get the lay of the room before we start," she explained. She ruffled the little horse's mane. "This is Honeybun. She's a seeing-eye horse." She pointed to the two smaller dogs closest to her. "The Irish setter there is Seth, and the little French bulldog is Elise. One of our volunteers is also bringing his Frenchie, named George Washington."

"Oh yeah!" Iris said, then remembered to shut her mouth before anything else came out of it.

"Have you met George Washington?" Denise wondered.

"No..." Iris shook her head. "It's just... a cool name for a dog."

The third dog Denise had brought was a large, completely tan shepherd mix. He trotted over to Iris and sat beside her foot, leaning into her leg. He looked up at her with his earnest brown eyes and panted slightly, as if he were smiling.

Iris grinned and offered the back of her hand for him to sniff. "And who's this?"

Denise laughed. "That's Angus!" she replied. "Looks like he really likes you, Iris!"

"Your name is Angus?" she asked the dog, giving him a little rub on the shoulder. "That's one of the best names ever!"

Angus wagged his tail.

One by one, volunteers began to trickle in over the next fifteen minutes, helping themselves to treats and coffee. By nine o'clock, they had assembled four dogs and a pony, a black cat named Ralphie, a small black rat named Ratrik, a huge green-winged macaw called Samson, and two chubby guinea pigs named Caramel and Mocha, who looked like the rodent equivalent of bed head. They were shortly followed by Bowie the hedgehog and his owner. Ironically last to arrive was a man wearing a stetson and carrying a twelve pound tortoise named Dale Earnhardt.

"Nine o'clock!" called a quaking voice in the hallway.

"Hello, Irene!" Iris called back. "Come on in, and meet all the wonderful animals!"

"Nine o'clock, and no BINGO. Says BINGO, right here." She waved her printed schedule. "Lois is coming for BINGO, and there's a... a..." she pointed. "...a *turtle* in her spot. No turtles at BINGO! Oh look, there's a pony!" She shuffled into the room, forgetting all about BINGO.

Lois followed several seconds later, gazed around the room, then took a chair beside the table where Ralphie the black cat was lying on a pet bed. The two of them regarded each other with peaceful expressions. A volunteer offered her a piece of chicken to give Ralphie. She took a bite out of it and gave the other half to the cat.

"Eres muy guapo, sí!" she chortled.

Startled, Iris looked at Candace. "I didn't think Lois ever spoke!" she gasped.

"She never has before!" Candace whispered. "She was homeless before she came here. We were guessing she didn't speak because of a stroke, or possibly because Irene does all the talking for her."

"I think I have a better theory," Iris whispered. "Maybe she doesn't speak English!"

"I'll put a note in her file to look into that!"

Walter shuffled in and looked around. "Jiminy!" he hooted. "I feel like I'm back at FBI headquarters!"

Doris wandered into the room behind him, eyes wide.

Walter poked his cane, which was black with flames painted on it, toward the rat. "Look, there's a politician I know!"

"Really?" Doris asked, looking alarmed.

"Stay and have fun," Candace said to Iris. "I'll do taxi time." She set off to gather more participants.

A white, curly head peeked around the corner. "Is that... a rat?"

"Hi, Betty!" Iris called to her. "Yes, but you don't have to see the rat if you—"

"Oh please, could I pet it?" Betty asked, stepping forward, hand eagerly extended.

A volunteer had her take a seat, and then set Ratrik in her lap. She squealed with excitement.

The guinea pigs in the bin next to her began to squeak in response.

Betty cackled, "Quick! I need leaves! The babies are hungry!" She cuddled Ratrik against her neck, reached for a handful of parsley from the tray, and gleefully rained it down on the guinea pigs' heads. She looked down lovingly at the little black rat on her shoulder. "Aw, what a little precious. He's *over*good!" Then she started to laugh. "He's made you a present! Look!" She handed the volunteer a small brown pellet.

Iris exchanged amused expressions with Denise, who shook her head in amazement.

Betty waved a trembling hand toward Iris. "Could you come over here, dear?"

Iris crossed the room and knelt beside her chair. "What do you need, Betty?"

"You're a nice girl," Betty said, still petting the rat. "I wonder if you could go back to my place and fetch Poppy. She would have a great time here!"

"Who's Poppy?"

"My Shetland pony."

Iris giggled. "You keep a Shetland pony in your room? I bet she could use some exercise!"

"They do get overweight," she sighed. "Oh good! Never mind, she's managed to find her way!" Betty beckoned at the empty doorway. "Come along, Poppy! Come meet this rat!"

"Bananas!" screeched Samson the macaw. "Dibs on bananas! Dance! Dance bananas!"

Caramel and Mocha squealed again, still munching on their parsley.

Candace returned, pushing Fred in his wheelchair.

He caught sight of Samson and pointed. "I used to hunt with them things! Rabbits, squirrels, pheasants."

Samson's owner brought him down from his perch and held him a little closer.

"Pretty falcon!" Fred grinned. "That's a biggun! Are you a hunter, too, big guy?"

Samson cocked his bright red feathered head. "I'm older than you!" he squawked.

Fred slapped his knee. "Well I'll be dipped!"

Chapter 5

Tucson, Arizona ~ 1965

Sunday morning dawned bright over Tucson. The threatening snow clouds had vanished, and Eugene was eager to set out.

He had waited impatiently for the rest of the week to drag itself out of his way. Three full, long days of work and teaching had passed, plus one day of packing and finalizing his trip plans. And, of course, making sure his new car was still spotless.

Four days since he had met Kat. He couldn't believe it had only been on Tuesday night that such an alluring and vivacious creature had appeared in his life. One moment, he had only academic achievement left to look forward to. Now, he felt an actual spark of something. He could be... *happy* again. He had picked Kat up at the theater every single evening and spent a few hours soaking in laughter and pleasant conversation with her.

He had planned to leave for Sedona on Saturday, but now that he'd invited Kat to come with him, they'd had to wait until after closing night of *My Fair Lady*. The loss of one day off his research trip would be worth it, he reasoned. He relished being alone, but he relished her company even more.

Best of all, Eva would never find out. She had been less of a problem than he could've hoped. Storming out on Wednesday evening and spending the entire night away had been a first, even for him. He came home Thursday afternoon in desperate need of a shower and shave, and a change of clean clothes, steeling himself for the diatribe that was sure to come. But he needn't have worried, as it turned out. To his delight, the little blue Beetle was gone, as were many of Eva's clothes, her toiletry kit, and her overnight bag. Another first.

Clearly, she doesn't want to see me, either. Now we're getting somewhere.

Eugene had embraced the freedom her absence had granted, spreading his maps and notes all over the table and working into the wee hours, whistling in the shower, devouring frozen dinners, and feeling only mildly curious about where Eva had run off to. *Probably went to her sister's. She'll be in good company since they both hate me.*

But just to be on the safe side, he had asked Kat to meet him around the corner from her residence hall this morning, away from the prying eyes of her dorm mates and his neighbors. She had accepted his explanation that he didn't want anyone mistaking her for one of his students and thinking there was some impropriety going on. *Partly true.*

When he rumbled up to the curb with the Mustang's top down, he was struck again by how stunning she was. She stood waiting with her red suitcase, dressed in tight fitted jeans and a cropped royal blue sweater. She had a matching polka dot scarf tied in her hair like a headband, while all of her lustrous blonde waves draped effortlessly down her shoulders.

"Hey, Brigitte Bardot!" he called. "Goin' my way?"

"Oui, monsieur!" she replied with a little wave.

Before he could put the car in neutral, she had slung her case into the back seat and plopped into the seat beside him without even opening the door.

"Wow, have you practiced that move before?" he laughed.

"Yes! In case I ever have to play a bank robber in a movie! Or escape from paparazzi!"

"Very impressive!"

"Merci beaucoup," she said in a perfect French accent. "Let's go! I can't wait!"

Kat's enthusiasm was contagious. Eugene almost felt himself getting younger as he gunned the engine and sped toward the freeway.

"This is going to be far out!" she gushed.

"You don't even know the plan yet," he laughed. "Aren't you the least bit curious what we'll be doing?"

"Not at all!" She stretched her arms skyward, palms up, and then rested her hands behind her head. "You promised me red rocks, gorgeous scenery, spending time with a genius hunk, and getting to avoid five days in Squaresville with my parents. And in this car, too! What else could I possibly need?"

Eugene was pleased, but couldn't help blushing a little. "You think I'm a hunk?"

"Obviously!" She rolled her eyes. "We established that when I said I'd see you. I do have standards, after all."

"Do you, now?" He gave her a side glance.

"I do. And it's working from every angle, as far as I'm concerned."

Eugene's eyes went wide.

She leaned toward him in her seat and ran her hand across his chest and into his jacket, until she found the pack of cigarettes he kept in his inside pocket. He almost hyperventilated.

He poked the car's cigarette lighter button quickly, before she could rummage through his pants pockets for his other one.

"So how did you manage to get away?" he asked, genuinely curious but equally eager to hide how unsettled she made him.

"I told my old man that my good friend Gene was doing a very important research project out of town, and really needed an assistant." She pulled out two cigarettes and slid the pack back into his jacket.

"Your parents were okay with it?"

"I may have led them to believe that your name is spelled 'J-E-A-N.'"

"Ahhh…"

"So it'll be just us girls!" she giggled.

The lighter button popped out. She put both cigarettes in her mouth and lit them simultaneously.

"You're crazy."

She put one of the cigarettes in his mouth. "I know."

He took a long draw and gazed at her. She sat peacefully, smirking at him as if she knew precisely what her presence was doing to him.

"So." He cleared his throat. "Originally, I was planning to camp. It's how I've always done these trips. But if you're not used to roughing it, I can probably… figure something else out."

"Hmm, that sounds cozy," she sighed. "I love camping."

"It's going to be pretty cold at night, are you sure?"

"It'll be fine if the tent's not very big," she replied. "It's not, is it?"

"It might fit two."

"Perfect."

Eugene drove north on Interstate 10. They stopped for burgers and shakes in Phoenix, and continued up Interstate 17 another hundred miles until the soil became rusty red. The saguaro and mesquite had given way to scrub oak, agave, and juniper trees dotted along the hills. They veered slightly west and then meandered north again for another nine miles on 179, past Martian-looking rock formations.

"There's Bell Rock," Eugene pointed out.

"It's gorgeous!" Kat exclaimed. "I feel like I'm on a different planet!"

"All these formations are sedimentary deposits. Amazing, right?"

"Sedimentary... I forget, is that the water one or the volcano one?" she asked.

Eugene laughed. "Water. This whole area used to be under an ocean!"

"You're pulling my leg!

"I'm serious!"

"How could water have left dirt way up there?"

"It was that deep!" He winked. Her amazement made him feel... brilliant. He realized that what he was doing was the scientist equivalent of bicep flexing, but he didn't care. "There's a bunch of igneous rock underground, though," he continued. "You know, the volcanic kind. It has magnetic properties."

"Like the magnets in cartoons?"

"Yeah, kind of."

"How in the world does that happen?"

"Well, the molten rock bubbling up from under the earth's crust has iron in it. As it's cooling, it orients itself to the earth's magnetic poles before it hardens." He smiled. "It gets even more interesting, because when those volcanic rocks break up, sometimes they shift around enough to create a magnetic anomaly. Other times, you can find large underground mineral deposits or even archaeological ruins that show up as anomalies. You can map those if you have the right equipment."

He looked over at Kat's face. She was squinting straight ahead.

"Sorry," he sighed. "I must sound like such a square. All that technical stuff is probably pretty boring."

"What? No way!" She gave him a reassuring grin. "I was just imagining what you were talking about. It sounds so major! I can't believe you know all that stuff!"

He smiled back. He wasn't used to feeling like anyone found him interesting.

"I wish I'd had a science teacher like you," she went on. "You explain things in a way I actually understand."

"Really?"

"Yeah! You're brilliant! So that's what we're going to be doing out here? Studying rocks?"

"Well, yes and no." Eugene put out his cigarette in the ashtray. "I've already mapped some neat spots where the electromagnetic readings are unusual. I did that my last three trips here. What I'm here to do now is measure the trees in those places. I have some theories about how the earth's magnetism affects plant growth. Might be useful to somebody someday."

"So how do you measure the trees? Like, tallness or whatever?"

"No, not really," he chuckled. "I'll look at girth and trunk shape a little bit. But what I'm really after is tree ring samples."

Kat looked concerned. "Don't you have to cut a tree down to see the rings?"

"Nope! I have a handy-dandy little tool called an increment borer. Takes a nice little sample so you can see a cross section of the rings, and the tree gets to live another day."

"So it doesn't hurt the poor trees, right?"

"Eh, not much. Like a giant bee sting. Gotta be a little careful—don't wanna get dirt or fungus in the hole, but usually the tree seals itself right off and goes on like nothing ever happened."

"That's so boss!" Kat squealed. "I can't believe I'm with a real scientist doing real research!"

"I can't believe I'm with a woman who actually thinks this stuff is interesting!" Eugene laughed.

"Yeah," she huffed. "People think that because I'm a female theater major, I must not have a brain. But you have to be really smart to memorize the amount of stuff I do. Plus, I do like science. I think it's fascinating. I just like acting more."

Eugene pulled off the pavement onto a dirt side road and parked.

"I would never accuse you of being unintelligent," he said. "What I meant before was… I think it must be *me* that women find boring, so my work seems boring, too."

"What!" Kat said. "You're the most interesting man I've ever met! You actually have goals in life besides partying and showing off. I love listening to you talk." She leaned in closer. "And even if I don't understand a *hundred* percent of it," she murmured, "it's still nice to watch your lips move."

"Is that so?" he whispered, leaning closer.

"Mm-hmm."

Up until this point, Eugene had reasoned with himself that his relationship with Kat was merely one of friendship—of mutual understanding and affection. Despite the interesting turn his thoughts of her had taken lately, he could still rationalize his interest in her. A man needs to be appreciated. A man needs fellowship. If he couldn't find that at home, it was perfectly innocent to seek it elsewhere.

It was at this moment, however, with her blue eyes inches from his and the strawberry scent of her hair so close, that he knew deep in his soul that his rationale was a load of garbage. He was falling for Kat, and he wanted to kiss her, here and now. He also knew that doing so would make him a cheat.

He didn't care.

Skliros narrowed his eyes. A distant plume of chalky pink dust arose as a car made its way across the desert. From a perch above his dilapidated cliff castle, he could make out the shapes of two human creatures. He emitted a low grumble of delight when he noticed something far more interesting: two shifting pockets of space near the humans where light seemed unable to penetrate. One clung close to the female like a parasite. The other was seated halfway inside the male's body like a disease.

"Vroma!" Skliros hissed.

An impish creature of wavering gray mist slinked toward him from the shadows beneath the crumbling walls.

"Yes, Great One?"

"More of those creatures approach. Two this time, in a car."

"More sightseers?"

"Possibly. But these are something different. They have guests."

"Hmm, this bodes well."

"Perhaps. None would dare attempt an incursion on my domain, but these beings may be on some errand of their own. We must... welcome them."

"I'll go make an introduction," Vroma snickered, and crept off in the direction of the vehicle, which had found a clearing off the abandoned dirt road and parked.

Thelo and Apateon could sense him before he was within speaking distance.

"One of our kind approaches," Thelo muttered.

"Interesting to see one so far from civilization," Apateon commented.

"You are in the realm of Skliros, Red Ba'al, lord of these lands since the time of floods!" Vroma announced.

"Congratulations to us," yawned Apateon. "Red, is he? Did he do most of the decorating here, then?"

Vroma sneered. "You will show due deference to the Great One while on his lands. The blood of many thousands of image-bearers is on his sword. He is not afraid to slay your hosts."

"Fine," said Thelo. "Send him our greetings. We will stay no longer than the humans."

"Then your business is with these creatures, and not with this domain?"

"Yes," Thelo replied. "I would not lose this one if I could help it. He is a most gratifying entertainer. He wants... *everything*.

Especially this female. His desires almost exceed my own. He will see that I am denied nothing I wish to experience."

Vroma leered at the woman in blue, who was pulling a red suitcase from the car.

"An exquisite creature," Apateon agreed fondly, "and in love with her own reflection. She is a lump of clay awaiting my artistic mastery."

"Very well." Vroma seemed satisfied. "I will tell lord Skliros of your business here."

"And you?" Thelo asked. "What keeps you tied to these uninhabited lands and bound to a master? Surely, there are more tantalizing prospects."

"These lands are not uninhabited," Vroma replied. "Human numbers are greatly reduced since the gatherers left for the plateaus. But more come all the time—restless seekers in need of enlightenment. I spread inspiration wherever I can," he sneered. "And... these creatures? What are they in search of? I'm sure I could... *assist*."

"Mine desires rebellion and sensation," Apateon answered. "Fame, too. Pitiful thing is still trying to figure out who she is. She needs me to tell her. I will see to it that she makes a spectacular end... like a mushroom cloud."

"This one is here for personal gratification," Thelo added, motioning to the man pulling camping supplies from the trunk. "Chief among his desires is this female. But he also comes in search of trees."

"Trees?" Vroma asked.

"Yes. He believes the trees will prove the caliber of his intellect. He must pierce and prod them. However, I have not yet decided whether he will fail or succeed. Despair drives desire as much as achievement."

"You will hear from my master shortly," Vroma said abruptly, and darted away.

"Looking forward to it," Thelo lied.

"Well. He's… delightful," said Apateon to no one in particular.

Once camp was set up, Eugene planned to hike to his first few plotted map coordinates and get as many tree ring samples as he could before he lost the light. But every time he caught sight of Kat, he wavered. It would be equally gratifying to just build a fire and sit with her cuddled against his side… especially after earlier today.

"What do you want to do this evening?" he asked her. "You hungry?"

"Nah, it's okay. I never eat after lunch," she replied.

Eugene gave her a quizzical look.

"Well c'mon, what should I want more? Dinner, or a killer figure?" she laughed. "I'm going to be in movies someday, after all."

He put his arm around her waist. "I think you're beautiful just the way you are."

"Exactly." She tapped his nose with her finger as she said it. "Totally worth it."

"And you…" She returned his embrace. "Well, you're absolutely perfect. I'm wondering how such a handsome, accomplished man finds himself available, right when I need him. How has nobody stolen your heart by now?"

He searched her face. *Would she understand if I told her?*

Eugene hesitated. "Life can be funny sometimes."

Had Eva ever made him feel like this? *No.* He plunged ahead. "Besides, someone *has* stolen my heart."

"Who?"

"I'm looking at her."

Her mouth curved in a slow smile, and she kissed him softly.

"I have an idea," Apateon whispered. "Let's see what she does with it." He drew close to her ear.

Kat's eyes sparkled. A strange look spread across her face, making Eugene's heart do an offbeat dance. "Let's get married, Gene!"

His eyes widened in shock. "What?"

Thelo cackled. "Good one!"

Kat laughed, the perfection of her beauty searing Eugene's soul with longing. "You heard me! Let's get married!"

"But..." Eugene's mind raced, searching for words. "We've known each other less than a week!"

"Long enough to know that you're everything I want," she said. "We make each other so happy!"

"You're eighteen years old! You want to be a wife?"

"Not *a* wife," she murmured. "*Your* wife."

He returned her kiss with a mixture of intensity and sadness. "You have no idea how badly I want that." He sighed. "But I can't."

"Why not?"

"I'm..." He scowled, hunting for words and suddenly furious with Eva for the agony he felt. Kat was the only right thing in his life. If she knew about Eva, it would break her heart.

"What is it?" Kat hugged him closer. "Don't I make you happy?"

"You make me happier than I ever thought I could be," he said with great sincerity. "I'm just not in a position to make you any promises right now. I wish I could."

"You still in pain because of *her*?"

Eugene's stomach lurched. "Who?"

Kat shrugged. "I dunno, whoever you didn't want to talk about the other night."

"Yes." He pulled her into his chest and kissed the top of her head. "That's exactly it. It's just a little complicated right now."

She sighed contentedly against his shirt. "I can wait."

"I won't keep you waiting long."

"Good."

A hulking shade fell over the campsite, making even the late afternoon sun seem filtered by smoke. Thelo and Apateon watched the approaching figure with wary expressions. He was a foul stench of a creature, consisting of no more physical substance than either of them, but he projected waves of crimson and gold into the atmosphere around himself with kingly arrogance.

"You must be Skliros," Apateon said drolly.

"Do not speak my name," Skliros spat.

Thelo could feel a chemical shift in Eugene's body in reaction to Skliros's presence. "Fine, we won't," he said. "But could you rein it in a little? You're frightening the humans."

Skliros compacted his bulky form to a thick, colorless mass. He pointed to Eugene. "Is this the piercer of trees?"

"Yes. He is in search of knowledge," Thelo replied.

Skliros grinned. "He will find more than that! You see, there is a tree in my realm that he would find particularly interesting."

"No... You have one of the Great Trees?" Thelo asked, his voice rising in pitch. "Oh-ho, that is brilliant! He won't be able to resist!"

"Those are heavily guarded, you know," Apateon droned. "Good luck getting near it."

"I'm well aware!" Skliros snapped.

"My master's great ambition is to strike down the Guardians of the Great Tree," Vroma cackled, peering out from behind Skliros. "He has promised me a position of prominence when we succeed."

"Oh, hello again," Apateon said. "Didn't see you back there."

Vroma hissed.

"Striking down Guardians?" Apateon continued. "Well, now. That's ambitious. Whatever for?"

"Because they annoy me," Skliros growled. "They worship The Three. They are thorns in my eye—a blight on my otherwise pristine lands. Besides, without Guardians, the Great Tree will no longer be secret. It will draw curious human creatures in great numbers."

"That's a terrible idea!" Apateon scoffed.

"You would dare challenge me?" Skliros barked.

"Think it over," Apateon continued, undeterred. "Great Trees are dangerous. The first human creatures to meddle with it would get killed and scare the rest away."

"Then I will teach them to worship *near* its mystical power."

"And… worship what, exactly? You? The Tree? In case you haven't noticed, literal idols are not exactly in fashion these days. Not around here, anyway."

"No, not me," Skliros grumbled. "Not anymore. We will teach them to worship themselves, and even the earth itself, as gods. The scroll is being written even now. We will channel it through the proper instrument at the proper time. Taking the Great Tree for ourselves is just the beginning."

Apateon shrugged. "As I said, good luck getting near it."

Skliros turned to Thelo. "We will show your host where to find it. His own instincts will no doubt take over from there."

Thelo smiled.

Eugene sighed. Having Kat in his arms felt entirely too good. But it was not his main reason for being here. He had to get at least a few samples before sundown.

"Well," he said. "I guess I should hike out for a while and get a couple tree stands sampled while I can."

Kat gave him one last squeeze and released him. "Want me to come?"

"Sure." He smiled down at her. "It would be nice to have someone give me a hand." He gathered his map, compass, borer, and several sample tubes into his satchel. "Ready?"

"Ready!"

They followed a bearing northwest, putting them into the upper left part of the quadrangle on Eugene's map. He intended to cover every point he'd marked over the next few days by methodically following a grid across the entire area.

When they reached the first tree stand, he was overcome by an unsettling feeling. He looked around, double checked his map, and frowned.

"What is it?" Kat asked.

"Not sure," he said. "We're in exactly the right spot, but I just... hmm..." He craned his neck into the distance. "I suddenly have this urge to go a little farther. I just want to see what's over that ridge right there. You game?"

"Absolutely!" Kat agreed. "It's gorgeous out here!"

The farther off-grid he hiked, the more driven Eugene felt. Thirty minutes later, they topped the ridge and looked into the small valley below.

"Wow," Kat breathed. "It's like a painting! And look..." She pointed. "There's a little house down there!"

Eugene's eyes were drawn to a stand of trees just at the bottom of the hill.

"What the heck is that?" he muttered. Without another word, he began his descent.

Kat followed.

Eugene pushed his way through a cluster of scrub oak and stunted juniper shrubs, emerging into a circular clearing about twenty feet in diameter. In the center stood a massive, shaggy-barked monarch covered in pale blue berries. Its thick trunk rose from the red soil in a perfect spiral, then split into seven perfectly spaced branches ten feet off the ground.

Kat emerged from the shrubs behind him. "Wow, that's a big tree!" she gasped.

"Big?" he said. "It's massive!"

"What is it?"

"*Juniperus osteosperma*," he replied. "At least... it *looks* like one. But it's gotta be at least ten meters tall. Most are half that, or less. The tallest are maybe eight meters at most."

"Well maybe he likes it here," Kat suggested.

"He shouldn't," Eugene said. "We're on the east side of that ridge. These trees aren't shade tolerant. *At all.*" He squinted up at it. "So... what's it doing, growing like gangbusters right here?"

He crunched through the dry grass toward the tree, unable to take his eyes from it. "Look at that... totally out of the wind, but twisted like a barber pole. I've gotta sample this one," he said. "I can't even guess how old it is, but I'm dying to know."

Ten steps away from the tree, Eugene stopped again. He shook his head, put a palm over one ear, and looked at Kat.

"What's that weird sound?" she asked.

"You hear it, too?"

"Yeah, it's like..." She frowned.

"There must be a generator nearby," he said.

"Maybe we should leave it alone," she whispered. "Aren't we on somebody's land?"

He looked around him. "Maybe. We'll be quick." He pulled the strap of his satchel from across his body and set the bag on the ground. He rummaged for a few seconds and found his borer and sample tubes.

"Excuse me," said a man's voice behind them. "You can't be here."

Kat let out a startled gasp. Eugene closed his eyes and mouthed a curse. He plastered on a smile and rose to stand, turning toward the voice.

The man standing before him looked to be about forty, with swarthy skin and a few silver hairs in his otherwise jet black ponytail. He was wearing tan work trousers and cowboy boots. His dark brown eyes bore a look of confidence.

"Hello," said Eugene, trying to appear casual. "I'm sorry, I thought this was federal land."

"You are on the land of my ancestors," the man replied. "I am Joseph Iwila. I live just over there." He pointed toward the small house they'd seen earlier.

"Nice to meet you, I'm Eugene Thomas." He gave the man a firm handshake. "And this is Kat, my… assistant."

She waved.

"I'm a scientist at U of A," Eugene continued. "I'm here to study the growth patterns of trees, so I wonder if you'd mind me taking a quick sample of this big guy. He's quite extraordinary."

"That will not be possible."

Eugene let out a small chuckle. "Let me explain… you see?" He held up the borer for Joseph Iwila to see it. "This makes a tiny little hole and takes a piece no wider than a drinking straw, just so you can see the rings. Won't hurt the tree at all."

"I'm afraid I cannot allow it."

"Aren't you the least bit curious how old this tree is? I mean, it's huge!"

Joseph Iwila just stood there, resolute.

Eugene frowned and exhaled his frustration through his nose. "What, is this tree sacred to your people, or something?"

Joseph simply gazed at him, unmoving.

"The tree will be absolutely fine if I—"

"It is not the tree's safety I fear for," he interrupted, crossing his arms. "It's yours."

"Are you actually threatening me?" Eugene shouted.

"There is no need," Joseph replied, still calm. "The threat is with you already. Be careful, Eugene Thomas."

Eugene poked his finger toward Joseph's face. "You're a *freak*."

"C'mon Gene, let's just go," Kat said, tugging his arm. She looked afraid.

Eugene glowered at Joseph, snatched his bag from the ground, and trudged off in the opposite direction. He hiked at double his previous pace until he and Kat reached the top of the ridge. Finally, he turned. His eyes were fiery.

"This isn't over," he seethed.

"What are you going to do?" Kat asked.

"He can't watch that tree forever."

Chapter 6

Vancouver, Washington ~ Present day

Zoo Day was the most fun Iris could remember having in her whole two months working at Rookwood. For two straight hours, she and Candace brought every resident who was mobile enough to interact with the animals, watching them experience true delight. She even remembered to "meet" George Washington the bulldog and his owner, the stamp dealer, for the "first time."

Will's animal party platter lay empty once everyone had a chance to feed a morsel to a rodent or watch a bird or dog do a trick. Ratrik, Bowie, Caramel, and Mocha were full and sleepy, and Samson the macaw had indeed gotten his dance bananas. Honeybun's mane and tail were full of braids and yarn, while Ralphie the cat had spent most of the time purring in Lois's lap. Dale Earnhardt, the tortoise, had delighted the crowd when he challenged Fred's wheelchair to a race, and won by a nose. Fred had been gracious in defeat, reminding everyone that "it's not polite to show up a turtle."

For another hour after that, Denise, Iris, and Candace took volunteers and their animals around to visit residents who couldn't leave their rooms. Iris couldn't help but feel a bit wistful as she passed room 105, which had sat empty for months since Angus had never come along after all. She was relieved, though, that his real old age was spent on his own terms, surrounded by those he loved. And she remembered the heart shaped mirror frame which hung in the chapel even now, which had held his secrets for over a century. She smiled.

At noon, she and Candace flopped into their chairs in the Activity Office, feeling both accomplished and ready for a break.

"Will's making curried lamb," Iris told her. "You gonna join?"

"Oh, not today," Candace waved her off. "I'm not a curry person. Besides, I'm sure you two would like time to chat."

"News travels fast, I guess," Iris said, turning a little pink in the cheeks.

"With James around? Yeah!" Candace smiled at her. "But it's not like I didn't see it from a mile away. What did I say from day one? He's totally into you!"

"Seems so! He's…" Iris laughed. "He's pretty great."

"Girl! You are smitten already! Get your tushie down there and have a great lunch break. I'm going to turn on my classical music and eat a bagel."

"Are you sure you—"

"Scat!"

"I'm going!"

"See ya!"

Iris laughed as she exited the office, only to bump into James, the office admin assistant.

"Hey, Iris! What's up? Going down for a lunch date with Will?" Sixteen year old James had no subtlety whatsoever, but Iris had come to love that about him.

"Yep. He's doing lamb. Wanna come?"

"Ick. Sorry, but no way. You guys are way too cute already. Whenever I hang around you, I feel like I ate a whole box of Twinkies."

"James, you've seen us together *one* time!"

"Twinkies!"

Iris shrugged. "Fine, suit yourself."

Even at the bottom of the stairs, Iris could smell the warm, heady scent of curry and saffron filling the air. Will stood alone in the deserted kitchen, plating the last bits of garnish on two picturesque dishes.

"I hope you're planning to take pictures of that!" she said from the doorway.

He looked up, his expression full of contentment. "I hadn't thought about it," he admitted. He wiped one last drop of stray sauce off the edge of the plate and presented it to her. "As promised, your curried lamb, m'lady."

"This is too pretty to eat!" she exclaimed. "Hang on, I'm taking a picture." She whipped out her phone.

"What for?"

"So I can remember it. It's the first curry you've ever made me!"

He chuckled. "It won't be the last, I promise. Unless you hate it."

"That's impossible, but let me check…" She sat on a stool, took a small morsel onto her fork, and savored it. She looked him in the eye. "I'm sorry, but I have really bad news, Will…"

"What?"

"I won't be able to eat Indian takeaway anymore. You've ruined it. Now anytime I want a curry, you'll have to make it for me."

His face was solemn. "I understand. I've brought this on myself. I'll just have to deal with the consequences." His dimples reappeared and his look of satisfaction returned. "I have a question for *you*, though. On a different subject. Something that's kind of… been on my mind. A lot."

"Sure, what's up? Oh my gosh, this is *so* good…"

"Iris, I need you to focus."

"Sorry. Please continue."

"Um, well… Y'know, we had such a good talk on our drive a few nights ago. I was feeling like things made sense. Like… yes, let's see more of each other. Take it slow. But the more I think about it, the more I have no idea what that even means."

"Seeing more of each other, or taking it slow?"

"Either one."

Iris set her fork down. "Well…"

She hadn't given it a lot of thought. Not practically.

"And then," he continued, "we said we're kind of… dating, but is that more serious than 'seeing more of each other,' or does it mean the same thing? I guess I just want you to tell me what you need, because I've never really dated anyone seriously, at any speed."

Iris smiled. He was hard to resist when he looked vulnerable. "I guess when we first met, and I was so… attracted to you, but I didn't know you very well, I was afraid it would turn out awful, like it did before. With Brett."

"Who's Brett?"

"That chef I used to work with," she sighed. "Went on two dates with him, and then he turned into a psycho."

"Oh, restraining order guy!" Will nodded. "You told me about him. That's why I gave you my number in the first place, in case you ever needed… anything."

"Yes," Iris breathed, relieved that that conversation had really happened, and wasn't one that had been wiped from this reality.

"And then you said that's why you never date anyone at work. Except… I guess you do, in my case. But I hope you're feeling okay about me. I haven't scared you, have I?"

"No!" Iris said quickly. "Just the opposite. Every time I see you, I want to see you even more."

He smiled. "I feel exactly the same way. But I just keep running into this 'take it slow' thing, and I never know how much to say." He studied her. "I would never want you to feel like running away."

"I don't." She met his gaze. "What would you say right now if I had never asked you to take it slow?"

Will reached across the counter cautiously, as if approaching a frightened animal, and laid his hand gently over hers.

She was touched to her core by the depth of respect and tenderness in his gesture.

"I'd probably tell you that I can't remember what I used to think about in my spare time before I met you. And… I don't plan on dating anyone else, pretty much… ever. If I'm honest, I hope…" He struggled for words.

"I don't plan on dating anyone else, either," she filled in the rest.

He smiled, relieved. "I was just afraid somehow you meant you just wanted to be extra good friends or something."

"I don't hold hands with my extra good friends. You can ask them."

He gave her hand a light squeeze. "Good. Because that would be a little weird." He smiled. "I guess the only other thing is… Man, it's hard to say it right. Basically, with anybody you meet in life, there's emotional distance at the beginning, you know? With most people, you keep that distance. Like with an acquaintance, or an old high school buddy, where you spend time with them, but at some point, they move on and you never see them again. And it's fine, because they were *in* your life, but not really *part* of it.

"But sometimes," he continued, "there's someone you keep getting closer to, like a best friend. You end up going out of your way for each other, and you both reach a point where you know you'll be in each other's lives for good. No matter what happens after that, you're invested. You either carry them in your heart for life, or you carry the scar of losing them. No going back. You know what I mean?"

"I think so. My roommate, Charlie, and I met in third grade. I think by fifth grade, we had reached that point where we knew we'd always be friends. I'd say we're more like sisters now."

"Exactly," Will said. "And I've reached that point with you, Iris. I hope that's not too much to say, but I wanted you to know. No matter what happens from here on, I can't stop caring about you. I'm not out to force a romantic confession out of you, but you need to understand me. I will never be able to go back to thinking of you as just a sweet girl I work with. I'm past that. I want you in my life, and I hope you want me in yours, in whatever way I can be."

Iris soaked in the full meaning and the safety of his words. He offered honesty without demands. She had little idea what had transpired in this version of their two months of friendship. In the only version she could remember, he had been her rock. He had trusted her when it counted and come through for her when she and Angus desperately needed him. He had saved them both. And she could never tell him. She knew she wanted him, needed him, in her life, too. *But how is it fair to get so close to someone when you can never tell them the truth?*

She wove her fingers through his, letting herself imagine the words she already knew she wanted to say. *But what will happen to us if he doesn't understand why I can't tell him everything?* She looked at his face. *It's too late for me, too. I'll just have to figure it out.*

"I want you in my life, too," she said finally. "I can't guarantee how fun it'll be for you all the time. I have some pretty crazy things going on, and it's getting crazier every day."

"I'm okay with crazy," he said.

"I hope you mean that," she said earnestly. "I'm not out to force any romantic confessions out of you either, and we don't have to come up with all the answers right now. But I need to make it clear what I'm doing right now, Will. I'm letting you in. What you say and do, from now on, stays with me."

"I'll be careful, I promise."

"I believe you."

"How do you feel about hugs?" he asked sheepishly.

"Umm, I think they're better than coffee, if they're done right."

He stood and pulled her into a tender embrace that was both electric and perfectly comforting at the same time.

Iris had just enough time to stop by the store for cupcakes before heading over to the Reynolds house after work. At any other time in her life, she would have considered eating dinner with her old science teacher and his bachelor son two nights in a row an incredibly odd thing to do. But there was nothing odd about it to her now. Jason and Gray had become a lifeline of vital information, and their home felt like one of the safest places she'd ever been, much like Darrick and Katie MacCrann's home had felt when she and Angus had taken refuge there.

Once they'd finished their meal of Gray's famous roasted chicken and dumplings and settled in with coffee and cupcakes, Jason asked her, "How's your reading going?"

"It's going super well," Iris replied. "Most of it makes sense. I get a little bogged down here and there, but whenever I do, I just research the passage for more historical context. Then I usually end up cross referencing it with different parts of the book. Like whenever I research the prophetic passages, I keep finding myself in the back where the prediction was actually being fulfilled. It's weird to me how it all connects when it was written down by so many different people at different times."

"It's still weird to me, too," Grayson admitted. "But cool."

"Yeah, but it's totally not in chronological order!" Iris exclaimed. "I'm skipping all over the place and it makes me crazy! I've had to make a chart just to keep everything straight!"

"That sounds like you!" Jason laughed. "But have you come across anything so far that doesn't sit right?"

Iris thought about it for a moment. "No, nothing like that. I just don't understand what's happening to my head."

"Happening to your head?" he asked. "Is it exploding or something?"

"I don't know, it's hard to put into words. If you'd asked me a year ago, I'd have called this book a bunch of rules, superstitions, and myths… without even reading it. And now that I'm actually seeing for myself what's in there, I'm starting to wonder why I had that attitude. It doesn't strike me as any of those things."

"That's pretty common, actually," Jason said.

"Really?"

"Oh, yeah. There's a particularly vicious type of blindness where the Histories are concerned. People are prone to more bias and intellectual dishonesty on this topic than just about anything else. And many who feel that way haven't given it a proper read, either."

"I can't understand why, though. It's so fascinating!"

"Well… *now* you think it's fascinating. What about *before* you walked in a different century, or saw a Messenger or a Great Tree for yourself?"

"I guess it would have been harder to accept."

"Yes," said Jason, "harder to accept, and even harder to take literally!"

"But I know there are millions of people who *do* take it literally," she mused. "And they haven't seen the crazy things I have."

"Yeah, that's what we call 'faith.' It's a great source of hope for people who have it. I know it is for me. It's never disappointed me."

"So then… faith is just blindly accepting whatever it says in there as fact?" She instantly regretted how condescending she sounded. "Sorry… you know what I mean, right?"

"Of course I do," he said gently. "I don't think you should ever just blindly accept what you hear. I think you should question anything that gives you pause, no matter the source. Investigate until you're satisfied. Truth will always stand up to scrutiny."

"I agree with you," she said. "But I've always thought that truth was proven in a lab, or with an authenticated artifact."

"That's to be expected. Our Western way of thinking does that to us. Truthfully, everyone has a paradigm, a model of the world through which they live and see, based on previous information. But you have to realize something, Iris… you see with your *mind*, not your eyes."

Iris furrowed her brow, absently stirring her spoon in her coffee. "I don't see with my eyes?"

"Not really," Jason answered. "Your eyes are just data ports that take in holographic and energetic structures, and then your cone cells decode them. But you *see*—meaning you decide what *reality* is—by filtering everything through your paradigm. If your paradigm is flawed, your conclusions might be, too. When that happens, you actually turn the information around you into a virtual reality, and live out a lie."

She laughed. "You mean there are people walking around living in their own pretend worlds?"

"Yep. It's not as odd as it sounds. People do it all the time without realizing it. Imagine a person who's never interacted with a dog before. His only paradigm has been fed by stories like 'Little Red Riding Hood' and conversations with people who were attacked by dogs. What's he going to *see* the first time he meets a real dog?"

"A vicious beast?"

"Precisely. Even a wagging tail and slobbering jowls could be 'evidence' of aggression to this person, because his paradigm dictates it. But *we* know that's not the truth, because we've been to dog parks and seen *Scooby-doo*. Different paradigm. It's a false reality he's created, but he lives by it as fact."

"Well, of course! It's easy to see what's real when you look at such an obvious example," Iris objected. "But some paradigms are so widely accepted, it's hard to know when they're false."

"That's very true," Jason agreed. "And it's good to be honest with ourselves about it. But we have to decide with great caution *how* we will see. It's crucially important, because when thoughts take root in your brain, they become a real, physical substance that travels along neurons with branching dendrites, like trees. The more traffic they get, the more those little trees grow and take up real estate in your brain. Essentially, we're still choosing which tree we're going to eat from. The garden used to be on the outside… now it's on the inside."

"Thoughts… have physical substance…" Iris murmured.

She thought of the long, pink scar on her shin. Less than two weeks ago, she'd dragged a sharp ax against her leg, opening a deep gash. It should still be hurting. She should have needed stitches. But it was healed in a day. Her old paradigm, which stated how impossible that should be, had turned out not to be reality. Reality was right here—a fully healed leg—caused by something she couldn't see.

"I don't think most of my old paradigms survived my last adventure," she admitted.

"It's no wonder," Jason chuckled.

Iris took another slurp of her coffee. "So the Guardians believe the Histories are true?"

"Yes."

And all of them are one hundred percent on board with that?"

"That's correct."

"Hmm."

"It wouldn't make sense for us not to be," Grayson added. "Our diaries date back at least that far, and always coincide with what's in the Histories. They've never conflicted. More importantly, our entire function is to partner with the unseen— safeguarding something that couldn't exist by chance. Something as complex as a time fabric that grounds all of reality doesn't just... happen."

Even as Gray spoke, Iris could feel the truth of it. Her journey to the past with Angus—the absolute precision required to set things right—had been nothing short of miraculous. To chalk that up to coincidence bordered on the absurd.

"And if I decide to take this mysterious job, that means I have to believe in all of it, too? I mean... I've only read half of it, so far."

"The Council understands your position, Iris," Jason said. "Their offer stands as long as you act in good faith and strict confidentiality. They're not going to force any beliefs on you. They couldn't, anyway."

"Why do you look amused?"

Jason laughed. "I'm just trying to imagine *anyone* telling you what to think and getting away with it."

"They're welcome to try!" Iris laughed with him.

"Okay, so!" Jason cleared his throat and set his plate aside. "Here's what the Council is proposing..."

"Yes! Let's have it!" Iris leaned forward in her chair.

"They want to put you in charge of some unusual missing persons cases."

"What? Seriously?"

"Seriously. Mind you, there aren't very many. We Guardians are excellent at our jobs. But every so often we get people like Angus, who find themselves a little stranded due to unusual circumstances. There have been some real head scratchers in the past few centuries—people we thought would have reappeared by now, but we can't seem to locate. Angus Armstrong was the strangest case we know about. He was missing for over a century, as you know. It worked out beautifully in his case, because you were there."

"Aw, it was nothing," Iris said. "He just seemed so lost. I wanted to do everything I could to help."

"I wouldn't call what you did for him 'nothing.' Don't dismiss the fact that you knew nothing about the Guardians or the Great Trees, but you chose to believe his story was possible. And you put yourself in serious jeopardy for his sake. Not many people would have done that."

"It was worth it." Iris warmed at the memory of Angus's face growing young before her eyes. "Besides, he would have done the same for me."

"Perhaps so. But imagine if you hadn't been there. Angus had no idea what had really happened to him, and no way to get the right kind of help. The MacCranns weren't aware he'd reappeared, and had no way to relocate him even if they had known. They're geographically limited, as all Guardians are. They needed an extra person to find Angus and bring him back. Someone like you."

"I just feel lucky that I was there," Iris said.

"Oh c'mon, you know better by now," Jason scoffed. "Luck had nothing to do with it. You were there because you were meant to be. The Council takes that very seriously."

"So what would I actually be doing, then? I felt like all I did for Angus was bring him tea and cookies, and then commit a series of felonies!"

Jason let out a hearty laugh. "Well, just imagine a scenario in which you could save someone like Angus again, but this time with some serious financial backing and a worldwide network of support on your side. And instead of stumbling around in the dark for information, you'd make use of all of the history you know, plus have access to the accumulated knowledge of the Guardians."

The magnitude of what they were proposing was beginning to sink in. Iris was speechless.

"We would provide you with a dossier on a missing person, detailing everything we know, recorded by the Guardian involved. You'd go to work with your research skills and see if that person has reappeared anywhere, or estimate where you think they're most likely to pop up. Once someone is found alive, you'd lead the extraction team."

Iris belly laughed. "*Extraction* team? What is this, the CIA?"

"Oh, give us this one," Gray chuckled. "We're excited! We've never had an extraction team before! We wanted it to sound cool!"

"How big of a team?"

"Three or four," Gray continued. "You'd need to liaise with the Guardian involved, bring the person back to the appropriate location, and if it's still possible, get them home. We saw what you went through with Angus. With support, you could do in a few days what it took you two weeks to accomplish alone."

Iris's mind was spinning. "Okay, this all sounds… amazing. I guess I just wonder… why *me*? Why doesn't the Council just appoint some of its own members to do this job?"

"Uhh… that's a great question," Jason said. "It has about four and a half answers, though. As I said, the Council takes it seriously when someone like you is surrounded by miracles—what seem to be coincidences. They admire your tenacity and your heart. Intervening on behalf of someone who was lost because you knew it was right, and then keeping it confidential, showed a lot of character. They also feel that your comprehensive grasp of world history would uniquely qualify you to handle these cases. And since you're not a Guardian responsible for a Great Tree, you're free to roam. But y'wanna know the biggest reason of all?"

"What?"

"They're old!" Jason laughed. "They've served their entire lives, and they want a break!"

"I can't say I blame them," Iris giggled. "So are you going to join the Council when Grayson takes over your spot? You did just turn fifty, after all."

"Yes, I'm nearly ancient." He sniffed. "Well, to be honest, I've already told them I would join. It all depends on you."

"Me? Why on me?"

"Guardian culture, again. No one is forced to work alone, especially not the young. If you took the job, you'd be considered an honorary Guardian Heir—like an apprentice. Trouble is, you're not the child of a Guardian. So they would assign you to someone. That Guardian would be responsible to bring you up in Guardian knowledge, and see that you get the support you need. Then he would report directly to a Council member."

"So who would be my boss?" Iris wondered.

"Well, not so much a boss as a mentor," Jason said. "The Council discussed that. They want you to feel at ease. You're familiar with Gray and me, so one option is to work with us. But you've also worked closely with Darrick MacCrann. They've already spoken with Darrick, and he's excited to have you, if you choose to go there. Their only stipulation is that your choice not draw attention or arouse a lot of questions."

"So if I chose to work with Darrick, I'd have to move back to Scotland?"

"Yes. And you'd have to do it on some other believable pretense."

"And if I stayed here, I'd work with you?"

Jason hesitated. "Not me, officially. I'm always here if you need me, of course. But if you stay, you'd be assigned to Gray. He'd take over as Guardian here, and I would be officially retired and join the Council. Gray would report to me."

"Jason, I can't make a decision that's going to determine the direction of your life like that!" Iris blurted.

"Oh, we're faced with life-altering decisions all the time, and we aren't even aware it's happening," he said gently. "Listen, you just make your decision for yourself. I'm happy with either outcome."

She let out a breath and nodded.

"And Iris? Take your time and really think about things, okay? Remember that you can always say no. Taking on this life… it's not going to be easy. I just want you to be sure you're prepared to go through with it."

"Yeah. Like travel, and research and stuff?"

"No… I mean having a whole side of your life that you can't tell anyone about."

Iris's stomach dropped. *This isn't going to be so simple.*

Chapter 7

Sedona, Arizona ~ 1965

Eugene and Kat hiked back to the first map point in silence. When they reached the tree stand, Eugene plunked his bag on the ground. He began to assemble the borer, attaching the handle to the shaft and stuffing the core extractor into his back pocket, muttering to himself the entire time.

"I don't know why you're so hot under the collar about all this," Kat finally said. "It's just one tree."

"I don't expect you to understand," Eugene answered without looking up. "You don't know trees like I do."

"So tell me."

He huffed, and rummaged for a sample storage tube—a simple paper straw. He found one and put it into his other pocket. Finally, he looked up at her. "It's not *just* a tree. It's the weirdest tree I've ever seen. Its growth is unprecedented. I could do an entire paper on it!"

She sidled up to him and traced her finger down his forearm. "So it would be a really important paper, then?"

He let out a sardonic laugh. "I don't do anything that *isn't* important."

"Well... what about this project?" She gestured to the trees next to him.

"I could do both," he said. "It would blow their doors off back at the U!"

"Then let's get back down there!"

"You're funny," he said. "Am I supposed to just tie that Indian up?"

Kat smirked. "There's more than one way to tie a man up. Trust me."

A devious grin spread across Eugene's face. "You little devil!"

"I say we go at sunset, and see how this... *Joseph* guy likes my acting skills."

He laughed. "For science, of course!"

She pursed her lips in mock seriousness and nodded. "Of course."

The last orange hues had begun to disappear from the sky when Joseph Iwila heard a timid cry coming from outside his house. He opened the door and listened intently.

"Dad, what gives?" asked the fifteen year old boy who sat at the table doing algebra.

"I thought I heard an animal," Joseph replied. "Might be that coyote that's been after the sheep."

"I'll check it out," the boy said. "If I have to look at one more math problem right now, I'm gonna lose it."

"All right," Joseph replied. "Take the rifle."

The boy stood eagerly and stretched his lanky arms.

"And Benjamin?"

"Yeah?" He always paid a little extra attention when his father used his full name.

"Don't be long. You have homework to finish."

"Looking forward to it," he told his father with a roll of his eyes. He grabbed the gun from the rack by the door and disappeared.

"Teenagers," Joseph mumbled.

Ben set out in an easterly direction, toward the sheepfold, which was half enclosed by an open barn. His feet made almost no noise as he listened in the still evening. Just as he was about to give up and tell his old man he must be hearing things, a faint whimper floated toward him from his right. He turned south and rounded a small formation of rocks about ten feet tall. He stopped in his tracks.

Seated at the base of one rock was the most beautiful woman he'd ever seen. She was holding her ankle, and had large tears rolling down her cheeks.

He rushed to her side and knelt down. "Are you all right, miss?"

"Oh, thank goodness!" she cried. "It's getting dark, and I'm so lost! I thought I'd have to spend the night with rattlesnakes!"

"Why are you out here all alone?" Ben asked.

"I wasn't, but my friend went to get help and I think she must be lost, too! Oh, this is so *frightful!* It was just supposed to be a fun hike!"

"Are you hurt?"

"I think my ankle is broken," she whimpered.

Ben set his rifle against the rock and examined it in the fading light. "It looks bruised. We should get you back to my place and put some ice on it. You'll probably need to see a doctor."

"Oh, thank you so much. You're my hero!" She gazed up at him with soulful, adoring eyes.

"Can you hang tight here while I get my dad?"

"Yes. I'm sorry I'm so distraught. I was just... so frightened! I can't thank you enough!"

"I'm Ben, by the way." He smiled shyly.

"I'm Lola."

"Okay, hang on. I'll be right back."

From his hiding place behind a boulder halfway down the ridge, Eugene watched a teenage boy dash back into the small house. A minute later, both he and that annoying older Indian emerged and quick-footed it in the opposite direction.

Eugene made a break for the trees, keeping his steps as quiet as he could. He had reassembled his borer while he was waiting for Kat to make her move. Now with it in hand, he broke through the shrubbery surrounding the giant juniper in the same spot he had before. He heard the strange humming sound again. It was so subtle, it seemed almost to come from inside his head.

He set the sharpened tip of the auger into a furrow of the juniper's bark at chest height. With one hand steadying the shaft, he pressed the bit into the tree and turned the handle hard. The humming sound became slightly more pronounced.

Is that noise coming from the tree? He listened. *It can't be.*

He continued to turn the borer with pressure until the auger's threads engaged and began to sink into the tree with every turn. Then, it was just a matter of turning the handle with both hands as smoothly and quickly as he could until he had sunk the entire length of the shaft straight into in the center of the tree, past the pith. He wanted a core sample that was longer than the radius.

He looked around him. He still couldn't hear anyone coming, so he moved quickly. This was a critical stage, especially with such a huge tree. If he didn't get the borer out soon, the pressure inside the tree would rebound and clamp down on the steel shaft, making it almost impossible to remove. He pulled the long metal extractor from his back pocket and slid it all the way inside the auger shaft, then gave the borer's handle two full counter-clockwise turns. As soon as he felt the core he had drilled snap away from the inside of the trunk, a pronounced moaning hum arose from the depths of the tree.

His eyes went wide. *What is going on with this tree?*

He gently pulled the extractor from the shaft, bringing with it a perfectly cut cylindrical radius of the tree. He carefully set it flat on top of his leather satchel. If Kat were here, he would have had her store the sample in a tube immediately, but there was no time for that now. He feverishly continued to turn the handle counter-clockwise, feeling the resisting pressure inside the tree. Drops of sweat began to collect on his forehead. The shaft was backing out a little bit, but mostly spinning with every turn. The auger wasn't engaging as well as he'd hoped. He exerted some additional force, pulling on the handle while turning. The tree hummed louder.

Kat waited impatiently for that kid Ben to bring his dad to help her up. To stave off boredom, she tossed pebbles at a lizard, while trying to remember to stay in character. Finally, she heard their voices approaching, so she put her distressed face back on.

"She's right back here…" Ben was saying.

Joseph and Ben Iwila stood above her in the deepening twilight.

"Oh, thank goodness you're back!" She looked up at them with as pitiful an expression as she could muster.

"Dad, this is Lola."

Joseph looked her over with a critical expression. "Nice to see you again, Kat."

"Joseph." Kat nodded.

Ben frowned. "Wait, you two have met?"

Without a word, Joseph scooped Kat up from the ground and strode toward the small house with her in his arms. Less than a minute's walk put them right in the living room. He set her on a cushy armchair.

"Now, tell me exactly what you are doing on our land," Joseph said. His expression was not angry, but stoic.

"Dad, she hurt her ankle hiking. That's what she said."

Joseph's eyes traveled to Kat's ankle. "You did an excellent job on this," he complimented her. "But it is not as convincing in the light."

"What are you—" Kat began to protest.

Before she could say anything else, Joseph stooped down and swiped his thumb across her ankle. He showed Ben the blue eye shadow that had stuck to his thumb. Ben's mouth fell open.

Suddenly, the boy and his father grew still and alert. They looked at each other.

"Did you hear—" Ben began.

"It's the Tree!" Joseph jumped to his feet.

For the first time since Kat had met him, he actually looked distressed.

"I hope you are satisfied," he said soberly. "You may have just killed that man."

The tree had begun to hum at such a pitch now that the sound was genuinely painful to stand next to. Eugene found it so distracting that, in his rush to remove the borer from the tree, he pulled too hard on the handle. It detached from the shaft and sent him tumbling backward. He scrambled to his feet, swearing in new and creative ways, and reattached it. He yanked a leather glove from the side pocket of his satchel and slipped it onto his right hand. He used it to grasp and pull on what little of the shaft he had managed to unscrew from the tree, while continuing to turn the handle with his left hand. The maneuver was beyond awkward, but it was his best idea in the short time he had left to work. He couldn't rely on the handle much for pulling, and he couldn't touch the steel shaft with his bare hands until it cooled down from all the friction inside the tree.

After another full minute of labor, the threads on the bit engaged and the borer started backing out of the tree without pressure. He kept up the turning at a feverish pace. He was trying to listen for footsteps and voices, but could hear nothing over the odd hum of the tree.

Finally, the borer came free. The tree immediately quieted. At this point, he would have normally spent time cleaning bits of wood out of the auger bit, but now, he didn't even take it apart. He just tucked it into his bag as it was, knowing he'd pay for it later with a chipped bit and lacerated notebooks, but he didn't care. He slid the core sample into a couple of paper straws from his bag, and disappeared from the clearing at the same moment that Joseph Iwila and his son came through the trees on the other side.

Eugene and Kat each circled back to camp in the last diffuse rays of dusky light. As soon as they caught sight of each other, they laughed.

"We're a regular Bonnie and Clyde!" she giggled.

"I don't know what you did, but it sure worked! They both came running!" Eugene beamed at her.

She struck a dramatic pose with the back of her hand against her forehead. "Ah broke mah poor ankle! Whatever shall ah do? Save me, fearless knight!"

Eugene laughed again, spun her, and dipped her into a passionate kiss. "You're amazing."

"Yes, that's true."

He released her, and his face grew serious. "You know, we probably shouldn't stay here," he said. "We stick out like a sore thumb, and I don't know what those guys will do."

"It's not like they're going to want your sample so they can stick it back in the tree!" she laughed.

"No, of course not. I was thinking of something more practical, like not getting arrested for trespassing on private land, that kind of thing. I just don't want to get you mixed up in anything that would give you a criminal record."

Kat grinned.

He raised an eyebrow. "You don't already *have* a record, do you?"

"I'll never tell!" she giggled.

He shook his head, smiling at her.

"Well…" She bit her lip. "You're probably right. Let's pack up. But where are we going?"

"We'll get a motel room in town. We can find a better camping spot tomorrow."

Joseph and Ben stood beside the Great Juniper, listening to its pained vibration. Joseph shined his flashlight on a steady stream of dark, inky sap that dribbled from the pierced trunk.

"It is just as he said," Joseph sighed. "A small hole."

"You saw that guy before?" Ben asked.

"Yes, he was here earlier. I warned him of the danger, but his heart was prideful."

"I wonder how long this will take to heal over."

Joseph turned to his son. "Do you remember the story of the Lost Carpenter?"

"Of course. That took forever! But this wound isn't as severe."

"I'm afraid that's hard to judge with Great Trees, son. Yes, the carpenter took a branch, while this scientist took only a sample. But he has cut across a major artery, so to speak. This could also take a long time, unless it is repaired before the healing begins."

"We have to get that piece back!" Ben's face took on a fiery expression. "And I'm a little annoyed at that chick who tricked me. It'd be nice to—"

"Guard your heart, Benjamin," Joseph said sternly. "They are ignorant."

"So are we going to do this in the dark, or wait until dawn?"

Joseph frowned, contemplating the seeping wound in the tree. "The sooner, the better, I think."

Eugene made sure he put the top up on the Mustang before he gathered his overnight bag and Kat's red suitcase, locked the doors, and trotted up the stairs to where Kat was waiting outside the open door of their motel room. It was a cold night, full of stars. Kat leaned against the balcony railing, cigarette in hand, staring at the sky.

He threw the bags onto the bed and joined her, sliding his arm across her shoulders.

"Gene, did we do something awful?" she asked absently.

"What do you mean, awful?"

"With that great big tree."

"I didn't hurt the tree. That old fellow is hale and hearty. He'll be just fine."

She looked at him, her eyes clouded with a disturbed expression. "Those two guys seemed so upset about it, though."

Eugene scoffed. "Who knows, with Indians?"

Kat shook her head. "Y'know the older one, Joseph? He said something to me…"

"I'm sure he was just trying to scare you off." He pulled her into an embrace. "Don't worry about that guy, okay? Put him out of your pretty little head."

"If you think so."

"I do. We'll never see him again. Let's go in where it's warm, huh?"

"Sure." She flicked her cigarette over the railing and watching it spit a few sparks on the sidewalk below.

"Actually," Eugene said, "you go on in. I just want to grab something from the car. Be right back."

Kat shrugged and went inside.

As much as he wanted to begin his evening with Kat and see where it led, Eugene couldn't shake his curiosity about that tree. What a racket it had made! It was the most surreal thing he'd ever encountered. He just wanted to get a better look at the sample in good light, and then make sure it was stored properly. No sense in letting it get ruined after he'd gone to all that trouble to get it.

He unlocked the passenger door and reached under the seat where he'd hastily stashed his leather satchel. Being careful not to brush his fingers against the razor sharp auger bit, he retrieved the paper tubes that contained the sample, along with a roll of masking tape. That borer still needed cleaning, but he'd have to bother with it later. He stuffed the bag back under the seat, locked the car, and headed back up to the room.

Kat was in the bathroom when he returned, so he set the sample and tape on the little side table and pulled the chain on the lamp. He found a notepad emblazoned with the motel's logo at the top and used it as a placemat. Carefully, gently, he pulled the straws apart, revealing the sample from the tree. For half a second, he thought he heard the tiniest high pitched vibration, but it quickly faded. He slid the wood completely out of the tubes and set it on the notepad.

What he saw in front of him completely baffled his brain. The entire piece of wood was uniform in appearance—there wasn't a single tree ring anywhere. Instead, the entire length of it was covered in a shimmering patina, the color of pyrite. He gasped, and bent closer. As he squinted at it, he could see what looked like tiny metallic waves, rippling up and down. The motion reminded him of the way ocean currents eddied in and out of a tide pools, or how an electromagnetic wave oscillated. It was such a subtle movement that if he was any farther away than twelve inches, he couldn't see it.

"Wow," he whispered. He gingerly touched the wood with his fingertips. As he did, the high pitched vibration returned. He pulled back his hand in shock and examined it. The pads of his fingers were stained dark. He picked up one of the straws and held it up to the light. It, too, bore dark stains on the inside. "What the heck *is* that stuff?"

"What stuff?" Kat stood in the doorway of the bathroom, holding her makeup bag. Her head was wrapped in a towel and she had changed into an oversized t-shirt.

Eugene looked up, his face in awe. "Kat! This tree sample is unbelievable! It has no rings! There's this crazy sap I've never seen before..." He held up his stained fingers.

"Whoa..." she said. "Wait, how can there be no rings? Don't trees get a new ring every year?"

"Yeah, give or take. This one's gotta be hundreds of years old by its size, and no rings! None!" he cried. "Like it's ageless! No wonder that crazy coot wanted me to stay away from it!" He stared at the sample again. "This is going to rewrite science! And I'll be the guy who—"

Kat shrieked and dropped her makeup bag, scattering its contents across the tile floor.

Eugene frowned. "What's gotten into you?"

She pointed straight at him, her eyes wide in horror.

"WHAT?"

"Gene! You... you look like a ghost!" Her voice trembled.

"What are you talking about?"

"Your hands..." she couldn't stop staring.

He looked down at his hands. They had become transparent. He could see that the inky sap stain had spread down his fingers onto his palm, but he could also see his own lap right through it. A chill of panic swept over his body. He jumped to his feet, sending the chair over backwards.

"Oh God! What's happening?" Kat cried, still rooted to the spot. "I can barely see you!"

He looked up at her, awash with terror. The room began to fade from view, replaced by blinding light.

Skliros roared in frustration. His billowing black form hovered over the trembling woman who stood alone in the motel room, staring in shock at a toppled chair.

"Oh, cheer up," Apateon drawled. "It's the closest you've ever gotten to that Tree, am I right?"

"Silence!" he boomed. "What good is it now that the creature has disappeared? I told that worthless partner of yours not to let him touch it!"

"First of all," Apateon growled, "he wasn't my partner. I don't *do* partners. Second, I don't know what else you expected from those two. They want what they want. That human can't keep his hands off anything. You really think *Thelo* was going to stop him?"

The woman below them fell to her knees and began to cry.

"And now look what you've done. My poor pet creature is upset!" he snickered.

"There is no one to write and spread word of the Great Tree," Skliros snarled.

"Oh, he's around someplace," Apateon shrugged. "You'll just have to keep an eye out."

A menacing grumble arose from Skliros. "Your attitude irks me. You forget your place. Shall I dispose of this creature for you? She does seem too upset to go on." He descended into the room and hovered near the woman, his hand near the base of her skull. "I could give her some wonderful perspective on the subject of suffering. Then, when I'm finished, I could inform the other princes of how you've failed me. They might be interested to know where you are."

"Oh, relax," Apateon sighed. "Fine, you win this round. You want humans to come worship in your realm? I'll work on it.

You'll have to give me some time with this one, though. She's raw material. But I think she's seen enough that we can put her to work."

"That's the first sign of intelligence I've seen from you," Skliros said. "You have some past experience in religions of this sort, don't you? You will start now."

"Is the scroll prepared?"

"I just received it." Skliros produced a small parcel that looked like a roll of filthy toilet paper. "It's a twist on some old classics."

Apateon absorbed it, enveloping it like an amoeba and digesting it. "I can work with this," he chuckled. "Like I said, it'll take some time. She's got too much to lose at the moment."

"She needs a hero!" Skliros laughed. He rippled, bending the energy waves in the motel room, causing the lamp to flicker and then crash to the floor.

The woman screamed and scrambled onto the bed, clutching a pillow to her chest.

"You... killed... him..." he whispered loudly enough for a human to hear.

She whimpered.

"You're... nexxxxt!" he hissed.

She hid her face in the pillow as her whole body shook.

"All right, don't overdo it," Apateon said so only Skliros could hear. "We need her to be conscious!"

With a sinister chuckle, Skliros rose into the air, through the ceiling. "I'll be watching." He streaked away into the desert.

Apateon rolled his eyes. Then, after careful consideration, he floated in front of the frightened woman. He manipulated the spectrum of lightwaves until he had reconstructed a pleasing facade—an old favorite. He appeared as a slender bearded man with a friendly smile, wearing a white cloak with a sword and scabbard at his side, and holding a staff. It resembled the face of a host he'd occupied for some time in the British isles many centuries ago. Those were glorious days back then, when the putrid, superstitious creatures believed he was a god inside an oak tree. He could make them do anything... right up until the day the Messengers of the Three had routed him, led into battle by Albion, the commander of that dominion. Now he was banished, reduced to such inefficient means as actually befriending these filthy humans.

"Everything is going to be all right, dear one," he said in a soothing baritone. He'd opted for a British accent, too, for a bit of extra flair.

She gasped and looked up at him in shock. "Who are you?"

"My name is... *Albion*," he continued with a wry smile. "I am one of the White Brotherhood. I'm here to help you."

Tears streaked down the woman's face. "Are... are you an angel?"

"I am a messenger," he replied. "I have great knowledge to impart to you. I will help you realize your own potential."

"There was something really scary in here a minute ago," she whimpered. "That wasn't you, was it?"

"That was a being of great evil, intent on your destruction," he answered truthfully. "I have vanquished him with my sword on your behalf, for you are of utmost importance."

"I am?"

"Never doubt it, dear one."

"Wh-what happened to Gene? Is he really dead?"

"He may yet live. But you must follow my instructions exactly. Can you do that?"

She nodded dumbly.

"Very well. First, you must take the keys and open the car."

"What? Why?"

"There is something you must see."

Kat obeyed, padding down the cement steps barefoot in the cold darkness. She unlocked the passenger door, and sat in the seat. "Now what?"

"Open the glove compartment."

"What am I looking for?"

"You'll know it when you see it."

She rummaged through it, feeling a thick owner's manual, a few receipts, a pack of gum, cigarettes… then her fingers found a small, round object. She held it in her palm. *A wedding band?* It swam in front of her eyes, blurred by tears.

"He's…" she sniffed. "He's *married?*"

"I am so sorry, precious child," Apateon said in his most soothing voice. "He deceived you. You needed to see the truth."

"How could he?" she screamed. She clutched the ring in her fist.

"He saw your beauty and took advantage." His voice was like silk. "If you listen to me, I will never let that happen to you again."

Kat shuddered, the chill night soaking through her t-shirt, adding pain to her tormented sobs. "Albion, what do I do?"

"We must speak to no one of Eugene, ever again. He is a traitor. I will show you the safest path to your true destiny. Do you trust me?"

Her chin quivered as she nodded again. "Yes."

Chapter 8

Vancouver, Washington ~ Present day

I ris replayed yesterday's conversations in her mind as she made the drive to her parents' house on the outskirts of Vancouver. Everything Jason and Gray had said about the possibilities of her future swirled together with everything that had passed between her and Will. She wanted to help the Guardians find lost people. It burned in her like a growing flame. But Will was right—at a certain point, you know when someone is going to be in your life forever. With some, you know it sooner. She wasn't sure if she could do life without Will anymore… at least not without considerable pain. But how could she ever hope to have both?

And that wasn't the only thing that occupied her brain. The words of the Histories stood in her mind like a castle under construction. She had spent hours last night finishing the older part of the book. Although she was paying for the lack of sleep with a slight headache, it had been worth every moment. The power of the stories and the force of this God's passion for His people awed her. She found it a little frightening, if she was being honest with herself. He was so many things.

The way He protected His own and dealt with His enemies was positively fierce. But the way He invited people to walk in the garden or talk with Him on a mountain seemed so… *personal.* If the stories were to be believed, then those people would have seen firsthand that He was truly everything He said He was, and had the power to prove it.

But if He was so amazing, powerful, and wise, then why didn't the people want to be with Him? she wondered. *The first people had the perfect setup, and they screwed it up. Then the chosen nation was invited up to a summit with God Himself, and they actually refused!*

Iris frowned. *Had they really said, "Sorry, God, but you scare us. Just give us rules to follow, punish us when we break them, and we'll go through a middleman if you need to talk to us"? Who does that?* Then she had a realization: *Actually, I guess a lot of people do that.*

So then… He set up a whole system that way, with laws and punishments, at their request. The more history progressed, the harder it was to stay on God's good side, even for people who really wanted to. Who can begin to keep up with all the rules there must be now? How do the Guardians live like that?

Iris pulled into her parents' long driveway and parked in the same spot that she'd used since learning to drive. She let out a big yawn. Her mother had decided that a morning visit would fit their schedule best, and she expected Iris to show up not only on time, but in a chatty mood. Both her parents would want to hear all about her trip to Granny and Granddad's in St. Cyrus—at least, the part she could remember without blurting out official secrets. Iris looked in the rearview mirror to see how awake she looked. *Marginal.* She hoped there would be coffee.

Even though she had to mentally prepare to converse with her mother, it would be great to see them both. Especially her dad. Finn Jacobs had been the driving influence behind her love of research and history, as well as her analytical, wide-angled perspective on life. The two of them could sit happily ensconced among pots of coffee and stacks of books, and not emerge for days. But thanks to her mother, she had always had a very full and "proper" social calendar to balance her out… including being forced to make intelligent conversation before nine in the morning on her day off. She trudged past the neatly manicured shrubbery and let herself in through the oversized oak door.

"Hello!" she called out, hanging her scarf and rain jacket on the old fashioned coat rack in the entryway.

"In here, lass!" her father's voice floated toward her from the living room.

She smiled and kicked off her boots.

Finn was seated cross-legged on his favorite corner of the brown leather sofa, coffee in hand. He was reading a paperback titled *Prehispanic Religions of Ancient America*. Iris recognized the soft green sweater he was wearing as the one she'd gotten him for Christmas two years ago.

"I've missed you," she said, plopping down next to him.

He set his cup on the coffee table and enveloped her in a tight hug. "Is that all?"

"No," she giggled. "I've also *really* missed you!"

"I thought so." His short, neatly trimmed beard tickled her face as he planted a quick series of kisses on her temple. "My sweet girl. You've been missed round here, that's certain. I'm not sure I can endure another of your mother's Christmas Eve parties without you. I had to decorate the tree, y'know."

"Yes, she told me."

"I'll bet she did. And I still cannae tell what's so awful about it. I thought the trick was to stand about ten feet back and toss the ornaments at it for even distribution, am I right?"

Iris laughed. "Absolutely! It's how the pros do it."

"Arright, then."

Iris looked over at the Christmas tree by the fireplace. *Hmm.* She could almost believe the ornaments *had* been tossed at it from ten feet.

"It looks great, Dad."

He shook his head and chuckled.

"What's that you were reading?"

He handed her the worn book. She scanned the table of contents.

"You're into studying religion now?"

He shrugged. "I'm into everything. Y'know that. With some cultures, you cannae understand their lives properly unless you study what they believed. It dictated everything from when they planted crops to how they decided when to go to war."

"Yeah, I could see that." She set the book on the coffee table. "I've been doing a little bit of study myself lately."

"Is that so? What about?"

"Oh, just…" Iris searched for the right wording. "I guess just trying to decide how I really feel about all that stuff we used to learn in church."

He studied her face. "What brought that on?"

She smiled, thinking of Angus when he said to her, *"God might as well be holding up a massive sign that says, 'I SEE YOU, IRIS JACOBS!'"*

"I've just met some really interesting people lately. I guess it's got me thinking."

"I see."

"Hey Dad, how come we never went to church after we moved to the States?"

"Hmm, good question," he said, reaching for his cup. "Honestly, I think there was just so much going on with immigration paperwork, finishing my doctorate, teaching, finding a house… we just never made it a priority. Then we got out of the habit, I suppose. It was always really more my parents' thing, anyway. Church was a decent way to connect with people in a small village, but round here, it's hardly necessary."

Iris leaned into her dad's side, digesting that thought for a moment.

"But what about… God?"

"Well, I suppose He exists. It seems likely He does, or at least some kind of higher power. But if that's so, then He's everywhere, isn't He, lass?"

"I guess so," she conceded.

"Don't need a building for that."

"Well *there* you are!" Heather said from the breezeway that led into the kitchen. Her ginger curls were neatly pinned back from her face, and she wore an apron made of thistle print fabric. "Nice to know you've arrived so I'm not keeping the food warm!"

"Sorry, Mum. Nice to see you," Iris said, rising to embrace her mother.

Heather gave her two pats on the shoulder and continued, "Let's get on before I have to reheat the oven. Call us next time you'll be late, Iris."

"She wasn't late, dear," Finn said, getting up from the sofa and following them to the table. "She was snared into conversation by the old man in the sitting room."

"And you both know better," Heather said with an air of finality, removing and folding her apron.

Finn raised his eyebrows and gave Iris a side look that made her have to stifle a giggle.

"Let's get you some coffee," he said with a wink.

"Iris, do you still have that caffeine habit?" Heather asked as they sat at the table. "It's not healthy for someone your age, you know."

"Oh, leave her be," Finn grumbled, filling a mug for her. "I want to hear all about your visit with the folks. How are they?"

"They're doing so great," Iris replied, accepting the coffee and taking a long sip.

"So *well*," Heather corrected.

Iris let out a sigh, but tried not to make it a loud one. "Yes, sorry. They're doing very well. Granny made some amazing pies, as always. Granddad is as busy as ever with his commissioned work. He's been doing more furniture lately."

"Dad does love his rocking chairs," Finn said fondly.

"Yes he does," Iris agreed. "We talked about you a little bit. And he loaned me a really interesting biography about the master craftsman who got our family started in woodworking."

"Oh, aye! The uh... oh, what's his name... Armstrong," Finn said.

"Angus."

"Yes! Interesting you should bring that up, actually."

"How come?"

"Oh... I'll tell you later. It's a great story, though. I've read the book myself. Too bad it wasn't written yet when I was a twelve year old, trying to make my dad happy by picking up a hammer and making some truly hideous birdhouses. I might've tried harder if I'd known more of the history."

"I doubt it," Iris giggled. "But I think your career suits you perfectly. It's led you here. I love it here. And I want to do exactly what you do, maybe even more."

Heather passed a tray of roasted fingerling potatoes, tomatoes, and sausages. "What do you mean, more?"

Iris shrugged, taking a little of everything on the tray. "Maybe travel?"

"That's brilliant, Iris!" Finn said. "You should!"

"And what about this man you're seeing... any plans of marriage?" Heather asked as if she were asking Iris to pass the jam.

Iris had expected this question, but not three minutes into breakfast.

"You're seeing someone?" Finn asked, his fork frozen mid-air.

"Nobody panic," Iris chuckled, trying to lighten the mood. "It's still really new. I've only known him for two months, okay? There are no diamonds involved."

"And does this man have a name?" Heather asked.

"His name is Will Donovan. He's a chef."

Heather pursed her lips, then sipped her tea. "I'm surprised you'd go for that, after last time."

"Mum, he's a sweet guy! Not every chef is a psychopath. Anyway, I wasn't even looking for anybody. We just became good friends and then decided to see what happens next. He's been really great about everything."

"Well he's a lucky guy," Finn said, raising his mug in salute and taking a sip. "You've got a great head on your shoulders, sweet girl. And I know you can handle yourself out there. Any man tries to treat you poorly, you'll do exactly as you did last time and fight back."

Iris smiled. "Thanks, Dad."

After breakfast, Iris helped wash the dishes and Heather excused herself to get ready for some kind of ladies' charity fundraiser committee meeting. Once she'd disappeared upstairs, Finn and Iris sneaked their third cups of coffee and sank into the couch.

"So, my girl, did you really mean what you said about getting out there and doing some traveling?" he asked.

"Actually, yeah. I've been considering a job that would involve a lot of research and travel."

"What job?"

"Uh… I don't really know a lot of the details just yet. And if I do it, I'd probably only do it part time. But it's something, at least."

"Well, good for you. I was a wee bit worried when you took the job at the old folks' home that you'd given up on your dreams a little."

She shook her head. "Nah, I just needed rent. But actually, I really like it there! Never a dull moment!"

"And does this charming chef of yours understand your dreams?" His eyes twinkled.

She laughed. "I don't remember saying he was charming!"

"You didn't have to."

"Dad!"

"I know my girl! What can I say?"

Iris turned slightly pink. "Well I'm not sure if we've ever talked about that specific subject," she said truthfully. "But we will."

"Good. And you stick with whatever keeps you curious and full of wonder, arright? Just like I taught you. Even if it's a dusty old book that preachers drone on about every Sunday."

"I'm starting to think it's a lot more than that," she said earnestly. "Have you ever actually read the whole thing?"

"No, can't say that I have," he replied with an amused wink. "Shall I? I can add it to my stack if you want to compare notes like in the old days."

"Oh, will you? I'd love that!"

"Anything for you!"

She kissed his cheek.

"Now for your present!" he announced, and plunked his empty cup on the end table. He hopped up, went to the tree, and snatched the lone box from beneath it. It was wrapped in green tartan paper with a gold bow. "It's a bit of history, you see. I've been waiting ages to give it to you."

Iris tore the paper away and opened the black box. Inside lay a small antique pendant. The outside edges were loops of gold in the shape of a crown, studded with tiny diamond chips. A dangling seed pearl hung from the bottom of the crown. In the center lay three tiny irises in cobalt and purple enamel, with a single petite amethyst set into the flower on the left.

"Oh Dad, it's exquisite!" she gasped. "And that's my birthstone, too!" She looked up at him. He was beaming.

"I thought you might put it in your collection, but there's also a new chain in the box if you'd like to wear it."

"I can't believe how perfect it is! What did you mean, it's a bit of history?"

"Well, it's been in our family since the late Victorian period, always handed down. It's been the tradition that the next girl in line receives it on the Christmas after she turns twenty-two years of age."

Iris tilted her head. "That's kind of a strange number. Any idea why?"

Finn shrugged. "It's always been done. My guess is that it's a carryover from the days when wearing jewelry was only considered proper after a woman was a bit older. Why that specific age, I have no idea."

Iris took the pendant from the box and held it in her palm. "Gosh, I love the design. It's so intricate."

"Oh, that's the other thing I was going to tell you. As I was saying before, it's interesting you brought up Angus Armstrong, because he's the one who commissioned the piece."

Iris's mouth fell open. "What?"

"He did! The iris was well known to be a favorite of his. It shows up in a lot of his earlier works, especially. He even named his first child Iris."

She smiled. "Okay, so how did we end up with it? Why isn't it in *his* family?"

"It *is* in his family."

"I don't quite follow, Dad…"

"Well I'll tell you! I'm glad I looked all this up, because I knew you'd ask."

Iris grinned. "You trained me well."

"Aye," he chuckled. "Not sure if you've read the whole biography, but Angus Armstrong and his wife had four children—two sons and two daughters. The first was Iris, as I said. She married the son of his best friend. But his other daughter, Marjorie, actually grew up and married her father's apprentice, Ewan Jacobs. Their first child, Angus's granddaughter, was also named Iris, in honor of her aunt. So Angus had this…" Finn pointed to the pendant, "made for her by a jeweler in Edinburgh."

Iris was dumbfounded. "So there was *another* Iris Jacobs, over a hundred years ago… and she was Angus's grandchild?"

"Aye, the original Iris Jacobs! It's a lovely bit of history."

"Is that why you named me Iris?"

He nodded. "Your mother and I wanted to give you a family name. We were looking back over the family tree and chose that name because it symbolizes wisdom and courage."

Iris gaped at him. *This is insane. I'm named after myself. And now Angus is one of my many-great ancestors?* She looked down at the elegant pendant. *Twenty-two years old, indeed. Very convenient, Angus.* She chuckled to herself.

"Something funny, lass?"

She shook her head. "It's perfect, Dad." She looped the sparkling chain through the bail on the pendant and slipped it over her head. "Thank you for holding onto it for me all these years."

He touched her cheek. "It suits you."

Iris put in her earbuds on her way out of her parents' house and dialed her phone. As she pulled out of the driveway, Jason picked up.

"Hi, Iris!"

"I want the job."

"You absolutely sure?"

"Yes. Absolutely."

"What are you doing right now?"

"I think I'm coming over to see you, am I right?

"Bullseye."

"See you soon."

Iris sped up. Now that she'd made her decision, she was impatient to get on with it. She felt butterflies as she imagined what might lie ahead. Her mind was so preoccupied that she reached the Reynolds' house with very little memory of driving there.

When she knocked, Grayson threw the door wide. With a huge grin on his face, pulled her into a hug.

"I never thought my first Heir would be a girl!" he laughed.

Surprised, but delighted, she returned the hug and said, "Well, get used to it, Boss!"

"Heyyyy! There she is!" Jason said from behind Gray. He hugged Iris into a sandwich.

"I guess we're hugging today!" she laughed.

"Well this is a historic moment!" Jason said. "C'mon in. The second after we hung up, I announced your decision to the Council. Your database thread is absolutely blowing up. They wanted a conference call with you. I hope that's okay."

"Of course!" Iris agreed, taking off her jacket. "I'd love to get to know some of them. How many will be on there? Three or four?"

Gray and Jason laughed.

"What?"

"Do you remember me telling you they've always been fond of get-togethers?" Jason asked. "This is no exception. Two hundred and eighty-six of them are actually on there to welcome you. I'm sure we would have gotten more, but word only got out ten minutes ago, and with all the different time zones..."

Iris gasped. "But... how can that many people have a conversation at once?"

Gray chuckled. "The Guardians have developed their own software for it. It's like video conferencing, but a little more advanced. It'll be fun! You'll love it!"

They went into a home office that had two mahogany desks facing each other in the center of the room. One wall was lined with monitors, one large and several small ones displaying camera feeds of a tree in the adjacent cemetery. The monitors were surrounded on all sides by floor to ceiling bookshelves loaded with journals.

"Wow, this is a lot like Darrick's study," she commented.

"Yes, it's very avant-Guardian," Jason said, wiggling his eyebrows.

"Oh Dad," Grayson groaned. "Didn't I forbid you to make puns in here?"

"Yes, son, you did. I'll try to *monitor* that more closely."

"Ugh."

"I'll *screen* out unwanted comments…"

"Dad."

"Hehe! Sorry."

Iris watched the exchange like a ping-pong match, in absolute delight.

Gray waved her over to his desk, where another huge monitor showed a video conference in progress. Most of the screen was filled with small rectangles, each with the faces of men between the ages of fifty and ninety, from every race and color imaginable. In the upper right corner of the screen lay a world map with dots lit wherever a participant was located. Directly below that lay a running comment box. Some comments were preceded by a name and region, but most were preceded by a number.

"What do the numbers mean?" Iris asked.

"Oh, here?" Gray pointed to the comments. "That's how many people have said that particular phrase. The software converts everything that's spoken into text form, and then tallies up all of the comments with similar content and transmits them as one. Then it's translated into your native language on the monitor so you have a transcript of what's being said, even if you can't hear it. So right now, it's telling us that ninety-three of them have said 'Congratulations,' two hundred fifteen have said, 'We are so glad to have you,' and all of them have said 'Welcome.' The comments with names are unique and translated individually."

"Wow." Iris sat in Gray's chair. The chatter fell silent. Every man beamed at her with rapt attention. Iris didn't know what to say. She couldn't put into words the emotion she felt as she saw the support and regard these special men held for her. Each of them had served a lifetime doing what Darrick and Jason were doing, gladly building their lives and legacies around the protection of others.

Smiles broke out over dozens of faces, and there was a low murmur of several voices speaking at once, but Iris couldn't understand them. She looked at the comment box. Almost all of them had said the equivalent of "Wow, it's really her." About fifty others had voiced the sentiment, "It's all right. Don't be afraid."

She smiled. "Thank you for believing in me," she finally said. "I will do my very best… to… honor this Council, and to help as many people as I can. I think all of you are amazing. It's truly a privilege to be here."

Several heads nodded up and down. About eighty of them said, "You will do great things," and all of them said, "We're behind you."

The frame around one box glowed while the man spoke in a language Iris had never heard. In the comment box, his words showed up in English.

Gavin MacCrann, Scotland, United Kingdom: *I am so pleased to see you with us. My son Darrick speaks so highly of you. He is already planning something to welcome you. I should coordinate with Jason about it.*

"I think very highly of him as well!" Iris replied. "I can't wait to find out what he's up to! Please tell him and Katie hello from me!"

The elderly gentleman, who looked about seventy years old, gave her a boyish grin and a thumbs up.

Gray bent over her shoulder so that his face showed on camera. He spoke several rapid phrases in the same strange language that Gavin MacCrann had used. Iris stared at him. The translation popped into the comment box a second later:

Grayson Reynolds, Washington, U.S.A.: *Thank you all for welcoming Iris. She is an eager student and will do us proud. I have much to go over with her now that she has joined us. Gavin, my father will touch base with you shortly. I will keep the rest of you updated.*

Several responses popped up, most carrying the sentiments of "Great to see you all," "Looking forward to it," and "Let us know how we can help."

One by one, the little boxes disappeared as the dots on the map went dark.

Iris was still staring at Gray. "What language were you speaking?"

He smiled. His wavy auburn beard couldn't hide the slight blush on his cheeks. "Forgot to warn you about that. It's Chaldaic. When that many Guardians gather at once, we automatically switch to it."

"Chaldaic? That's like… an ancient, dead language, isn't it?"

"It's really *not* a dead language."

"How in the world did you learn it? Does it get passed down?"

"Uh, no. We don't learn it. We just… know it. It's the original language that was spoken by Guardians before everyone scattered. The rest of the world forgot it, but the Guardians were allowed to keep it. Now, when there are too many different languages in one place, we just revert to the original. Most of the time, we don't even realize we're doing it."

"That's trippy," Iris said.

"Maybe so, but it's also highly convenient not to have a language barrier." Gray looked over at Jason, who was standing by the monitors. "Dad? Did you hear—"

"Yes, I heard. Taking charge already, I see." He winked at Iris. "I'll get in touch with Gavin. Can I have the room?"

"Yeah. Thanks, Dad. It'll help if we can divvy up a little right now."

"Of course."

"Iris, let's grab a seat in the living room." Gray motioned to the door.

She followed him from the office to the airy living room and sat on a cream colored sofa opposite the brick fireplace. Gray sat beside her and turned his whole body to face her.

He grinned. "I'm so excited about this! It's one of the most unprecedented ideas the Council members have ever come up with!"

"I'm excited too!" Iris said. "Although it all seems rather fast!"

He laughed. "It's anything but fast. Honestly, they've tossed around the idea of bringing someone in since Angus Armstrong disappeared in 1844, but some weird stuff went down during both world wars that made them get more serious about it. Then you and Angus happened, and now the journals document that period both ways. Once the Council saw how much your involvement changed things, it practically decided for them."

"So what's first?" Iris tapped her fingers together.

"Well, we have a few cold cases we can start you on. But until then, let's talk practicalities. The Council has guys from every walk of life, but we have quite a few lawyers, businessmen, and financial wizards among us. They've been thinking a lot about how to make life simpler for you if you decided to join us. They realized that a bunch of old guys shoving money under the table without a paper trail, especially to a young lady, wouldn't look so good. We function largely outside of most governments, but they understand that *you* can't do that. So they created a private research foundation. That legal entity will be your official employer, where your title will be 'Research Specialist.' You'll get tax forms and everything. That way, you never have to lie when people ask you where you work, because now it's a thing."

"What a relief!" Iris felt easier in her mind already. Now she'd have something to tell her dad. And Will. And Charlie. "Do I get health insurance?"

"Yes. Here's the plan… if you get sick, we'll pray for you."

She laughed. "No, really, what's the plan?"

Grayson just looked at her.

"You're serious?"

"Yes, it should cover most things. But if the timing is delayed for whatever reason, send us the bill and we'll cover it."

"That's it… just prayers and a promise?"

"Yes, Iris. That's how we do things. There's no need to overcomplicate it."

"But—"

"How's your leg doing, by the way?" He winked at her.

"It's… oh, I see. Fine, you win."

"Next… pay. They discussed it, and they think with your current living expenses it would be best to start you at twelve."

Iris thought that over. "Well, I get fifteen at Rookwood, but I guess twelve is still pretty good for now. How do they figure up my hours?"

Gray shook his head. "I think you misunderstood. I meant twelve *thousand*. Per month. Plus expenses."

Iris's mouth fell open.

"It's hard to put a price on what you'd be doing," Gray continued. "They tried really hard to be fair. Most of them wanted to pay you far more, but some felt that it might arouse too many questions if they did that right away. But they do intend to give you raises periodically. I hope that's okay."

Iris nodded, then remembered to close her mouth. "I guess I won't need to stay at Rookwood anymore."

"Actually, it would be a good idea if you did, at least for now. Huge life transitions raise questions. Besides, you wouldn't want to get bored in between cases. Do it for the joy of it."

Iris smiled. "That actually sounds really nice."

"Excellent. Okay, well, there are just a few forms for you to fill out so we can square away all that boring money business." He handed her a manila folder that he'd brought out from the office. "And then we'll just have to schedule some study sessions."

"Study sessions?"

"Yes. I know we said you're a 'Research Specialist,' but before that, you're officially a Guardian Heir. *My* Heir. That's an honorary title, but we're treating it like it's not. That means I'm now your teacher. You'll be expected to know the Recitation, understand the Histories and the nature and behavior of the Great Trees, Guardian culture, and how to document your accounts. It's going to be a challenge, but we'll get there. You can certainly learn as you go."

A confident smile spread across Iris's face. "Challenge accepted."

Gray smiled. "Good."

Chapter 9

Eugene squinted against the light. "Kat?" he yelled. "Can you still see me?"

Finally, his eyes adjusted to his surroundings. He was standing in a pool of late afternoon sunlight that streamed through the open window of a modestly furnished living room. There was no sign of Kat or the motel room in which he'd just been standing.

Instead, there was a petite woman peering at him from the hallway. She looked to be in her mid thirties. She had long, curly brown hair, and wore jeans and a t-shirt that said "Coffee and Chill."

"Where am I?" Eugene asked her.

"Gabe?!" the woman yelled.

"Yeah!" said a man's voice outside the window.

"Visitor!"

"Oh, is that what we're calling it now, when you need me to kill a spider?" he called back.

Eugene stood frozen, unsure what to do next.

"Gabe? Seriously! Get in here!"

A man opened the front door and came inside. He had short, dark hair and brown eyes. He was followed by a ten year old boy who was the image of his father, but with hazel eyes. His black hair was wavy, tied in a long ponytail with a leather string.

"Who are you people?" Eugene demanded.

"Well now," the man said casually. "Interesting you should ask, since you're the one who showed up in *my* living room." He approached Eugene slowly. "You look just like my grandfather said you would," he commented.

"What are you talking about?" Eugene was starting to feel like he was having a nervous breakdown. "Where am I?"

"You're in the house of the Guardians of the Great Juniper. I am Gabriel Iwila. This is my wife, Brittany, and my son, Danny. You are welcome here. We've been waiting over half a century for you to show up."

"That's ridiculous!" Eugene spat. "I'm only twenty-eight years old. You must have me confused with someone else."

"You're Eugene Thomas, the scientist. Yes?"

"Yes, but…"

Gabe strode up to him and looked closely at his eyes. "You haven't cut yourself or anything lately, have you?" He held the back of his hand against Eugene's forehead.

"Knock it off!" Eugene jerked his head away. "Of course I haven't! What are you doing?"

"Just making sure you aren't sick. Sometimes, a cut can—"

"Well, I'm fine, okay? I must have blacked out or something. Or maybe someone poisoned me! I don't know why you people brought me all the way back here, but you can just leave me alone."

"My grandfather told me you were a little surly." Gabe smiled. "But that's okay. I know you've had a really weird day. Would you like to sit? There's a lot you should know."

"Your grandfather? That wouldn't be Joseph Iwila, would it?"

Gabe flashed a brilliant white smile. "That's him, all right!"

"You're as much a freak as he is." Eugene headed for the door. "I gotta go. Kat's waiting for me."

"I really think you should listen to wha—"

"Have a good one!" Eugene waved without looking back as he strode toward the trail that led up the ridge and out of the valley.

Danny looked up at his father. "Does he even know what year it is, Dad?"

Gabe patted Danny's shoulder. "I doubt it. But he's not my prisoner. He can figure things out his own way, if he wants to. I'm sure he'll be back."

"Interesting…" The word radiated out of the formless, dingy haze that hovered on the ridge above the little stone house. Skliros billowed into the air for a better vantage point. Apateon, that worthless hack, had been right after all. The ambitious male creature had indeed reappeared. Skliros descended until he was close enough to touch the human and addressed the slithering mass on the man's back.

"When did you last look upon me?"

"Yesterday," replied the creature.

Skliros let out an echoing chuckle. "Thelo, is it?"

"It is."

"You let me down, Thelo. It was not yesterday you saw me. The human touched the forbidden Tree, though I warned you. I told you to take from the Tree, and let the human bring it fame. Instead, you allowed this imbecile slip through a crack. Now he is utterly displaced!"

"What?" Thelo hissed. "How am I to blame? The man withholds nothing from himself. I merely bring inspiration."

"Your thinking is tiny, as you are tiny," Skliros growled. "Does no one understand how to start a proper religion anymore? Sacrifices must be made!"

"As I recall, that is precisely why your last disciples left you," Thelo snickered. "You have a heavy hand."

Skliros let out a menacing rumble. "Do not question me, or I will end him right now, and send a host of hornets behind you."

"What would you have me do, then? He is seeking hard after answers. Nothing will persuade him to stay here."

"You will seek answers with him. The human Guardian has predicted his return to my realm. You will report to me then."

Eugene muttered under his breath as he stomped away from the little red stone house and down the rusty trail that wound between the scrub oak and junipers. His body was complaining of fatigue, but anger kept his brain alert.

This stupid land is crawling with stupid Indians! How long was I even unconscious? Kat must be so worried, wondering where I am.

He craned his neck as far as he could into the distance, but saw no sign of his Mustang. Only more red rocks and shrubbery.

So I didn't drive here. Did those jerks kidnap me or something? Who do they think they are, anyway? This trip is turning into a nightmare!

Thelo relished the rise of fury in Eugene's body. He whispered something.

Eugene had another thought. *Those clowns better not have touched my sample back at the motel, or I'll kill them.*

He held up his hand. *Huh. Those weird black stains are gone.*

Eugene looked back from where he'd come, and then took in the length of trail ahead. He swore. It was going to be at least an hour and a half of hiking, maybe longer, to get into town on foot. It would be well after dark by then. He checked his watch. It read 10:15. He frowned and looked at the sinking sun on the horizon.

It can't be later than six, by the looks of it. Why is my watch so fast?

He put it to his ear. *Still ticking.* He shook his head.

At least I escaped. I'll just have to get back as quickly as I can.

Eugene had to walk for closer to two hours. Since he had no flashlight, dusk had slowed his progress. He'd resorted to picking his way down the trail just fast enough to make headway without twisting his ankle on a rock, spearing himself on an agave plant, or running straight into a cactus.

Finally, he emerged onto a blacktop highway and headed north. His feet felt like lead. He couldn't remember the last time he'd slept. If he squinted, he could just make out groups of buildings dotting both sides of the road ahead. They were illuminated here and there by the glow of dim porch lights and indoor lamps shining through the windows, but there were no street lights on.

Eugene tried to flag a passing car, but the driver honked at him and sped away. He grumbled. At least the motel was only another half mile up this road. He could make it.

At last, he plodded across the deserted motel parking lot. Still no Mustang. *Did someone steal my car?*

He felt in the pockets of his jacket. He found his room key on its tacky leather keychain in one pocket. In his other pocket still lay the rhinestone earring that Kat had accidentally left on the seat of his car. Inside pocket… *Great. Out of cigarettes.*

He took the metal and cement steps slowly, his legs almost drained of energy, and shuffled to his room, readying his key. But something was different. In the place where a keyhole should be, there was just a box with a slot in the top. He frowned and tried the knob. Locked. He tried knocking.

"Kat?" He waited, then tried again. "Kat, are you in there? I'm back!" There was no answer from within the darkened room.

A janitor rounded the corner at the far end of the building, pushing a large trash can on wheels toward him.

"Excuse me!" he called out. "What's wrong with this lock?"

The janitor continued toward him, in no hurry. He stopped in front of the door. "Looks fine to me."

"My key won't work, though."

"Keys aren't my thing. See the front desk." He rolled on.

"Fine," Eugene replied. "Hey, any idea what's with the blackout? The Ruskies or the Viet Cong finally decide to drop the big one?"

The janitor stopped and turned. "What?"

"Y'know, nukes?"

"What are you talking about, dude?"

"The street lights are off!" Eugene exclaimed. "The whole town's dark. What's the deal?"

"It's always dark at night, weirdo. Sedona's been a dark sky city for almost twenty years. Y'know… light pollution and all that?"

"Light pollution?" Eugene scoffed. "What the heck are you talking about? They were on when I was here yesterday!"

The janitor shrugged and continued to walk away.

"Can I bum a smoke?" Eugene hollered after him.

"I don't smoke!" the janitor replied without stopping, and disappeared around the corner.

"Figures," Eugene muttered. He turned toward the stairs, fuming. Now he'd have to deal with some half asleep moron at the front desk, when all he wanted to do was let Kat know he was okay, make sure his sample was still where he left it, and fall into a soft bed.

"Excuse us, sorry," said a couple as they passed him on their way up the stairs.

They stopped in front of Eugene's room, slid a little card into the slot, opened the door, and went in. Eugene's eyes went wide. He scrambled back up the stairs and banged on the door.

The man opened the door a crack. "Yes?"

"What are you doing in my room?" Eugene demanded.

"Uh…" The man peeked out a little more, looking around to see if Eugene was alone. "Wrong room, dude."

"No, see?" Eugene held up his numbered keychain. "Number's right on there. Worked yesterday!"

The man looked as if he were trying to decide whether to laugh or call someone. He held up a small plastic card. "Keys look like this."

Eugene frowned, and then felt a sudden rage well up in him again. "Did that Iwila guy put you up to this?"

"Who? Listen, I don't want any trouble…"

Eugene pushed his way past the man into the room.

The woman who had entered a moment ago yelped in surprise.

"What the heck are you doing? Look, we don't have any cash on us!" the man was saying, but Eugene just scanned the room. Everything looked different—the bedding, the carpet, the furniture… even the lamp that Eugene had used.

"This has to be some kind of trick," Eugene muttered, raking his hands through his hair. His sample, his bag, Kat's luggage, his car… everything was gone.

"Is he on meth?" the woman whispered to her husband, who shrugged in reply.

With an expression of deep concern, the man spoke slowly. "I'm just going to call some help for you, okay, man?" He reached toward his back pocket.

"Stop right there!" Eugene yelled. "No funny business!"

"I'm just going to make a call…" the man tried again.

"Well, the phone's over there, genius!" Eugene shot back. "I'm going, okay?" He edged toward the door. "I don't need to get knifed or shot or whatever it is you were about to do. Obviously, there's been some kind of… mistake." He backed out of the room. "I'm going. Just… chill out."

He turned for the stairs and ran. Once he was back by the road, he turned south and walked aimlessly, trying to decide what to do. He could call the police and report his missing car, but that couple at the motel, not to mention Joseph Iwila, probably already had the cops looking for him. That Gabriel guy had said he needed to tell him something… *But there's no*

*way I'm walking all the way back there and spending any more
time with those freaks.*

And where in the heck is Kat? Maybe, if he'd been unconscious
and kidnapped, she had too? *Or... maybe she got scared and hitched
a ride back to Tucson? That's gotta be it. Poor thing didn't know
what to do, so she went home. She must be so worried. I should get
back down there and find her. Maybe she's got my stuff.*

He crossed the road so he'd be on the same side as the
southbound traffic. He had seen very few cars, but he'd make
sure the next one stopped. He kept walking, though his entire
body felt like a bruise. His tongue felt spongy and dry. He realized
he hadn't had a drink of water in at least a day.

A glow of headlights slowly cast Eugene's shadow in front
of him. He turned and stuck out his thumb. A Volkswagen bus
puttered to a halt beside him, and the dark haired passenger rolled
down her window. She wore heavy eyeliner and black lipstick,
and had piercings in her nose, lips, and eyebrows.

"Where you headed?" she asked with a smack of her gum.

"Tucson," Eugene replied.

"No way!" the driver said, leaning across the cab to look at
him through the window. He was a slender man, arms covered
in tattoos. His long hair was twisted into a bun. "We go to U of
A! We're just heading back there now. Totally hop in!"

"Thanks." Eugene opened the door and slid into the seat.

"What's your name, man?" the driver asked as he pulled
back onto the road.

"Eugene."

"Old school, I like it. I'm Jaden, this is Kayla."

"Pleasure." *Nice to meet you, weird people with weird names.*

Kayla turned in her seat and looked at him in the dim lights
of the dashboard. "No offense, but what are you doing out here
on foot if you're headed to Tucson? That's like, kind of a long
walk!"

Eugene sighed. He was so tired. "Someone stole my car."

"Oh man, that sucks!" Jaden said.

"Yeah." Eugene's throat was so dry, he almost couldn't choke out the word. "Sorry, do you have any water?" he croaked.

"Oh, totally!" Kayla said, and rummaged in a bag at her feet. She passed a metal container to him. "All I have is my Hydroflask though, sorry. Hopefully you don't mind sharing. I don't have any, like, scary diseases."

"Thanks." Eugene paused a little at her distinction between "scary" diseases and none at all, but he decided it was worth the risk, and took a long drink. "So you guys go to U of A?"

"Yeah," Jaden replied. "We're out here for the weekend on a meditation retreat. Took a vortex tour, learned about the medicine wheel, met our spirit guides. It was dope."

Dope? Are they on drugs? Eugene had little idea what most of that meant, but didn't have the energy to ask. "I go there, too. I'm teaching and doing graduate studies."

"Sweet! So were you out here on a retreat, too?"

"No. Research."

"Nice. Research in the great outdoors totally rocks."

"Trees this time, actually."

"Dude, you're hilarious!" Jaden laughed. "So are the cops like, looking for your car?"

"I'm sure they are," Eugene replied with an edge to his tone. "But that doesn't do me any good now. I really need to get back."

"Well, we should roll up in like, three and a half hours. Cool?"

"Sure. What time is it, anyway?"

"It's about nine thirty."

Eugene reset his watch. "Thanks again." He rested his head against the seat, feeling suddenly dizzy with fatigue. The hum of the engine buzzed in his ears like a saw. He closed his eyes and tried to tune it out. But even the seat felt like it was trying to chafe his skin off. He rubbed his eyes with his fists and tried to breathe slowly.

"You okay, dude?" Kayla asked.

Eugene felt self-conscious. He must look ragged. "You got any cigarettes?"

Kayla opened the glove box and handed him a brand new pack.

He opened it like a child on Christmas morning and took two, then handed it back.

She shook her head. "Keep it. Looks like you could use 'em."

"Thank you." Eugene dug in his jeans pocket for his lighter.

"You need a spark?"

"I got it." He lit up and took several long draws. His body began to relax. A fresh wave of exhaustion hit him. He savored every millimeter of the cigarette, then shakily reached across to the ashtray and put it out. He fell into a deep sleep on the seat about ten seconds later.

Eugene's groggy brain awoke to the sound of whispering voices.

"He's out. Maybe we should just let him sleep."

"In the car?"

"It's not going to hurt anything!"

"Jaden, it's freakin' cold out here! It's like thirty-five degrees!"

"Fine, you wake him up."

Someone shook his shoulder. "Eugene?" It was Kayla.

Eugene sat up, completely disoriented.

"Hey, sorry. Our exit's coming up. Is there someplace you want us to drop you off?"

"Um…" He shook his head, rubbed his eyes, and tried to think. "Yeah, just uh… can you take me to East Sixth and Euclid? I can walk from there."

"No problem, that's right on the way," Jaden said. "You gonna be okay?"

"I'm just tired. Nothing a shower and a bed won't cure."

Minutes later, Jaden took a left on Euclid and pulled over. "Well, good luck, man. Sorry about your car. I hope they find it."

"Thanks for the lift," Eugene said, shaking both their hands. He slid out into the cold night, stuffed his hands into his pockets, and walked toward his neighborhood.

Everything seemed so surreal. He couldn't tell—maybe it was the chill in the atmosphere that made the street lights seem a different color or the buildings seem so unfamiliar. He turned onto his street, toward the familiar sight of the Spanish style house he and Eva rented. Still no blue Beetle.

She must still be at her sister's. Or wherever she went.

He stepped under the adobe arch onto the porch and put his key in the lock. It wouldn't turn. He flipped it upside down and tried again. Nothing. Obviously, she'd been here and changed the locks while he was gone. She might even be in there now, with her car parked out of sight around the corner. His anger returned in force. *If she thinks I'll take her back after this…*

"Eva!" he yelled, pounding on the door. "Eva! You can't hide in there!" He grabbed a rock from the flowerbed and shattered the window next to the front door. He reached inside, undid the lock, and let himself in.

A light flipped on in the back bedroom.

A man about thirty years of age emerged from the hallway and stood there in boxer shorts and a white t-shirt. He gave Eugene a fierce glare. "What do you want?"

"I want to know what you're doing in my house!" Eugene shouted. "Are you Eva's new fling, or something? At least I have the decency not to bring them home!"

"Man, you need to calm down. There's no Eva here. Now get out of here or I'll call the cops."

"Of course she's here! Do I look like an idiot? You think changing the locks is going to just make me go away? Eva!" he yelled toward the hallway. "Why don't you introduce me to your new boyfriend!"

He heard a feminine gasp come from somewhere behind this hulking man.

"C'mon out!" he called. "What do you think I'll do? Throw a vase at your head?"

"E, hand me my phone," the man said quietly.

"Oh, is that a pet name? Just 'E'? That's the best you could do? Are you a neanderthal?"

A frightened woman appeared behind the man and slipped a black, shiny object into his hand. He barely took his eyes away from Eugene while he slid his finger across its surface and then held it to his ear.

Eugene went cold. *That's not Eva.* He looked around him, and realized for the first time that this room looked totally different. In his blind rage, he hadn't noticed before. There were photos of these people on the walls, and a plaque that said "John + Emily, est. 2015."

This was just like the motel room. Nothing the same. Everything wrong.

Eugene stood glued to the spot, trying to comprehend his surroundings. Sounds and thoughts blurred together. *"You look just like my grandfather said you would..."* He shook his head, trying to force something to click. *"We've been waiting over half a century for you to show up..."*

Eugene realized that the man was talking to someone on that device.

That's a phone?

He was giving a description of a burglar, who was... *him.* He looked into this couple's stubborn, frightened faces. *What am I doing? I just... broke into someone else's house? But...*

He suddenly heard the wail of a siren a few blocks away. Adrenaline coursed through him. He bolted for the door and fled into the night.

Eugene ran east toward campus, but skidded and swung hard right when he saw flashing red and blue lights. He heard someone behind him yelling at him to stop. Instead, he sprinted all out toward the huge brick buildings. He didn't stop when he crossed Park, and paid for it with the sound of a honking horn from the car that barely missed him.

Gasping for air, he didn't stop. He ran down Lowell, keeping himself in the shadows between the buildings and the landscaped trees. His chest was aching, burning. His legs felt like rubber. He dived behind a thick hedge of trees along the back entrance of a tall, X-shaped building. He bent over at the waist, body convulsing as he gulped in oxygen. After two minutes standing in the dark, he heard voices passing close by. He quieted his breathing as much as he could, as the beams of two flashlights swept across the ground just inches from his shoes.

At last, all was quiet. He checked his watch. One thirty in the morning.

He peeked out from the trees. Not a soul in sight. He considered seeing if his key to the lab under the stadium would work, but he didn't have much hope for that. Not after his last two experiences. Where could he go? A lone park bench sat to his right, just beyond the edge of the trees. Could he sleep there? It looked cold and exposed. He sat on the ground. At least here in the shelter of the buildings and trees, it was a few degrees warmer. He lit a second cigarette from the pack. He'd have to ration these. No telling when he could get more.

What's happened to me? He took a puff and adjusted his back against the brick wall behind him. *Everything got weird the second I touched that tree sample. The tree sample with dark sap... and no rings. Maybe it was poisoned by nuclear waste or something.* He thought that over, then shook his head. *Don't be stupid, Eugene. That was the biggest, healthiest juniper on the planet. There's no way it was poisoned.* He took another puff. *What were those waves inside the wood grain? Energy? What if I really am over fifty years in the future? What does that make me... eighty or so? Dead? Is Eva dead, too? Or Kat?*

Eugene twirled the butt of his cigarette into the soil and leaned back against the wall. He shivered. *I'll just have to get some answers in the morning.* Fear and anger twisted inside him, mixed with gnawing hunger. The impossibility of his circumstances threatened to overwhelm his emotions, but he refused to think of the *what,* and focused his mind instead on the *how.* He pretended he was warm, and entertained every scientific theory he'd ever heard about time, until his thoughts distorted into erratic dreams. The voice of Joseph Iwila echoed in his head: *"It is not the tree's safety I fear for. It's yours."*

Chapter 10

Vancouver, Washington ~ Present day

I ris lugged her suitcase into the apartment and shut the front door as quietly as she could manage. She peered down the hallway to see if Charlie's bedside lamp was on. Sure enough, a crack of light glowed at the bottom of the door, even though it was close to midnight. Charlie would normally be asleep by now, but she'd been staying up later than usual ever since Iris had gotten her hooked on D.M. Hawthorne novels. She slipped her keys onto the hook in the kitchen, wriggled out of her wet boots, and hung up her jacket.

Iris sighed, glad to be home. She'd just finished the busiest five weeks of her life. Ever since accepting the job of Research Specialist for the Council of Guardians' foundation, newly named Grove Research and Antiquities Conservation Enterprises, her brain had been going nonstop. There was so much to learn.

She'd almost memorized the Recitation—the oral tradition known to all Guardians—which she'd first heard spoken by Darrick MacCrann on the day he'd caught her and Angus lurking in the woods by the Great Hawthorn.

She was steadily working her way through the newer portion of the Histories as well. For some reason, it was taking a lot longer to wade through, even though it was shorter. She kept finding herself stopping to ponder. Gray said there was no hurry, but Iris felt a sense of urgency that she couldn't explain.

Thankfully, understanding the Trees had been the easiest part so far. Her adventure with Angus had been like a crash course on the world of the Great Trees. She had experienced first hand what the Guardians had spent centuries of accumulating and sharing knowledge to understand. This had made the past five weeks of study sessions with Gray feel less like a review of mundane case files, and more like a process of collaborating and putting pieces together.

It had all culminated this past weekend, when she went on her first mission. Gray had been right—with the support of the Council, she had accomplished in three days what would have taken her weeks to do alone. With a little ingenuity, a good deal of research, and a lot of sunscreen, history had been preserved and another soul was back on the right timeline. The only drawback was her late return. She'd had to fly a commercial airline home because the private jet she'd flown out on had been needed elsewhere.

She shook her head. *One minute I'm waiting tables and almost late with rent, and the next minute I'm acting like private jets are a normal part of life.*

She tiptoed toward the hallway with her suitcase in tow.

Suddenly, Charlie's door swung open and she emerged wearing a tank top and flannel pajama pants. She was carrying an empty water bottle in one hand and was totally absorbed in the book in her other hand.

"Hi."

"Gah!" Charlie dropped the water bottle and flung the book in the air. It landed face down on Iris's foot.

"Sorry…" Iris felt sheepish, even though she'd genuinely tried not to startle her roommate.

Hand on her belly, Charlie let out a huge breath. "Geez! I about peed myself! I was at this really scary part!" She picked up the book.

"I'm so sorry, I tried to be quiet!"

"It's okay, I'll live." She let out another breath. "Hey, what's with the suitcase?" Charlie gestured. "I didn't think you even owned one."

"Yeah, I… didn't, but I had to buy one for—"

"Kona?" Charlie gaped at her luggage tag, and then back at Iris. "You went to the big island? I thought you said you were going to be working late all weekend!"

"I was!"

"In… Hawaii?"

"Yes?" Iris blushed.

Charlie put a hand on her hip.

"Not all research can be done on the internet, Charlie! For some stuff, you have to be there!"

"Uh huh. And… did you research some beaches while you were there?"

"Um… really only two," Iris said truthfully. *One in Hawaii, one in Canada.*

"Okay." Charlie shook her head, then gave Iris a warm smile. "Well I'm glad the new job is working out so well. You deserve it."

"Thank you!" Iris picked up Charlie's fallen water bottle and handed it back to her before heading to her room. "Sorry again for almost making you pee yourself."

"Lucky you caught me before I filled this thing!" She headed into the kitchen. "Oh, by the way," she called, "you got a stack of boxes delivered today."

"Really? Where are they?"

"Living room!"

Iris dumped her suitcase and came back out to the dim living room. Brand new computer equipment. From the looks of the boxes, quite a bit of it. Jason had said they planned to "update" her equipment for her. This looked more like they were outfitting her to run a sting operation.

I thought we weren't raising questions, guys. Where am I supposed to put all this?

Charlie came out of the kitchen with her water bottle filled and sat on the sofa. "So you must've scored some serious overtime this weekend to bankroll this getup," she commented.

Iris shrugged casually. "Actually, it's from work. Everyone in their organization has computers like this at home."

"Sheesh."

"Yeah. I don't even know how to set it up. I'll have to get my boss over here."

"Your boss makes house calls?"

"Mentor, I guess. I don't exactly have a boss…"

"What kind of place do you work for, anyway?"

Iris was starting to wonder if she'd already said too much, or how she'd even know when she'd crossed that line. She had always admired Charlie's incisiveness, but the receiving end of it was not a comfortable place to be.

"Well… they work all over the world," she hedged, "so they find it's better to network through computers rather than have a central location. I've worked with them in the past. It was kind of a… pro bono thing."

"Really? I don't remember you ever telling me about them before. When was that?"

In the nineteenth century? "Uh, it was a long time ago."

"Huh."

"I was pretty surprised to get the job, honestly, but it's been great so far."

"Well, if you're happy, I'm happy," Charlie said, rising from the couch and wandering back toward the hallway. "Just don't put all that stuff in the living room. I need space for my pilates."

"No worries. I'll just…" Iris scanned the apartment, then muttered, "I'll just get rid of my bed or something."

Bed. Oh, man.

Her eyes drooped, even as her brain refused to stop retelling her weekend adventure. She shuffled back to her room. All of her gadgets were begging for attention, but she had very little to give. She mechanically unzipped her suitcase and brought out three charging cables that had inexplicably tangled together during her flight. Shrugging, she plopped the entire mess on the floor, plugged them in one by one, and managed to find each of the opposite ends for her watch, phone, and ancient laptop.

Her phone screen lit happily, promising to be fully charged within two hours, and announced that two missed calls, three texts, eight emails, one alarm, and a weather report needed her immediate scrutiny.

Sighing, she climbed into bed without undressing, shut off her light, and scanned through the notifications with one eye. She deleted seven of the emails without opening them, and tapped on the one from her dad:

Hello, my girl! Interesting reading! I see what you mean. Chat soon. Love you! Dad

"Huh," Iris said aloud. She could tell there would be some interesting conversations ahead.

She checked the texts. One was from Candace, two were from Will. Candace wanted her to come in an hour later tomorrow, but left no explanation as to why. Iris gladly reset her alarm. Extra sleep is extra sleep, no matter why it happens.

Will's texts were from yesterday, two hours apart, and both the missed calls were from him. Iris cringed. She'd had no service in some of the places she'd been this weekend, and hadn't even seen these. But she also hadn't told Will she was leaving town, only that she'd be working overtime. Like Charlie, Will knew that she'd accepted a research gig that would take up a lot of her time during the training phase. But she'd been hesitant to tell him anything beyond that. Any details she could think to add just felt like lies. Telling him more would risk the secrets of the Guardians and the Trees, putting her in jeopardy of forgetting everything that had happened since she'd met Angus. The idea was horrifying.

She had begun to feel that her life had always been leading up to the moment she'd walked into room 105 and met a man out of his time. Her experiences since then had redefined her and given her soul a divine calling. To risk losing that was unfathomable, even if it meant letting others down sometimes. And it looked as if she'd done just that.

(1/2) Hey Iris! I miss you! I know you're busy but I want to talk to you about something kind of important. How about over our dinner tonight?

(2/2) Hi again. Are you still coming? They will hold the table another fifteen minutes. Let me know. I hope you're ok.

"Oh NO!" Iris cried, sitting up. "That was supposed to be yesterday?" Frantically, she opened her calendar app and scrolled down. There it was. *Date w/Will 7pm.* She'd stuck it into the wrong week. Normally, she wouldn't have even needed to set a reminder for something like that. She would have been looking forward to it for days. But Will had called and asked her out right in the middle of a study session with Gray. She'd been so distracted in the moment that she'd stuck a reminder in her calendar, meaning to ask him more about it later. But then this mission had come up at the last minute and absorbed all of her focus.

"Aaagggh!" Iris flopped onto her pillow, berating herself. *I am the worst.* She imagined Will, waiting alone at a candlelit table for two… his sweet, handsome face filled with concern. Texting her. Waiting. Calling. Wanting to share something important with her while she was a thousand miles away, thinking nothing of him.

She couldn't stand it. She turned on her light. It was now well after midnight. Although Will might not see it till morning, she had to try to make this right. She replied to his last text.

I can't believe I put our date in the wrong week of my calendar, and my phone wasn't getting calls. I am SO SORRY! I feel like the worst person ever! Will you please forgive me?

Ten seconds later, her phone began to play "More Than A Feeling" and Will's picture appeared. She pressed the green button.

"Hi."

"Hey." Will sounded sleepy. "I'm glad you're okay."

"I'm not okay, I'm a total dork face! I can't believe I stood you up!"

"Things happen." He yawned. "You can't fix it by beating yourself up."

"I can try! Will you forgive me?"

"Already did."

Iris sighed. It was so good to hear his voice. "I don't deserve you."

"Why not?"

"You should at least be mad at me for a few days or something," she said glumly.

"I'd rather not," he chuckled. "What would that accomplish?"

"I dunno, assuage my guilt or something. And now you're up late because of me."

"That's true. How dare you, or something."

She laughed.

"Nah, I was actually just headed to bed," he said with another yawn. "I've been working on a project."

"What project?"

"That is absolutely none of your doggone business."

"Ha! Well now, aren't *you* mysterious!"

"Darn right, lady. I've got secrets."

She giggled.

He paused. "Y'know, I've really missed you lately. That's probably not too secret. I know your new job has you pretty

153

busy, but… I just thought… I guess I was hoping to see more of you outside of work."

She closed her eyes, feeling a sizable portion of her guilt returning. "I know. I've missed you, too."

Wait, is that true? Have I even had space in my brain to miss anybody? She felt worse.

"I feel awful that I haven't been around much, and I really want to make it up to you. I want to hear what's on your mind."

"I'm glad," he said. His voice seemed lighter. "It's more of an in-person kind of discussion, though."

"I have something I want to talk to you about, too," she said. "How about a do-over?"

"I don't know, are you gonna show up this time?" he teased.

"Oh *there* it is!" Iris laughed. "It was on a delay!"

"You feel better now that I've given you a hard time?" he chuckled.

"Much."

"Dinner tomorrow?"

Ugh. I can't put him off again, but I'm supposed to debrief with Jason and Gray tomorrow after work. They'll want to set up the computer, talk about my trip…

"You still there?" he said.

"Yes. Um, dinner tomorrow. Let's do it. Can we make it a little later, like eight?"

"Uh… I have early mornings, so that might be a little tight… I guess I could work it out, though."

"Well… no, I'll just… it's okay. Let's do seven."

"Thanks, that helps. Pick you up?"

"I'll be ready!"

He paused again, as if deciding how to sign off. "Sleep tight."

She smiled. "You too."

Vancouver was seeing a dry morning at last. Iris enjoyed her drive to Rookwood Senior Home through the simultaneous fog and sunshine. It was so much brighter when she came to work an hour later! It made her look forward to spring even more.

She stashed her purse in her locker, clocked in, and peeked into the kitchen. *Hm. No Will.* She saw Joy, the cook who had helped with Zoo Day, working the griddle and calling out orders. Had Will put her in charge of breakfast service?

She headed up the stone staircase and down the cherry paneled corridor to the activities office. She could see through the window that Candace had left her thermal coffee mug and a half eaten bagel on the desk, but the door was locked. Not that unusual, if she had to step out. She had once explained to Iris that unattended offices were sometimes mistaken for... *other* facilities. But where was she?

Iris wasn't sure what was on the calendar for this morning, but the Activity Room was a safe bet. She headed in that direction. As she approached, she noticed the lights on and heard voices inside, but the blinds had been drawn. *Is there a meeting in there or something?* She opened the door a crack and peeked inside.

"SURPRISE!!!"

Iris gasped. Candace and James, along with James's mother, Becky the receptionist, stood just inside the door, grinning at her. The entire room was decked with silver and lavender streamers and balloons, with a giant H-A-P-P-Y-✿-B-I-R-T-H-D-A-Y banner strung across the back wall. The room was packed with Rookwood residents—most smiling at her, a few asleep.

"Oh my gosh!" Iris laughed. "You guys! This is amazing!"

"Happy New Year!" yelled Betty. She threw a handful of confetti in the air over Iris's head.

"I thought there would be cake!" said Fred. He was wearing a fetching party hat.

"Don't worry, there's cake." Will's voice came from the back of the room. The sight of him took Iris's breath away. He looked even taller today, in his crisp white chef jacket. He stood beside a table laden with trays of hors d'oeuvres and a stylish potted iris in the center.

Iris beamed at him. He winked back.

"We should get started!" Candace announced. "Who wants snacks?"

A general cheer went up from the room as paper plates were passed around and everyone tried Will's hors d'oeuvres. Iris made her way to the table, among cheers, tender pats on the arm, and murmured greetings from the residents.

"Welcome home!" cried Doris.

"Yes, mazel tov!" added Walter. "When's the due date?"

Iris couldn't help laughing, but kept moving. Finally, she wound her way to the back and stared at Will in amazement.

"I can't believe you did all this!"

His face was filled with delight. "Happy birthday, Iris."

"Thank you." Her face was pink as she leaned in and whispered, "I forgot it was today!"

He laughed. "Well you'd better cut the cake, then!"

She took the knife he offered and looked around the table. "Um… where is it?"

Will moved to stand behind her. He gently put his hand over hers and guided her knife toward the potted iris in the center of the table, until the point of the blade stuck right into the elaborately detailed flowerpot.

"That's a cake?!" she cried. "This is amazing! How did you do this?"

Will was all dimples. He had also gone slightly pink. "Well, the flowerpot is a modified sticky toffee pudding cake, filled with treacle buttercream, and then covered in fondant. The iris is made of gum paste… I was actually painting that when we talked last night. And uh, the dirt is just smashed cookies."

"I did that part!" James called out.

"Yes, James did smash the cookies. It was a crucial contribution."

"Anytime, dude!"

Iris grinned back at James, and then up at Will again. "I *love* sticky toffee pudding."

"Yeah, I figured it wasn't a huge gamble."

Candace stepped around a few people and joined them. "So? You going to cut this thing, or just stand around looking at it? Wow, Willy, this is a work of art. Y'know what? Nevermind. We should just look at it."

"I agree," said Iris.

"No!" Will protested. "The best part is inside! Just cut it!"

"Fine then, I'm keeping the flower."

He grinned at her, plucked the iris from its cookie dirt, and laid it carefully on a paper plate. "There. Eat your cake."

"Fine, I will. Will."

James came over. "Oh my gosh, you guys. Stop being cute. The people demand cake!"

Iris laughed and began to put slices of cake on plates for the guests.

First Irene puttered over and patted Will's arm. "Congratulations again!" she said. "I wish the two of you many happy years together!"

He choked back a laugh and patted her hand in return. "Thank you very much."

"Come here, son," Irene motioned to him.

He bent closer and looked into her eyes with a warm smile.

"You won't always know what she wants," Irene continued, "but if she knows you love her, then she has everything she needs."

"That is both wise and true," he replied, and kissed her wrinkled cheek.

"You're a nice young man. And a looker!" She patted his face. "Now don't forget what I said."

"I won't."

Iris dashed into her apartment after work, hoping to clean it up enough before Jason and Gray arrived that it wouldn't look like it was occupied by rodents. Gray was planning to do a quick debrief session about her trip while Jason set up the new computers and listened in at the same time. Then they were going to set her up in the central database so she could log detailed accounts of her work and access the vast library of Guardian journals.

Her room was always clean, but the places that she and Charlie shared were… less so. Iris still hadn't figured out where the computer would go, but she decided not to worry about it, and instead focused on unearthing the sofa and coffee table, and doing dishes.

She had just pressed the start button on the dishwasher when she heard a knock. She opened the door. The two Reynolds men had brought more boxes.

Grayson beamed. "We come bearing gifts!"

"I'll be lucky to find a spot for the first one!" she laughed. "Come on in, guys!"

"Well this second gift should fix that problem," Jason said. "It's a custom desk! I think you'll love it."

"Hmm, well I have a desk in my room already," said Iris.

"Right, but was it designed by a Guardian and then built to spec by none other than Liam Jacobs?" Gray asked. "Because this one was."

Iris gasped. "You're kidding me!"

Gray smiled. "Remember Gavin MacCrann telling us that Darrick was planning a surprise? He designed something he thought might work well for a small space and hired your grandfather to build two of them. He kept one, and had the other one shipped as a welcome gift."

"I can't believe this!" Iris laughed. "Did my granddad know it was for me?"

"Nope!" Jason chuckled. "Does it go in here?" He pointed to the first door down the hall.

"Uh no, that's Charlie's room. I'm the one at the end."

"Charlie?"

"My roommate."

Jason looked at Gray. "Did we know she had a roommate?" They both looked at her.

"Sorry," she said with a shrug. "I guess we've always just talked about other stuff."

"Man, I feel bad," Gray said. "We should have asked. I just get so impressed with you sometimes that I forget you have a real life."

"Don't feel bad," Iris said. "It makes sense that I've spent most of my time at your place because that's where everything is. Plus, Charlie might overhear, so…"

"So is Charlie your… boyfriend?" Gray asked, suddenly looking awkward.

"Charlie is short for Charlotte," Iris laughed. "She's been my best friend since third grade."

"Oh, okay." Gray seemed oddly relieved. "Well that's… really cool."

Jason gave Gray a strange look, then asked Iris, "So you're the last door down here?"

"Yep."

"Perfect. I'll set it up." He heaved a box off the floor, and trudged down the hall. "Oh, by the way, Iris… I talked to Gavin earlier today and he said that Darrick just found another letter tucked away in his study. It's addressed to you."

"No way!" Iris exclaimed. A broad smile spread across her face.

"Yes, way! But he's not sure whether it's from Angus or someone in their family. Would you like him to open and scan it? Or just mail it to you so you can open it yourself?"

Decisions, decisions.

"I'd love to see it for myself," she said at last. "Will you ask him to mail it?"

"No problem!" he said and disappeared into her room.

"Man," Gray said, shaking his head. "Some people have all the fun!" He picked up two of the boxes from the living room. "So Iris, it sounds like your first mission went off without a hitch. Did you enjoy it?"

"It was amazing!" She followed him to her room and sat on the bed. "I had no idea that a lost piece of timber could drift that far! But it was amazing—I put the word out that I needed ocean current data, and one of the Guardians in California got in touch with an oceanographer buddy of his who actually had a current simulator! We had a working model within hours, and tracked the wood to within ten miles of beach!"

"Ha, that's awesome!" said Gray. "And two of the MacCranns came along, right? Were they helpful?"

Iris nodded. "It was so great to see Katie again! And Callum was fantastic. It was because of him that we found what we were looking for so quickly. He could hear it! Saved us a lot of hunting. I think I ruined my sandals, though. Man, it's rocky there."

"Well, I reckon you can expense that."

She laughed. "I keep forgetting I can do that! Oh my gosh, now I want to go shopping!"

Once Jason was finished, Iris had the most functional, efficient workspace she'd ever seen. The burnished mahogany desk made a small footprint, occupying half the depth of a typical desk, but with various nooks and shelves above it that were suited perfectly for journals, a monitor, and a keyboard. The large monitor was the same size as Gray's, perfect for video conferencing. Iris also had a brand new laptop that could do screen mirroring with the larger computer. This way, she could still work remotely. Both computers could interface with the central database using highly encrypted software, and both had a keyboard shortcut that would hide the database's access portal behind an undetectable firewall and immediately toggle the screen to something mundane, like a search engine homepage. She would never have to worry about someone reading over her shoulder or getting into the database without authorization.

Jason had rigged a wifi hotspot and special router that were entirely separate from the ones on her utility bill, and she had no idea how they worked at such a blistering speed. The only explanation he offered was, "Well, we have our own network, so…"

Charlie came home from work just as they were finishing taking all of the flattened boxes out to the recycling bin.

"Well… hey there. Do you do windows, too?" she asked Grayson as she walked up.

He smiled at her. "You must be the famous Charlie! I'm Gray." He shook her hand.

"Yes, I suppose I am the famous Charlie. And what are you famous for around here?"

Gray laughed. "I work with Iris. We were just setting up some stuff, but we're done now, so we'll get out of your hair."

"We?"

"Yeah, my dad's in the car. I work with him, too."

"Well, great to meet you!" Charlie said.

"Yeah, you too!"

Charlie watched him walk away, then came inside and found Iris in the living room.

"Hey, you!" Iris greeted her. "How was work?"

"Let's talk about *your* work for a second, missy. You never told me your boss was a certified hottie!"

She's right, he kind of is. "You know, he's not really my boss…"

"Is he single?"

"I… think so. Well, I know for sure he's not married. I'm pretty sure he doesn't have a girlfriend, either. We don't actually talk much about our personal lives. But I do know he plans to get married and have kids someday. That's about it."

"He's already thinking about being a dad? That's so cute!" Charlie gushed.

"I don't really know what type of person he's looking for, Charlie."

"Well, put in a good word for me, okay?"

Iris chuckled and shook her head. "We'll see."

That could actually royally complicate things.

To be on the safe side, Iris had decided to keep the two areas of her life as separate as possible. The less she spoke of her regular life to Jason and Gray, the less crossover there would be. And the less she said about Jason, Gray, and the Guardians to Charlie, Will, Candace, and her parents, the less chance she'd have of slipping up and ruining everything.

She hoped.

Chapter 11
Tucson, Arizona ~ Present Day

E ugene's first sensation upon waking was a painful tingle on his left cheek, followed by fervent complaints from his neck. He opened his eyes. The soft gray light of dawn illuminated the dry, gritty soil in front of his eyes. He sat up. Somehow, he'd ended up asleep face down in the dirt. He reached up and brushed away the pebbles that had lodged in his hair and embedded themselves in his stubbled cheek.

He sighed. *How are the mighty fallen.*

He stood and stretched his neck, brushed as much dust off his clothes as he could, and smoothed his hair. It was going to be difficult enough to figure out what to do next, but it would be even harder if he looked like a hobo. When he was reasonably satisfied with his appearance, he peeked out from behind the wall of trees and shrubs. Thankfully, it was still too early for many people to be around.

He set out back toward Lowell and took a left, trying to get his bearings. None of these buildings looked familiar at all. According to the sign, he'd taken shelter beside a mathematics building, even though he distinctly recalled it being much smaller and on the other side of the street just a few days ago. He approached another alien building which looked to him like a cross between a tree and a spaceship, bedecked on all sides with vertical steel girders.

"Tree Ring Building…" he muttered to himself, reading the sign. "That should be named after *me*."

He peered into the distance, between more strange buildings. *The stadium is still there. So at least I know where I am.* He lit a cigarette and pondered for a moment. *Probably the smartest thing to do is go to the library and figure some stuff out. At least I know it's open and they won't kick me out.*

He turned north. It was several blocks, but the sleep he'd gotten had given him some energy, despite his growing hunger. It was a relief to finally see some familiar buildings. But as he crossed the lawn and approached the arched entrance, he stopped short, dismayed. *Museum? This is a museum now? Where's…*

A slender man wearing torn baggy pants rode past him on a skateboard. He had a pair of strange white plugs in his ears. *Hmm, I guess I don't look any worse than he does.*

"Excuse me!" Eugene called out to him.

The man stopped, tugged one of the plugs out of his ear, and looked at him curiously.

"Where's the library?" Eugene asked.

"Oh, you wanna go that way," he pointed east. "Just stay on University and you'll see it on the right. It's right by the stadium."

Eugene's shoulders slumped. "Thanks."

"Yep." The man rode off.

By the time he reached the library, Eugene's stomach was growling loudly enough to be audible in a quiet building. He found a restroom and washed his face. Then he gulped water from a drinking fountain, hoping that would quiet things down.

He usually preferred to work alone in libraries and find his own way around, but he had no idea where to start in this massive place. He headed for a desk beneath a sign that said "Ask Us." *Promising.*

The short, pink haired woman behind the desk was also wearing ripped jeans and a faded t-shirt. *Maybe everyone dresses like hobos nowadays.* She was watching a television on her desk and using a flat typewriter with no paper in it at the same time, which made her look a little insane, in his opinion.

"Excuse me," he said. "Do you have a telephone book I could borrow?"

She looked mystified. "I'm not sure."

He frowned. "How could a library not have a telephone book? I just need to find a couple people... one person, specifically. I just want to look up her address."

"It would be a lot easier if you Googled her," the woman replied.

"I beg your pardon?" Eugene snapped. *Did she just call me a peeping Tom?*

"Look her up online."

"What line?"

She huffed. "Are you for real?"

Eugene just stared back.

"Computers are that way." She pointed. "Log in with your NetID and... Wait, are you a student here?"

"Um..."

"The public computers are in the Weaver building. You'll need a valid ID to get a temporary card. You can get one there."

Eugene began to succumb to a strange feeling, similar to panic, but more confusing. It rankled him at the same time it almost brought tears. He gritted his teeth. *So this is what it's like to feel helpless.*

"I'm really sorry, maybe we got off on the wrong foot," he tried again, in as polite a tone as he could produce. "I've been... away... for a really long time, and I'm not very familiar with things anymore. Could I get your help?"

She looked at him doubtfully.

He gave her his most charming smile—one that had never failed to elicit a feminine response. "Please? I'd consider it a personal favor."

She sighed. "Fine, Cary Grant. Just this once. What's her name?"

"Thank you so much," he said. "Her name is Kat..." Eugene came up short. *I never asked her last name! How did I think I'd find her in the phone book?*

"That's it?" The woman tapped her nails on the desk. "Just Kat? Is that a stage name or something?"

A stage name...

"Sorry," Eugene said, feeling sheepish. "I'm drawing a blank on her last name, but I do know she attended here in 1965. She was in a play. Maybe... is there a yearbook somewhere?"

"Yeah, they're around. But I'll just pull up a digital copy..." She clicked a few keys. "You said 1965?"

"Yes."

"Okay..." Her eyes scanned the screen for several moments. "School of Fine Arts..." she muttered. "Ah, *My Fair Lady?*"

"YES!"

"Shhhhh."

"Sorry," he whispered.

"There are a few cast photos," she said, and turned her screen toward him. "Do you see her?"

Eugene scanned the grinning black and white faces. "That's her, right there," he said, suddenly feeling like crying again.

"Kathleen Tyler," said the woman. "Well, we can try looking that up, but she might have a different last name now. And addresses can be a little tricky to get."

"I'd be grateful." Eugene leaned against the desk, suddenly overwhelmed. *She might have a different last name. Of course she would. She wasn't going to wait around for me.*

Then his thoughts took a sharp right turn. *Why didn't I look Eva up first? She's my wife, for crying out loud! Did I think she'd still be angry after all this time?* He thought of what Eva must look like now, and shuddered. *If she's still alive.*

He imagined what he would say if he saw her. He couldn't string two thoughts together that would even come close to an explanation she'd believe, much less make anything right, ever again. A cold bleakness settled over him as he thought of Eva, and it dawned on him: He was afraid. *But am I afraid she's dead, or afraid she's alive?*

"Well, it's like I thought," said the lady at the desk. "I'm not getting much in a general search. But she might be on social media. You should check there."

"Social… media?"

"Man, you really have been away for a long time."

"Yeah, uh… Peace Corps."

"So you probably have no social media accounts at all, right?"

"None whatsoever."

The woman's expression softened. "I'm sorry you don't seem to be having the best day," she said gently.

Eugene kept control of his emotions, but only by a slim margin. "Thanks. It's definitely been… something."

"Here," she said, and pulled a black rectangle from her purse. "I'll just look around on my phone for a sec. Maybe we can find her. I'll start with the platforms that older people use more."

Older people.

She stared into the tiny screen for several long moments, her thumb flicking expertly across its surface.

"Oh my gosh, I think this is her!" she said. "She still goes by Kat Tyler! Look!" She held up the phone.

Smiling out from the screen beneath a floppy sun hat was a woman in her seventies with long, wavy silver hair, blue eyes, and a gleaming smile. Despite her wrinkles, she was still glamorous.

Eugene couldn't speak. *I can't go see her. Why would she want to see me after all these years? She wanted to marry me, and I just… disappeared.*

"Looks like she's online right now," said the woman. "I could message her if you want."

Eugene was startled. "Right now?"

"Well, yeah. Not sure how else you're going to get in touch."

"Uh… okay?"

"What's your name?"

"Gene Thomas."

"All right, gimme a second…" The lady tapped out a lightning fast message with both thumbs, and then waited.

Eugene could feel his nerves telling him to run.

"Hm. That's weird," she said. "She doesn't believe me, and is asking if I have a photo."

"What?"

She pointed the phone at him. "Smile!" The phone clicked. She looked at the result with an amused expression. "Yikes, you're not very photogenic. Oh well, I'm sending it anyway."

Several moments passed while the phone made a series of strange noises and the woman used her thumbs to reply.

"Okay, she's kinda freaking out. You're not some crazy stalker, are you?"

"Of course not!" Eugene said. "What is she saying?"

"Um, mostly like… 'No way,' and 'I can't believe it,' stuff like that. Oh, now she's saying she'll meet you at Starbucks. Is that good for you?"

"What's a Starbuck?"

"Ha. Good one. I told her to come to the one right here by the library. Just go down there and get some coffee. She said she'll be there in twenty." She looked up at him, eyes bright. "Well, that was fun! Is she your grandma or something?"

"Something like that."

"Cool, well have fun. She seems excited to see you. Anything else I can do for you?"

Eugene was too overwhelmed to think. He just shook his head. "Thank you again. I appreciate your time."

Eugene found the coffee shop easily enough. He took a seat in the back corner, facing the door. His heart pounded. He had thought he was hungry when he came in, but the more he considered what was about to happen, he just felt sick.

After ten minutes, a girl in a green apron approached him. "Sir, if you're going to sit there, you have to order something."

"I'm just meeting someone."

She crossed her arms.

"I'll just have a cup of coffee, then."

"You need to order at the register."

"Fine." He stood and walked over. "Cup of coffee, please," he said again, with an annoyed glare.

"So like... house brew, cold brew, nitro? Or like an Americano?"

Eugene's eyes goggled. "What's an Americano?"

"Shots with hot water."

He frowned. "Seems a little early to be doing shots."

"Espresso shots."

"Oh. Um, no... just regular coffee made from coffee beans. Like Folgers or something."

"Sir, we don't sell Folgers. This is Starbucks."

"Okay, whatever brand you have is fine."

"Brewed, or pour over?"

"Brewed, I guess?"

"We have dark or Pike Place today."

"Whichever one tastes the most like coffee."

She rolled her eyes. "Black?"

"Yes." Eugene actually preferred cream, but he'd already had to make too many decisions so far.

"Short, tall, grande, or venti?"

"Are we still talking about coffee?"

She narrowed her eyes. "Size..."

"Coffee cup sized."

She sighed and shook her head, but pressed another button. "What's the name on the order?"

He looked around the coffee shop. "I'm the only one here. Are you afraid it'll get lost?"

She sighed, waiting for an answer.

"Gene," he finally said, and reached for his wallet.

"Two dollars and thirty-three cents, please."

"Are you kidding me? Coffee used to cost fifteen cents!"

"Maybe when Kennedy was president," she said. "Are you like, a method actor or something?"

Eugene had no idea how to respond, so he just dug the money out of his wallet and handed it over.

"Tall brewed for Gene!" someone shouted on his left.

He shook his head, pocketed his wallet, and picked up the cup. It bore an overly detailed sticker with the word "JEAN" at the top. The coffee was bitter, but at least it was hot.

He had just returned to his table when Kat walked in.

She was still slender, and wore a long skirt with boots and a soft tan cardigan. Her wavy silver hair hung in a braid over one shoulder. She stood in the doorway, speechless. It looked as if she was struggling to move her feet, so he stood and slowly approached her.

"Kat?"

She covered her mouth with her fingertips as tears spilled from her eyes. "I thought this might be some kind of mean prank," she said.

"What do you think now?"

"I haven't decided." She looked him over in awe. "You're… really him?"

"I came and found you as soon as I could," he said earnestly. "Will you come sit?"

She nodded, and they moved to a table which was tucked away from prying eyes.

She shook her head in disbelief. "How do I know it's really you? I mean... it can't be! You haven't aged at all!"

"Look at me, Kat. I'm sad to report that I'm still wearing the same clothes I had on the last time you saw me. Here..." He dug in his pocket, produced her sparkling earring, and set it on the table.

She gasped. "Where did you get that?"

"You left it in my Mustang."

She picked it up and let it dangle for a moment. "I always wondered..." she murmured, and set the earring back on the table. Her eyes were full of tears. "What happened to you?"

"I don't know," he confessed. "We were in Sedona. I'd just touched a sample of that really weird tree, and before I knew it, over fifty years had gone by! For me, that was about a day ago. I've been trying to get back ever since!"

"Only a day?" she whispered.

"Yes!"

She squinted. "So that tree really *is* something secret. Did you know it would do that?"

"No! I promise you, I never meant for this to happen! I can't imagine what you went through." He searched her face, willing her to believe him. "I don't know what I hoped to accomplish by looking you up now. I guess... I just didn't want you to think I had betrayed you."

She processed that for a moment, then shook her head. "But you *did* betray me." Though she spoke softly, her words stung him.

"What? No! I—"

"I brought something for you, too," she interrupted him. "I fled with it in my hand that night, and I could never bring myself to get rid of it after that. I put it away and didn't think about it for years, until I got your message. I don't know why I've kept it all this time..." She reached into her cardigan pocket.

"Maybe as a reminder to myself to be more careful who I trust." She set his wedding band on the table and slid it across to him.

"Oh, God..." He bowed his head. *How in the world did I ever imagine no one would find out? Or that she'd be okay with it?* He looked at her. "I don't know what to say."

"I thought about sending it along to your wife," she said absently. "But in the end, when everyone thought you were dead, what good would it have done? I thought there was a chance she never knew about me, so I kept it that way."

"I really appreciate that," Eugene said with a sigh of relief.

She looked up. "I didn't do it for you. Eva had just become a widow, Gene. I had played a part in that. I thought it would be easier for her if I at least didn't disgrace your memory. I owed her that much."

"How... how did you find out her name?"

"I read it in your obituary. The courts declared you dead after only a month, because the police found your car and assumed you'd gone into the desert and been killed somehow. It was in the newspapers."

"Oh." He reached out gingerly and took his ring back. He rolled it between his fingers. He felt like he'd only taken it off last week. And now, he couldn't remember why he'd been so angry. He put it into the inside pocket of his jacket.

"Things had just gotten so hard with Eva," he said. "I don't know. We could barely talk without fighting anymore. And then you came along, and you were so..." He looked into her eyes, and realized that none of his words would land. The best years of Kat's life were behind her now, tarnished by the memory of the horrific night he'd put her through. She didn't see a handsome, intelligent, desirable man now. She saw a liar.

"When were you going to tell me?" she asked quietly.

"I honestly don't know. I wasn't really thinking about the future. I was only thinking about that night."

"It was the worst night of my life," she said, her eyes full of pain.

"What happened to you after I was gone?"

"You... faded away, like a ghost. I thought I was losing my mind. And maybe I did. You're going to think I'm nuts if I tell you the rest."

"Hey, I'm over fifty years in the future. It's not going to sound that crazy."

She took a deep breath, steeling herself. "Something... came to me that night."

He tilted his head. "You mean, like a realization?"

"No, I mean a thing. Some*thing*. It was... a voice. It knocked things over. It told me that I had killed you. I was so afraid that maybe I had."

"But you didn't! Why would you believe that?"

"Because... Joseph Iwila had said almost the same thing to me."

Joseph Iwila. I hate that guy.

"Then another being came in after that," she continued, "and told me he would save me. He said he would show me my true destiny."

"Had you... I mean... I'm sorry, but had you taken anything?"

"No. Nothing. I talked a big game back then, but I had only ever smoked cigarettes. No, he's real. His name is Albion. To prove I could trust him, he told me where your ring was."

Eugene's body gave an involuntary shudder, as if a cold wind had hit his back.

"He convinced me to forget about you, and go to New York without telling my parents. I thought it was to pursue acting. I was broke within two weeks. I ended up living with a group of kids in the Bowery for a while. They let me sleep on their couch. But Albion showed me how to read people, how to know about their pasts. He helped me do psychic readings to make grocery money."

"So how did you manage to get back?" he asked.

"I saw an old man one day. He was teaching chanting in Tompkins Square Park. The things he said made so much sense to me. My friends liked him, too. We called him our swami. And Albion told me I should learn from him, so I did. When he taught, I was right there. When he opened a little bookstore, I worked there. When he decided to take his teachings on tour, I went along. The teacher and a group of us traveled for six years. I was really proud, you know? I could really bring money in.

"Then, in seventy-one, I started to feel really strange when I did readings. I got sick. I felt dizzy. I couldn't control my visions anymore. Every time I went into a trance, I just kept seeing flashes of light. I think it was some kind of interference in the ethereal plane. So Albion just… left me one day. We were in Florida, and he said that he'd found a better instrument to channel knowledge through, but that he would return to me if I could prove myself worthy again.

"After that, I couldn't even do the readings. The teacher accused me of abandoning true enlightenment, and sent me away." She shrugged. "I had nowhere to go. My parents never knew where I was. I felt like I should at least let them know I was alive. So I called them."

"Wow, after all that time?" Eugene said. "That took guts."

"Yeah, I was terrified. I didn't expect them to forgive me, but they… wanted to. They asked me to move home and finish school, so I did. But I switched from theater to nursing so I could keep showing people Albion's teachings about energy healing. It's good karma."

"So you're a nurse?"

"Retired."

"Oh, right. I guess you would be."

"But I still lead meditations. I'm going back to Sedona soon to open my own studio. That's where I first met Albion. Maybe I'll find him again if I go back."

"Wow." Eugene swirled the coffee in the bottom of his cup. "Did you ever… y'know…"

"You mean did I ever get married?" Kat finished.

"Yeah." He felt awkward asking, but he had to know.

"No, I didn't." A hardness had entered her expression. "I guess after you, I didn't really feel like trusting anyone else."

"But it's been so long, and you were so—"

"Listen, I was a stupid kid when you met me. I still believed in love. But I saw plenty, doing readings on guys. Lots of them wanted to know if their lovers and wives knew about each other." She scoffed. "I was just done with all of it, by the end."

Eugene was shocked at her bitterness. The love of life she'd had, the joy bubbling from her, was gone. "I'm so sorry," he said hoarsely. "For everything. For what it's worth, you made me so happy. I thought I'd never be happy again, until I met you."

She squinted at him. "I thought you made me happy, too. But in my long life, I've realized that I don't want happiness that has to be stolen from other people."

Eugene hung his head, feeling another strange sensation tearing at his soul.

"Besides," she continued, "if you were willing to leave your wife, who's to say how long you would've stuck by me, before someone else came along?"

Eugene hadn't considered that, but he couldn't refute it. Not now. After all, hadn't he said a lot of the same things to Eva in the beginning? He shook his head. "You deserved so much better than me," he murmured.

"Well," she replied, her voice thick with emotion, "you were a good lesson." She shrugged, pushing away tears. "I helped people, and I took care of my parents. Hopefully there's enough good karma there to get me by. And in that vein, here's some good advice: go find Eva. Just do that for me. She's the one you should be apologizing to. I think she really loved you."

"She sure had a funny way of showing it."

"Gene, you need to grow up," Kat sighed.

He jerked his head up.

"Not everything is someone else's fault. Blame her if you want to, but you're the one who cheated."

Eugene would normally have fought back, but he felt deflated.

"I don't know where she is," he said lamely.

"Well, you found me. You can find her, too." Her face softened, and she spoke more gently. "You still have time to make something right. I think you should."

He nodded.

"You got any money?"

"Twenty bucks. Well… eighteen, after this terrible coffee."

"I figured. Listen… I have sort of a rainy day fund. I grabbed it on my way out of the house, just on a whim. I want you to take it." She drew a fat envelope out of her purse and slid it toward him.

"Kat, I can't accept this."

She leaned forward. "I don't know if you've noticed, but everything's about ten times more expensive now. You'll be lucky to get lunch and dinner on eighteen bucks. You wanna be stuck here, or do you want to find your wife?"

Eugene found himself fighting tears again. "Why are you doing this?"

"Because I'm old, and because I can," she replied. "Because grudges are bad energy. No matter what you did to me, you're also partly in this fix because I helped you get there. I'm just trying to bring some balance to the universe. At least let me do that. If I can set you free from this place, maybe I'll finally be free of you, too."

Her words tore at him. After a long moment, he sighed and accepted the envelope. "Thank you."

She nodded and stood. "Be well, Gene."

Kat slipped away quietly. Her earring still sat on the table, its mock diamonds glinting at him in the light.

"Goodbye, Kat," he whispered.

Eugene walked back into the library and up to the information desk. The girl with pink hair was still there.

"Cary Grant," she said with a little smile. "You're back. How was coffee with your grandma?"

"Productive," he said cryptically. "Listen, I know you said 'just this once' last time, but I was wondering if you could help me locate one more person. It would mean the world to me."

She took in his red eyes and pleading expression. "Are you okay?"

For once, Eugene made no attempt to be charming. "I am most definitely *not* okay. But I'm trying to be."

"Then let's see what we can do." She offered him a sympathetic smile, and turned to her computer. "What's the name?"

"Evangeline Thomas."

Vancouver, Washington

As soon as Jason and Gray left, Iris sat cross legged on her bed, getting familiar with her new laptop. It was exactly like the one Gray had been letting her use at their house. She spent some time documenting the final details of her first mission using the software that Jason had installed.

Gray had trained her on the finer points of Guardian journaling over the past few weeks, since it was done in a slightly different style than she'd expected. To her surprise, Guardians valued subjective impressions along with objective facts, and they used specialized vocabulary for both. Over the years, they had developed a software that tagged and categorized those items. If one Great Tree had separate, overlapping accounts, the software combined them into one continuous narrative. Thankfully, it was fairly intuitive to use. She typed in the last period, hit "Merge," and watched her sentences slot together like a puzzle with the accounts submitted by the three other Guardians she'd worked with.

The corner of her screen flashed: *Incoming Message…*
She tapped the screen and a window popped up.

From: Gabriel Iwila, Sedona AZ
To: Iris Jacobs
Cc: Grayson Reynolds

Greetings from sunny Arizona! I have a development to report on a cold case involving my family's Tree. I see that the dossier created by my grandfather, Joseph, is already in your queue, Iris. But I've bumped it to the top because I just spotted the guy! His name is Eugene Thomas. No advanced aging to report, but here's something fun: he's a real piece of work! I tried to fill him in on his situation, but short of tying him to a chair, there wasn't a feasible way to do that. Not sure where he's headed now, but I'm sure he'll be back once he realizes the level of crazy he's swimming in. I'll ping you if I see him again. Let me know if you need anything from me once you've had a look at his file. Excited to work with you!

Best, Gabe

P.S. My son Danny wants your autograph.

Iris giggled at the postscript, and then reread the message. "Wow," she mumbled. "A real piece of work, huh?" She switched screens to her case queue and clicked on the top entry. She read through the basic stats—*late twenties to early thirties, scientist from University of Arizona. Objective: Tree sample.*

"Oh dear, that is not good," Iris muttered, and continued reading aloud: "Belligerent… accompanied by a woman named Kat… hmm… ooh, nice, he drove a burgundy 1965 Mustang convertible." Her eyes continued to scan the screen. *Sample taken with a sharp instrument, through the trunk of the Great Juniper.* She zoomed in on the grainy photos of the weeping wound in the tree, and cringed. "Yikes, poor Tree…"

She read through Joseph Iwila's entire account from March, 1965, detailing how this man and his accomplice had managed to acquire a sample on their second attempt.

The old broken ankle routine, eh? Those turkeys.

In his last paragraph, Joseph said that he and his son, Ben, had already noticed the car parked at a nearby campsite earlier that day. They tracked the two perpetrators to the same campsite, now abandoned, followed the tire tracks out to the road, and then found the car at a roadside motel. Joseph had seen the woman look for something in the car and then return to the room. She had left the following morning on foot.

Before housekeeping could clean the room, Joseph had let himself in (no details on the method of entry used) and swept the place for clues. He found the Tree sample lying on a table and took it home. He had immediately attempted a repair by placing the sample near the Great Tree before it could heal naturally, but the piece had failed to reattach itself. It was incomplete. Joseph hadn't been able to hear the vibrations of any other pieces during his search, so he put the wood sample into storage in the house. This would ensure that anyone who may have fallen through time would reappear in that spot once the Juniper had healed.

No one in the Iwila family had seen the man or the woman again. *Until today.*

"Hmm," Iris mused to herself, "so the question is, where would Eugene Thomas go? First thing I'd do is look for familiar people."

She tapped in a quick search, "University of Arizona Eugene Thomas," and got nothing except general search results for the school. But it did answer one of her questions, which was what city Eugene was from. She tried a general people search for "Eugene and Kat Thomas, Tucson AZ" but came up empty. So she tried just "Eugene Thomas Tucson AZ," and found a newspaper article and an obituary.

She clicked the article, which was an image scanned from an archived copy of *The Arizona Daily Star*. The headline read, "Missing UofA Scientist Presumed Dead, Wife Pleads With Court." Iris read about how this man's wife had petitioned the courts for a death certificate on financial grounds, and had based her testimony on the circumstantial evidence of his character, current devotion to his work, and last known location. Apparently, it had been enough back then. Interestingly, the wife's name was Evangeline, not Kat or Katherine.

Iris made a few notes. All of this man's possessions, including his impounded vehicle, had been released to his wife. She had just begun another search when her watch alarm buzzed. Her brain registered the time. Five seconds later, she realized the significance of it.

"Will's going to be here in fifteen minutes!" she cried, chucking her laptop onto the bed. "Gah!! Why can't I keep him in my head for more than half a day? I have the memory of a goldfish!"

Thankfully, she'd already picked an outfit. She dashed to the mirror and began tugging her hair free of its french braid. *I'll just have to work some magic.*

Chapter 12

I ris had decided to wear her favorite lavender dress this evening. It was one of the rare shades that complemented her ginger hair and fair skin. When Will drove up, she could tell he agreed. She had left her hair down and wavy, and gone light on makeup.

"Happy birthday, beautiful. You look amazing," he said, taking it all in. "Your dress matches your name."

She blushed. "Thank you."

"Is that a new necklace?"

"Yeah, it's from my dad. I guess it's been in my family for a long time, but he gave it to me for Christmas."

"It suits you."

"That's what he said!" She smiled at him. "You look amazing, too."

And he did. He'd opted for jeans with a black button down and black shoes. Simple and perfect.

Will had chosen a high-end restaurant for Iris's birthday. There was a fireplace at one end, a stylish bar, and tall, cozy booths. Once they were seated at their table and had placed their order, she looked at him expectantly.

"So? What's the big thing you wanted to talk about? I've been wondering all day!"

He sipped his water. "I'm not sure if it's good news, but I feel like it is. Probably."

"Okay…"

He took a deep breath. "I'm leaving Rookwood."

"Seriously? That's… I mean, that's… wow."

"Yeah, that about sums it up." He gazed at her. "To be honest, I never intended to stay as long as I did. I've wanted to start working my way up into… well, places like this." He gestured around him. "Somewhere I could be more creative. But…" He reached across the table and lightly touched her fingers with his. "This really awesome activity assistant showed up one day, and then it was really hard to leave."

"Will, if you need to move on to keep your career on track, you totally should!" Iris said earnestly. She could feel herself growing warmer at his touch, but couldn't help feeling a little glum at the same time, as she imagined the kitchen without him.

He frowned slightly. "I had always planned to, but I thought once I did, I'd be happier about it."

"You're not happy?"

"Well I suppose I am, because an amazing bistro down on the waterfront just hired me on as a sous chef. I was blown away that they'd start me there instead of as a line cook."

"What! That's amazing, Will! Congratulations!"

"Thanks," he said, but his smile was subdued. "I'm really excited to start something new. It'll be a slight pay cut for a little while, but they said they promote from within, and it's well worth it. I just…" He frowned again. "If it wasn't for you raiding the kitchen for coffee and pastries at work, I would hardly ever see you as it is. If I leave…"

Iris felt another pang of guilt. *Will doesn't deserve what I'm putting him through.*

"I know what you mean. I've felt awful about that." She looked into his eyes. "I haven't been trying to put you off, or make you feel taken for granted. I want to see you more than anything! But two jobs…"

"I know," he said. "I really do understand. It just kind of sucks right now."

Her eyes brightened. "Well, I think I might have some good news on that front. I just went through a sort of... performance review... kind of thing. And it went super well. So I don't think the training part of things is going to go on much longer. Pretty soon I'll have more free time."

He let out a huge breath. "That is *such* good news. Because my last day at Rookwood is at the end of the week, and I don't think I can just quit you cold turkey."

Iris laughed. "You make me sound like coffee or something!"

"Yes, it's quite the compliment!"

"I will have to go out of town on the spur of the moment, occasionally," she said. "But it won't be that often, and I promise I'll tell you when I'm leaving."

"I appreciate that." He looked at her with a pensive expression. "I'm wondering something."

"What?"

"Well, when I say I miss you, it's the honest truth. I'm just telling you how I feel. But I think it's making you feel guilty, and I don't want you to feel that way. I just want you to go out and do exactly what you want to do with your life. If your new job makes you happy, then you should do it. I think my new job is going to make me happy, too. But it's also going to pull us apart. It's going to make us miss each other, even more than we do now." He smiled sadly. "And I don't think either one of us is willing to stay put, because we're both following our dreams."

"Yeah," Iris said glumly. "I can't imagine doing anything else. And I don't want you to be stuck at Rookwood just because of me. But I don't know where that leaves us, exactly."

"Hmm, I think this is the part where a lot of couples break up," Will said matter-of-factly. "This is when they say it didn't work out because they didn't fit into each other's lives anymore... or they wanted different things."

Iris hung her head. "Is that what's happening to us?"

Will leaned forward. "No. Absolutely not."

She looked up. A fire had come into his eyes.

"Remember what I said to you." He didn't intend it as a question. "No matter what happens from now on, you're part of my life."

She put her hand on his arm. "And you're part of mine."

"That means you have my loyalty, Iris. I understand that every decision I make is going to impact you in some way, even if it means distance. But I intend to cross that distance in every way I can, for as long as you want me to."

She squeezed his arm, savoring the warmth of his assurance.

Their salads arrived, along with a small loaf of freshly baked bread.

"Maybe I sound corny, I don't know," he said with a crooked smile, as he sliced off a piece of bread and handed it to her. "I might be way too serious, saying everything all wrong, and freaking you out."

"You're not!" Iris protested. "I don't think you're being corny at all!"

"Well, I think maybe I'm supposed to be more aloof for a while. Keep you guessing. Isn't that how guys do it?"

"Maybe," she admitted. "But I like the way you just say what you think."

"Good, because I'm pretty sure I'm stuck like this. You know you're the most incredible person I've ever met, right?"

She stopped halfway through buttering her bread. "Really?"

"Really. I hope that's not a lame thing to say, since you're the only person I've ever dated. But there's a reason for that."

"What's the reason?"

"My family."

"They didn't want you dating too young, or something?" she asked.

He shrugged. "I doubt they'd care. It was more about my little brother, Luke."

"You've never talked about him before," Iris said.

Will stared at his salad as he watched memories flicker in his mind. "Well, it's not the greatest story. I've never met my father. My mom raised me until I was five. Then my little brother came along. I don't know who his dad is, either. But after he was born, my mom kind of just… fell apart. My grandma would come over when I was at school, but otherwise I pretty much raised Luke." He finally took a bite.

"Wow, so you must've been pretty busy after school, huh?"

"Yeah. I learned how to change diapers and feed a kid when I was in first grade. Our mom was a waitress, or at least that's what she said. Maybe that was code for something. But she would bring groceries home and then sleep a lot. So I taught myself to cook from old recipe books my mom had around. Sometimes, she'd bring men home, but they always left. Once Luke got older, he had a lot of questions. Since our mother was hardly ever around, I just learned to be honest with him, about everything. It was so much simpler that way. Maybe that's why I'm so awkwardly frank all the time, and I've never had time to date. But Luke is eighteen now. He just joined the Navy. It's been kinda weird having the apartment all to myself."

Iris was overwhelmed. She had no idea that such tenderness could come from such a difficult life.

"Where's your mom now?"

"She died a year ago. She was… found. Someone took her life. The police were never able to figure out who did it, or why."

"Oh Will, I'm so sorry."

"I'm okay." He gave her a rueful smile. "It's like I said, I was never very close to her. But I do wish she'd been there for Luke. At least I was done with culinary school by then and had a good enough job to keep him out of foster care. He would have pitched a fit."

"So the two of you are pretty close?"

"As close as two brothers can be." He sighed and set his fork down. "Sorry, all of that is probably super depressing. And this is supposed to be a nice dinner for your birthday and everything."

"No, it's okay," Iris reassured him. "I want to know the real you. I'm glad you felt safe enough to share that with me."

"I do feel safe around you," he said, and picked up his fork again. "Safer than I've ever felt around anyone. I just thought if I told you, it might help you understand where I'm coming from. People always come and go, in and out of my life. Nothing ever sticks, unless I go after it with everything I have."

She slipped her hand into his, and smiled at him. "Well, I'm not going anywhere."

He smiled back. "I'm glad. I know I've got something amazing with you. Maybe it seems like I move at a glacial pace sometimes, but it's because I want to be careful, y'know? I used to watch my mother trade a kiss for a beer or a cigarette. I saw how those men looked at her, and it made me sick. I knew I never wanted to be like that."

"You're not like that at all," she said, with a reassuring squeeze.

The waiter brought their plates, and they dug into exquisite almond crusted sea bass and roasted garlic sweet potatoes. Will savored and analyzed each flavor, explaining to her how he would probably replicate it later. She loved watching how his face lit up as he talked about it.

Once he could focus on normal conversation again, he asked, "What was it you wanted to ask me?"

"Oh! Yes. Well I've been doing a lot of reading lately, and I guess I was just wondering where you stand on the whole... *God* issue."

"God," he mused. "Interesting question. Well, my grandmother believed in God. She died when I was nine. She was Eastern orthodox. I think she was onto something when she said the world is too beautiful to have happened by accident.

But uh… I don't know. Beyond that, I've never given it much thought. Seems like most people who believe in a divine being just worship in their own way. I've certainly sent up a prayer or two on my worst days. Maybe it's just that there's a divine spark in each of us, so we connect with that in whatever way gives our lives meaning. Whatever the concept of God means to you, I don't think there's a right or wrong way to go about it."

A waiter sidled up to the table. "How is everything here tonight?" he asked.

"Wonderful!" Iris told him sincerely.

"Yes," Will agreed. "Please send our compliments to the chef. This sauce is perfect."

The waiter nodded. "I'll be sure to tell him. He sometimes comes out to thank guests personally, so you might even see him." He took the empty bread board and glided away.

Will turned back to her. "So is that what you've been reading about?"

"Hm? Oh yeah," Iris replied. "Just trying to decide what I think about it. I'm almost done with the whole book. So far, it seems pretty legit to me."

"I confess, I've never been able to get into all that. It just seems so… old. How do we know any of it's even true, if it was written thousands of years ago?"

"Oh, you did *not* just ask a history nerd a question that might take the rest of the night to answer!" Iris laughed. "There are several pretty reliable ways to verify manuscripts, but with a lot of it, I guess you just kind of… have to decide whether you really buy it or not."

"Well now I know who to ask if I ever get curious!" He winked. "Now, the big question of the moment is, do you think you might want dessert?"

"Oh my gosh," Iris sighed contentedly. "I don't know where I'd put it. Plus, I still have a slice of sticky toffee pudding cake at home! I can't imagine they've got anything here that's better than yours."

"It's possible, but do you want to risk it?" Will asked with a wry smile.

"I think I'll manage. That cake in my fridge is calling me. I don't think Charlie would eat it with all the death threats I wrote on the box, but I shouldn't tempt her for long. Just to be safe."

Will chuckled. "All right. I'll get the check so you can get home to your cake." He looked past her and tilted his chin at the waiter, then gave him a polite smile. His eyes shifted slightly and he spotted a man in a white jacket having a friendly conversation with a group of diners three tables down. "Oh look, I think that must be the chef."

Iris turned to look behind her, and did a double take. A chill of dread splashed her like cold water in the face. She whipped her head back around and stared, unseeing, at the table top.

"Iris, what's wrong?" Will asked.

She gripped the seat and shut her eyes, trying to fight off the image of a sinister face, full of hatred, spewing threats just inches from her ear while a forearm pressed her into a wall, threatening to cut off her air.

"Iris?" Will's voice was alarmed.

She looked at him, eyes pleading. "We have to go. *Now.* Please, Will."

"Sure…" He grabbed his jacket. "What's going on?"

"It's him." Tears of panic started to come, but she took a deep breath to steady herself. "The chef… it's Brett."

"What?" He narrowed his eyes. "Okay, sit tight. I'll get you out of here." He intercepted the waiter, glanced at the bill for about two seconds, tucked two fifties into the little black folder, and said, "No change."

"Thank you, sir. Have a good night."

Iris had put on her coat by the time he returned less than a minute later.

"C'mon," he whispered next to her ear. "We'll have to walk past him, but try to stay behind me, okay?"

She nodded and followed him.

They had nearly made it past Brett when he caught Will's eye and reached out for a handshake.

"Ah, good evening! I was just about to come say hello," he said. "I'm glad everything was to your satisfaction."

"Yeah, it was great." Will tried to hide the edge in his voice as Iris stood behind him.

"And… your charming date—"

"Isn't feeling so good all of a sudden," Will finished Brett's sentence. "I'm just going to get her home."

"Oh, I'm sorry to hear that…"

They began to slide past him.

"Too bad I didn't know you were coming, Iris," he continued. "Or I would have made you something special."

Will stopped. "What did you say?"

Brett smiled.

"Don't speak to her," Will said quietly. "Don't even *look* at her."

"I can look where I want," Brett replied with a cool glare. "You're in *my* house, big boy."

"I won't make that mistake again, believe me." Will gave Brett a withering stare, then put his arm around Iris and escorted her outside.

Will had barely closed the door on Iris's side of the truck when Brett strode up behind him.

"Just a friendly word of advice," he said with a smirk. "You're wasting your time with that one. She couldn't find her way to first base with a flashing neon sign."

"Or," Will countered, "maybe she just doesn't have a taste for scumbags."

Without warning, Brett drew back and threw a punch at Will's face, but Will sidestepped it a split second before Brett's fist impacted the window instead.

Iris let out an involuntary shriek.

Brett cursed and doubled over, cradling his knuckles.

"Here, let me help you with that," Will said, and brought his knee up hard into Brett's stomach.

Brett went to the ground with a gasp.

"Wow, that looks like it hurts," Will sympathized, "but I'm sure you see my point." He turned toward the truck and said over his shoulder, "Good talk!"

A glowing being over ten feet tall stood next to the groaning man on the pavement. His sword was still sheathed, but he smiled with satisfaction.

"Nice move," said Brennus, who was leaning against the passenger door of a black pickup.

"He brought it on himself," said the other. "I just helped mine get out of the way."

"Still." Brennus approached and saluted. "You must be Varick. I was told you were coming."

"I am." Varick returned the salute. "And you are Brennus, Watcher of the Heir. I admire your work."

"It is an honor," Brennus replied. "She is growing beautifully. The Master whispers to her about the Histories in almost every quiet moment. But she is in a season of great turmoil. Challenges await, and she must be ready."

"Indeed." Varick nodded. "My charge has his heart set on her. Their destinies become more intertwined by the day. Though he is full of courage, he is not yet her equal."

"Have you been sent to redirect him, then?" Brennus asked.

Varick shook his head. "Merely to stand watch."

"Shall we?"

They rode on the cab of the truck as it pulled away.

A thick, hazy mist hovered a hundred feet away, cloaked in black shadow, watching them disappear into the distance. Although it had pretended to accompany a group near the building's entrance, it had kept its eyes on this fascinating exchange. *"Brennus, Watcher of the Heir,"* it hissed under its breath. *"Interesting."* That name was well known in this dominion.

It slinked back along the ground toward its host, who had just become even more useful than expected. The man had risen to one knee, trying to catch his breath.

"She'll pay for that," it whispered to him.

The man's eyes flashed with fury.

"That's right," it snickered. *"We'll find her."*

Will hopped into the truck and they roared away, leaving Brett on the ground behind them. He drove in silence for a few blocks, then looked at Iris.

"You doing okay?" he asked.

"Actually, yes." She had calmed considerably ever since watching Will drop Brett like a sack of spuds. "I'm feeling better about Brett than I have in a long time, to be honest!"

"Gosh, he's a nice person," Will said through clenched teeth.

"You didn't hurt your knee, did you?" Iris asked.

"Nah, that guy's got a soft belly."

They looked at each other. Iris snickered. Will chuckled. They both burst into laughter.

"Man, I wish his food sucked! That's the only bummer part," Will said. "He actually is a decent cook. I wish I could just hate everything about him. He won't even give me that!"

Iris laughed. "Well I don't think he actually made any of it, if that helps you feel any better. He always preferred to run the pass."

Will nodded appreciatively. "I *love* that you know what that means!"

"He was always happy to take credit, though." She smirked. Then she sighed as her face grew somber. "Will, what you did tonight was… beyond amazing. But… he might not let it go. I wouldn't be surprised if he tries to bring charges."

"I thought about that," Will said. "But I think he learned his lesson last time, because he picked this fight out of the range of security cameras. It'll be his word against mine. And you were my witness—the poor fellow banged his hand on my truck. What a klutz!"

She giggled. "Yeah, gosh. He might have a few broken fingers."

He stopped at a red light and looked at her. "I'm glad you're okay. You know I'm here for you anytime, right? I don't know what that guy's glitch is, but if he ever comes back, I'll be here."

"I know."

"And as much as I dislike him, I do understand why he'd have a hard time being rejected. There's something about Iris Jacobs."

"Oh, please."

"What? There is! Just accept it."

She huffed, but smiled. "Well, thank you. Let's just hope he got the message this time."

"Let's hope."

Iris made her morning rounds at Rookwood with a light step the next day. As she delivered the residents' mail, her mind was full of last night. She kept thinking about how Will had stood up to Brett. He wasn't angry—he was perfectly in control—but he wasn't about to be bullied. It was a side of him that gave his words new meaning. Having someone like him in her life was a gift. That's all there was to it. With Will, what you saw is what you got. And even though some of his past bravery had now officially never happened, she had seen for herself how far he would go to protect her.

She had also finished reading the Histories last night. The ending had felt both fitting and completely unexpected at the same time. The last section had sounded more like the older parts, full of symbolism that tied everything together. And it all seemed to converge on one person: the Son. She would have to ask Jason about it soon.

"Nurse?" called a little voice from the doorway she'd just passed. "Help me, please?"

Iris smiled. This happened almost every time she went by this room. Leaving the wheeled cart full of mail in the hallway, she entered with a patient smile and approached the frail woman on the bed.

"How can I help you today, Eva?"

"I'm worried about my wedding ring," Eva replied. "I haven't seen it since I did the dishes, and last time it went down the drain, he got so mad! He had to take the pipe apart for me, even though he was supposed to be studying. I felt just awful about it. Will you look for it, dear?"

"Eva, I know exactly where your ring is, and it's perfectly safe," Iris said, patting her hand.

"Oh, goodness! You found it?"

"Yes, so don't you worry your beautiful head, okay?"

"Bless you, dear. It's my favorite thing in the whole world. It's all I have left of him."

"I remember." Iris grinned at her. "I think your breakfast tray will be here soon! Won't that be nice?"

"Oh, I can't eat that," Eva protested. "I have to watch my waistline."

"But I know the chef personally!" Iris teased. "What will he say if you don't enjoy the beautiful bacon omelette he made for you this morning?"

"Well, maybe a bite."

"Good girl. I'll see you later, okay?"

Iris went back to her mail round, stopping at a few more rooms. When she turned the corner, she saw an unfamiliar man walking toward her. He wore classic Levis and a vintage Harrington jacket—slightly unusual choices for someone who looked like he was under thirty. Though he was freshly shaved and his hair was combed, there was a raggedness to his features, as if he were deeply exhausted. He was reading every brass name plate as he walked slowly down the hallway. *Maybe he's lost.*

"Hi!" she said.

He jumped. "Oh, uh… hello."

"Sorry for startling you," she said. "Do you need help finding somebody?"

"Um… Eva Thomas?"

"Oh, sure. I was just with her, actually. I can show you where her room is. Are you… a relative?"

"Yeah."

Iris got the strangest feeling, looking at this man. She couldn't put her finger on exactly what it was about him. He was being a little cryptic, maybe. But he didn't have to explain himself to her. Family members came and went all the time.

She gave him a friendly smile. "She's just around the corner. Follow me."

"Actually…" The man stopped. "Um, maybe I should come back another time. I'm sorry to bother you."

"Oh, okay," Iris said, looking at him quizzically. "Are you sure? It's just right here…"

"I have to go." The man turned and strode toward the lobby.

"Huh." Iris shrugged and pushed the mail cart to the next room.

Then a thought came to her… a tiny connecting thread, almost as if someone had whispered it to her.

"Thomas…" Iris whispered, eyes wide. *Eva Thomas. The widow of Eugene Thomas was Evangeline Thomas… could that be Eva? Of course Eugene Thomas would come looking for his wife!* She jerked her head up and looked around the empty corridor. *That might've been him!* She dropped a stack of magazines and sprinted toward the lobby, dialing Grayson at the same time.

The man was gone.

"Hello, Iris!"

"Gray!" she panted. "I think he's here! The guy from Arizona, I think I just saw him!"

"What? Why would he be there?"

"His *wife* lives here! I just put it together!"

"Where is he now?"

She pushed the heavy front door open and peered around the parking lot. "Well, he just left, but there are no cars leaving the lot. I think he must be on foot."

"Can you follow him?"

"No, I'm on the clock…"

"Okay, don't worry," Gray said calmly. "State testing at school today, so I'm actually off right now. I'll hop in my car and see if I can intercept him. What's he wearing?"

"Jeans, black windbreaker, looks kind of… I dunno, vintage or something."

"He looks *vintage*? That's a new one."

"Oh, you know what I mean!"

"Okay, I'll let you know if I spot anyone vintage looking."

"See you tonight, right?"

"Looking forward to it, as always," he said with a chuckle. "Should be interesting."

Chapter 13

I ris counted down her last hour at work, checking the clock every three minutes.

This is torture! No wonder Guardians try to make sure they only have to work for the fun of it!

At last, four o'clock came. She grabbed her purse from her locker and called Gray before she had even left the break room.

"Hey, hey! There's my favorite Guardian Heir!"

She smiled in response. "Hiiiii, Grayson. So? Did you find him?"

"Find who?"

"What ya mean, who?" She breezed through the employee entrance and walked out from under the portico into the afternoon sunshine.

Gray laughed. "You mean Vintage Guy? The guy who's currently on my porch, lighting up his third cigarette in a row? Yes, I found him."

"Oh, man. I'll be right there."

When Iris drove up, there was no one on the porch, but she saw several cigarette butts smashed into the doorstep, and could detect a faint smoky odor. She let herself in without knocking, as she'd grown accustomed to doing, and walked into the living room.

The same man she'd seen in the hallway at Rookwood was sitting on the sofa, minus his jacket, and looking at her with a critical gaze.

"Hello, I'm Iris," she said to him. "Eugene, right?"

"Sure." His face was deadpan.

"Do your friends call you 'Gene'?" she tried again.

"Yes. Call me Eugene."

"Okay…" She looked over at Gray, who was seated in the armchair beside the fireplace.

He rolled his eyes.

"Eugene had a couple of sandwiches while we were waiting for you," Gray said. "And he was just telling me his theories about why he thinks we're all a bunch of trained psychotic killers. Y'know, the kind who give you pastrami and swiss before they bump you off."

"I see…" Iris said, taking in the stubborn set of Eugene's jaw. "Well. That's colorful. Is Jason here?" she asked Gray.

"Strangely, no," he replied, crossing his arms. "He suddenly had the urge to go grocery shopping. You know how it is, when you've got a cheeky time traveler on your sofa. You find yourself in need of supplies. Ice cream… duct tape… sedatives…"

Iris bit her lip, trying not to laugh. She turned back to Eugene, whose eyes had widened slightly. "Well, ice cream would be nice." She sat opposite Gray, in Jason's matching armchair. "So, Eugene. You've come a long way from Tucson."

Eugene looked startled for the second time that day. "How come you people know so much about me?" he demanded.

"You messed with a strange Tree, am I right?" She tilted her head toward him. "One that you were warned to leave alone?"

He opened his mouth to argue, but thought better of it, and frowned. "Maybe I did, but somehow I ended up waking up in that Iwila guy's house! What I did, I did for science. Is that any reason to kidnap or poison a person?"

"Definitely not," she agreed. "We don't do stuff like that." She leaned back in her chair and looked at him calmly. "What's happened to you is both unfortunate and rare. And I know you didn't intend this result. But you're a scientist, Eugene. *Think.* Is there a kidnapper or a poison known to man that can fling you half a century into the future?"

His frown took on a tinge of desperation. He stubbornly refused to answer for several moments, but finally let out a breath. "No. I guess there isn't."

"Good." She nodded. "Now we're getting somewhere. The Tree you cut isn't actually a juniper. You might have noticed."

"Yes, Einstein, I noticed."

"Okay, first of all, some basic ground rules," Iris said, leaning forward, elbows on her knees. "Let's keep the conversation civil and sarcasm-free, arright? You're in the home of Guardians. We're here to help you. I'm going to do everything I can to get you back where you belong, but it'll go a lot faster if you cooperate. And I could do without the cigarette butts on the porch. Simple enough?"

Eugene slumped. "Yeah, sorry. I've just had a rotten few days. I just spent forty-five hours on a train after being chased by cops and sleeping under a tree. And now I've been picked up by the Ghost of Christmas Present over there."

"What did I just say about being civil?" Iris raised her eyebrow.

"Sorry. I just… I don't even know why I came here in the first place."

"I know why you came. To see Eva."

He glanced up sharply, then back down at the rug. "Yeah. But I don't think she'll want to see me. Not after everything…"

"You might be surprised. She never remarried, you know."

"I don't know why not," he sighed. "She wasn't all that attached to me."

"If you say so," Iris said gently. "I think it would do her a world of good if you would talk to her. I have a feeling she could fill you in on some things. But… you should know that she's changed a lot since you last saw her."

"Well yeah, I imagine she's really old."

"Not just that. Eva has dementia, Eugene. What she can remember varies from one day to the next. But I do know she's got a great long term memory. And she thinks about you. A lot."

"She does? I can't begin to imagine what she's said about me."

"Well, just today she told me that the wedding ring you gave her was her favorite thing in the world, because it's all she has left of you."

He looked at her, eyes red, struggling with some inner turmoil.

Iris looked back at Grayson, who was watching the entire conversation with a look of satisfaction and pride. One side of his mouth lifted in a reassuring smile. He nodded encouragingly at her.

"Anyway, it's good that you're here," she continued. "I would've had to track you down either way, so at least you've saved me that trouble."

"Why you?" Eugene asked, brows furrowed.

"I… specialize in cases like yours," she said with a smile. "It was just today that I realized who you were."

"Kind of a coincidence that I met you, then," he said.

"Oh, I don't believe in coincidences anymore," she chuckled. "I think Eva ended up at Rookwood for a reason. But I digress. You're probably wondering what in the heck happened to you."

"Uh, yes. I very much am."

"Okay, let's start with the Tree. You should understand that when Joseph Iwila warned you to stay away from it, it was because it's not actually a tree. It's one of thousands of anchors holding the fabric of space-time in place around the globe. The anchors are shaped like trees because that's a favorite design of the Creator's. We see it everywhere, from roots, to blood vessels, to river deltas. The energy fabric that conducts time has a similar structure. The physical trees are merely a camouflage for what's underneath. Every single Great Tree has a Guardian watching over it, to make sure no one gets hurt like you did."

"Are they all Indians? I really don't like Indians," Eugene muttered.

"That's a little racist, arright?" Iris said calmly. "No, there are Guardians of every race on the planet, from the darkest Africans to the most translucent Scottish people like myself. All of them are completely brilliant individuals, and they spend their lives selflessly protecting the Great Trees from people like you. So regardless of his DNA, Joseph Iwila was just doing his job. And you only got by him because you played on his compassion. Kind of a jerk move."

Both Eugene's and Grayson's eyebrows went up.

"Is she always like this?" Eugene asked Gray.

He shrugged. "Is she wrong?"

Eugene shook his head and stared at the floor.

"So…" Iris continued, "can you accept that there are no Guardians out to get you, and that it's a good idea to listen to them?"

Eugene sighed. "Yeah."

"Wonderful. It gets even better. When you reappeared, you ended up in the house where Joseph Iwila's grandson lives now, instead of a landfill somewhere. That's because Joseph had the decency to track you down and take back the piece of wood you stole."

Eugene narrowed his eyes. "*He* took it?"

"Yes, Eugene, he took it! And it's a good thing he did! You touched it, right?"

"Yeah, I got some kind of weird, dark sap on me."

"That wasn't sap. It was a concentration of dense particles. That's why you followed that piece of wood. Your body had sort of… magnetized to it. At least you were only displaced a few miles. A friend of mine ended up on the wrong continent once! And you're even luckier that you didn't cut yourself."

"What is with that, anyway?" Eugene asked curiously. "That Gabriel guy asked me if I had cut myself."

"It's exactly what he was supposed to ask," Iris replied. "Gabe wanted to make sure you weren't dying. Time Tree poisoning is a medical emergency. I've had it happen to me, and let me tell you, it is no picnic."

"Wow, that's heavy." Eugene raked one hand through his hair. "I guess I should've been nicer to the guy."

"Then do better next time you see him," Iris said soberly. "We'll have to take you back there to get you home."

"But how?" Eugene asked. "Everything I've learned about time theory is that the arrow only points one way, and that's forward."

"Well…" Iris squinted, hunting for words. "Particle physics has come a long way since your day. We don't completely understand why, but at the most subatomic level, a sort of reverse entropy is actually possible. And that's how the Trees work. They self-repair, so if you have all the missing pieces, you can actually reverse the damage. That puts the timeline back where it was, and if all goes to plan, puts you back where you were. It takes some precision, though."

"And these Trees are everywhere?" Eugene asked, his curiosity growing. "Has anyone ever done a paper on it?"

Iris and Gray exchanged amused looks.

"No, they never have," she answered, "and I'll tell you why. The moment you sit down to write it, you'll forget everything you were about to say."

"Ha!" Eugene laughed. "I guarantee you, this experience is something I'll never forget!"

"That's what I said, too, when I didn't know any better," Iris said sympathetically. "But knowledge of the Trees and the Guardians is safeguarded by the spirit realm. Only Guardians themselves, and those they tell directly, can retain it. If you try to relay that knowledge to a third party, it gets wiped."

"The *spirit* realm?" Eugene was incredulous. "You mean I can never tell anyone about this, or some unseen force is going to erase my mind?"

"Oh, not the entire thing," Iris said with a wink. "You can try to write that paper if you want to, I suppose. I guess it depends on how badly you want to remember all this."

"Geez."

"We do have a minor setback to deal with, though…" she continued.

"Setback?"

"Yes. If Joseph Iwila had your piece of the Tree in 1965, then why isn't it fixed? You're still here, which means he didn't have it all. He was careful to take everything he could find, but obviously it wasn't complete. Do you have any idea what might've happened to the rest of it?"

Eugene frowned, deep in thought. "I guess a little piece could have jammed inside the borer," he said. "I was kind of in a hurry that night."

"Where was the borer when you disappeared?" Iris asked.

"In my bag, under the seat of my car." His face filled with concern. "But there's no way we'll ever find it. I'm sure they impounded the car and tossed everything inside it decades ago."

Iris and Grayson looked at each other.

"Really galls me, too," he muttered. "I had those wheels for less than a week! Brand new! And poof… gone. Who knows where it is now?"

"This could be a little complicated," Iris agreed. "But I've seen some pretty impossible things come together, so I'm not ready to throw in the towel just yet."

"I think you're dreaming," Eugene said bleakly.

"If you'd seen what I've seen, you might feel a little better," Iris said gently. "I can't make any guarantees. But for now, I'll do my best to track down the car—see how it changed hands. Maybe your stuff is buried in someone's garage, or in an evidence room somewhere. Who knows?"

"Okay." Eugene seemed overwhelmed.

"You can stay here with us in the meantime," Gray offered. "And try not to worry. Iris is great at what she does. I bet you'll be out of here before you know it."

"Thank you, I… I appreciate that. I didn't really have a plan once I got here. I guess I just thought if I could talk to Eva, something might start to make sense."

Gray nodded.

"Joseph's account also said that you were with someone named Kat," Iris said. "She didn't touch the wood too, did she?"

Eugene hung his head. "No, she's…" he huffed. "She's right where she's supposed to be. In a manner of speaking."

"You saw her?"

"Yeah, the girl at the library helped me find her and Eva both. Kat was still in Tucson. She's… really different now. Kind of weird, actually. I'm pretty sure I ruined her life."

"I'm sorry, Eugene." Iris looked at him sadly. "But let's see what we can do to make things right, okay? And I'll make sure you get over to see Eva tomorrow."

"Thanks." Eugene rubbed his eyes and stood. "I think I'll step outside for a few."

"Oh, good, it'll give you a chance to clean up the porch," Iris said with an unflinching gaze.

"Yes, and if you see any weird trees out there," Gray added, "don't touch 'em."

"Trust me, I won't," he mumbled, and clicked the front door softly behind him.

Iris watched him through the window. "I feel bad for the guy," she sighed. "When Angus went through this, he at least had his faith to keep him sane."

"Yeah, that makes all the difference," Gray agreed. "But I can tell this whole situation's really got him thinking."

"The more, the better." She smiled. "So, you got dinner plans? I could rummage through your cupboards again and whip something up, if you like."

"I really liked that noodle thing you made last week," Gray said with a twinkle in his eye.

"That was mac and cheese from a box with some stuff from your fridge thrown in!" she laughed. "Not exactly fine dining."

"What? It was good!"

"Okay, I'll look around," she said, and stood to leave.

"Iris?"

He caught her hand. It made her feel strangely warm.

"Yeah?"

His blue-green eyes were full of sincerity. "I just… want you to know that I'm really proud of you. You handled yourself so well just now. No one could have done better." He looked awkwardly at her hand and released it. "I just thought you should know that."

After a dinner of salad and frozen pizzas doctored up with extra olives, mushrooms, tomatoes, artichokes, and pesto that Iris had found in the kitchen, Eugene had seemed more cheerful. Iris had used Gray's computer to email Gabe Iwila and tell him the good news—Eugene Thomas had been found in good health, he had been fully briefed, and was as surly as ever. Jason had asked her to stay for ice cream, but Iris was eager to get home and go into full research mode. She was sure that Eugene's Mustang must hold the answer, or at least a strong lead.

Gray walked her to the door.

"Great job again today," he said, leaning on the door jamb. "I'm starting to wonder if there's anything left for me to teach you. It makes me a little sad."

"Aw, poor thing. You've done too good a job, I guess," she chuckled. "But you can't get rid of me that easily. You're still my boss. And if it weren't for you, where would I stash Eugene?"

"I'm not your boss." He looked at her with the same serious expression he'd had earlier.

"Mentor, then."

"Better…"

"Friend?" she suggested.

"Definitely friend." He put one arm over her shoulders and gave her a quick squeeze. She caught the faintest scent of his cologne.

"Iris, I was wondering…"

"Hm?"

His expression was indecipherable. Finally, he shook his head. "It's okay. Maybe some other time."

She shrugged and headed for her car. "Okay. See you later!"

"Hurry back," he mumbled.

Iris had just parked outside her apartment when her phone rang. It was Will. Before answering, she combed through her brain to make sure she hadn't forgotten anything important. She was pretty sure they hadn't said anything about getting together today, so hopefully he was just calling to chat.

"Hey, you!"

"Hi." He sounded bashful. "I uh… I'm doing it again."

"What are you doing?"

"Thinking about you."

"Oh, goodness," she laughed. "There's gotta be something better on TV!"

"Nope."

Iris sighed. "I still can't get over what you did last night. You know, you're quite dashing when you're making a point."

He chuckled. "Listen, I was wondering… would you ever want to do a group hangout with some people? Because, y'know… I've never really met your friends."

"Actually, I'm such an introvert, I think you probably have met most of them. They have gray hair, white hair… sometimes pink…"

He laughed. "No, c'mon. You have to have other friends besides that! What about Charlie? You talk about her so much, it would be great to get to know her."

"Actually, I'd love that!" she exclaimed. "I'm sure Charlie would, too."

"Great! And you could invite whoever else. Maybe Grayson?"

Iris's heart skipped. "Uhh… Grayson? Have I ever mentioned him to you before?"

"Well… no," Will admitted. "But I heard you talking to him on the phone today, so I assumed he must be a good friend of yours."

"You heard me talking on the phone?"

"Yeah, today in the break room, after work? I was just grabbing my stuff when you came in."

She frantically searched her memories. She had clocked out, opened her locker… called Gray… *Will was there?*

"I feel like such an idiot!" she cried. "You were standing right there and I didn't even say hi to you? Who *does* that?"

"Well it was a *little* surprising," he said. "But it seemed important, so I just figured I'd call you later…"

"I can't believe this," Iris whispered. "How did I not see you? You're six-two!"

"Well if it helps, I wasn't six-two at the time. I was tying my shoe."

"Gahhhh…"

"It's no big deal, Iris!" he laughed. "It was actually kinda cute."

She groaned and leaned her head on the steering wheel. *I am the worst.*

"So anyway," he continued, "is this Grayson someone you'd want to include if we did a friend thing?"

"Um. Can I think about it? He's actually more like my… supervisor. At the other job."

"Ohhh…"

"I mean we get along great, but…" *Did we actually have a couple of moments today?* She shook her head. "I'm not sure we're on a hanging out for fun kind of basis." *Except that we spend time together almost constantly.*

"Okay, well just think about it. Maybe we can get something on the calendar soon. I don't want you to feel isolated from everyone else in order to spend time with me."

"I don't even understand how you're a real person sometimes," she said. "You're so completely good to me, even when I'm a total doof. Don't you ever get upset about anything?"

"Absolutely."

"What do you get upset about?"

"Today, I found an entire pan full of dried out, overheated lasagna in the oven. I made that lasagna perfect, and then one of my sous chefs brutally murdered it."

"That *would* be upsetting."

"Then I said something harsh, like… if you wouldn't serve that to your own grandmother, then don't serve it to someone else's!"

"Well, that's actually a valid point."

"Yes, but…" Will chuckled. "I may have overreacted just a teensy bit when I gave him that lasagna for lunch. Seriously, it was like jerky."

"Well, you were provoked," she giggled. "And here I was beginning to think you didn't have any weaknesses."

"I don't fold laundry, either," he confessed. "I just stuff it into the drawer."

"Man, I don't know if I can date such a deeply flawed person."

He laughed.

"Well, I should probably get out of my car and get to work on some stuff," she sighed.

"You've been sitting in your car all this time?"

"Yes, because sometimes it's nice to talk to you without Charlie making faces at me." Iris got out of the car, grabbed her purse, and locked the door behind her. "So how many days do you have left at Rookwood again?"

"Three more. Then I get a week in between before I'm off to run with the big dogs."

"That's going to be so amazing for you, Will! I'm so excited! We should do something during your week off."

"Definitely," he agreed. "You have time?"

"Well, not tons. But I'll make something happen." She considered how to get away from Eugene's case for part of a day. It wouldn't be easy. She unlocked the door of the apartment and turned to go inside, when something caught her eye.

Her stomach dropped.

Brett was leaning against her car. He gave her a little wave. *How long has he been standing there?*

"Oh my gosh," she squeaked out, almost inaudibly. "He's here!"

"Who is?"

She dashed inside, slammed the door, and locked it. She stood with her back to the door, suddenly out of breath. "Brett's here," she whispered. "He's leaning on my car. Will, he just saw me go inside. He knows where I live!"

For the first time, Iris heard Will use an expletive. "Call the cops," he growled. "I'll be right there, I promise." He hung up.

Iris looked around the dark apartment. Charlie wasn't home yet. Iris was alone. With shaking fingers, she dialed 911.

The longer she spoke to the dispatcher, the more frightened she became. There was a list of questions, and she'd had to answer "no" to every one of them. Had the suspect entered the home?

No. Physically assaulted or verbally threatened her? No. Spoken to her? No. He had done none of those things… *today.*

They couldn't do anything except send an officer to check on her and give Brett a warning if he was still around. *But he knows where I live! What good is a restraining order?*

She peeked through the blinds. Her car stood alone, pale in the moonlight. Nobody was around. *Did I imagine it?*

A plume of white smoke blew across the window directly in front of her, coming from the right. She shifted her eyes to see its source. Brett was leaning with his back to the wall beside her window, taking lazy puffs on a cigarette. He took one long draw, turned to face her eye to eye through the glass, and blew the smoke toward her face. She gasped and drew backward, trying to close the gap in the blinds, but one slat was stuck. She heard him laugh. Iris backed away from the window until she bumped the dining table. She watched Brett's silhouette reach up and extinguish his cigarette against the window pane. A burst of orange sparks flared and died right by the opening in the blinds.

Within ten minutes, a black truck zoomed into the parking lot. Will looked like an angry grizzly bear when strode up the front walk, glaring around him.

But Brett had disappeared.

When she heard Will's voice, Iris opened the door, eyes red and streaming with tears. Will locked the door behind him and held her for ten minutes while she cried.

"I'm here," he soothed her. "I'll stay as long as you need me, okay?"

Will was true to his word. They watched a movie and said nothing about Brett. But Will kept his arms around her, stroking her hair or giving her a comforting squeeze whenever he felt her tense or saw her face get a certain look. She jumped when a police officer knocked on the door, so Will answered it and helped her get through another series of questions. As she had feared, there was very little they could do unless Brett was caught in the act. When Charlie came home, Will introduced himself and filled her in about what had happened. The whole time, he spoke softly and stayed close, a balm to her ragged emotions.

Iris had intended to begin her research about Eugene's car tonight, but her brain had canceled those plans and informed her that moving away from Will's side would be a terrible idea. She concurred.

As her body relaxed, her eyelids fluttered closed and she began to drift. Sometimes, a line from the movie on the TV would make its way into her conscious thoughts and try to draw her back into the living room. But eventually, she found herself in Scotland.

She stood on the bluff overlooking the North Sea, with her beloved village behind her. Miles of strand the color of butter toffee stretched out before her, dotted by dark brown and gray rocks. The sea breeze rustled her hair and swayed the vibrant purple wildflowers that grew scattered along the emerald cliffs.

"Come along, Iris!" said a voice just behind her. She turned. There was a man with dark, curly hair and strong, muscled arms. He wore a plain shirt, work trousers, and boots. He sat on a little picnic blanket that was set with a child's teacup and doll, a basket, and a jam sandwich on a napkin. He was smiling, his blue eyes reflecting the sunlight.

"Angus?" She tried to say it loudly enough for him to hear, but it came out a whisper.

A little girl in a cream colored linen dress ran past her, into his arms. She was no more than two years old.

"Will you help your Dad make something special?" he whispered in her ear. She grinned at him and nodded, her blonde curls bouncing. He drew a piece of paper, pen, and a bottle of ink out of the picnic

basket and began to write. The little girl picked up her sandwich and took a bite that spread strawberry jam across both cheeks. She watched her father with fascination, slowly backing toward him until she had plunked into his lap. He continued to write, working around her little body while occasionally nuzzling her cheek with his. She put her sandwich up to his mouth, so he took a small bite and murmured his thanks in her ear, causing an eruption of giggles. She watched him for another minute, and then reached down and put her sticky hand on the paper, leaving a jam handprint. He looked at her. She looked at him. A smile spread across his face. "Well that's a message I'd not thought to send," he chuckled.

"Iris?" Will whispered.

She opened her eyes. She was on the sofa, still dressed in yesterday's outfit and covered with a fleece throw blanket. Will lay on the floor beside her in jeans, t-shirt, and a hoodie. He was resting his head on his hands and looking up at her with an expression that she assumed only morning people understood.

"It's six," he said. "I just wanted you to know that everything's okay, in case you heard me leaving."

She closed her eyes again, but smiled. "Thank you," she whispered back. Then she frowned and looked at him with one eye. "Did you sleep on the floor without even a pillow?"

"Yeah. It's fine, I don't mind. I used to do this a lot for Luke."

She reached out for his hand. He laced his fingers into hers.

"Thank you," she said again.

He kissed her hand. "I'll see you at work, okay? I'll make you breakfast if you come fifteen minutes early."

"Are you baiting me with bacon again?"

"Yes."

"See you at 7:45."

Chapter 14

I ris stayed awake after Will left, even though it was early. Her mind longed to remain in the ethereal dream she'd been having. It had felt so real. And unlike so many other dreams, it didn't fade from her memory once she woke up. The sweetness of the scene made her yearn to see her friend again. Angus had had a beautiful soul. His heart was completely devoted to his God and his loved ones. Helping him get home was the best thing she'd ever done. No one could be more deserving.

Her mind wandered to Eugene. She couldn't imagine anyone more different from Angus. Eugene was brash and blunt, driven by achievement, and burdened by guilt. Unlike Angus, he'd been warned by a Guardian before damaging the Tree and did it anyway, through trickery. He hadn't even been with his wife at the time. He'd been with some other woman! Iris realized that she didn't even like the guy. *Would it be so bad if he was stuck? Perhaps the past was better off without him.*

She chided herself. *It's not for me to decide who deserves saving. I just need to do what I do. The second I get off work, I'll get going on research so he can get out of here.*

After a long, hot shower, Iris dressed for work and went in search of coffee.

"I really like Will," Charlie said as Iris came into the kitchen. She was eating toaster waffles and reading the end of the same book that had flown through the air when Iris had startled her a few days before.

Iris smiled. "I really like him, too," she replied. *Quite the understatement.* He had kept her calm enough to drop peacefully off to sleep last night, despite the scare Brett had given her.

"Seems like he's really serious about you," Charlie pressed.

Iris dumped coffee grounds into the french press. "What makes you say that?"

"Um, I came out for a glass of water, and I saw him sleeping on the floor. Guys don't usually do that just for the challenge of it."

Iris had no answer for that. She'd been just as surprised to see him this morning as Charlie had been. And yet, why was she surprised?

"Anyway, I just wanted to tell you that I approve," Charlie continued, "since I know that would be a deal breaker for ya."

Iris chuckled as she filled the kettle. "Well, thank you. I was on pins and needles about that, hoping Will wouldn't get too attached to me before you made up your mind about him."

"Actually, I'm kind of surprised you haven't had him over before," Charlie said, closing her book. "Haven't you guys been a thing for like a month and a half?"

"Yeah, pretty much."

"Are you still on the fence about him, or what?"

Iris frowned. "No, I don't think so. I've just had a lot going on."

"Well I suggest you make sure that cutie is one of the main things you have going on," Charlie said.

"I'll work on that. He did say he wants to get together with you. Like for a group friend thing."

"Sweet. I'll give him the straight skinny about you!" Charlie set her plate in the sink and hip-bumped her on the way out of the kitchen. "See ya. Tell Will I said thanks for watching out for my best friend."

"I'll tell him," Iris laughed, and nudged Charlie's back with her shoulder. She checked her watch. She could get to work just in time to see Will for a few minutes before her shift, if this water would ever boil... Then she remembered she was supposed to pick Eugene up this morning. They had arranged the whole thing over dinner last night—Eugene would get to see Eva while Jason and Gray were across the street teaching their classes. The unspoken subtext seemed to be that they also preferred not to have Eugene lurking around their Tree unsupervised.

Iris grunted in frustration and texted Will:

Unavoidable errand came up. Breakfast for lunch?

Will had told her he would start keeping his phone in his pocket instead of his locker after all this nonsense with Brett had started. She hoped he would see her message in time, especially since he put so much care into his cooking. His answer arrived:

Good timing. See you at 11.

"Of course he understands," Iris mumbled. "He's Will." She stuffed her phone into her back pocket and poured the hot water. *I did say I wanted an interesting job, but I had no idea it might involve taking care of an overgrown man-baby. Ugh. Be nice, Iris. Eugene can't help it that he's not Angus.*

Eugene was just putting on his black jacket when Iris came to the Reynolds' front door. He was dressed in one of Jason's plaid shirts. His hair was combed to perfection, although Iris could see that he'd cut himself shaving.

"Good morning," she greeted him. "Sleep okay?"

"Not a wink," he groused. "Today is going to be unreal. Could you sleep if you were me?"

"I don't know." She tried to muster some compassion. "Probably not."

Jason appeared in the doorway behind Eugene. He was holding an apple in his teeth while slipping into one of his classic gray blazers.

"Hey Jason!" Iris greeted him.

"Guh nohning!" he said around the apple, then pulled it out of his teeth with a grin. "It's going to be a fun day, I can feel it!"

"Ugh. I'll be outside," Eugene said, reaching into his pocket for cigarettes.

"You know those will kill you," Jason said.

Eugene rolled his eyes. "You sound like my wife. And anyway, who cares? I should be dead by now, right?" He stepped onto the porch and dug out his lighter.

Jason feigned shock. "You mean you have a wife who wants you to live longer? What a bummer that must be."

Eugene thought that over for a moment, his expression sober. He looked at the cigarette in his hand, frowned, then he put it between his lips and turned to Iris. "Can we stop for more cigarettes on the way? I'm almost out."

"You won't need 'em," Jason said.

"What are you talking about?" Eugene asked, the cigarette waving up and down in his mouth as he spoke. He lifted his lighter.

Jason smiled. "I'm talking about you. Your body is free of those."

Eugene gave him a perplexed look and lit the cigarette. As soon as he inhaled, he let out several barking coughs. He looked at Jason, wide-eyed. "God, that burns! What did you do?"

"Me? Nothing. I was just told to let you know."

Eugene attempted one more draw, but hacked and spluttered again, followed by a gag.

"Very good." Jason nodded. "Probably shouldn't try that again, if you want to keep your breakfast." He picked up his briefcase and stepped outside, as if what he'd just seen was the most ordinary thing in the world. "Have a great day, kids! Iris, I can pick him up at eleven, okay?"

Iris nodded. She and Eugene stood agape, watching Jason jog across the street.

Just behind Eugene, Thelo recoiled in horror.

That man… How dare he speak against what is mine? He could feel one of his tethers dissolving like smoke. Although his first instinct was to strike, he checked himself. The last time he had assailed a creature with the Seal, he'd been cast into the desert. It would be best to bide his time.

"You people are a trip," Eugene mumbled. He looked at his smoldering cigarette with distaste and ground it out with the toe of his shoe. "Let's go."

Eugene sat in the passenger seat of Iris's hatchback.

"Seatbelt," she reminded him.

He sighed and yanked the strap into place.

Iris pulled out onto the main road, aiming for a break in the traffic that was perfectly navigable as long as she got up to speed in second gear and then skipped straight to fifth.

Eugene whistled. "Wow. For something that looks like a toy, this thing really moves."

"Uh, thank you," she said, shaking her head.

"You're welcome," he said. "Seems like you drive really well, too, for a woman."

"For a *woman*?"

"What? It's a compliment! It's a well known fact that—"

"We're changing the subject now." She rolled her eyes. "So," she began, "We should talk about *your* car."

"What about it?"

"Well, it's just about the only lead we have. I'm not saying your bag is still in it. You're right about the likelihood of that being pretty small. But maybe someone saw it. I'd like to start with a VIN search. Maybe we can figure out where it is now, and work backwards. You don't happen to have anything with that number on it, do you? Like a receipt from the dealer, or an insurance card, or… something in your wallet?"

"Yeah, I had all of that, but not in my wallet. It was all in the car."

"Hmm…" Iris tapped the steering wheel. "The car went to Eva after you were declared dead. Any idea what she would have done with it? Would she have traded it? Sold it? Driven the wheels off it?"

"Sold it, probably. She never wanted me to buy it in the first place."

"Maybe we can find out who she sold it to."

Eugene frowned. "That's great. So all we have to do is find a missing bag by finding a missing car, by using a VIN we don't know, but we'll get that number from the missing paperwork by asking a person who can't remember squat. I see no downside."

"Always so cheerful," Iris sighed.

They rode quietly the remainder of the trip to Rookwood as Eugene stared out the rain-streaked window. He broke the silence only once to wonder aloud how anything ever photosynthesized in this weather.

"Listen to you," Iris said wryly as she parked and shut off the engine. "You're even clever when you complain."

"I'm just tripping out, that's all," he admitted.

Iris looked at his frightened face and felt a twinge of remorse. "It's going to be okay," she tried to reassure him.

"What if it's not? What if she doesn't even know who I am?"

"She's still your wife."

"Not legally. I'm dead, remember?"

Iris laid her hand on his arm. "That's not how it works with promises."

He let out a long, shaky breath. "Let's just get this over with."

Once they were inside, Iris had Eugene follow her to the Activities Office.

"It's going to look weird if I bring a visitor up the back stairs without an explanation," Iris told him. "So who do you want to be today? A relative? Not sure the exact truth will get us the response we're looking for."

"I don't know, I guess I can say she's my great aunt or something," Eugene suggested.

"Okay. I prefer not to lie, so I'll keep the talking to a minimum, but now at least we'll have our story straight if anybody asks."

Eugene nodded.

"Remember not to mention anything about the—"

"I know, I know," he snapped. "Jason already reminded me about the hocus-pocus forgetting spell."

Iris raised an eyebrow. "I see that you're nervous, but could you at least be nice to my boss when we get in there?"

"Sorry."

Candace was shuffling through an inch-thick stack of paperwork on her desk. The flamingo-pink reading glasses that often sat atop her frosted, spiky hair were instead perched at the end of her nose. She looked up. "Well, well! Good morning! Who did you find?"

"Candace, this is Eugene Thomas. Eugene, Candace Wood, my boss."

"Pleasure to meet you." Eugene gave her a disarming grin and shook her hand.

"I met Eugene in the hallway," Iris explained. "He was hoping to visit Eva." Two truths, assembled out of order. Iris was starting to feel terrible every time she spoke this way.

"Oh, wonderful!" said Candace. "Eva doesn't get a lot of family around. Well Iris, tell you what… I'm a little busy, but I'll see if I can borrow James to help with morning rounds for a few minutes so you can show Eugene where to go, and maybe stick around if he needs you to. Sound good?"

"Perfect," Iris said, and tilted her head for Eugene to follow her. "Thanks, Candace!"

"Will is making cheese danish today!" Candace called after her. "But you probably knew that already!"

Iris turned. "Actually, I didn't, but you've just changed my entire outlook for today!"

Candace laughed. "Nice to meet you, Eugene!"

He waved, cast her another charming smile, and followed Iris. His furrowed expression returned almost immediately, and remained all the way to Eva's room.

"I should warn you," Iris said to him as they walked, "Eva's mind isn't always in the right decade. She still converses really well, but she might say things that don't sound right. It's a lot less confusing for her if you just kind of… go along with it. Okay?"

He looked a little alarmed, but nodded. "I'll try."

Eva was always awake and dressed at this hour, so Iris didn't even pause outside the open door. She didn't want to give Eugene even the slightest opportunity to hesitate.

"Good morning, Eva!" she greeted her in a cheerful voice. "I've brought someone to see you!"

"Oh, goodness! Who is it?" Eva asked, patting her hair and straightening her pink blouse. "Is it Jennie?"

"Nope, it's someone else," Iris said, and patted her hand. She looked back. Eugene had not followed. "He'll be right in," she said toward the doorway.

Eugene peeked his head in, then slowly made his way toward them.

"Gene!" Eva cried. "There you are! I've been waiting. Is it time to go?"

Eugene looked shell shocked. He tried to answer, but no words came out.

"Would you like me to give you a minute?" Iris asked him.

"No, uh… could you stay?"

She nodded and moved to a chair in the corner to make room for him.

He stepped forward, eyes on Eva. His face held a mixture of fear and confusion. He pressed his lips together and shook his head at Iris. "That's not her," he whispered under his breath. "It can't be."

"Yes it is," she whispered softly, nodding toward Eva. "Don't be afraid."

"I'm all packed," Eva continued. "Do you think everything will fit in that little car?"

Eugene glanced back at the door, but stood still. He finally found his voice, though it was hoarse. "Um… packed?"

"Yes! For our trip! I've been wanting to go for ages. I'm so happy you're taking me."

Eugene squinted. "Where am I taking you?"

"You kidder!" Eva laughed. "Why, to Sedona. I've always wanted to go."

He looked at Iris, bewildered. "This is pointless," he whispered. "She thinks this is our wedding day!"

Iris nodded in encouragement. "She remembers you, though!" she whispered back.

He turned back to Eva, who was gazing dreamily out the window.

"Did I ever tell you *why* I wanted to go there?" she asked him.

He crossed his arms. "Uh… cowboys?"

She glanced at him sharply. "You don't believe that!" she chided. "I said that to get your goat. I only watch those silly movies so I'll have something to talk to Father about when he has us over for supper." She sighed. "No, I really wanted to go because I thought you'd like the rocks."

"You thought… I'd like the rocks?"

"Of course! You love rocks! My parents were engaged there, you know." She looked out the window again. "Mother said the rocks are like red castles. Can you imagine, Gene?"

He stood motionless, jaw clenched.

"I think it must be suppertime," Eva commented absently.

"I can't do this," Eugene growled. He turned on his heel and strode from the room.

Iris followed. "Eugene, wait."

He stopped. "She… is completely out to lunch," he whispered, pointing back toward the room. "Talking to her is getting me absolutely nowhere."

"Well maybe it's getting *her* somewhere," Iris returned. "Did you consider that?"

"What good could it possibly do her to talk to me?"

"You left her, Eugene. She was a widow. And yet, the moment she saw your face, she went back to one of the happiest days of her life. That's the longest I've ever heard her stick with one train of thought!"

He put his hands on his hips and stared at his shoes for a long moment, then let out a derisive chuckle. "You weren't there, okay? That woman couldn't stand the sight of me. The last time I saw her, she was chucking pottery at my head. You can both romanticize the past all you want, but if *that*…" he pointed again, "is what it comes to, then people are better off alone."

Iris stood speechless for a moment. It wasn't hard for her to imagine why someone like Eugene would get something thrown at him. But before she could give in to the temptation to verbalize that thought, she took a deep breath.

"I'm sorry that didn't go the way you hoped," she offered. "But I just need to see if she remembers anything about the car, okay? Do you want to wait out here?"

He stuffed his hands in his jeans pockets and leaned against the wall with a huff.

She shook her head and went back into Eva's room, pulling out her phone and doing a quick image search for a burgundy Mustang convertible.

"Oh, hello, dear!" she called to Iris. "I think I forgot to eat lunch. Can I make you a sandwich while I'm at it?"

"No thanks, Eva," she replied. "I just wondered if you remember this car…" She showed her the phone.

"Oh dear," Eva said, shaking her head. "Oh dear, that's Gene's car."

"Yes, it is," Iris nodded. "Very good. Do you remember—"

"It was such a beautiful car," Eva continued. "I wish I hadn't said such awful things. I've had nightmares about it."

"I'm so sorry, Eva. I'm sure it must be difficult to think about that. But the police gave you this car, didn't they?"

"Yes." Eva began to cry. "He went away and never came back!" Her slender shoulders sagged as she spoke through tears. "Then suddenly I had this car. What could I do with *that*?"

Iris plucked two tissues from the box on the bedside table and handed them to her. "So you didn't keep it?"

"I couldn't even look at it," she sniffled, "and think about how I'd driven him away… how he went on his research trip, thinking I didn't love him. Did he fall? Was it wild animals?"

"Oh Eva, I know it wasn't that," Iris said as tears gathered in her own eyes. She put her hand on Eva's shoulder.

"I didn't want that car, I just wanted *him*!"

"Of course."

"When that Murphy boy asked me, I didn't think twice about selling it." Eva went back to staring out the window. She clutched her tissues in her hand for several moments, then sighed. "The breeze is very big today," she commented. "It shouldn't be so hot out. Maybe you can play outside."

"So… Murphy?" Iris pressed. "What was his first name?"

"Whose first name?"

"The Murphy boy you said bought the car."

"Oh, I don't know. They have too many children to keep track of, those Murphys. They're Catholic, you know." Eva blew her nose. "Gosh, I must be getting a cold."

Iris sighed. *Well, that's that, I guess.* "Thank you for the lovely chat," she said. She patted Eva's hand and turned to leave.

Eugene was standing in the doorway, eyes red. He had heard every word.

Iris could barely focus on lunch. Her mind was a tangle of thoughts. Eugene had spent the rest of the morning staring at the canaries in the lobby and wandering the garden. True to his word, Jason had picked him up and taken him somewhere for burgers.

The sight of Will in the kitchen warmed her, especially today. She was still in awe of how he'd come to her rescue last night. But she also couldn't get over what she'd just witnessed in Eva's room. Eva seemed to have almost perfect clarity about anything related to her husband. Everything else was a little mixed up, but it was like she kept Eugene in a special, untouched place in her mind. When she spoke of her wedding day, Eva had seemed more at peace than Iris had ever seen her before.

Yet Eugene seemed to pride himself in his hard exterior, afraid to reveal a vulnerable human being underneath. Did he really not care about anyone else besides himself? It seemed so, and yet, Eva had fallen for him *some*how.

What if I do get Eugene back home? Will he still just leave Eva? Maybe he's right… maybe he really is better off alone.

"Iris?" Will's voice cut into her thoughts.

"Hmm?"

"Are you okay? You seem like you're somewhere else."

"Oh my gosh," she said, shaking her head. "You're right, I kind of… got lost in my thoughts there for a minute."

"Are you getting worried again? About Brett?"

"Uh, no… I just have a really weird… case. That I'm researching. There just seems to be a lot more to it than I initially thought there would be."

"Oh, okay."

"I'm sorry about that. What were you saying?"

"It's fine." Will shrugged. "I just asked if you wanted to go out for Valentine's Day tomorrow."

Iris put her palm flat on the counter. "How did I forget that's tomorrow?"

"I don't know," Will chuckled. "I thought it might be on your radar, but who knows? You forgot your own birthday, too. Are you just not a holiday person?"

"I thought I was!" Iris laughed. "But I'm really starting to doubt my ability to multitask during cases."

Will nodded. "Duly noted. Well listen, it's fine if we pick a different day."

"But it's Valentine's Day, though!" Iris objected. "I could try and work something out."

"Nah, who needs all the crowds?" Will smiled, but Iris could see that it was only with some effort. "We'll just have our own Valentine's Day when your case lets up a little. How about it?"

Iris eyed him doubtfully. "I mean... I guess I kind of do have a ticking clock with this one... but I don't want you to be disappointed."

"Oh, I'm fine." He put his hand over hers. "It'll be that much more fun when we get around to it. Just let me know when."

"Thank you, Will."

Iris went home immediately after work, got into her most comfortable lazing-about-the-house clothes, and went into research mode.

After she had logged every detail of Eugene's case up to this point, she did a search for the Murphy that had bought Eugene's Mustang. She had asked Eugene as Jason was picking him up, and he'd told her that the Murphys were their neighbors a block over. He didn't remember their first names either, but it had been enough to go on.

The City of Tucson had a fantastic online map with historic aerial overlays. Every parcel of land had the current owners listed. She found Eugene's old house and checked the surrounding streets. To her surprise, one of the homes was still listed as belonging to a Donald Murphy. A quick people search led her to Donald and Betty Murphy, both age 89, and the names of their five grown children. Iris checked social media platforms for the three sons, located one of them, and sent him a quick message to see if he remembered the car. Now, she could only wait.

Her phone pinged. It was an email from her dad. She clicked it open.

Favourite Daughter—

As promised, I've finished the reading and I'd love to compare notes. I find the narrative compelling and the historicity impeccable. What are your thoughts on the mystical aspects?

Tea and shortbread, Dad

Iris looked over at the book she'd borrowed from Jason, sitting atop the stack of notes she'd compiled about it. The Histories had taken on a life of their own in the past weeks, almost like an addiction. She had chased after anything that stumped her, tracking down texts from the original languages and educating herself on the historic perspectives of the original readers. She had been voracious, even sacrificing precious hours of sleep, to get to the bottom of it. Now that she'd finished reading it, she couldn't help feeling a little sad, like she'd only scratched the surface somehow.

Ever since Eugene had shown up, she'd had to put her reading on the back burner. But now that she'd done everything she could with Eugene's case for today, she reached for the book and flipped through it, rereading certain pages she'd marked. It was as she'd thought. The entire story as a whole, although it was about so many things, seemed to revolve around one idea… one Person. But something wasn't sitting right with her. It was like her mind and heart couldn't settle into a proper rhythm with each other. Maybe if she talked to Jason…

She looked at her watch. It was still plenty early in the evening. She considered driving over to the Reynolds' house, as she often did. But she dismissed that idea. She'd seen enough of Eugene for one day. They wouldn't leave Eugene by himself, and neither of them would come here. They both felt strongly about not spending time alone with her, which she thought seemed a little old fashioned, but the protective sentiment behind it still touched her heart.

Finally, she decided to send Jason a text:

Done with the book. Feeling odd. ALLOFTHEQUESTIONS. Pie?

His reply came back in under a minute:

Same place as last time in 20? π *+ SOMANYANSWERS?*

She sent a quick thumbs up, changed back into clothing that was free of holes, and headed into the rainy night.

Concealed, yet towering behind, Brennus drew his sword and escorted Iris. Whenever she met with Guardians, things always got a little agitated around her. But he would be ready. This could be the day.

Chapter 15

I ris walked into the restaurant fifteen minutes later. The usual crowd of retirees had dissipated and given way to a sparse, unprofitable assembly of hermits huddled in ones and twos behind laptop screens and headphones, consuming mostly coffee and the occasional plate of chili fries. The staff had reached skeleton crew status, so her presence went largely unnoticed. She scanned the faces in the room and finally spotted horn rimmed glasses and a gray low fade haircut in a back booth near a window.

Just then, a middle aged woman in a brown apron approached. "Table for one?"

Iris nodded toward Jason, who had just seen her and waved. "Actually, I'm—"

"Oh, meeting that cutie back there?" the waitress filled in. "Hm?"

"He said he was waiting for a red haired girl."

"Yep, that's me."

The woman offered her a grubby vinyl menu.

Iris shook her head. "No thanks, I'll just…" She headed toward Jason with a polite smile.

The waitress shrugged and stashed the menu back into the wooden slot next to the cash register.

Iris sat opposite Jason, who regarded her with a fatherly expression for a long moment, then broke into a contagious smile.

She grinned back. "What?"

He shook his head. "I'm just proud of you, kid. Grayson keeps telling me such great things. And you've finished the Histories already, huh?"

"Yeah, it actually didn't take as long as I thought it would," she replied. "It was the most absorbing thing I've ever read!"

"I feel the same way about it," Jason agreed.

The same waitress who had greeted Iris brought two cups of coffee and two plates of peach pie with ice cream. She ignored Iris, but made sure there wasn't anything else she could get for Jason before batting her eyelashes and sauntering off.

"Thanks! I love peach pie!" Iris said. "How did you know?"

"I didn't," Jason chuckled. "I told Gray I was meeting you for pie, and he said 'Iris likes peach,' so I took the liberty. Worst case scenario, you'd want something else and I'd have to eat both of these myself."

"Wow, I can't believe he remembered," she mused. "I said that forever ago!"

"Gray retains a lot of trivia. One of the multitude of reasons he's a great teacher."

"He's going to make someone very happy someday."

"I'm certain he will," said Jason. "He's been thinking about it more lately, which I'm glad about, because I'm retiring and I find my lack of grandchildren vexing." He swigged his coffee, frowned, and scooped half of his ice cream into it. "But we didn't come here to talk about Gray's dating habits. What questions did you have for me?"

Iris giggled. "Well, if I've understood everything correctly, it seems like the whole book is the story of God trying to partner with mankind through His Son. Am I close?"

"Right on the money," Jason nodded. "But that's not much of a question."

"Fine, maybe it's not." Iris stabbed her pie. "I guess I just need to babble for a minute, and then you can tell me what I got wrong. Fair?"

"I've had a lot of practice doing that," Jason said with a wink.

"Okay... My biggest overall impression is how much the Creator really loved people and wanted them to know Him. I think it's interesting that He kept adapting His relationships with people. Seems like He tried it about five or six different ways."

Jason stirred the last lump of melted ice cream in his coffee. "Okay, describe the ways."

"Well, for the first people, He gave them the entire planet and everything on it. He straight up lived with them and chatted face to face. But they allowed themselves to be talked into attempting greatness without Him, which gave evil access to the world and it messed up everything. And it got crazy with rebellious angels, giants, and all kinds of violence. Which you'd *think* would make God super angry. But it doesn't say that. It says He was grieved. So He had to clean up that mess, and try again with Noah. But those people did the same thing—they tried to be great without Him, *again*, by turning themselves into a world superpower. So He also had to clean up that mess too, by giving them different languages and, as you said, 'inspiring them to go fulfill their destinies.'"

"Yes, it sounds better than... how did you put it? 'He zapped their brains'?" Jason smirked.

"Ha! I guess I did say that," Iris laughed. "Potato, potahto. But then He tried again, with that guy Abraham. I've studied the types of contracts and covenants people used to make in the ancient world, and I think it's cool that God kept wanting to be in grant covenants with people... in other words, saying, 'I'm going to just promise you things with no strings attached.'"

"Exactly," Jason said. "They didn't have to hold up their end of any deals, because both sides of the deal were on God. Abraham was sound asleep when his deal was sealed."

"Right! And God totally proved He was different from other gods. I remember from a class I took that child sacrifice was a pretty common way to make a deal with a pagan god back then. Abraham had to be familiar with the practice. But when God tested Abraham's loyalty by telling him to sacrifice his son, Abraham knew He'd never make him go through with something as sick as that."

Jason nodded. "Yes, God is very much against child sacrifice. Abraham didn't walk up the mountain with his son and say to the servants, '*I'll* be back.' He said, '*we'll* be back,' because he knew that God must have another plan up His sleeve. He really believed what God had said about all the promises coming true through his kid."

"Yeah, talk about trust!" Iris shook her head. "I can't even imagine that. But God did what He said and made the family into a nation. What really surprised me, though, was that God never even made a legal code for them at that point," Iris said. "It seems like all proper nations have legal codes, but they didn't. He just kept dealing with them as things came up, forgiving them, keeping His promises and everything. Which is why it absolutely baffles me that, after all the promises He made to Abraham's family had come true, and after how patient He'd been with them, they made the stupidest move in history!"

"Oh? Do tell…"

"They essentially blew Him off!" Iris took another bite of pie and talked around it. "Everything happened just like God told Abraham it would. They were slaves for four hundred years, and led to freedom by God Himself though a bajillion different miracles, whining the entire way, and were *finally* free to get back to chatting with God face to face! He offered them another grant covenant like Abraham had, but they didn't want it! Why? I mean, I'm sure it was really scary when they came to the mountain and everything was thunder and lightning and smoke, so I kind of get why they might've been afraid. But still!"

"True, I'd probably be freaking out," Jason said.

"But after everything He did for them? Come on! Even the people themselves acknowledged that they could hear God's voice and live through it, which is saying something. I mean, they knew the story of Adam... why didn't they want to get back to that kind of relationship?"

"People are puzzling, aren't they?"

"Definitely. I mean... my gosh, they actually *heard* God's voice, and their response was 'Uh, no thank you. Just give Moses some rules for us to follow, and we'll hold up our end of the deal.' Which of course, they never did for longer than five minutes. If I was God, I would have told them right off that it was a stupid idea and they had no clue what they were asking for. I would have *made* them take the first deal!"

Jason smiled. "You would have said, 'I command you all to *want* a close friendship with me'?"

Iris paused. "Well, that sounds bad, too. But it's better than allowing people to bind themselves to a covenant that requires strict obedience on pain of death! God never treated them that way *before* they had the law. The worst they ever got was a reprimand. But *after* they asked for laws? Holy crap!"

"Yes, almost literally," Jason agreed. "It was a terrible system. Why they asked for it, I don't know either. But I have a feeling they just wanted some control, you know? Maybe they wanted to feel like they were earning their place."

Iris looked at him doubtfully. "They had to see how impossible that was."

Jason picked up his cup and swirled it. "Not just impossible... *offensive*. It's like offering to pay someone back for a Christmas present while telling them how much you deserve it."

"Yeesh."

"Yeah. But it was so much worse," Jason continued. "People refused to see how offensive it was when they tried it in Eden, or at Babel. I know you don't have kids, but as a dad, I can tell you that sometimes the best thing for a stubborn little kid who won't listen to reason is to tell him, 'Have it your way,' and let the chips fall where they may. Gray went through a few phases of that. Sometimes, I just had to let him see how his bad ideas would pan out. Of course, I protected him, but I also let him experience the consequences of his choices. He didn't get to be this amazing all by himself!"

Iris laughed. "You sound like a great dad!"

"Well…" Jason sniffed. "I do all right. It was mostly his mother who was great at that, if I'm honest. But God is the absolute best parent there is. He let His people experience the consequences of their foolishness, while at the same time protecting them from it. Every year, he let them make a sacrifice to cancel their debt to the law and re-up their covenant. And when they abandoned Him completely and worshipped false gods, He allowed them to be captured by their enemies occasionally. Sounds brutal, but under the covenant they asked for, it was actually one of the most merciful options—it took away their ability to feel good about their choices and made them realize they should turn back to Him."

"And that could have gone on indefinitely, but I'm glad He didn't let it," Iris said. "Seems like the longer they lived under that system, the farther off the mark they got. God kept offering to be their king, and they just wanted to have a human king. So dumb."

"Well…" Jason mused. "Maybe they were. But I have to wonder if I would have done any better. It's easy to sit here now, knowing everything I know, and make a better decision. But all of us are flawed. We live in the same atmosphere of evil that invaded creation because of Adam. We're all susceptible to terrible ideas."

"I suppose so," she agreed. She licked the last bit of peach pie filling off her fork. "And most of the kings they had were awful, but at least they found David. He seemed better."

"Yeah, he was known as a man after God's heart," Jason said. "Did you notice that?"

"I did, but it didn't make a ton of sense to me," Iris admitted. "He was a decent military leader, but he was also an adulterer, a liar, and a murderer."

"That's true, but remember, you said it yourself—God's heart toward people was always grant covenants. He wanted to hold up both ends of every deal so He could just relate to people personally. David was pretty unique in his generation, because whenever he screwed up, his first response wasn't to say, 'I've gotta find a way to fix this myself.' He knew he couldn't. Instead, he went straight to God and asked for a clean heart. He knew the only real way to rule his nation was to rely on the grace of God. And because of his attitude, he understood God better than most. He was able to write songs with words like 'Give thanks to the Lord, for He is good; His steadfast love endures forever.' Heck, he danced before God in his long johns and didn't care who saw!"

Iris laugh-snorted. "Oh my gosh, I almost got coffee in my nose!"

"Sorry," Jason said with a sheepish grin.

"I guess it makes sense why God wanted someone in David's family to be the one to sign a better covenant," she commented, dabbing coffee off her chin.

"Absolutely."

"More coffee, hon?" the waitress asked Jason.

"Sure! Iris, you good?"

"I should probably switch to decaf."

The waitress rolled her eyes. "I'll have to brew a fresh pot."

Jason grinned at her. "Janice, that would be wonderful, thank you."

Janice perked up a little and hurried away.

"Which brings me to the newer part of the book," Iris continued. Oh my gosh! It's crazy!"

Jason chuckled. "Crazy, huh? How so?"

"Well, it's like one of those movies where you think you're waiting for a certain character to show up and fix everything, but then you find out he was actually there the entire time… you just didn't realize it was him at first!"

Jason grinned and wagged his finger. "See there? I knew you were one perceptive cookie!"

"Ha! If you say so. I felt like it took me a while to figure it out, but the Son of God—the visible, physical manifestation of God—didn't show up as a baby first. He was with His people the entire time in different ways, right?"

"Very good," Jason said. "I'm impressed!"

"Well it's all in there. I mean there's one of those songs David wrote, that lays it all out. It says the same One who created everything is the One who led the people out of slavery and did all those amazing things. When you get to the book written by John, he makes it clear that it was the Son of God that made everything, so He had to be the one from the song, right?"

"Yes. John called Him the 'Word of God.'"

"That was weird to me at first," Iris mused. "But not after I looked at the whole pattern. Every time God spoke, things would happen. It's like the Son is the part of God who gets things done."

"Hmm…" Jason tilted his head and thought it over. "I guess that's not a bad way to think of it. Another way to say it is that the Son is 'God's mind made up.' All of His ideas, truth, grace, and love… every good idea He's ever had, and everything He wants to do, plus all of His authority, can be found in the person of the Son."

"Um, how in the heck did He manage to cram alllllll of that into a human body without it blowing a gasket?"

Jason let out a hearty laugh. "Well, luckily the human body has no gaskets! But beyond that, we also read that He set aside His glory. That's the really overwhelming part of Him that humans have trouble dealing with. So when He came, He left that part back home and just came as a humble man, and brought God's mind, heart, will, and authority with Him."

"Wow. So that kind of seems like a miracle in itself."

"It definitely is."

Janice brought her orange pot, filled their cups, and gave them both strange looks.

Jason grinned at her again. "Would you like to join us, Janice?"

"No, thanks…" she said, brow furrowed. "I'm good." She meandered away.

"She's been eavesdropping for a while now," Jason whispered. "I don't blame her at all. This is great stuff."

Iris giggled, and added cream to her coffee. "I just think the end of the story is magnificent, though," she sighed. "All of the prophecies about a better covenant came true. The Son showed up as a human, and taught people what God was really like, instead of all their awful, misleading religious ideas. The people finally got another chance to see what He'd been trying to tell them since the beginning. He put Himself up as the atonement sacrifice, like the lambs they'd been killing every year, except by doing it as a human being, He essentially regained authority over the planet for mankind. Right?"

"Yep, like a second chance Adam," Jason agreed. "First Adam gave it away, second Adam took it all back. Not only that, but He's fulfilled every promise He ever made to Adam, Noah, Abraham, Moses, and David. He didn't skip over a single one."

"I just love that," she said. "And then He was like He was in the beginning—He just wanted to love people. He only had harsh judgments for the people who kept trying to make it all about the law again."

"You notice He never went back on what He said about the law, though," Jason pointed out. "He didn't say, 'never mind, forget all that.' He actually taught that following the law was even harder than they thought! But he didn't teach that because

He wanted them to try harder. He was just pointing out how impossible the standard had been from the very beginning. Then, He went ahead and *fulfilled* all the law's requirements when no one else could, and signed a new covenant with God, using His own blood, on behalf of mankind. That means people don't have a covenant with God by themselves anymore. They stand within the Son's agreement. Their debt to the law is pardoned. Failure to fulfill the covenant is no longer possible, because the Son can't fail."

"Amazing," she said wistfully. "And He made his followers so powerful! That was because they got their authority back, right?"

"Yes," Jason agreed. "And because they had the power of God's Spirit living inside them like He did when He was on earth. The same Spirit that resurrected His dead body the third day after He died."

"That was kind of a mind bender for me too! But if I can accept that He spoke the world into existence in the first place, then it's not a real leap to say He raised a dead body. After all, He had done it before."

"For sure. He wanted people to understand that even death itself has no power over Him. And no power over them, if they have His Spirit."

"Seriously? He just… sent His Spirit behind Him after He left? That is such a trippy idea! That was basically God without a body, right?"

"Yes."

"Living inside the bodies of people?"

"Yep."

"Crazy. Well no wonder they were walking around doing miracles by the end of the story! I mean, He said, 'go do the stuff I do,' right?"

"That was the idea," Jason said, grinning. "The Son didn't leave so much as scale the operation. He wanted more and more people healed, and more and more people to understand that they could relate to God without fear. There was only so much He could do as one person. But living inside of thousands, He could bring heaven back to earth."

"And then everything He predicted about the end of the awful system happened, too," Iris added. "He warned his friends in person, but he visited John later and told him again in a dream. That's in the last book. And it all happened! I read up on the historical background around that time. What a brutal time in history! Nero was widely known as 'the Beast' and people really were forced to worship him before they could go grocery shopping. I can't imagine that. They would actually check if you had ashes from the altar on your hand or your head before they let you buy stuff! They were burning God's followers right and left, and some of the worst persecution of all was coming from the Jews."

"Hard to imagine, right?" Jason said with a grim expression. "They had been reading about His coming for so long, but they had a totally wrong picture of what He would do when He came. They thought He would bring about political freedom from Rome, but He meant He would free them from the law that was killing them. They found that *so* offensive because they took great pride in following the law. They couldn't accept the kind of freedom He was offering, and wanted to kill Him and anyone else who taught about it."

"His followers had to be crazy brave," Iris said. "Obviously they were convinced this was the truth, or they wouldn't have kept dying for it."

"Very true. But the Jews really had to sit up and take notice in 70 A.D., when the Roman army leveled the temple. I mean, it's only in the book as a prediction, but did you go read about that afterward?" he asked her.

"Yes, of course! I wanted to know what all the dire predictions were leading up to! I mean, it's crazy… God used to live in that temple, right? But He sure wasn't attached to it, because when he sent His Son, He wanted it *gone*. He started by ripping the curtain in half, and then years later, the whole thing went up in flames. Not one brick on top of another by the time it was all over. Well, there's that smidge of outer retaining wall still there, but not a speck of actual temple left. He wasn't kidding when he said that desolation would stand in the holy place. Titus's army devastated the whole city. The only survivors were the ones who heeded the warnings to leave. Everyone who stayed wished they'd never been born."

Jason looked sad. "I hate that part," he admitted. "At least He gave them decades to get on board with the new promise before yanking the old system down. I know it had to be done, but still. It was Jerusalem's darkest day. God's wrath completely sucks."

"Was He that angry with the Jews?" Iris wondered.

"No," Jason said, shaking his head. "His wrath wasn't so much for people. He was angry at the system that had veiled His face for so long. He was angry at His enemies, the deceiver and his minions, who plagued His people. He wanted to make sure that the system could never be rebuilt. The priests could only be put in office to make sacrifices if they could prove their lineage. The siege at Jerusalem not only removed that priesthood, but destroyed their records so they'd never be able to rebuild."

"I guess... given their past, they'd probably be tempted to try it," Iris said somberly.

"I sincerely hope they never do," Jason said. "The only agreement God will ever stand by now is the one He has with the Son. All they have to do is agree to it. Then they'd finally have the peace they've been searching for."

"You mean, all they had to do back then, right?" she said, swirling her spoon around in her cup. "I mean, it's one of the coolest stories ever, and I think God is brilliant how He handled it. He considered the cost of making a planet full of willful people before He even started, and realized He'd have to put something in place to keep up a relationship with them without turning everyone into mindless puppets." She sighed. "I just wish He was still doing it."

Jason leaned forward on his elbow. "You what?"

Iris looked into his eyes. "I wish it could be like that now," she said. "People back then had it so great! Miracles, and God actually talking to them. He gave it such a great ending, too. But I don't know where that really leaves anybody nowadays."

Jason's eyebrows went up. "Iris, it still *is* like that now!"

She frowned. "How? I mean, maybe Guardians are kind of special because you guys hang out with spirit messengers and do a specific job for the Creator. But besides that, I've never once seen people like the ones described in the Histories. People might talk about the stories in church, but they're half asleep. I've been there. They might as well be talking about the weather."

Jason sighed. "I'm sad to hear that's been your only experience. It really shouldn't be that way, because God meant it when He said that His dwelling place would be with people from now on, and that His body on earth would be His followers. He meant *now*."

Iris felt a stirring of… *something*… deep in her soul. "Now?"

"Yes! Now, and for the rest of beyond time! Remember the story He told about the tiny seed that grew into a giant tree?"

"Yes, I think so…"

"Well that metaphor completely applies to today. He's on His way back, and His kingdom isn't ever supposed to stop. It's supposed to get bigger and bigger, until the whole world is fed and sheltered by it, and gets to rest in its shade. The last book talks about the tree whose leaves are for the healing of the nations… that's now. And it talks about a city whose gates are always open… that's the church!"

"But which church? There are a million different kinds!"

"Well… 'church' is just a made-up word," Jason said. "Its origins are a bit dodgy, actually. Thank your English translations of the Histories for that. It replaced a Greek word, *ekklesia*, that meant a governing body—literally, a gathering of summoned citizens who took responsibility to make sure their land was governed well. It had no religious connotation whatsoever when it was first used. When God said His followers would be His governing body, He was fulfilling that part in Isaiah: 'For to us a child is born, to us a Son is given, and the government will be on his shoulders.' If He's the head, and His followers are His body on earth, then the government of His kingdom is put on His followers. He decided not only to make them His new priests, but also kings. The only way He could do that is by adopting them into His family and making them His heirs, just like His Son. All they have to do is put their total trust in the new covenant He made, and He makes them into royalty."

"It's that easy?" Iris was aghast. "If His people are royalty, then why don't they act like it?" she wondered.

"Well… again, not wanting to judge anyone too harshly here, but we're all in process. Some believe, but just haven't realized everything they've inherited. They're still learning. Some don't read the book at all, and never learn. Some are blinded by dark forces. I mean, did you notice all the parts about the enemy or the accuser who wants to destroy mankind? He's already been defeated, but he keeps shouting and cursing and doing what he can to drag people down with him before the end. I'm sad to say that many succumb to it."

"But… you're saying there *are* people… right *now*… who look like the ones in the book? Who act like God's Son and actually live powerful lives?"

"Absolutely. They're all over the world! In fact, you've met at least one besides the Guardians you know."

Iris pondered that, wracking her brain. "Who was it?"

"According to Darrick, a certain man prayed a powerful prayer over his dying friend. Within minutes, she was restored to life and her leg completely healed. Sound like anyone you know?"

"Angus?" Iris's jaw dropped. "He *did* say he was praying right before I was healed. I didn't connect the two, though. I saw that huge man in the cloak and thought…"

"Hey, the Messengers of The Three are on our side. We partner with them all the time. It's not a rare thing at all to see an answer to prayer arrive with one of them."

Iris stared at the table, incredulous. "So you're saying that… God is still letting people in? It's not over? Because…" Her throat constricted with emotion. "I sure would like to be part of it."

"It's *not* over," Jason whispered with passion. "It's just beginning!"

"Y'know what?" Iris was startled by her own level of conviction as she spoke. "I really think that's true. I think it's *all* true!"

Jason leaned forward. "Would you bet your soul on it?"

Her face spread with the most profoundly joyful smile she could remember. "Absolutely."

Brennus spiraled into the air like a rocket, flashes of fire sparking in every direction. He let out a glorious sound—a shout of triumph mixed with a song of joy—that sent waves rippling through the ether for thousands of miles. Others who heard joined him, harmonizing across leagues of space. When the chorus reached the eastern shore of Scotland, it was taken up again in majestic merriment, this time led by Caledon of the Great Hawthorn, and soon thereafter joined by Albion of the Great Oak. From the mind of the Master Himself came the lyrics:

What was lost has been found! The Guardian of the Lost has been born!

Chapter 16

I ris awoke before her alarm. As she slowly opened her eyes, she thought she could hear music. As she became more aware, she realized it must be the remnants of a dream, like when a song is stuck in your head and it only feels like you're hearing it. But this was achingly beautiful music, complicated and peculiar. She sat up. The song faded away.

Something is different.

She looked at herself in the vanity mirror across the room from her bed. The girl looking back at her was the same girl as yesterday morning… long ginger hair, sleepy eyes, crazy bed head.

"I don't feel like I'm by myself, though," she whispered.

You're not.

Her eyes widened. *Am I talking to myself?* She remembered last night's epic discussion with Jason. *It's the same now as it was in the book!* She whispered again, "I believe you! So that means we're family, right? You live with me now? Are we sharing a body or something?"

The response did not contain words, but instead, the most tender impression—much like the residual feeling that lingers after a long, tender embrace.

Her eyes grew moist, and she nodded. "Good, I'm so glad."

Iris showered and dressed quickly, so she could be out of the bathroom before Charlie needed it, for a change. She was ready for work just as her alarm went off, so she reset it for five minutes before she needed to leave, and sat down at her computer.

She located and scanned through some archived Arizona law enforcement procedural manuals to find out what the chances would be of Eugene's property still being stored as evidence somewhere. It didn't look good.

Even in cases where police suspected foul play, evidence wasn't stored this long. And from what she'd been able to find out, Eugene's missing person case hadn't been much of a case. After examining the scant circumstantial evidence, searching the desert, and waiting a month, the authorities had ruled his death accidental and closed the case. That meant if his old bag was anywhere, it would either still be in the car, which was highly unlikely, or possibly stashed somewhere by a subsequent owner. Or it was just gone, along with his chances of ever getting home. It was a grim thought, but Iris refused to entertain it for more than a moment. Everything leading up to this point had filled her with hope. It was too soon to give in. She would just have to double her efforts—track down and talk to every previous owner she could, and see if she could locate the car at the same time. That bag had to be somewhere.

She clicked on her social media tab. There was a response waiting from Randy Murphy, the man she had messaged yesterday about Eugene's car:

Hello, Yes I am the same Randy Murphy from Tucson whose father is Donald. I do recall widow Thomas selling that Mustang but it wasn't me that bought it, it was my oldest brother Steve.

He had it for a good ten year I want to say but he sold it to his buddy Norm and Norm's kid drove it to school for a while. Steve doesn't do the Online but we just watched the game on Sunday had good pork ribs I can get you the recipe if you want that too and I asked him about it. Told him a girl was trying to find out the VIN so he thought that was funny but you know what He regrets selling it because it was such a chick magnet! But the wife said sell it so you know how that goes. He don't know what Norm did with it and he don't recall seeing no bags or tools or nothing in the car But he might have some of the papers still and might find that number for you because he was always such a packrat and I keep telling him to throw stuff out but now he's going to say I told you so if we end up helping you. So he's looking in his garage today and God knows if he will ever come out again without a tow rope but I will keep you posted. Maybe I'll help the old geezer so he doesn't get lost haha

Iris had to reread several sentences to make sense of this man's rambling style. Even though his message gave her an intense craving for coffee and commas, it was also encouraging. All she had to do was find one person with a record of that VIN and she could move straight to a database search in the National Motor Vehicle Title Information System for a real shot at finding some solid information. Knowing how many owners the car had had, and whether it had been junked, could save her a lot of time.

She sent Randy a quick reply, thanking him for his help, and asking for Norm's last name.

Her watch buzzed. *Five minutes...* She composed a quick email to her dad:

Favourite Dad—

I agree with both your literary and historical assessments and I'm eager to see your notes. My opinion on the mystical aspects:

100% real. You know me, never one to mince words. At the risk of sounding like I've lost all objectivity, I see no other honest way to deal with those ideas other than to embrace them fully. You?

Coffee and cheese danish,
Iris ♡

Valentine's Day at Rookwood Senior Home was a grand affair. Will made heart shaped mini crustless quiches and pancakes for breakfast. Because there would be a party later, Iris had begun to set up a little craft area in the back of the dining room. She did her best to keep a straight face as she shamelessly eavesdropped on the diners.

Fred held a mini quiche upside down and asked, "What do I gotta do around here to get food that isn't shaped like a butt?"

"Your chin is shaped like a butt," Walter retorted.

Doris giggled. "You're always *so* funny, Hank."

"Who's Hank?" Fred demanded.

"Party at ten o'clock!" First Irene announced over them.

"At yours or mine?" Doris wondered, wide eyed. "Shall I make a dip?"

"Dip for what?" Irene asked.

"For dipping!"

"Dipping what?"

"Dipping *things*!" Doris frowned at Irene. "Pretzels, chips, carrots…"

"Elbows, knees, toes…" Fred added.

They continued to discuss particulars until they all agreed that a dry white wine would go best with the turkey.

Meanwhile, Betty ate three of the little pink pancakes on her plate before she decided the last one couldn't be trusted, and flung it into the chandelier.

"Nice arm!" Walter said with admiration. "Was that one bugged?"

Betty nodded gravely. "Coulda been."

He leaned in and whispered, "That'll show 'em!"

After breakfast was cleared away and the errant pancake rescued, Iris and Candace festooned the dining hall with crepe paper streamers, paper doilies, cupid cutouts, and balloons in red, pink, and white.

After Candace had blown up ten balloons in a row, she stopped to catch her breath. "So Miss Iris," she puffed. "What's new on the romance front? You and Will got something big planned for later on?"

Iris felt her face flush, but ignored it and continued separating paper doilies. "Actually, I've been doing some side work lately… I picked up a research gig a while back and I'm working on a case that needs to get done ASAP. So Will and I are kind of… postponing—"

"Okay, what?" Candace looked aghast. "First of all, when were you going to tell me you got another job? Congratulations are in order!"

"Thanks," Iris said, looking sheepish.

"Second of all… *what*?" Candace put one hand on her hip. "You're going to keep that fabulous man waiting?"

"He said he understands."

"Of course he does," she said, and stretched out another balloon. "He's one of the good ones. But it's for that reason I hope you don't keep him waiting too long. Don't get me wrong… I really think that doing work you love is vital. But if you're serious about Will, start getting in the habit of building time into your schedule for him. Otherwise it'll only get harder."

Iris paused. "That's good advice, actually. I guess I'm not very good at doing that." She shrugged. "I thought it would be easier if I kept those areas of my life separate."

"Does that feel natural to you?"

Iris sighed. "Not really. But a lot of my work is confidential, y'know? I can't really involve him. But now I just feel like I'm constantly disappointing him."

"Has he said that?"

"No... but he's gotta run out of patience eventually. Anybody would! I mean, how do I know if my life's too complicated to involve someone else? Will might *think* he wants to be with me, but if it means spending his life waiting around for me to show up and being in the dark half the time, I don't think that's very fair to him."

"Well..." Candace blew up another balloon, her cheeks puffed out and her forehead going red. "That's for him to decide, isn't it?"

"I guess," Iris replied glumly. She tore open a bag of confetti hearts and scattered them on the table in front of her. "But if there's some sweet little chef somewhere who could spend all her free time adoring him, I think he deserves a chance to find her."

"Will's not interested in Joy." Candace opened her scissors and began curling strands of thin pink ribbon.

"I didn't mean her specifically—"

"I know." Candace winked. "But maybe you should just keep being honest with Will and let him decide if he'd rather settle for someone else. Unless you truly don't feel the same for him as he does for you. That's different."

"I... I think I do. I'm pretty sure. It's not that. I mean..." Iris frowned. "I just don't know if I'm good for him."

"Well, there's a balance there somewhere. I'm sure you'll find it."

"I hope so."

They finished decorating just before ten o'clock, then made the rounds to gather the largest crowd possible. The gala included Iris's craft table, an hour of song and dance featuring hit love ballads of the forties and fifties, and a screening of *Singin' In the Rain*.

Will had outdone himself on his last day, creating miniature chocolate cupcakes with sugar hearts and personalized monograms piped across the tops for each resident. While Candace handed those out, Iris sat at the craft table, helping party goers decorate heart shaped name signs for their doors using lace, buttons, sticky gems and letters.

Betty lingered for an especially long time, arranging and rearranging her gems and stickers until they were "just so."

"You have such a pretty name," Iris commented as she helped her place the letters in the right order. "Is Betty short for Elizabeth?"

"No, it's short for 'You Betcha!'"

Iris giggled.

"Probably can't fit it all on here, though," Betty sighed. "So this will do just fine." She made a fist and gave the stickers a good smash to make sure they were firmly attached, then showed it to Iris. "That's overgood, ain't it? I'm gruntled with it! Thanks, honey!" She waved her paper heart at Iris as she shuffled toward the door. "Come back when you can stay longer!"

"Okay, You Betcha!" Iris waved back. She chuckled, and began cleaning up. She reached under the table and pulled out the empty plastic tote for the art supplies. In the bottom lay a solitary lavender heart bordered with plastic diamonds. Across the center, it had glittery silver letters that spelled "Iris."

"What the…" She picked it up and turned it over. In Will's slanted script, undoubtedly written with the customary black ballpoint that he kept in his sleeve pocket, it said:

This is what happens when you leave unattended art supplies in my dining room. I'm really going to miss being here. Looking forward to whenever I see you, anytime I see you. ~ Will

"Me too," she whispered. Her heart ached a little. *Am I bad for him?*

She sensed absolutely no response. She frowned and continued to pack up.

Her phone buzzed, interrupting her thoughts. It was a text from Gray:

When do you get off today?

Candace had made the Valentine party today's main event, figuring it was the most people could handle in one day. That meant she was off early. She replied:

Early - 1:00. Why?

Gray's next message arrived almost at the same time hers went out:

Could you come update Eugene? He's driving me nuts.

She smiled, feeling a little bad for him.

I'll be right over after work, ok? Don't kill him.
It'll waste all my research.

When Iris arrived at the Reynolds' house, Eugene was seated in Grayson's chair by the fireplace, reading back issues of *National Geographic* from the early 1960s.

He glanced at her for a second, then muttered, "Are you the new babysitter?"

She shrugged out of her jacket. "Why? Do you need one?"

Eugene glared. "There's nothing to do around here. They won't let me watch television. I can't even smoke anymore!"

She opened her mouth to let fly with a snarky response about sleeping in the rain, but something stopped her. The longer she looked at Eugene, the more she *saw* him. The more she saw, the more deeply her heart grieved for him. She walked over and sat in the opposite chair.

"What?" he snapped.

"I'd be scared, too," she said softly. "And I know you can't do the things you'd normally do to get your mind off it."

He narrowed his eyes. "I never said I was scared."

"Anyone would be."

He didn't answer.

"I'm glad you're here, Eugene," she said sincerely. "I'm doing my absolute best for you, okay? I want you to know that. And I've got some good news, actually."

He lowered the magazine and gazed at her.

"I talked to Randy Murphy, your old neighbor. He remembers the car. He and his brother Steve are looking for the old paperwork on it. Meanwhile, I'll track down Norm, the next guy who owned it, as soon as I find out his last name."

"Probably Norm Jackson," Eugene said. "They were tight in school. Can't believe that clown ended up with my car."

"Randy said that Norm let one of his kids have it," Iris said.

"Oh, even better!" Eugene rolled his eyes. "He reproduced! Well, Norm has the intelligence of a moldy stump. If his kids are anything like him, we can kiss that car goodbye, I'll tell you that much."

"I'm going to hope not," Iris said, undeterred. "In the meantime, hang in there, okay? Shouldn't be too much longer before we get some real answers."

"And what then? Once nobody's seen my stuff and I'm stuck here for real? Am I supposed to just live under a bridge like a troll? Or go stay with Eva in the loony bin and sleep in a chair, like usual?"

"Let's only worry about that if it happens," said Gray from the hallway. He walked into the room several steps, then crossed his arms. "We'll take care of you, okay? You're not going to end up under a bridge."

"I don't take charity," Eugene grumbled.

"Sure you do," Gray countered. "You do it every time you take a breath. God's good like that."

Eugene shook his head and went back to his reading.

"I'm going to do a walk around," Gray said to Iris. "Wanna come?"

"Sure." She rose and donned her jacket. "See you later, Eugene."

Eugene grunted.

Gray rolled his eyes and opened the door for her.

The day had grown warmer as the clouds parted, revealing the first tiny spikes of daffodils cutting through the soil. Shy white crocus blossoms peeked around green blades, and hot pink buds the size of pinheads adorned the shrubs along the front walk.

Iris and Gray picked their way across the graveyard toward a towering two hundred fifty foot grand fir that was nestled in among several tall headstones and slightly smaller evergreens. Iris could detect a faint hum in the air as they drew closer.

"I still can't believe this place is so close to a road and a school, and you never get people in here," Iris said.

Gray waved his hand in front of the motion sensors one by one, making sure his watch buzzed at each one. "Well this place is inhabited by spirits," he said, eyes twinkling. "My great grandfather may have embellished a little about that, but the rumors are alive and well. I keep my ear to the ground at the school, and apparently, living here has done wonders for my street cred."

Iris laughed. "Charlie and I sure knew better than to mess with Mr. Reynolds back in the day! The kids all said he could communicate with the spirit world."

"Hmm, accurate." Gray chuckled, and continued to make his way around the tree.

Iris read the names on the headstones closest to the tree. "Wait a second, these all say Reynolds on them," she said. "Your family lost that many people at once?"

"Heck no," Gray replied. "They're not real graves. My ancestors founded this site when it was mostly woods and farmland around here and nobody would know the difference. The headstones nearest to the tree were just put there to prevent anyone from digging too close."

"Why, what would happen?"

"No idea, but I don't think I'd like to find out." Gray lowered himself onto a stone bench with a sigh and leaned back against the Great Fir. "I think I'm going to sit out here and enjoy the fresh air for a while before I head back in there with Mr. Sunshine." He patted the spot next to him. "Wanna sit?"

"Sure." She rested against the tree beside him.

He gave her a gentle nudge. "You good?"

"Yeah. Just wish I could get answers faster for Eugene."

"Oh, I've been keeping up with your case logs. I think you're doing the best you can," he said.

"Thanks."

They watched a squirrel doing acrobatic leaps from one branch to the next, twitching its tail after each graceful landing.

"I've been meaning to tell you something," he said.

"Sure, what's up?" she asked casually, still watching the squirrel.

"I think I'm in love with you."

Iris felt her stomach drop into her shoes. Slowly, she turned to face him.

His expression was full of the same sincerity she'd seen before, but had taken on a new fervor.

She couldn't answer. Her mind just kept flashing back to moments, looks, smiles... *peach pie... Oh God, I should have seen it sooner...*

"I didn't know how else to say it," he laughed. "You've been such an incredible friend, Iris. You don't know how long I've waited for someone like you, who understands what my life is really like. Someone I don't have to hide from, or pretend I'm just a teacher." He took her hand.

Like the last time he'd done that, she grew warmer. His hand was large and soft against hers. Comforting. She tried to answer, but couldn't speak.

"I asked some of the men I trust for advice... if it would be out of line to tell you all this. They said it would be worth the risk, and I agree with them. You are... more perfect than I could imagine," he said, pulling her hand a little closer. "I think we've got possibilities." He searched her face. "At least I hope so."

She looked into his blue-green eyes. *What do I say?* Everything Gray was saying made complete sense. On paper, they *were* a perfect match. He was an amazing friend... a beautiful person. And he knew... everything. Suddenly, all of her frustration and anxiety about Will welled up to the surface. Every moment, she was terrified of saying too much and putting her memories of the Guardians into danger. Every day, she berated herself for not being there for Will like he deserved. She wanted Will with all her heart, but could never have him without making his life incredibly complicated.

Her eyes welled with tears.

"What is it?" Gray murmured. "Did I upset you?"

"No..." Iris shook her head. "I just..." She looked into his concerned face. He was wonderful. She would never have to worry about *him* forgetting her. The idea suddenly felt like magic to her, a way to heal her divided existence.

He leaned closer.

It would be so easy with Gray. So warm and uncomplicated...

His lips were inches away.

But...

She quickly turned her head to the side, and his lips pressed against her cheek, at the corner of her mouth. She closed her eyes. The shock of intensity from this tender gesture made her lightheaded. But she couldn't just fly away in the feelings of a moment. Not when her heart was with someone else.

She hung her head. A tear fell from her eyelashes into his lap. She was kidding herself. This would never be easy or uncomplicated.

"I'm sorry," she whispered.

"No, don't be," he said. "Tell me what's going on. Help me understand."

She squeezed his hand, and found her voice. "You're right… It's been amazing for me too, having a friend who really understands everything the way you do. I don't blame you for seeing the potential in that. But I've been having a hard time navigating all of this. I didn't grow up with it like you did. And I don't have the luxury of getting to keep it in my head no matter who I talk to."

"That's true. I didn't think of it that way," he admitted. He released her hand, but kept his gaze trained on her. "You just seem like such a natural part of things now. I keep forgetting how strange it must feel to you."

She nodded. "I already feel like I have to lie too much. So one of the ways I've been trying to avoid that is by keeping my two lives as separate as I can. I haven't told other people much about you, and I haven't said much to you or Jason about myself, either. Including the fact that, uh…"

He let out a knowing sigh, and gave her a sad smile. "You're seeing someone?"

"Yes."

He hung his head. "I'm such an idiot."

"No, you aren't." She bumped his shoulder with hers. "You couldn't have known."

"I could have if I'd bothered to ask first! I just assumed that if there was someone special in your life, you'd mention him once in awhile. But you never have, so…" He shook his head. "But that's no excuse. I'm really sorry."

"Don't worry about it," she said. "I completely understand. I promise it's okay."

"If you're sure. I haven't ruined everything, have I?"

"C'mon," she gave him a side eye. "Of course not. We can be grown ups about it. And for the record, I love that you thought I was worth the risk."

"Well you are. Never doubt that."

They leaned back against the tree, staring up into the branches for several minutes.

"You going to be okay?" she finally asked.

"Yeah," he said good naturedly. "Thankfully, I spoke up before things got to the point of excruciating, so recovery shouldn't take as long. I can compartmentalize."

"Very sensible."

"Thanks." He turned his head toward her. "How serious is it with this guy, anyway?"

She whacked his leg with the back of her hand.

He laughed. "Do I at least get to know his name?"

Iris thought of Will's dimples, and the beautiful Valentine he'd made for her. She smiled. "His name is Will Donovan."

"Will…" Gray mused. "Must be a stand-up guy."

"He is."

"What are you going to do?" he asked. "Can't keep him in the dark forever."

Iris shook her head. "I don't know."

"Well, just remember you're not in this alone, okay?" He turned to face her, eyes serious. "You're the first non-Guardian we've ever adopted and given rank to—that means you're totally unique. None of us are sure how the memory thing would work with someone like you, so of course we have to tread carefully.

But if Will is important to you, then…" Gray swallowed. "He's important to us. You're one of us, and you have our total support."

Iris nodded, her heart filling with relief. The thought of keeping everything the same, juggling two worlds on her own for even one more day, seemed daunting.

"C'mon, I have an idea," Gray said. He stood and offered his hand to help her up.

She followed him back to the house. "What are we doing?"

"You'll see." He led her straight through to the den, where Jason was grading tests.

"Hey, you two!" he greeted them. "Tell me you've come to distract me!"

"Definitely," Gray said. With a look of intense focus, he sat at his computer and pinged every Council contact in the database. He created a conference call screen, pulled up an extra chair for Iris, and waited.

"Oh, very interesting!" Jason chuckled as his computer chimed. He clicked and his face popped into one of the little boxes on the left, and a dot appeared over Washington on the map.

"This one should be better attended than the last one," Gray said to Iris. "I used a special code for urgent meetings."

Iris blushed to her roots and sat down. "Gray," she said in a barely audible whisper, "my love life is *not* urgent!"

"It's not just that," he whispered back. "It's your life in general that's urgent. You're important. You need to realize that."

"But what about the guys eight time zones away who are trying to sleep? This can wait!"

"Someone's always asleep. That's how it works with globes. Trust me, they won't want to miss this. They're huge fans of yours."

Several faces popped up, then more and more. The map lit up with scattered dots. Iris was stunned. Within five minutes, there were over eight hundred members of the Council of Guardians looking at her. She suddenly wanted to hide behind Gray, but forced herself to sit still.

Just like last time, a general murmur began, as their various greetings combined and popped into the comment box, translated into English.

Gray took in her petrified expression. "I got it," he whispered reassuringly.

He turned to the camera and spoke in the same strange language Iris remembered from last time. The translation appeared:

Grayson Reynolds, Washington, U.S.A.: *Greetings, everyone. Thank you for meeting us. Iris has told me of her great concern that being one of us will compromise her outside relationships. Those whom she loves know nothing of us, and keeping it from them is hard on her conscience. She would like your advice.*

Hundreds of tiny heads nodded, and voices arose. Comments began to come in.

(587) Sympathies. That is not easy.

(712) Your loyalty is appreciated.

The software highlighted and magnified the video feed of one man as he spoke:

Zhang Wei Shú, Anhui, China: *The wives keep the memories. Have you considered this?*

Alessandro Albero, Aosta Valley, Italy: *Yes, that would confer first-party status.*

A general murmur of agreement followed.

(5) Grayson, have you spoken to her yet?

(826) Wait, what?

(644) Grayson wants to marry Iris?

Gray turned to Iris, pink in the face, and whispered, "Sorry. They're very transparent people."

Jason chuckled behind his monitor.

Gray leaned over. "I heard that!" He held up his hand to the camera and spoke rapidly.

Grayson Reynolds, Washington, U.S.A.: *Guys, that's not happening. She already has someone else.*

There was total silence and blank stares for a few seconds, followed by hushed comments of tsks and sympathies. Fifty-nine asked if she was sure, while seventeen more shared the thought that it could fix the whole problem. Three wondered if Iris just didn't like beards.

Jason was almost beside himself trying not to laugh.

"Welcome to the Council of Guardians. You now have a thousand grandpas!" Gray whispered under his breath.

Iris felt a little sorry for him, but couldn't help smiling.

He spoke a quick three word phrase, which translated: *I'll survive. What should Iris do?*

The men deliberated for ten minutes, and came to a consensus. They sent their love and signed off. As their video feeds went black, their resolution came onto the screen:

If anyone Iris loves is a loyal and worthy friend, either Jason or Gray may fully inform them, in private, of anything Iris wishes them to know. She must understand that by telling them, she puts them at risk of telling a third party and subsequently forgetting everything they heard, and possibly even parts of their relationship. Longer term relationships survive such a memory loss largely intact, but shorter term ones are more difficult to predict. Some people might even forget her completely, depending on how deeply rooted their memories of her are. She must judge the risk for herself. If a man ever desires to marry, she must tell him everything. We will continue to seek wisdom about how Iris's rank affects her first- or second-party status. Will advise as soon as more is known.

Iris read it twice to make sure she fully understood.

"Is there anybody you want us to talk to?" Jason offered.

Iris mulled it over. *Shorter term relationships are more difficult to predict? I completely trust Will, but what if he makes a mistake? What if he talks in his sleep and his little brother overhears him someday? And he would never agree to as much lying as I do on a regular basis. He might even wonder if he can ever trust me again. What if... I dunno...*

She forced a smile. "I'll let you know."

Chapter 17

B rennus escorted Iris home, keenly aware of the tense energy in her body. The Master had settled her at the deepest level of spirit, but great human dilemmas still stirred in her heart. She was worried. It permeated the atmosphere like chum in shark infested water. He didn't analyze, he merely drew his sword and kept his eyes ahead. She was young. She'd learn to train her mind eventually.

As they neared her door, he could sense another warmth close by. Sure enough, his old friend leaned casually against the kitchen counter, waiting.

"Aimsir! It's been a little while!" Brennus greeted him.

"More than a little while for me, my friend," Aimsir replied, smiling. "I came the long way around, remember?"

"The carpenter did live a good, long life," Brennus agreed. "What brings you here?"

"My last task on his detail. A message. After that, a reassignment."

"Who's your new charge? Anyone I know?"

Aimsir smiled. "The Guardian of the Lost."

Brennus let out a joyful laugh. "That's perfection!" Still grinning, he raised his sword in salute. "I'm looking forward to working with you again."

"As am I," Aimsir replied, returning the salute. "What news from Varick?"

"All is well at present. There is one beast who seems to be dividing his time between us, but it's unclear which human is his true target. His behavior so far has been aimless and spiteful. His last appearance was three nights ago."

Aimsir nodded. "We'll be ready."

Iris got home in the late afternoon to find a slew of waiting messages—some paper, some electronic. She could tell that Charlie had been here on her lunch break and left a stack of mail on the kitchen counter. Iris had been ignoring the postal service for over a week. The pile was bordering on embarrassing now, so she started there. She barely glanced at most of it, setting aside the tax stuff and shuffling the ads, coupons, and flyers into the recycle bin. At the bottom of the pile lay a stiff cardboard mailer bearing a registered number and a customs form from the U.K.

It's from Darrick!

She ripped the tab across the top and peered inside. There was a sealed antique envelope inside of a plastic sleeve, along with a loose sheet of Darrick's personalized stationery with a handwritten note, which read:

Dear Sis,

> *As promised, here's the letter I found, addressed to you, I presume. I stuck a bit of extra hurry-up on this because I think you're probably as impatient to read it as I would be. My dad may have told you how I found it tucked away among Éamon MacCrann's later journals. I'm sure you have a guess who it's from. Seems like blind luck I found it now, but we both know*

*that's a ridiculous notion. It's yours to treasure, but I confess I
do hope you share!*

*Katie still speaks of your whirlwind trip together, and was
so excited to help out on your first mission. It'll be several years
before I get someplace tropical myself, but I've promised to take
her. She sends her love, and so do Callum and Brody.*

Cheers,
Darrick

Iris turned to the envelope. Her name was written with a
distinctive capital "I" that she'd seen once before, on an envelope
hidden behind a secret panel in a mirror frame. She smiled.

The idea of tearing into this pristine envelope horrified her,
so she did the next best thing: she located the sharpest knife she
could find in the kitchen and sliced through one of the short
edges of the rectangle. She slid the letter out and opened it.

Iris had hoped for more photographs, but this letter was
dated 1847. That was only three years after he'd gone home,
long before he'd written the letter she'd found in the frame.

Dearest Friend,

*I find it's at this time of the year that I think of you most
often, because it was on an April day much like this one when
I found myself beneath a Hawthorn tree, having had my entire
destiny saved by someone who believed me.*

*I hope this letter finds you well. The Guardian says it's a
risk, writing to you, but I've made certain no one will see it.
Except little Iris. That's her there.*

There was a smudgy toddler handprint, browned with age.
He continued his flowing script below it:

Heaven knows what color the strawberry jam will be by the time you see it, but I knew you'd enjoy her message as well. She's so lovely, like my Gillian. I named her for you because she wouldn't be here if not for you.

But there's been something else on my heart that I wanted you to know. I think of it every time I pray for you, and it's this: Life is fragile, but God is not.

In the version of the world that I'm glad to say never happened, the two of us, only in our twenties, had the very life drained from us. Even Gilly, the strongest woman I know, was struck down in an instant. As I consider my time there as a daft old man, I realise that at any given moment, we may break through the veil. Our grip on this world is tenuous at best, yet the One who arranged us in perfect order holds our very fragile lives with a most capable and loving iron grip. To this world, we are fading flowers. To Him, we are permanent. I hope you've found, as I have, how very worthy He is of your trust. Because you can trust a God whose specialty is the impossible. Remember that, my dear friend.

Lovingly,
Angus

P.S. One of these days, time won't matter anymore. I'm looking forward to seeing you then. I'll have a modern American hug waiting for you. In the meantime, I intend to commemorate our journey every April with some kind of project. If I live to be very old, then the number of irises I end up leaving behind will be, as you would say, "ridiculous."

Iris laughed, and realized that her eyes had gone blurry as she read and reread the lines. She traced the little handprint with her finger. What a gift this was.

Just like in my dream. Was it a dream, or was I actually there?

She hated to disappoint Darrick, but there was little information in the letter that would be of any value in adding to the Guardians' knowledge base. She sent him an email anyway, thanking him, confirming that the letter was indeed from Angus, and returning her love to the family. She said nothing more than that. She knew he would understand.

She might share the letter, someday. But not yet.

Iris was grateful to spend most of the following day doing research. The Murphy brothers had apparently emerged from Steve's garage alive, because Randy had come through with another rambling message that contained not only a VIN for Eugene's Mustang, but a recipe for "killer" pork ribs. Despite the fact that it called for copious amounts of cola, she made a mental note to show it to Will.

Then she chose a national title search vendor whose logo she liked the color of, and submitted the VIN to their website.

Records found. Sweetness. She typed in her payment information.

A little popup opened at the top of her browser, which had a Grove Research and Antiquities Conservation Enterprises logo at the top, followed by the message, "Hi, Iris! Would you like to claim this as a business expense?"

She chuckled. *The Council made me my own browser plug-in? Of course they did. Why am I surprised?* She clicked "Yes." The window flashed the words, "Reimbursement Forthcoming," and disappeared. *You clever people, you.*

The website's little thinky dots waved up and down for so long that she began to wonder if it would ever load. Finally, a smattering of information filled the screen, with a large green "Download Full Report" button at the bottom. She clicked, and was relieved to see that the car's general description matched the one Eugene had given. She scanned through the list beneath:

Current Title Records 1
Historical Title Records 5
Title Brand Records 2
Junk and Salvage Records 1
Insurer "Total loss" Records 1
Recall Records 0

She scrolled through the rest of the report, making note of the year each time the title changed hands. "Okay..." she mumbled. "Five owners, all in Arizona. Two in 1965, that was Eugene and then Steve Murphy. One in 1975, that was Norm Jackson and his son. Next one was 1989... who was that?" She scratched another note on her page. The car had been branded a total loss in 1994. The final record was another Arizona title with a "Junk - 08" brand in 2016. The fifth owner had to be a scrap yard.

Hmm. She tapped her finger on the desk. It wasn't great news, but at least she knew how many missing pieces she had left to find.

She managed to track down Norm Jackson's current location, which, unfortunately, was a cemetery in Phoenix. His obituary showed that he had passed away six months ago.

On a whim, she tried calling both of the last phone numbers she found listed for Norm. One was out of service, but someone answered the second one. It was Norm's son Billy, who was there helping out his elderly mother.

As Iris talked with Billy, she had a hard time imagining why Eugene regarded the family with such disdain. Billy was a kind man, incredibly sharp, and spoke of Norm with great affection. He had dealt with his father's estate, and was absolutely positive he'd never seen Eugene's bag or any strange looking tools lying around, nor did he remember finding anything like that in the car when he was driving it, well into the late 1980s.

Billy remembered that a friend of his, whose name was Jake Johnson, had bought the car after that, driven it for a few years, then totaled it. When Iris asked for details, Billy just chuckled. Finally, he said, "Parking brakes are important, especially near a lake."

Oh dear.

She shook her head and wrote "Lake Johnson" into the number four slot on her list, then scratched out "Lake" and wrote "Jake."

The only other thing Billy knew for sure was that Jake had hung onto the car for quite a while, thinking he would enjoy fixing it up on weekends. The last he'd seen it, it was up on blocks in Jake's backyard. Where it was now, Billy had no idea, but he suggested she "check with the idiot."

Did *he* have Jake's contact info? Of course not. They'd lost touch about a decade ago, but if it helped, his wife's name was Karen.

Brilliant.

Iris thanked him, and hung up. "Jake Johnson..." she muttered. "How many hundreds of those are there? Might as well be called John Smith."

She got up to make herself a distracting cup of tea, because she was fighting discouragement a little more than she cared to admit. *Now we're dealing with not only a totaled car, but a flooded and subsequently junked one?* She let out a sigh and put the kettle on.

At least the details were starting to fit together. Jake Johnson had to be the final piece of the puzzle, as long as he hadn't given the car to anybody else and forgotten to transfer the title... *the same way he forgot to set a parking brake.*

She set out a cup and rummaged in the cupboard for her favorite earl grey.

Was it really possible that this guy had kept a junker in his backyard for twenty-two years? It seemed unlikely, but then again, she didn't know very many middle-aged men. Her own father's projects were only on paper, and Finn's idea of doing automotive work was to call a mechanic. Maybe some guys did hang onto giant rusty piles of hope for that long.

She returned to her desk with tea, cookies, and renewed determination. A people search for Jake Johnson in Phoenix, Arizona netted over one hundred fifty results. Undeterred, she filtered for age. He had to be in his fifties or sixties. That narrowed the results to thirty-seven. Still too many to call one by one. She filtered out anyone named Jack, then scanned for the name "Karen" under known family members.

Beautiful. Down to two. I can deal with two.

She called the first number listed.

"Mmmmyello?" said a bassy voice.

"Is this Jake Johnson?" Iris asked.

"Depends on who's askin'!" He let out a boisterous laugh. Apparently, he enjoyed his own sense of humor.

She forged ahead. "My name's Iris. I'm trying to track down a sixty-five Mustang convertible you might've owned."

"Uh…" There was a pause. "Look, that was a completely legitimate claim, okay? I did *not* drive it into that lake on purpose! Can you even investigate that after this many years? There's gotta be a statute of limitations—"

"Mr. Johnson," she interrupted him. "I'm not from an insurance company, I just want to find the car."

"Oh. Well you must be reading a really old want ad then, because I already sold it, like years ago."

"I can see that. I'm looking at the title report."

"Uh… okay, so… why are you calling me, then?"

"Because I wanted to ask you—"

"Frank!" he yelled. "Get outta there! Go on!" The phone made a scratching sound, then he came back on. "Dumb dog," he muttered. "Sorry. What were you sayin'?"

"I just wanted to ask you who bought the car," she continued, taking a sip of tea to fortify herself.

"That big scrap yard out the highway that does classic restorations and stuff," he replied.

"I'm nowhere near Phoenix, so I'm going to need you to be a little more specific."

"I forget. Desert something."

Desert something. Wonderful.

"They'll haggle ya, but they pay good," he added. A large dog began to bark in the background.

"Did anybody else have the car after you got it?" she asked.

"Nope, just me. Finally got around to it, but it weren't great once I got lookin' at it. Couldn't see my way to sinkin' ten grand into that thing no more."

"Makes sense," she said. "Last question… did you ever find a leather bag under the seat, or notice any weird looking tools in the car?"

"Weird tools?"

"Yeah, like a long, skinny drill with a handle, about eighteen inches long?"

"Heh. Nope. I ain't even gonna ask what that's about!" He laughed again. "Never saw your purse or nothin' like that in there. Sorry, lady."

"It's not my p—y'know what? Never mind. Thanks for all your help, Mr. Johnson."

"Yep. Frank! Git over here!" he yelled. There was another shuffling sound, followed by a click.

Iris looked at the phone. "Mmmkay. Bye, then." *Colorful man.*

She did a general search for any auto salvage yards in Arizona with "Desert" in the title.

Eureka. Every result on the first page was for the same place—acres and acres of deceased vehicles, specializing in American classics. She smiled.

"Gotcha."

Both her back and her attention span were beginning to ache, but she was so close to a mile marker that she couldn't stop yet. She composed an email.

From: Iris Jacobs
To: Gabriel Iwila, Sedona AZ
Cc: Grayson Reynolds

> *Greetings from rainy Washington! I've tracked the car to a junkyard in Phoenix. Even chances it's a dead end, but it's all we've got, right? Can your dad spell you for a bit in Sedona so you can take a little field trip? I need a guy with sharp ears. Let me know when you're available, factoring in that Gray is really enjoying his time with Eugene. :)*

> *Cheers,*
> *Iris*

She sighed. Done for today. Once she heard from Gabe, it looked like Eugene might finally be on the last leg of his crazy trip home... hopefully wiser for the wear. She checked her watch.

Wow, it's only five o'clock. Could I actually manage a date tonight? Imagine that.

It would be a relief to see Will. Her last interaction with Gray had completely unsettled her. It wasn't like she had... *cheated* or anything. She hadn't said yes, after all. And she and Will had been careful so far, being honest about their present situation rather than making any grand promises. They had agreed to be there for each other, that was all. And she had never led Gray on, or *asked* him to fall for her. But she'd had an undeniable reaction to it, all the same. It was confusing.

She tried to put her finger on what had been so tempting about it, especially when she'd thought her feelings for Will were so strong. Gray was stable and kind, and he cared about her. She smiled. The Council sure had been rooting for him. *Poor guy.* He'd been such a good sport about it.

But Will had all of those qualities, too. The fact that Grayson knew more about her life right now wasn't exactly Will's fault. But fixing that would be a massive risk.

And then there was God. She had just entered a beautiful relationship with Him, captivated by the undeniable beauty of His goodness. Gray and Jason both understood what that was like, while Will merely acknowledged His existence. But that could change, given time.

She hoped.

But in the meantime, none of this would be resolved by staring at the bottom of an empty teacup. She realized she missed Will. If he was free tonight, she made up her mind just to enjoy being near him. Maybe answers would come.

She dialed his number.

"Hey," he answered. "I love that song."

"What song?"

"Your ringtone."

"What is it?"

He chuckled. "I can't tell you that."

"C'mon…"

"Nope."

She laughed. "Are you being intriguing again?"

He sniffed. "I can't help it. It's just my nature to be intriguing."

"Well, it's working perfectly. I'm calling to ask you out."

"Moi?"

"Yes, if you're available on such short notice, that is."

"Hmm…" he sighed. "I'll have to cancel some things."

"Like what?"

"Well, I definitely can't start folding my laundry *now*."

"Were you ever planning to?"

"Of course not!"

"Schedule's all clear, then?"

"Yeah. Can I pick you up in like thirty seconds? Because that's when I'm hoping to see you next."

"Ha. Trust me," she said, "you don't want to see this. Give me at *least* fifteen minutes."

"Hmm, I'll give you eight."

"Twelve?"

"Ten, and that's my final offer."

"Done."

Will took her to his favorite Italian restaurant, a little dive tucked away in the historic district of an adjoining town. They had been there once before. The fresh pasta and homemade bread at this place were divine. Iris agreed with him that the thirty minute drive was worth it.

After her last befuddling conversation with Gray, it was refreshing to reconnect with Will on the way there. They fell into an easy rhythm, working their way through what they'd missed over the past three days. To Iris, it had felt like much longer, because so much had happened. But she wasn't sure where to start, so she mostly listened to Will talk.

When they arrived, Iris could tell that Will had called ahead. The host took them straight back to a cozy booth. Their table was lit with a tiny candle in a jar and decked with clunky stainless steel flatware rolled up in paper napkins. The wood paneled walls were adorned with fake ivy, framed newspaper reviews, and an Italian flag, while the rafters glistened with twinkle lights.

She had missed looking at him. His dimples and soft spoken manner made him *seem* shy, but she knew better now. She'd seen his entire kitchen staff happily operating like a well-oiled machine at his command. When Brett had threatened her, he'd come to her defense more than once with a ferocity she hadn't realized he was capable of. She'd never known anyone else more self assured.

Tonight, he seemed more intent on her than ever. She had crafted a well thought out explanation of what she'd been up to—truthful, mostly vague. He rested his hand on hers, squinting in an odd way as she spoke, as if he was searching for something beneath her words. The look in his eyes had weakened her resolve. He deserved to know what was really going on in her life. Yet he never asked pressing questions. *How much longer can I keep this up?*

Iris did her best to focus on Will's funny story about teaching James how to poach an egg, but she was distracted by thoughts of Gray. She imagined how she'd feel if Will had suddenly formed a close relationship with another woman, spending hours working with her almost every day… and then refusing to give any details about it. *Ugh.*

She thought about yesterday, when Gray had leaned in, about to kiss her. She had seen the look on his face. She'd known what he was about to do. What had kept her from turning away until the last second? Was the momentary notion that being with Gray might be so much easier really *that* appealing? Enough to pull her heart away from Will?

Gray had been so confident in what he felt for her that he had come right out and said it. *What would Will say if I asked?* Her stomach did a tiny flip at the intense memory of his lips on her cheek. She hung her head, pushing away the thought and the twinge of guilt that came with it.

"Iris?"

She looked up.

Will was gazing at her with the same squint. There was no suspicion in his expression, only curiosity. "You okay?"

Caught.

"Yeah... I guess. It's just been crazy lately, y'know?"

He nodded.

"I've missed you," she continued. *True.* "And I've thought about you a lot." *Also true.*

"I've missed you, too." His smile was disarming.

"So... Will?"

"Hmm?"

Iris set her fork down. "Can I ask you a question?"

"Of course."

She took a deep breath. "How do you feel about... the 'L' word?"

"Linguine?"

Iris laughed, relieved at how it eased the tension in her soul a little. "No, not linguine. I already know how you feel about that."

"Well," he mused, stroking the back of her hand, "I think the 'L' word is super important. But I wouldn't just throw it around." His gaze intensified. "I fully admit that I'm wildly attracted to you. You're my favorite person. I hate being apart. And for the record, I don't even like the word 'girlfriend.' It doesn't come close to describing what's going on here. Not to me."

Iris's stomach did another tiny flip.

"Call me old fashioned," Will continued, "but I just think the word *love* is on another level. Maybe it's just semantics at this point... but to me, saying I love someone means I'm taking on a huge responsibility. It means I'm willing to give that person everything, to put them first for the rest of my life... and if necessary, give up my life." He gave her an odd smile and released her hand. "Wouldn't be fair to put that kind of pressure on someone who wasn't completely sure she wanted me to do all that."

Iris couldn't speak. Will's smile was peaceful, not accusing. And yet, he hadn't missed a thing. He had seen right through her conflicted soul. Even when he didn't know all the details, there was no such thing as keeping secrets from Will. Not really. And there he sat, calmly skewering chicken alfredo with his fork, waiting for her to make up her mind. Trusting her.

At last, her thoughts found their way into words. "Will, you're not the one putting pressure on me. It's everything else. There's just... so much you still don't know about me. And I want to tell you everything. I do. But it's not that simple..."

"Listen," he said softly. "I know you've got a lot going on. You've been a complicated person to know since the beginning. I know your life is about more than me, or work. It *should* be. I'm not going to put demands on you. I just want you to know... you're worth it to me. That's why I'm willing to sit here being confused with you."

Iris was overwhelmed. "Will, I don't deserve you."

"Well that hardly matters," he chuckled, "since I don't deserve you either. Just... promise me something."

"Anything."

"Don't change, okay? Just be happy with your life. Be you. And if, somehow, you can't do that with me in the way, just... tell me as soon as you can. The sooner, the better."

His words pierced her. "What do you mean? Will, you're not in the way of anything."

"I just want to be fair to you while you figure out... whatever it is. I want you to be sure."

Am I sure? She gazed at him for a long moment. "Okay. I promise."

"And you'll keep me posted?"

"Absolutely."

Chapter 18

After paying their tab, Will helped Iris into her blue cardigan. She slid her arm around his waist as they stepped into the twilight. The streetlights had blinked on. A shower had just passed through, plastering clusters of early fallen flower petals to the sidewalk like pink polka dots, and leaving the asphalt gleaming with reflected lights from the closed shops along the street. He put his arm across her shoulders, warding off the chill in the air. She loved the feeling.

Iris had decided something. Telling Will everything about herself was currently impossible, but living life without him was going to be equally impossible. And like every other seemingly impossible situation she'd found herself in for the past six months, she would just figure out how to have it both ways. She hugged him a little tighter and smiled up at him.

"Hey, I like that old smile!" he chuckled. "It's one of the originals!"

"Yep, this one's yours. You were the first to put it there."

"Good." He turned and pulled her into a bear hug. He sighed into her hair. "I want to tell you something else, because you've probably been wondering."

"Oh? What's that?"

He looked down at her, his eyes full of tender emotion. "I want to kiss you."

279

"Oh." She could feel warmth rise in her cheeks, but ignored it. "That would be all right."

He frowned slightly. "But I don't think I should. Maybe not yet."

"How come?"

"Because," he said, playing with a strand of her hair, "you're so beautiful."

"Is… that a problem?" she murmured.

"I could get lost in it. I'm not sure I could ever let go of you again if I kissed you now. But I've just told you to be happy… and to let me know if I don't fit the picture. Imagine if I didn't fit, but I kissed you anyway." He touched her cheek. "I don't need that kind of addiction. Not if I can't keep you."

Iris's eyes swam with tears. The longing in his voice washed over her, awakening within her a clarity and determination that almost frightened her. How could she have missed it before? Grayson was an amazing man—kind, considerate, wise, and understanding. She never had to be careful what she said around him. He was a loving, loyal friend. In fact, he was ideal in every way… except for one crucial thing. He wasn't Will.

She searched Will's face as an idea came to her. *Could I really do that? If I have Gray tell him everything, then he'll at least know what he's getting into. But then he'll be saddled with secrets that could make him forget me.* A pang of fear tried to rise inside her, but she forced it back down. *It's a risk I'll have to take.*

She couldn't keep Will in the dark any longer, nor was she going to give him up.

He looked troubled. "Have I made you sad?"

"No." She shook her head. "You've done just the opposite."

"I have?"

"Yes. There's no way you don't fit in my life. You're one of the best things in it. But you need to understand what you're getting yourself into. I want you to know everything… so you can decide if I fit into *your* picture."

"What are you talking about?"

Her heartbeat quickened. "Will you come with me somewhere?"

He gave her a quizzical look. "Of course."

As they headed down the sidewalk, she slipped her phone out of her pocket and fired off a text to Gray:

I need you to tell Will everything.

His reply came back ten seconds later:

If you're sure, then bring him over.

She smiled. *I'm really doing this.*

They had almost reached the truck when they heard a gruff voice ahead of them.

"There she is! Hey, Gorgeous."

Brett.

Iris froze. Her arm tightened on Will's back.

Brett stood twenty feet away, unmoving, leering at her. He looked clean cut as ever, sporting designer everything, not a hair out of place. His long, black coat gave him a menacing presence, despite his casual posture.

"What do you want?" Will called out. He turned to face Brett, pulling Iris protectively into his side.

"Oh, y'know," Brett shrugged, closing the distance another five feet. "Answers."

"Answers about what?" Iris demanded, trying to sound tougher than she felt.

"A *restraining order*? Seriously?" Brett chuckled. "You're so dramatic, Iris." He took two steps closer. "You realize, your little hissy fit last year cost me my job… which cost me my car… and a place to *live*. Replacing all of that has been extremely inconvenient. And all because I told you how much I care about you."

Iris choked. "*Care* about me? You shoved me into a wall and threatened me!"

Brett looked unconcerned. "Well, some people can't take a joke."

Angry tears pricked her eyes. "If that's your idea of a joke, then I want to be as far as possible from you!"

"Then why did you come looking for me?" Brett's voice had taken on a seductive growl. "You miss me, I can tell."

"Brett, I didn't come looking for you." Her heart pounded. "It was pure coincidence that we ran into you that night. We were just…" Her voice quaked, despite all her efforts to appear confident.

"No, I know exactly what you were doing." He smirked, his eyes sweeping down the length of her body. "You just wanted to take another look… see if *this* guy…" he jerked his chin toward Will, "measures up to what you know you can get. Clearly, you have a type." He cocked his head to one side. "Bit of a step down, though, I gotta say."

Iris could feel Will's arm muscles tense.

"Why don't you give it up?" Will snapped. "If she was into you, she'd be standing over there."

Brett's eyes grew malevolent, almost black. "If she was into you, *fat boy*, she'd believe you could protect her instead of shaking in her pretty little boots!" He looked Iris over again, eyes narrowed. "Just look at you," he scoffed. "Pathetic. I despise weak women." He stared her down for a long moment, shaking his head. Then he slowly raised his arm. "I think we're done here."

Iris saw only a dim reflection of street light glinting off the cold black steel in Brett's hand, as Will threw himself in front of her, followed by a flash and an explosion. The sound assaulted her ears with such force that it made every other sound seem like it was underwater. Her brain registered nothing but shock as Will rocked backward, letting out a pained gasp.

Iris clutched his shoulders, trying to stop him from falling. He teetered forward and went to his knees, a look of confusion across his face. Finally, he crumpled onto his side on the wet pavement, a stream of crimson spreading across his shirt in a circle, running too quickly from the shredded fabric over his heart.

"Will!" Iris shrieked, throwing herself to the ground beside him, cradling his head.

"Iris," he breathed with a ragged gasp. "Are you okay? Where is he?"

She looked back toward Brett, but saw only his retreating form walking into the inky shadows of a distant alley.

"I don't know!" she cried. "Gone? I think? He left." Her face crumpled into sobs. "Will, what do I do? I don't know what to do..." She ripped her cardigan off, wadded it into a ball, and pressed it into the wound. Will moaned. She could vaguely remember seeing something like this on TV, but it dawned on her that she had no idea how much pressure to apply, or even if this was the right thing to do. *Am I hurting him?* He moaned again, intense anguish on his face.

"Oh Will, I'm so sorry..." she whimpered. "I'm so sorry! Oh God..."

She snatched her phone from her back pocket and dialed with one hand, keeping pressure on with the other. She spilled as much information as she could to the person who answered, feeling a desperate panic rising inside her at how slowly and professionally he seemed to ask his questions. At some point, after she had emptied her brain of everything she could think of to say, the phone sank to her lap. All she could do was stare in disbelief.

Will trembled. His lips began to turn blue.

"Oh God, help him..."

She held both hands against the wound, as blood began to seep between her fingers. Her cardigan was soaked through, and still more blood came. She could hear a tinny voice urging her to stay on the line until help arrived, asking her to respond, but she couldn't.

"Iris," Will whispered. "I..."

She lowered her head to his. "I'm here."

"I love you," he breathed.

Iris closed her eyes, allowing tears to escape. She rested her forehead against Will's, which had grown cool and clammy. "I know," she answered. "I—"

Her reply was cut short by the sound of sirens and echoing shouts above her. People calling her "miss" and telling her she'd have to stand back.

"Miss, you'll have to let go of him."

They kept asking her things while they lifted him onto the gurney, but none of it made sense. Iris couldn't comprehend what she'd just seen.

Someone was screaming as they closed the doors and drove away with Will.

A police officer wrapped a blanket around her. It was only when her throat began to hurt that Iris realized where the screams were coming from.

The next six hours refused to make sense. Will had come through the surgery to repair his heart, but he'd been too unstable for them to remove the bullet that had lodged in one of his vertebrae. The doctors weren't sure if he would ever walk again. They couldn't even say with any certainty how long he'd be on life support. No one was sure whether his brain had been affected by a lack of oxygen, or when he would wake up. If he woke up at all.

Because she wasn't family, the nurses wouldn't tell her much more than that. Will's only next of kin was his little brother, on duty aboard an aircraft carrier somewhere in the middle of a faraway time zone.

Iris could only wait.

Eyes red, she sat. She kept vigil into the morning hours, afraid to move from the vinyl chair beside Will's bed in the ICU, while monitors beeped the minutes away and a whooshing contraption kept him breathing. She asked questions, but understood little of the nurses' minimal answers.

He was so still.

She rested her cheek against the warmth of his arm and closed her eyes.

Aimsir, Brennus, and Varick stood back to back, swords drawn, ready to engage. Brennus and Aimsir watched Iris, while Varick's eyes scanned the planes beyond the four walls of the fluorescent room. They came to rest on a flickering smudge, billowing and oppressive.

As it approached, its darkness thickened at the center, but its edges remained hazy, ever shifting. Two glowing eyes appeared, staring down at the patient in the hospital bed.

Varick narrowed his eyes and pointed his sword. "Be gone, Thanos. You've done enough."

"Oh, not nearly," the creature snickered, his almost-human face constantly shifting in and out of phase. He descended, hovering just above the man's head. "This is one of ours. He's *always* been one of ours, just like his mother was. I took her, too."

Varick began to advance, but suddenly stopped short.

"Varick?" Brennus said.

Varick shook his head, eyes horrified. "The Master has stayed my sword."

"See?" The word hissed from the center of the putrid mist. "Ours." The creature reached down with a black, amorphous fist and plunged it through the man's chest.

Piercing alarms brought Iris back to consciousness as a nurse in scrubs breezed past her, felt Will's neck for several seconds, and then began yelling at people in the hallway. Lights above the doorway began to flash. Within seconds, bodies began streaming into the room, bringing carts full of equipment with them. A cacophony of voices filled the air as blankets, wrappers, and bits of plastic scattered across the floor.

"Miss, you'll have to wait in the hallway, please."

Iris's rubber legs carried her into the corridor. She watched helplessly through the window, catching only glimpses of Will in between the dozen people working over him. Suddenly, everyone stepped back. His body jerked lifelessly in response to shocks from a defibrillator. Stunned, Iris yelped, both hands over her mouth.

A nurse standing near the window heard, and turned. With a pained look of compassion, he reached up and closed the blinds.

Iris shook. Unable to stand, she slid down the wall until she was seated on the cold linoleum, eyes wide, brain frozen. The yelling inside the room had intensified.

Brennus leaned down and whispered to her.

Without thinking, she grabbed her phone and dialed the first person she thought of. It rang so long, she thought it would go to voicemail.

"Iris? Are you okay?" Grayson's voice was muffled and sleepy. "It's 3 a.m."

"Gray..." her voice shook. "I... I need help. I can't... I can't do this by myself."

"Iris, what do you mean? Where are you?"

"Hospital. ICU."

"What!?" Gray shouted. "Are you okay? What happened?"

Iris took a shaky breath. "It's Will. He's been... shot." The last word was choked.

"Shot?!"

"It wasn't supposed to be him! Not him. He was just... Gray, I need you to pray for him. I don't think I can. I'm not doing it right. Maybe if you…" She fought for control of her voice. "He can't be dying! What am I going to do?"

"Iris, just hang in there, okay? I'm coming. I'll be right there." The line clicked.

Ten minutes later, the noise in Will's room died down. An eery quiet fell. Iris stayed planted to the spot where she'd sunk to the floor. Her heart pounded. One by one, doctors and nurses filed from the room. She couldn't look into their faces, for fear of what she'd see there. At last, the nurse who had closed the blinds looked around. Spotting her on the floor, he knelt beside her.

"I'm so sorry." He spoke just above a whisper.

Iris jerked her head up and searched his face. "For what?"

"He's gone." He touched her shoulder in a gesture of comfort. "Is there anyone we can call for you?"

"What are you talking about?" she demanded.

As the nurse struggled to put an answer together, the last doctor emerged from Will's room, ripped off his latex gloves with a sharp snap, and dashed them to the floor in angry frustration. "What a waste," he muttered, raking his hands through his graying hair. It was then that he noticed Iris on the floor with the nurse beside her, and came to himself, trying to resume a more professional demeanor. "I'm sorry," the doctor said hoarsely, and walked away.

Iris looked back at the nurse, horrified. "No." She rose shakily, leaning on the nurse's strong forearms for support. "He can't be gone."

The nurse gave her the same compassionate look he'd had earlier, as if he'd seen this a thousand times before. But he hadn't seen this one. Not Will. He was one of a kind.

"I need to see him."

"I'm not sure that's a good idea," the nurse began to protest. But at the look on Iris's face, his shoulders sagged. "I guess there's no harm in you sitting with him for a little while… if you're sure you're okay."

Iris nodded numbly. He squeezed her shoulder and left.

She stood motionless in the doorway. The white shrouded form on the bed suddenly seemed monstrous to her, as if it were a priceless work of art that had been slashed apart, threatening even the memory of its former beauty. Still, she forced her feet forward, inch by inch, toward the place once occupied by beeps and whooshes, progress and hope. Only stillness remained.

Will's face was covered, but his hand lay exposed. She slid her fingers into it, feeling its coolness, remembering the first time she'd held it. It had been cool then, too, from a chilly morning drive in his black pickup, blasting classic rock through the stereo on his way to work, as he did every morning. That was the first day he'd told her she was beautiful.

She was overwhelmed with longing to see his face one more time. The nurse's words filled her with dread. She wondered if it really wouldn't be such a good idea. But without further thought, she gingerly tugged the sheet down.

"Oh, Will…" Her face crumpled. He was ashen. The ventilator tube was still taped in place over his mouth. His bare chest was sutured, bruised, bloodied, and covered in wires. She touched his beautiful, perfectly messy brown hair. Still so soft.

"God, what is wrong with you?" she growled, suddenly furious. "Look at him! Is this okay with you?" Her eyes blurred. Her shoulders shook.

A few moments later, Iris felt a presence beside her. She could smell the faint scent of Gray's cologne at the same time she felt his hand on her shoulder.

"Oh, no," he murmured, gazing at Will. "When?"

"About twenty minutes ago." She clung to Will's hand, though it had grown colder.

"I'm so sorry, Iris."

"He was protecting me," she said dully. "The gun was aimed at me, and he saved my life." She stroked Will's arm. "He was only twenty-three, Gray. Twenty. Three. He's saved me over and over. He's supposed to be in my life. I need him. And now he's gone." Hot tears sprang forward again. "He's gone, while that animal is out there, still alive, roaming around!"

Gray stood by her for a long time, warming her with his presence, helping her feel safer. In the brief moment she glanced at him, she could see tears in his eyes. She could hear him once in a while, whispering under his breath, but she couldn't make out his words.

Suddenly, Gray removed his hand from her shoulder and took several steps back. Iris turned to look. Gray was standing very still, eyes closed, resting his hand against Will's shrouded ankle.

"Grayson, what are you doing?" Iris asked bleakly.

"I'm not exactly sure," he answered, eyes still closed. "Just… listening."

Iris frowned. "Listening?"

"Yes," Gray whispered, bowing his head. "I feel the strongest impression right now, and I just… I want to make sure I heard right."

Iris shook her head, battling anger. She thought Gray was here for support, but now he was acting weird… almost disrespectful.

Gray opened his eyes and raised his face to look at her, his expression filled with awe. He turned to Will, and spoke without hesitation in a strong, confident voice.

"Father, I ask that this man's life be returned to him. Death, you are not welcome here today. Will Donovan does not belong to you."

Overhead, a malevolent fog streaked skyward, screaming curses.

Iris gasped. *Was that…* She looked down at Will's hand. It twitched. She looked up at Gray. He was smiling, full of assurance.

Will inhaled and coughed. Iris shrieked, covering her mouth. She stared intently at Will. He was still once again.

Gray rested his hand against Will's chest. "Heart," he said calmly, "you will beat now. Get to work." He laid his other hand against Will's neck, waiting. Listening. He closed his eyes. Moments later, he nodded, a smile spreading across his bearded face.

Will's chest began to rise and fall in tiny, shallow breaths.

Gray stepped back. "I think he'll wake up soon."

Iris was still covering her mouth, eyes wide. She grabbed Will's wrist and pressed it with her fingers. His pulse was slow, but steady. She let out a hoarse laugh, bewildered.

"What did you do?" she cried.

"I was told to pray for his life, so I did," Gray replied matter-of-factly.

"That's it?"

"That's it."

A nurse approached the room, followed by someone from the coroner's office who was conversing quietly with her about examining the "male murder victim." They stopped short just inside the doorway, taking in the silent monitors, the mess on the floor, and the exuberant faces of the two people standing beside the bed.

Will's hand fluttered again.

Iris squeezed it, smiling at the nurse. "He's waking up!"

The nurse's face grew concerned. "Hon, I'm sorry, but... he's gone. Sometimes, the body—"

"No," Iris interrupted. "Feel his pulse."

The nurse cast a sad glance back at the coroner, and approached. Her face lit with a different expression when she saw the color beginning to return to Will's face and hands. She felt his carotid artery. Her eyes widened. "But that's impossible... he was... How can his heart be beating? There was almost nothing left!"

Will frowned. His breathing began to speed up, coming in short, shaky gasps through his nose. Eyes still closed, he whimpered. His hands tightened against the sheets, clutching handfuls of fabric.

Iris grew alarmed. "What's happening? What's he doing?"

The nurse shook her head, trying to open one of Will's eyelids to shine a light on his pupil. "I don't know," she admitted. "I've never seen this. It's not a seizure. I don't think he's fully conscious, but it looks like he's… panicking."

Will arched his back and began to moan in earnest. The nurse stuck her pen light back into her pocket and gently pressed his shoulder.

"Will? Are you with us, buddy? Are you in pain?"

Will tried to cry out, which made him cough and gag on the tube in his throat. He clawed at the tape around his mouth as tears streamed down his face.

The nurse slammed her fist against a button on the wall, yelling for help. Two more nurses appeared, a man and a woman.

"We need to extubate him, stat, or he's going to do it for us!"

The two newer nurses each steadied one of Will's thrashing legs. "Isn't this the guy that died an hour ago?" one of them asked.

"Yep," said the first nurse, doing her best to insert a small suction tube into a moving target.

"But I thought his spine was—"

"Clearly not!" This time she managed to insert the suction tube in the right spot. "I don't know any more than you do right now, okay? Except he's back, he's breathing well, and he's not too happy at the moment."

"Should we push some lorazepam?"

"Well, given the fact that I didn't memorize his chart…" she pulled the suction tube and began trying to loosen the strap behind Will's neck, "I don't know what or how much he's already got on board, so let's just do this the old fashioned way, okay? He's a big kid, but we've got him outnumbered."

Will gagged and coughed again, thrashing against the nurses holding his feet.

Iris had shrunk against the back wall of the room, her joy melting away into cold fear. Even Grayson's reassuring arm around her did nothing to mitigate her dread.

"I've never seen him like this," she whispered to Gray.

He squeezed her shoulder. "He's been through a lot," he said, trying to comfort her.

"But…" Iris's eyes widened as she watched the nurse, who was now chasing Will's bloody arm with a large padded bandage, attempting to stop the bleeding from the site where he'd just managed to yank out his IV.

"I need a little more help in here!" she yelled, catching his wrist and pressing the bandage into place.

Another nurse rushed in.

"Don't ask, just hold his hands down for me."

He obeyed, looking at Will in wide-eyed amazement.

After another minute of struggle, the tube came out. The moment it did, Will vomited. The nurse in charge had anticipated that, and was ready with a pan.

Eyes still closed, Will screamed. Deep, wrenching sobs tore from his already lacerated throat, filling the ward with the sound of otherworldly anguish.

Iris couldn't take any more. She didn't know what would happen next, but she couldn't just stand and watch. She rushed to Will's side and touched his arm. He snatched it away as if she'd scalded him.

"Will, I'm here," she soothed. "It's me." She tried again.

This time he let her touch him, and quieted to whimpered sobs.

She stroked his face, his hair. "Shh. I'm right here."

Will's face still held its pained expression while the tears continued, but he was responding to her.

The nurse looked on approvingly. "I'll page a doc. Let's give him a minute. Then we'll have to figure out what's going on here." She signaled the others, who left with a nod.

Grayson stepped forward. "Well, I think that's my cue, too."

"Wait, where are you going?" Iris objected. She stepped toward the doorway where Gray stood and spoke in a hushed tone. "What if I need you?"

Gray smiled. "Iris, *he* needs you," he whispered. "I'm a stranger to him. Let's not complicate things for him. Besides, you're not alone here. Your guardians are right over there keeping watch." He pointed.

"You really see someone?" Iris gasped, turning to stare at the empty corner.

Brennus smiled. Aimsir nodded. Varick crossed his arms.

"I sense them," Gray said. "Everything's going to be okay."

She squeezed his arm. "Thank you for being here. I don't even know what to say, or how to thank you for what you did... for Will."

"It's God you should be thanking. Looks like He's not done with Will yet." He looked back into the room at Will's tormented face, and his brow knit with concern. "I have a feeling that things are going to be very different for him from now on. Try to be patient with him." He attempted a final reassuring smile, and left.

Iris turned back to Will. His tears had slowed, but his face was still anguished. She bent and pressed her lips to his forehead, staying close so he could feel her presence. She rested her hand against his damp cheek, wiping the tears that trickled down.

"Will, where are you?" she murmured.

His forehead knit with despair, and he let out a long, shuddering sigh.

Iris lay on the bed beside him and hugged his arm. "Come back to me," she whispered.

He turned his face toward her and lifted a hand to touch her cheek.

"There, see? It's me." she reassured him. "Open your eyes."

For the first time, he spoke. "I can't." His voice sounded like gravel.

"Why not?"

"Because." He pulled her closer, until their foreheads touched, and struggled to hold back a fresh wave of tears. "I'm so scared this isn't real."

Chapter 19

Will had finally fallen into an exhausted sleep. He'd been hooked back up to the monitors and gotten a new IV. A doctor had pulled his chart, written whatever the medical term was for "never mind" across his death certificate, and straightened out the question of which drugs he was allowed to have. He thought it best to give Will a sedative, since his behavior had been so unpredictable. His entire medical team wanted to give him a full workup and take new images of his heart, but his current psychological state was making it impossible. Restraining him only made him more agitated. He seemed to do best either asleep or with Iris close by.

Shortly after Will fell asleep, the first nurse who had helped remove his breathing tube came back.

"Do you need to get some rest, hon?" she asked Iris. "He should be out for awhile."

Iris was numb with fatigue, but afraid to go anywhere. "No, I'm okay."

"Well…" The nurse tilted her head and looked Iris over with a doubtful expression. "All the same, that chair reclines. Maybe you could inspect your eyelids for a few minutes while we take him for some tests. Shouldn't be long. I'm just going to clean him up a little and get him a fresh gown."

"Okay. Thank you." Iris tried to settle into the chair, but couldn't get her eyes to close. She decided instead to watch the nurse, who gently cleaned Will's face with a damp cloth and wiped the dried blood off his arm.

As she began to pull the wire leads away from his chest, she gasped. "What the?"

Iris felt a stab of fear. "What's going on?"

"Um…" A frown crossed the nurse's face as she touched the left side of Will's ribcage. "There's supposed to be about a twelve centimeter incision right here, from the… Huh. Maybe it's…" She checked his right side and frowned again.

Iris rose and stood beside the nurse. "You mean from his surgery? It's not there?" she asked.

"Yeah… I mean, I think…" She grabbed his chart and flipped through it. "Yeah, it's right here. Penetrating thoracic trauma, emergency left resuscitative thoracotomy," she muttered, then looked at Iris. "This *is* your boyfriend, right? Same guy?"

Iris looked at her like she'd lost her mind. "Of course he is!"

The nurse yanked her pen light from her pocket and shined it directly on Will's side. "Oh, wait a minute…" She wiped a few smudges of dried blood from the area with the washcloth. "There it is. It's exactly where it should be, but it's… completely healed over. How is…" She stared at the curved scar, utterly bewildered. "Has he ever had this kind of surgery before?"

Iris shook her head. "No, I'm pretty sure he hasn't."

"Huh." The nurse rested the heel of her gloved hand on the bed rail, deep in thought. She reached forward and touched a spot on Will's chest, also light pink and barely noticeable. "There's the entry wound."

Iris's mind spun. She couldn't get over the similarity between these scars and the one on her leg.

The nurse continued her work, still wearing a dumbfounded expression. She rolled Will slightly to one side to pull his bloodstained gown free.

"What have we here?" She reached down and picked up something that had been on the bed behind Will's back.

It was a bullet.

Iris listened to the rhythmic beep of the heart monitor as she breathed steadily in sync with the rise and fall of Will's chest. The nurses had brought him back from his tests with an inexplicably clean bill of health, and he was still sleeping off the sedatives they'd given him. She lay next to him with one arm over his chest, just in case he could subconsciously feel her presence.

The nurses had finally convinced Iris that Will was in no more danger of dying than she was, and that she had time to go home and shower before he awoke. But she'd ridden here in a police car, and Will's truck was still parked outside the restaurant where they'd had their last meal together the night before. Besides, the thought of getting a ride home and then driving back in her state of blind exhaustion seemed not only difficult, but dangerous.

She drifted in and out of sleep. Here, she was at peace, content in the knowledge that she would be the first to know when Will awoke, and hers would be the first face he saw.

Her mind floated away to the eastern shore of Scotland, to her little home village, where one of the best friends she'd ever known was now buried… where he had saved her life almost two hundred years ago, and then they had shared a meal at the pub. And somehow, he had known she would need him again.

"Life is fragile, but God is not."

She could almost hear Angus's voice speaking the words that had come to her at the perfect time.

"You can trust a God whose specialty is the impossible. Remember that, my dear friend."

Though she was half asleep, a tear slipped from her eye and soaked into Will's sleeve.

"God, I trust you," she whispered. "I know you didn't do this to him. You brought him back to me."

After another hour of solid sleep, Iris felt a change in Will's breathing and drifted back to consciousness. As he began to breathe more deeply and deliberately, Iris worried that he might panic again, so she found his hand resting next to her and held it tenderly.

"Will?"

He took a long, steady breath and lightly squeezed her hand.

"Everything's okay," she murmured. "I'm here."

He turned his head toward her, and after several moments of struggle, opened his eyes halfway.

"There you are." She spoke softly, careful not to startle him.

"It's really you," he said in a hoarse whisper.

"Of course."

"I thought I'd never..." He made a sound like a soft hiccup. "I thought I'd never see you again."

"I thought the same about you," she replied, fighting tears.

"The pain..." he said groggily.

"Oh, do you need something for—"

"It's gone." He frowned slightly, and then sighed. "There's no more pain."

Iris breathed more easily, relieved.

Will relaxed, still sleepy, but Iris could tell he was trying to stay awake. Finally, he spoke again. "Why are you here? I mean... why are we..." He frowned again. "Where is this?"

"Do you remember anything that happened?"

He tensed. "I... I can't. I can't talk about that," he said, squeezing his eyes shut. "Please... just... tell me where I am now."

"You're in the hospital." She caressed his stubbled face, trying to soothe away the look of fear that had returned.

"Are you sure?"

"Yes, of course. I've been here with you the whole time."

He opened his eyes again, a little more this time, and studied her face. He took in his surroundings for the first time. "Okay…" He nodded. "Okay. I just…" He closed his eyes again and let out a shaky sigh. "God, I can't believe this is happening."

"What?" Iris was getting worried at how out of touch he seemed.

He looked at her for a long moment. "That I'm *here*."

"Well, you *are*. You're here with me." She pressed his cheek with her hand and rested her forehead against his. "I love you, Will. I'm so glad I didn't lose you."

"And I love you." He put his hand over hers, and shuddered. "I do." He looked at her with desperation. "But it's no good. I… I've never been so… *lost*."

"What do you mean, lost?"

"They're still here." His eyes moved slowly, warily around the room and then closed again. He gritted his teeth. "What are they waiting for?"

Iris looked around. She felt a chill. "Who?"

Will just shook his head.

A nurse walked in with a styrofoam cup of ice chips and another with water. He looked at the monitors, then at Will.

"Nice to see you awake," he said, offering a friendly smile as he set the cups on the bedside tray. "I brought you something to sip on. I'm sure your throat hurts a little, but I want you to try, okay? If we can get you hydrating on your own, then you can go home pretty soon."

Will sat up slowly. He didn't look at the nurse, but nodded and chose a cup.

Iris stood and gave the nurse a pointed look, tilting her head toward the door. "I'll be right back okay?" she said to Will.

He nodded again.

When she and the nurse had stepped into the hall, she spoke bluntly. "Why is he seeing things?"

"Sorry?"

"He says he sees… something. In there. Does he have something wrong with his brain?"

"That could be the medication," the nurse said, with a look of mild concern. "It's not super common, but hallucinations are on the list of side effects."

Iris let out her breath. "So that's all it is? Just a side effect?"

"Probably." The nurse checked his watch. "He hasn't had a dose for about six hours, though. So whatever it is, he probably won't see it much longer. I can page a doctor if you're really concerned about it."

There was a small crash inside the room.

Iris and the nurse both peered through the doorway. Will was staring at the empty chair beside his bed. He'd just thrown his cup of ice at it.

"Yeah, let's let those meds wear off and then we'll see where we're at, okay?" whispered the nurse. "I'll make a note that he's having an adverse reaction. And I'll call housekeeping."

Iris nodded at him and rushed back to Will. "You okay? What happened?"

Will looked up at her, then back to the chair, and up at her again. "Am I crazy?"

"No, you're definitely not," she said as confidently as she could manage.

"There was a… a black… shadow. With glowing eyes. It was just… *sitting* there a second ago," Will said just above a whisper, as if he were afraid of being overheard.

"Will, no… it was—"

"It said, 'You won't get away that easy.'" His expression was bleak.

Iris felt another chill. "The nurse said you might be having a reaction to the drugs they gave you for sleep," she explained, despite her misgivings. "You'll be back to normal really soon."

Will leaned back on the pillow and stared at the wall. "No. I won't."

Will seemed unable to rest again after that. He spent most of his time gazing at his blankets and fighting sleep, unwilling to close his eyes. Iris stayed near him, hoping that her presence would comfort him, but every time his eyes came to rest on her, he looked worried.

When a police detective came to question her about the shooting, Will barely noticed. She stepped out of the room and spoke with him in the hallway. Although Detective Coleman was compassionate, his questions were methodical and businesslike. He took her statement about the previous night and asked followup questions about the incident that led to her taking out a restraining order. She told him everything she could think of, except the part about Will giving Brett a knee to the stomach.

He pulled out a laptop and showed her some surveillance footage of a man walking down a dark alley, and asked whether it was Brett. Iris recognized his gait and his long coat, but couldn't see his face. The detective clearly wasn't satisfied with that. But he seemed to cheer up when Iris remembered from seeing Brett cook, and hearing him brag about it, that he was ambidextrous. He could still have fired a gun with his other hand, despite the fact that he was likely walking around with a few broken fingers. He put the misshapen bullet from Will's bed into an evidence bag, and then handed her a card with his direct number on it and told her to call if she thought of anything else. He gave her what she assumed must be the customary assurances that he was doing everything he could, and promised he would follow up with her soon.

Iris felt drained. She wished she'd never met Brett. The man was a walking nightmare. Would she ever feel safe again? She looked through the window at Will, who still sat motionless.

Anger flared up in her again. *How is it fair for someone like Will to get caught up in this?*

She approached his bedside. "Will?"

He jumped. His bloodshot eyes darted around the room, and finally came to rest on her face.

"Sorry, it's just me," she whispered.

"I don't like it here," he said in a hoarse voice. "Maybe I should just get home."

She nodded. "Maybe. The doctor just wants to see you acting more like yourself, y'know? So they can be sure all the drugs are out of your system before they release you. How do you... feel like that's going? Are you still... y'know, seeing... things?"

He frowned and glanced around the room again. His eyes lingered on one corner for a moment before he looked back at her. "No, I'm not." He stared at the blanket again. "I'm fine."

She squinted. *Did he actually just lie to me?*

"Well, if you really want to get out of here, I can call a nurse and see what they think."

He nodded.

To her surprise, they agreed to release Will within a few hours. Despite his strange behavior, they had no medical reason to keep him. His tests were clear, his vitals were strong. He was mentally responsive, and didn't pose a danger to himself or others. Being terrified was not a valid medical reason to stay. One nurse did offer him a pamphlet about PTSD, which he didn't even glance at, and recommended that he seek counseling, before she bustled off to gather his final paperwork.

There was a timid knock at the door. A teenage hospital volunteer stood in the doorway holding a brown bag. "This was just dropped off for you out front," she explained.

Iris took it and thanked her. The girl flashed a grin full of braces and disappeared.

Inside the bag were a couple of sandwiches—turkey, bacon, muenster, and tomato on sourdough—Jason's signature. Beneath them lay a clean t-shirt and a pair of blue sweatpants. Iris was touched. Will's clothes were trashed. She hadn't even considered what he would wear home. Now she didn't have to. *What would I do without those two?*

"Will, would you like a sandwich?" she offered.

He looked at her like he was trying to translate a foreign language.

She held one up and smiled. "Turkey and bacon!"

"I think I probably *should* want that," he said absently. "Right?"

Iris came back to the bed and sat on the edge of the mattress. "Well, there aren't any hard and fast rules about wanting sandwiches," she said. "But you must be getting hungry."

"I just don't see the point."

Iris felt the weight of his words on her chest. She touched his arm. "Maybe later, okay?"

"Yeah. Maybe."

She stood and rummaged in the plastic bag that contained what was left of his personal belongings until she found his keys. "I'm going to go get your truck, okay?" She fished out his phone, turned it back on, and slipped it into his hand. "I'll be right back. There are some comfy clothes for you in that bag there. Might feel nice to put those on, huh?"

"Probably."

Will's phone began playing "Danger Zone" in his hand. He jumped again, but made no move to answer it.

"Will, should I…" she asked.

He shoved the phone away.

She snatched it off the bed. The screen said "Skywalker."

"Hello? Will's phone," she said.

There was a pause on the other end. "Uh… hi. This is Luke Donovan, I'm Will's brother. I'm guessing this must be Iris?"

"Hi Luke. Yes it is." She pressed the button to put him on speaker so Will could hear.

"Can you tell me what's going on? I got a Red Cross message that Will's been shot. Now I got another message saying he's just fine. Which one is it? I'm kinda freaking out, here."

"Um… it's kind of… both?"

"Iris." Luke let out a long breath. "Is my brother alive?"

"Yes, he's alive."

"Look, I'm in Singapore right now. I got offered emergency leave, but I gotta know if he needs me to come home, otherwise I'm back on a COD. I got ten minutes to decide. Tell me what he needs me to do."

Iris looked at Will, who was fighting tears again. With a tender pleading on her face, she offered him the phone.

Reluctantly, he accepted it. "Hey, buddy."

"Will! Holy crap! Are you okay? I've been so worried! You weren't answering your phone!"

Will took a deep breath, struggling to keep his voice even. "Yeah, sorry about that, they made me sleep a bunch. Listen, they think I'll be out of the hospital in a couple hours. I can handle things here, okay?"

"Are you sure? Geez, I thought you might be dead!"

Tears fell, but Will kept his voice cool. "Nah, I'm good. But it's great to hear your voice, bud."

"Yours, too. I'm glad you're okay. You sure you don't need me to come home?"

"Do your thing, Skywalker. I'll see you in the summertime anyway. That's not too far away, right?"

"Right."

"I'll email you, okay?"

"Love you, Obi-Wan."

"Love you too," Will whispered, pressed the red button, and rested the phone against his chest.

"Will," Iris said softly. "Why didn't you want Luke to come?"

He looked as if his heart had broken. "He can't see me like this. I'm all he's got."

"Oh, Will." Iris let out a breath and touched his arm. "Try to eat, okay? I'll be right back to take you home."

He nodded.

She kissed his temple and left.

As she made her way through the lobby, Iris unlocked her phone and tried to decide which ride sharing app to use.

"Hey, you," said a voice off to her left.

She stopped. "Jason! Oh my gosh, you're here!"

"Yeah, after I dropped off the bag, I kinda thought I'd hang out and pray for a bit. Looks like you're headed out. Do you need a ride?"

"Actually, that would be amazing. I was going to pick up Will's truck from where we left it last night."

He stood. "No problem, let's go."

They headed through the double doors into the sunny afternoon.

"I really appreciate you coming, Jason. The stuff you brought..." Iris felt strangely emotional, but held back. "It was just really thoughtful."

"Oh, I'm happy I could help. Couldn't really get it out of my head this morning."

"I'm glad you stayed, too."

"Couldn't get that out of my head, either!" he said. "It's getting a little crazy up in that room."

Iris gazed at him in awe. "How... how do you know that?"

"Oh, y'know..." Jason smiled. "*He* knows everything."

They got into his car and buckled in. Iris pulled up the location she needed on her phone and stuck it on Jason's dash mount before settling into her seat, face grim.

"Will's acting so weird, Jason. He's looking around all the time, saying he sees black shadows and glowing eyes. I offered him one of your sandwiches and he said he doesn't see the point! I'm really scared for him. It's like he's living in an alternate reality."

Jason considered that, brows knit with concentration, then looked at her with a grave expression. "Iris, he's not living in an alternate reality. It's more like *we* are."

"What are you talking about? He's… seeing things!"

"Yes, he's seeing things. That doesn't mean the things he's seeing aren't really there. Given that he left the physical world not even twelve hours ago, it shouldn't surprise us."

Iris gasped. "You mean there really are monsters or… evil beings in there with him? Talking to him?"

"I wouldn't doubt it. You think they *like* the fact that he's living proof that death doesn't always get to win?"

"But…" She shook her head. "Is he going to be okay?"

"Yeah. Definitely." Jason said. He pulled onto the main road and settled into a comfortable speed before continuing. "There's a powerful purpose at work here. But there's also a real tension in that room… like… a standoff. It's almost like no one has permission to move yet."

Iris nodded, mystified. "Will said, 'What are they waiting for?' But I sure didn't see anything going on in there. How could *you* tell from the lobby? Is that a Guardian thing?"

"No," Jason replied, "it's not a Guardian thing. It's part of your inheritance, too. It's not all the time, but there are certain times we have to become more aware of what we're dealing with. I know it took you a little while to realize that the good parts of the Histories are still happening today. You need to understand that a lot of the bad parts are, too."

She stared out the window, processing his words. "Was Brett…" she trailed off, unable to decide what her actual question was.

Jason glanced at her. "He may have had a little help, yeah."

Her mouth fell open. "You mean it's not just Brett that's after Will?"

Jason frowned. "It's not just Brett, and it's not just Will he's after. Gray told me he was aiming at *you*. Isn't that what you said?"

"Yeah…"

Jason stopped at a red light and looked at her. "Iris, this isn't just some petty vendetta or bad luck. It was an assassination attempt."

"But… why?"

"You've become a threat. You have a uniquely important role to fulfill, and you understand who you are. There's nothing the enemy hates more than that. His main focus is stealing from God's people, destroying God's work, and killing whatever he can get his hands on."

"You're kind of scaring me."

He shook his head. "I'm not trying to scare you. But you should know what you're up against. Still…" He smiled. "It's not all bad. You're rolling with some big guns."

"Big guns?"

"C'mon. The Spirit inside you—'God without a body,' as you called Him? All that authority He gave you, along with every promise He's made? Plus some spirit guardians. Big ones."

"Really?"

"Oh yeah." The light changed, and Jason drove on. "Check the book, it's all in there. It's like having a badge and a gun, and serious backup. He doesn't expect you to handle it all by yourself, but He does expect you to handle it."

"But… I'm not even sure what I'm supposed to do!"

"Just stay close to Him where it's safe. He'll show you what to do. Go back and read how He handled Himself while He was here. But most of all, remember who you serve. He's already won. His enemies are like mosquitoes compared to Him. They get a little spooky sometimes, but they're liars. They're not even creative at all… they can only take what's there and distort it. Just know your stuff, and you'll spot it."

Iris's face filled with concern. "I feel like I barely know anything, though."

"Read through the Histories again, especially the newer part," he suggested.

"I've already read the whole thing!"

He chuckled. "I know. But that was when you thought you were reading a wonderful story about days gone by. Read it again, and it'll hit you in a totally different way. The Spirit will tell you what it means. Don't look for formulas, just be with Him in it, and He'll meet you there."

"Is that what you do?"

"Every day."

"Is that how you specifically knew to bring clothes and two turkey sandwiches?" She gave him a wry smile. "I don't remember reading that part."

Jason laughed. "Actually, that's exactly how I knew! It was a combination of 'I was sick and you visited me' and 'do for others what you would have them do for you.' Me personally? I'd want one of those sandwiches, and I wouldn't want to share. And, I'd want to ride home without my butt in the breeze. So there you go."

Iris shook her head and laughed.

After another few minutes, they pulled into the little historic district where she and Will had parked the night before. Iris could see Will's truck a block away. What she saw next made her catch her breath.

"Jason, stop!"

He slowed way down and swung into the nearest slanted parking space along the street. "What are we doing?"

"You've gotta be kidding me…" Iris mumbled as she strained her eyes ahead, staring at a figure on the sidewalk down the block. Brett was leaning lazily against the building, smoking, and glancing around him occasionally.

Jason followed her gaze. "That can't be *him*," he said incredulously.

Iris gave him an ominous nod and pulled out her phone. "I had no idea he was this stupid, though…" She dialed the number from Detective Coleman's card.

Jason looked back at Brett and squinted. "Uh, I don't think he's totally under his own power right now. I think he might be waiting for you."

Iris's heart leaped as she listened to the phone ring.

"Coleman."

"Hi Detective, it's Iris Jacobs. We spoke at the hospital earlier?"

"Hi, Iris. Anything new?"

"How about a perpetrator? I'm looking right at him."

"What? Where are you? Are you safe?"

"Yes. I'm in a car he doesn't know. I came back to get the truck and he's right next to it."

"He's… he's at the scene of the shooting? Right now?"

"Yeah."

"Idiot. Okay, stay put. Don't approach him. I'll get down there." He hung up.

"I can't believe this," she murmured.

Jason's face was concerned, but confident. "I sort of can. Usually the tactics are more subtle, but this…" He looked back at Brett, shaking his head. "You're clearly in the way of something big, if they're willing to be this open about it."

Iris looked at Jason, wide-eyed.

"Don't be afraid." He gave her arm a gentle squeeze. "It's not going to work."

They watched Brett for another minute. He flicked his cigarette into the gutter and began to shuffle toward them. He seemed to walk aimlessly at first, but as he drew closer, his jaw clenched and his face grew malevolent.

Iris plastered her back to the seat, hoping to make herself invisible, but Brett locked eyes with her and grinned. He stopped on the sidewalk in front of Jason's car.

"Iris!" he shouted, arms wide. "How many boyfriends you got, anyway? Dang, girl! This one's way too old for you!"

Iris felt her insides coil with dread.

"Don't be afraid," Jason said again.

"How's the other guy?" Brett yelled. "Did he ever get that leak fixed?"

Iris's eyes welled with angry tears.

People on the sidewalk began to cast awkward glances in his direction. A few pointed and whispered.

Brett bent at the waist and peered through the windshield at her. "Do you think dumb luck and a few felonies makes you good enough to run with Guardians?" he growled in a strange voice.

Panic filled Iris's face. "How does he…" she whispered.

Jason calmly unbuckled his seatbelt and opened his door.

"Jason, no! What are you doing?"

Jason planted his feet and looked calmly at Brett.

Brett sneered. "So what are you, her watchdog? Lap dog? Some kind of—"

"Shhhh." Jason held up his hand. "Quiet."

Brett opened his mouth to continue, but coughed instead. A look of rage came over him. He clenched his fists, staring with steely eyes as his breath came in heavy puffs through his nostrils.

"You will answer my question truthfully," Jason commanded in a sure, even tone. "Why do you seek this woman's life?"

Brett's voice came out half an octave lower. "She protects a man beyond his time. She must fail." He grinned. "More are coming. The Guardians will be taken and the Great Tree will be revealed."

"That's enough."

He fell silent, but his grin only widened. He reached behind him and pulled out the same gun he'd used last night.

"Bind his hands and feet, please," Jason said calmly.

Within seconds, Brett lost his grip on the gun, which clattered to the sidewalk, and his feet slid backward until his back was against the building behind him. Though he struggled, he was unable to pull his wrists or ankles away from the wall.

"Thanks, guys," Jason said, not taking his eyes from Brett. "You're a lot safer right there," he told him. "You go pointing a gun at people with cops on the way, you're going to get yourself shot."

Brett spat at him, but Jason dodged it.

Iris opened her car door and stood behind it, watching with horrified fascination.

"Now," Jason said. "I'm going to send you away from this man, but before I do, I warn you not to get any big ideas. I command you to go to the driest uninhabited desert you can possibly find, and park yourself there. You will avoid living things from now on. Got it?"

Brett bared his teeth and growled.

"Answer me."

"I got it," he seethed.

"Then go."

Brett's body arched and then crumpled to the pavement.

By now, a small circle of onlookers had gathered, whispering.

Panting, Brett looked up at Jason with a vacant stare. "Who *are* you, anyway?" he asked, his voice back to normal.

"Yeah, man, who are you?" said a bystander.

Jason looked around at their faces and replied with a half smile, "I'm a Tree Guardian, everyone! We were once thought to be legends, but now you've seen one in the flesh. Make sure you tell the next person you meet!"

The onlookers exchanged befuddled looks and dispersed, murmuring to each other.

One woman unlocked the car next to Iris and opened the door to get in. "Do *you* know who that guy is?"

Iris pointed at Jason. "That guy?"

"Yeah, he just said he's… he's a…"

"A what?"

"Hmm?"

Iris frowned at the woman. "You were just talking about that guy over there."

"No, I wasn't." She gave Iris a final confused look, got in her car, and drove away.

Suddenly, two squad cars approached with a squawk and wail of sirens. Brett's head snapped up. A look of panic swept his face.

"I think your ride's here," Jason commented.

Brett scrambled to his feet, grabbed his gun, and sprinted toward the street.

"No! don't—" Jason called after him.

There was a screech of tires and a sickening thud.

Iris gasped.

The police officers who had just arrived ran toward the sound amidst confused shouts.

"Oh no…" Jason moaned. "Please give him more time!" he said, and dashed after him.

In shock, Iris followed.

Jason was already kneeling beside Brett, whose face was bloodied. His arm rested at an unnatural angle. Jason's hand gently cradled Brett's head as he spoke softly to him for several moments. Brett looked at Jason for a long time, and then whispered "yes," before closing his eyes and exhaling for the last time.

Jason bowed his head for several seconds, then stood to make way for the EMTs.

Iris caught his eye, a question in her face.

Jason shook his head.

Iris was both relieved, and ashamed for feeling so relieved.

They sat on the curb, still in shock.

"He's safe now," Jason finally said.

"Didn't he just die?"

Jason nodded. "Yes. But he died alive."

Chapter 20

I ris opened her eyes and blinked at the sunlight shining through her window. She checked her watch and thought very hard, trying to decide what day it was. Finally, she remembered the last lucid thing she'd done before falling into bed—she had emailed Candace to call in sick for Monday. Which was now. And it was ten in the morning. She'd been asleep for thirteen straight hours.

She had driven Will home yesterday evening and made sure he had his phone charged and all of his favorite ingredients in his kitchen before she left. Even though she'd offered to keep him company for a bit, the way he'd been there for her the other night, he had shooed her home, urging her to just take care of herself.

I'm still not sure that was a good idea. He looked so… strange.

He had even started speaking to her in that same overly brave, placating tone he had used with Luke on the phone. He must've thought she'd believe him and go skipping merrily away if he gave her a convincing enough demonstration of how much better he was doing. But what could she do? Refuse to get off his couch? He was a grown man. He probably just needed some space to work through everything.

She checked her phone. There was one group text from Jason and Gray:

(J) How are you and Will doing today?
(G) Let us know what you need. That's an order.

She replied:

Don't know yet about Will. He's home. Thanks so much, guys. I'll let you know.

While it had been nice to get cleaned up and sleep in her own bed, she felt strange about being away from Will—almost as if she had somehow put him in danger by leaving. But that couldn't be. Brett was gone. Will's body was completely healthy. He was independent and capable. If he could raise a kid five years younger than himself and protect her when she was afraid, he could certainly take a shower, make himself dinner, and get some sleep. Still, she sent him a text to ask how he was doing. She'd know soon. He never took longer than a few minutes to reply.

She went to her computer and pulled up her email. Gabe Iwila had replied to her message two days ago. *Oh man, he's probably starting to wonder where I've been.* She clicked the link.

From: Gabriel Iwila, Sedona AZ
To: Iris Jacobs
Cc: Grayson Reynolds

Sweet! Yeah, I'm up for a field trip. I'm driving Jeep tours all day Monday thru Wednesday this week but after that, totally. Ben, my dad, is around a lot anyway now. It's been weird here lately—this past week we've had so many hikers, campers, and trippy hippies coming around that I've really needed the backup. I don't expect Danny to fend them all off. He's only ten. I'm starting to wonder if our little valley ended up on a tourist website by mistake or something. I hate to pile more research on you, but if you uncover any rumors about that, I'd love to get to the bottom of it and put a stop to it. It's getting a little stressful. Let me know when to expect you and I'll pick you guys up from the airport.

Best, Gabe

Iris frowned. Why were the Iwilas suddenly seeing increased traffic? Is that what Brett—or the creature using his voice—had meant by "The Guardians will be taken and the Great Tree will be revealed"? If there was some kind of plot to get rid of Ben, Gabe, and Danny and expose their Tree for what it really was, why did that mean *she* would have to fail?

She sent Gabe a quick reply:

> *Gabe, be careful. I don't think it's a tourist website that's bringing people. I heard it first hand from one of the dark ones that you're being targeted, and so am I. The goal is total exposure through the failure of this mission, but I haven't put the pieces together yet. I'll figure out flights and send you a time soon, but let's shoot for Thursday. —Iris*

She checked her phone again. Will still hadn't replied. That wasn't like him. She dialed his number. It rang until his voicemail picked up. She tried again, two more times, with the same result.

Maybe he's asleep… No. At ten thirty? Will's a morning person. Maybe… Hm.

Something just didn't feel right. She slipped into shoes and a sweater, grabbed her purse, and headed out the door.

In less than ten minutes, Iris pulled into an unmarked space next to Will's apartment. His truck was right where she'd left it. She knocked on his door.

No response.

She knocked harder. "Will?"

Nothing.

She dialed his number again. A moment later, she could hear a tinny, indistinguishable ringtone playing inside. *So he's in there, and his ringer's up.* Her concern morphed into dread.

"Will!" She banged again.

Ten long, quiet seconds passed. Then she heard the sound of the deadbolt sliding slowly out of the door jamb. She watched the knob turn at the same agonizing pace, until the door opened one inch and stood still.

Expecting to see Will standing just behind the door, she spoke more softly. "Will, are you okay?" She pushed the door open several more inches. "Why weren't you answering your—" She frowned. Will wasn't there. He wasn't even in the living room. The apartment was dark, shades drawn.

Iris pushed the door the rest of the way open. "Hello?"

The moment she stepped inside, a sick sensation of dread descended on her like a wave. With great effort, she moved forward, leaving the door open behind her.

"Will?"

She passed through the living room, her apprehension deepening. She peered into the kitchen. Only the light over the cooktop was on, but it illuminated the bizarre sight of a shattered ceramic mug lying on the floor beside a box of tea bags and a spent fire extinguisher on its side. The floor, wall, stove, and steel kettle were covered in a layer of white powder.

"Please," croaked a voice. "Please just stop this."

Iris whirled around to see Will standing in the dim hallway. His face was haggard, filled with desperation. He had three days' worth of stubble, and dark circles ringed his eyes. He still wore the same t-shirt and blue sweatpants, and stood as if his tall frame were sagging under some invisible weight.

"Will, what's going on?" Iris cried.

He didn't move. He just stared at her with vacant horror.

She stepped toward him, but he backed away.

"Why show me *her*?" he growled. "Anyone but her!"

The front door slammed shut.

Razor sharp fear stabbed through her like ice.

Her voice shook. "Will, what's happening in here?"

His face distorted and he let out a choked sob. "You sound just like her," he murmured.

"It *is* me!" She stepped toward him faster than he could retreat.

"Get away!" he yelled, his back pressed against the wall in the hallway. "Not again!"

"It's really me, okay?" she said softly, reaching for his hand.

When she made contact, his expression cleared a little. He slid to the floor. She knelt beside him. His breathing was unsteady, leaving small wisps of vapor in the air between them. Iris felt a cold breeze across her face.

"They said they killed you," he whispered.

"Who?" She could see her own breath now.

Will looked past her, then above him. "Them."

"Well, they lied to you."

"It's really you?"

"Yes."

"Because I see you come to me sometimes... but if I fall for it, they..." He made another choking sound and shook his head. "They show me what they did to you." His face crumpled. He covered his mouth with his fist as a strangled sob escaped, but no tears fell.

"Will, look at me," Iris said firmly. "They didn't do anything to me."

"It's almost like the last place," he said in a hoarse whisper. "Except I couldn't breathe there." He coughed, releasing a cloud of vapor into the freezing air. "And it hurt more."

"What place? The hospital?"

He shook his head. "No, before that."

That can't be right. Iris felt her gut wrench. *God, there's no way that's right.*

"I'm worried about you," he said absently, squinting at her with bloodshot eyes. "I thought you were going home. You need to get some sleep."

Her eyes widened. "Will, I *did* go home. I left you here over fourteen hours ago."

He gazed back at her, his eyes glassy and uncomprehending. "Haven't you slept?"

He thought for a moment, then shook his head.

"Have you had anything to eat since Saturday night?"

His eyes scanned the carpet. Finally, he looked up at her again. "There was too much fire."

"Have you at least had something to drink?" she asked, her voice rising.

"I…" He shook his head. "I can't really…"

"Can't really what?"

"Swallow."

Her mouth fell open. She looked over his hollowed eyes and cracked lips. A warming rush of fury swelled inside her, pushing her to her feet. "This is ridiculous!"

A framed photo of Will and Luke fell off the wall and shattered at Will's feet, causing him to scramble into the living room.

"Really?" Iris yelled at the hallway.

She looked over at Will, who was now on the couch. His head lay back against the cushion, his face contorted with pain. He clawed at the seat, laboring for each raspy inhale of breath.

Iris rushed to his side. "Will? What's happening?"

He couldn't answer, but Iris could see the imprint of three large fingers against his neck.

A shock of cold ran down her arms. "Stop it!" she shrieked.

Will remained where he was. Iris heard a faint, guttural growl to her left.

An even firmer voice arose within her. *Don't be afraid.*

Though she was incredibly afraid, Iris squared her shoulders and spoke fiercely. "I command you to let him go!"

Will took a huge breath. The indentations in his neck vanished, replaced by three long, bloody scratches.

"Nobody touch him!" she snapped. "Will, we're getting out of here." She sat beside him, hooked his arm across her shoulders, and helped him off the couch. She supported him all the way to the door, grabbed his sneakers off the floor, and led him out to her car. "Nobody follow us, either!" she shouted over her shoulder. She drove straight for the Reynolds' house.

When she pulled into the driveway, Jason was standing on the front walk, arms crossed. The sight of him comforted her. He always seemed to know what was going on without her telling him. He would know what to do next.

She had no sooner shut off the engine than Jason came around to Will's side of the car and opened the door. His expression was both pained and angry. He reached down, pulled Will's arm around him, and hefted him to his feet.

"Well," said Jason as he walked Will slowly into the house, "I guess now we know why there was a standoff."

Iris frowned. "What do you mean?" She opened the door for them.

"It was you," he said simply. "You're under heavy protection. He's not. All it took was for him to be alone."

When they walked into the living room, Eugene was sitting on the sofa thumbing through old records in a crate on the coffee table.

"What's with him?" Eugene asked, gesturing to Will.

"I don't have time to explain," Jason replied. "You're welcome to stay, but I need the couch. Scoot."

Eugene frowned, picked up the crate, and relocated to Jason's armchair, while Jason eased Will down on the sofa and arranged a pillow under his head. Will let out a long sigh and drifted off almost instantly. Grayson emerged from the office, took in the scene, and looked at Iris for a clue.

Jason spoke instead. "Son, you probably want to follow up a little more closely with stuff like this from now on."

"What happened?" Gray rushed to Will's side in five long strides. "Oh, no." He grimaced at the scratches on Will's neck and gave his father a troubled look. "I... I knew for sure he'd have questions. A *lot* of questions. But I never thought they'd... torture him. Not now."

"Rookie move, I'm afraid." Jason's face was grim.

Gray rubbed his forehead. "Iris, I am so sorry," he whispered.

"I don't know what you're apologizing for," she replied. "You didn't do anything except pray for him."

"But I could see that he'd retained a lot of awareness of where he'd been. That's why he was so scared when he was coming out of it. I should've stayed with him."

As Gray spoke, Iris remembered Will's words: *"just like the other place... except I couldn't breathe there..."* The same thought came to her as before, but this time, she spoke it aloud.

"You're saying he was in the *bad* place? That's ridiculous. That's... impossible!"

Jason looked at her with compassion. "Why is it impossible?"

"Because Will is the most selfless man on the planet, that's why! He gave up his childhood to raise his little brother. He's saved my life... at least twice. All he ever does is care for other people." Tears began to well over. "And now you think you can sit there telling me that someone like Brett, a murderer who wasted his entire life bragging and bullying people, can go be with God after thirty seconds on the right side, while someone like Will gets destroyed? You're out of your mind!"

Tears shone in Jason's eyes. "I know it seems backwards when you look at it that way, but you know full well that isn't how it works."

She stood. "Well maybe it *should* be!"

Eugene watched her warily as she paced.

Jason spoke softly to her. "Didn't you tell me that you loved how God approached people personally and offered them a relationship without judgment? You said it yourself, He only had harsh judgments for people who made it all about the law. Following rules or being a good person in order to get to God is essentially the same thing."

"But Will didn't deserve this!" she protested.

"God holds each of us responsible for what we know," Jason said. "And He makes sure every person knows enough to understand. But evil permeates this world, remember? It got here when Adam opened the door and welcomed it in. After living under it, each of us reaches a point where we buy into its delusions, and it *kills* us—even the very finest among us, like Will. We don't die physically right away, but our spirit—the very essence within us that was able to respond to God's voice, dies. And we go on like that. Walking tombs. Alive on the outside, but in reality, walking in the realm of the condemned dead."

Iris frowned. "How can people possibly be good and kind like Will, and enjoy life, if they're one of the condemned dead?"

"Because God's sun shines on everyone," Gray answered. "Anyone, even people in rebellion, can enjoy the things He made. But the physical realm is the only, and last, source of grace the dead will ever experience." He looked sadly at Will. "Once the final vestiges of God's light and presence are gone, nothing good remains."

Jason continued, "The suffering and death Will experienced weren't new for him. He was already there. He just became fully aware of it once God's physical presence was no longer there to alleviate it. He went to a place that was never designed for humans to go. It was meant as a dwelling for those who wanted nothing to do with God."

"You mean… darkness, torture, pain… that's—"

"That's what naturally occurs when the light, protection, and life brought by God's presence just aren't there anymore. But we weren't made for that, at all. It breaks His heart."

"Then why does God allow it?" she said through gritted teeth.

Jason looked at her tenderly. "You mean, why doesn't He force us to stay in His presence?"

Iris sat on the floor, deflated. She looked at Will. Another tear escaped the corner of her eye.

"Iris, you read it for yourself," Jason said gently. "He considered the risks of making a planet full of people who would choose to reject him. And He knew our rebellion would put us at the bottom of a pit a million miles deep. As much as we think we can claw our way up, or see how far we can get with whatever little ball of twine we have in our pockets, He knows we'll never get out. So He made a rope to pull us up. His cross wasn't Plan B. It was what *had* to happen. The Son put Himself up as the solution, and it was a done deal before He even spoke the first light wave into existence. He did that because having us in His life was worth it to Him."

"Will believes in God," Iris sniffed. "He probably would have gotten there eventually."

Jason nodded. "That's a great start. But the monsters who were messing with him also believe in God. Their passion is to see as many people stay in that pit as they can, keeping them busy, distracted, and deluded until they run out of time. Telling someone all they need to do is be a good person is one of their favorite tactics. But in that state of death, all the altruism in the world is nothing more than rearranging rocks at the bottom of the pit. Nothing anyone does matters down there… except whether they choose to grab the rope."

"That's the only thing? Just trusting the Son to rescue them?"

"Yep. Accepting rescue and trusting the free ride to the surface where life really begins. When He said He's the only way out, He wasn't bragging. He was stating fact. There's literally no other way. Saying 'no thanks, I prefer to climb' is the worst kind of tragedy. And to answer your question about Brett, yes… he *is* with God. Because he grabbed the rope. He believed in the name of the Son, which is 'God rescues.' Brett came to life, even as he died."

"He didn't deserve it." Iris stared at the floor. "But I guess that's not the point."

"No one deserves it," Gray said. "Thinking we ever could is nothing more than pride. God loved Brett and didn't want to lose him, just like He loves Will and doesn't want to lose him either. He wants all of us with Him in the land of the living."

"I really did feel like He came to me, when I believed everything I read," Iris said. "Like I came to life, somehow."

"That's exactly what happened!" Jason smiled. "He made you a completely new person!"

Her face was troubled. "But I took the time to read through the whole thing and research it. Will is in so much danger, he can't go home. He can't even swallow! He doesn't have that kind of time!"

"Well," Jason said, tilting his head at her with a fatherly expression, "the Spirit works with each of us differently. In your case, He worked with that big brain of yours. Maybe because it was the biggest thing in the way." He winked at her. "But with Will, He rescued him from death and gave Him another chance. That's something Will would understand."

Iris sighed. "I'm so worried about him. Maybe he should go back to the hospital."

Gray touched her shoulder. "Normally I'd agree with you," he said, "but what's wrong with him didn't come from the physical realm. It's not going to be fixed there, either."

Her face creased with concern. "I'm starting to get why those creatures don't like *me*. But I just don't understand why they'd go after *him* like this."

"Well," Jason replied, "creatures of evil don't know the future. Only God does. But they can certainly tell when He's gearing up for something. Whatever it is, Will is part of it. So they're sticking true to form—whatever God does, they're against it. Just the miracle of Will's return is enough to create a serious backlash. But whatever's in store for him now must be pretty remarkable."

"I'll stay with him, okay?" said Gray. "Until he wakes up. We'll get him better."

Iris nodded. "Thank you, Gray. But I'll stay too. I can't leave him again. Not until I know he's out of the woods. He hasn't had anything to eat in over twenty-four hours."

Gray smiled. "Well luckily, neither have I."

Iris gave him a befuddled look. "What... why? Are you sick?"

"No," he chuckled. "I just kept getting the impression I should hold off, and keep praying for you two instead. Now I see why. Looks like we're going into battle."

Will opened one eye. "So you're Grayson," he croaked.

"Will!" Iris gasped. "How long have you been awake?"

"Who said I was asleep?" he slurred. "I'm just... tired." He opened his eyes and fixed them on Gray. "You're her boss, huh?"

Gray smiled.

"You... prayed for me?"

"Yes, I did. I'm sorry I didn't check on you sooner..."

Will shook his head. "But you came, for Iris... after I was gone. And then you... asked for me back? Why would you do that?"

"Because the Spirit wanted you here. He invited me to be part of it."

"You didn't have to agree," Will rasped, then coughed.

"I wanted to," Gray said with great sincerity. "You're important to her."

Will gazed at him steadily for a long moment. Finally, he spoke. "You're a solid guy. I can see why she was torn."

Gray looked at Iris, whose face had gone pink, and smiled back at Will. "Oh, I'd like to think she took me seriously for a minute or two. But there was never a real contest."

Will offered his hand.

Grayson clasped it.

"Thank you," Will said, "for taking care of her when I couldn't. And thanks for bringing me back."

Gray nodded. "It's been an honor."

"Iris," Will turned to face her. "Don't be mad at God."

She shook her head, unable to reply, as hot new tears sprang to her eyes.

"No, don't," he insisted. "What I said to you before... I was wrong." He coughed again. "The Son of God is everything. He's... *everything*. Where I went, everyone knows who He is. The worst part about that place is knowing. I thought I was still there when I first got back. They kept telling me I belonged to them..." His voice grew more raspy. "They said they would kill everyone I love, and that I'd never get away... that He'd never forgive me." He took a deep breath to steady himself, and looked at each of their faces.

Iris stroked his hair. "What do you think now?" she asked.

"I think they lied."

Iris smiled.

"I've been so wrong. I see that. But I don't know how to be right." He looked at Jason. "But if what you're saying is true, then I'm grabbing the rope. I'm trusting Him."

Huge grins spread across the faces huddled around Will— Jason, Gray, Iris, Aimsir, Brennus, and Varick.

"In that case, happy birthday," said Jason.

Will stared at Jason for a moment, then let out a hoarse laugh and grinned. "I have no idea what just happened, but I feel... different. I'm..." He laughed again. "I'm not afraid now."

"You never have to be afraid again, Will," Jason said. "You're not their prisoner anymore. Death can't have you, either. He's just made you more alive than ever. You're never going to stop finding out how much He loves you. He's got so much kindness for you, and so many big things planned for you to do! Sorry if I'm shouting, I just get really excited!"

Iris and Will laughed.

"Oh my gosh, what is that?" Will said. He sat up.

"What?" Iris asked.

Will bowed his head and remained still for so long that Iris began to wonder if he'd fallen asleep sitting up. Finally, he looked up, his expression filled with awe. "My throat doesn't hurt! It felt like something was wrapped around my neck before, but…" He swallowed. "It's gone!"

Jason grinned. "Sweet, sweet freedom," he said, and wiggled his eyebrows.

"Could I have some water?"

"Brother, you can have whatever you want. I bet you're getting hungry, too."

Will set his feet on the floor. "Actually, yeah. Maybe… would it be okay if I made you guys something? I hope it's not too much to ask, but I've really missed cooking."

Jason laughed. "Do you actually think I'd turn down an offer like that?"

"I think I'll hold off for a bit, but I'll show you the kitchen!" Gray offered.

As Will moved to stand, he looked across at Eugene, who had been in the armchair listening to the entire discussion.

Eugene was seated sideways with his stocking feet on the chair, arms resting on his knees. His eyes were red. He seemed to be pretending not to hear, but the slump of his shoulders said otherwise. He swiped a bit of moisture from his eye.

"You okay, man?" Will asked him.

"Oh sure," Eugene replied with feigned enthusiasm. "It's all fine for you. Just a quick little change of heart and all your problems are solved. It's not that easy for some of us."

Will regarded him with sympathy. "Well, we've never met, so I can't say for sure what you're up against. I wouldn't say *all* my problems are solved... I've still got an apartment full of crazy that I have to deal with, and I'm pretty sure someone's trying to kill my favorite person. But the difference is, I'm not afraid now. I have hope. Looks like you could use some, too. You could be rid of that thing."

Eugene squinted at him. "What thing?"

Will pointed. "There's a shadow on you."

Thelo hissed.

Eugene's eyes widened. He looked behind him, and back at Will.

"I'm not trying to freak you out," Will said gently. "I'm just telling you what's there. I've been able to see those things ever since I got back. But they don't scare me now."

Jason and Gray exchanged looks.

Iris watched Will in amazement.

"This one..." Will tilted his head and studied the space next to Eugene's head. "Not super big, but he thinks he owns you. You don't have to put up with that, okay? Just ask God to get you where it's safe."

"That's it, huh?" said Eugene. "Just..."

"Grab the rope, dude. Trust me, you'd be an idiot not to."

Eugene's face fell, and he stared at his socks. "I don't think God would want someone like me."

"Oh quit it," Will said.

Eugene's head snapped up.

"I'm serious! You heard what they said. That's not how it works. The guy who *murdered me* is with God now. You really think it matters what *you've* done?"

Eugene stared at Will. Finally, he laughed. "No, I guess it doesn't!"

"Why are you laughing?" Iris asked him.

"Because I just realized I'm an idiot!" he replied. "And it feels good to admit it!"

"So how 'bout it?" Jason asked Eugene. "You going to let Him rescue you?"

Eugene thought it over, and nodded. "I can't think of a smarter move."

The thunderous celebration which followed caught every invisible ear within a thousand miles, even inspiring several dozen dogs to bark happily. Amidst the symphony of fanfare, one dark, squirming creature lost his grip. He was forced to retreat so far from his quarry that he became a distant speck on the horizon.

In his place settled Elias, a newcomer, outfitted not only with a shining sword, but a quill and ink. His comrades greeted him with salutes and cheers.

"I've been kept at a distance so long, waiting for this moment," Elias laughed. "The Master has given this man so much to write!"

Chapter 21

Will tied Jason's "Pie Are Round" apron around him and rummaged in the refrigerator. He found, to his delight, that Jason and Gray kept a respectable supply of fresh herbs and vegetables in their kitchen.

He poked his head out of the fridge and called into the living room. "Hey Gray?"

"Yeah?"

"How attached are you to these leftovers?"

"Take anything you want, buddy!"

"Sweet," Will mumbled to himself, and began to stack an assortment of seemingly incongruous items on the counter. He located a knife and chopped an onion with surgical precision.

Iris sat on a stool next to the counter and watched in awe. It wasn't just because this was her customary reaction to watching Will cook. He had also undergone a complete transformation. He had his color back. Even barefoot, he looked taller than before, and walked with a light step. His chocolate brown eyes were full of light. Even though he had enough stubble now for it to be considered a short beard, Iris could still see his dimples when he smiled.

He grinned at her. "What?"

"You," she replied, shaking her head.

He chuckled. "I know, right? Man, I feel better."

Will managed to create a frittata from a dozen eggs, chunks of leftover bacon and roasted butternut squash, bell pepper, chives, sour cream, and gruyere. While it was in the oven, he pulled a salad together and made his own dressing while Iris set the table. Just as the timer went off, Will brought out a cast iron skillet full of sizzling, creamy transcendence.

When Jason, Gray, and Eugene came to the table, they looked appropriately impressed.

"What happened?" Eugene gasped. "This looks amazing!"

"Will happened," Iris stated proudly.

Will laughed. "Major respect on that kitchen, you guys. You have just the right stuff to get things done in there."

"And yet we've never managed to arrange our leftovers in this order!" Gray chuckled. "I should've been watching how you did this."

"I watch him all the time, and I still don't know," Iris said. "He's too fast!"

"Thank God for three-day weekends," said Jason. "To think how close I came to missing this by being at my desk with a sandwich on the wrong Monday. It boggles the mind!"

Gray murmured his agreement.

"So Iris, should we…" Jason nodded at Will.

She gave Jason a quizzical look.

Gray leaned in. "You want us to fill him in?"

"Yeah, you know, I think Iris was going to tell me what it is you guys do," Will said, poking his salad. "Something with research, I know that much."

"You're kidding," Eugene said. "Iris, you've never told him about the—"

"Tssst!" Jason cut him off.

Eugene raised an eyebrow.

"Sorry," Jason chuckled. "But the last thing I need right now is an amnesiac wandering around my house."

Will looked completely bewildered.

"Um… where to start?" Iris began. "So…"

"Ahem," Jason said, eyes wide.

"Oh! Right, sorry," Iris answered.

"This is getting really weird," Will whispered to her.

She smiled. "It's okay, I promise. It's just that Eugene and I… *literally*… cannot explain it to you. But Gray will."

"Yes, I'd be happy to." Gray cleared his throat and set his water glass down. "Will, Iris has wanted to bring you in on this information since the beginning. But it's very need-to-know, and it's under powerful protection. She took a big risk coming to work for us, and she's taking an even bigger risk by asking me to tell you about it."

"Are you guys spies or something?" Will asked.

"Ha, no. Nothing like that. But in order to understand what we do, you have to understand our purpose. So I'll start at the beginning." He shifted in his seat, and began an oration thousands of years old:

"When the Master created the infinite universe, He put into it creatures who were too fragile to withstand infinity. They needed their existence marked out by the movement of celestial bodies, by the changing of seasons, by the passage of days and years. He created the finite fabric of Time, and wove his creation into it.

"Far above us, where days and months are sufficient to mark the passage of Time, it is the stars and planets which anchor this fabric in place. On earth, the fabric is bound into moments… therefore, the anchors must be more closely spaced. The Great Trees are the anchors and conduits of time on earth.

"The Trees were once guarded by Messengers of The Three. Mankind had become corrupt, yet a single man could live almost a millennium. Men had too long to ponder the source of Time, and too much temptation to interfere with it. Thus, they were never told of the Great Trees. But after the time of floods, when the lifespan of mankind was barely a century, the care of the Great Trees was passed to them. Messengers of The Three now watch over the human Guardians. Each Guardian must protect his Tree with utmost secrecy, and teach his son to do the same, down through the generations," he finished.

Will sat completely enraptured. At last, he squinted at Gray. "Time fabric?"

"Yes, lovingly referred to as 'spacetime,'" Gray replied.

"Anchored… by trees?"

"Yes."

"Okay. So, not *all* trees, obviously."

"No," Jason chuckled. "Specific ones, that aren't actually trees at all. They look like trees. They grow like trees. But underneath, they're something else entirely. They're spaced across the planet about every four or five hundred miles, give or take. Although it gets interesting over the oceans. But we won't go into that."

Will tilted his head, still processing. "So which one of you guys is the Guardian?"

"Dad used to be," Gray replied. "But officially, I am. He still spells me from time to time. The Great Fir is just outside. It's our job to see that no harm comes to it, and that its existence is kept secret. That's why we live and work so close to here."

"So there are Guardians like you guys all over the world?"

"Yep."

"Where does Iris come in?"

"Ah yes," Jason said, smiling at her. "She's our Research Specialist. You see, Guardians are geographically limited. We have to stick pretty close to home. But with the population of the world growing, we're seeing a slight uptick in… unusual occurrences. Iris did some excellent work last year on a case involving the Great Hawthorn of Scotland. The Council of Guardians was so impressed with her that they asked her to come help us on a more permanent basis. We could see how much more she could accomplish with the right kind of support."

Will turned to her. "I don't remember anything about that. What work did you do?"

Iris smiled and shook her head. "I can't tell you."

"I'm confused. We're all here in the same room. Does it matter who tells me?"

"I know it's really odd," Gray admitted. "Information has to flow through the right channels or it gets lost—I'll explain that in a second. But God put Iris in place Himself. She met a man named Angus Armstrong at the nursing home several months ago. He had mysteriously shown up one day, and Iris could tell there was something different about him. He was almost two centuries out of his time, because he had cut into a Great Tree when its Guardian was unaware. It's a pretty rare occurrence, but it does happen. The piece of wood he took, he used for a project, but exposure to the energy within it caused his body to follow it through time to wherever it was when the Tree finished healing. That was Rookwood. He was as good as dead. Yet because of her amazing research skills, Iris was able to spot a time traveler amongst dementia patients. She then had the tenacity not only to gain his trust, but to strike out on her own to get him back where he belonged. You must understand how extraordinary this woman is!"

"Oh, I know." Will smiled proudly at her, and rested his arm across her shoulders.

"Granted, she bent the law a little bit, and was subsequently fired from her job and had the authorities searching two countries for her…"

Will's eyes went wide. "Wha—"

"Her boss was *not* happy," Jason added ominously.

"Candace?" Will asked, incredulous.

"Yes, I think that was her name," Gray replied. "But it all worked out perfectly in the end!"

"Wait, wait, waaaait a second," Will protested, holding up one hand. "None of that actually happened! Iris started at Rookwood in November… November fourth, actually. That's the day we met." He smiled at her. "But she still works there. She's never been fired or chased by cops!"

"Well, that's true too," Jason said.

Will frowned.

"Dad, quit being enigmatic just for the fun of it," Gray said with a long-suffering smile, and turned back to Will. "What he means is, time travel creates separate timelines. When Angus cut the Tree, it created a timeline that shouldn't have existed. Everything that happened to him, including what Iris did to save him, was undone when they fixed the Tree. So because she did that, it turned out in the end that she never did, because she'd never met Angus to begin with. Make sense?"

"Uh…" Will looked at Iris, who gave him a sheepish smile. "Yes. I'm with you so far."

"Now here's where it gets weird…" Gray continued.

"Oh, *now* it gets weird?" Eugene muttered, but smiled.

Will cast him an empathetic glance.

"Guardians can retain two timelines in their memories at once," Gray said. "So Darrick, the Guardian Iris met in Scotland, can remember two different versions of Christmas day last year. In one, they had pie. In the other, they nearly blew a hole in the space-time continuum."

Eugene burst out laughing, then cleared his throat. "Sorry," he said. "It's probably not as funny as it sounded."

"But non-Guardians can only remember one version of events," Gray went on. "Iris only remembers the second one— the one that never officially happened. She remembers spending a day in 1844. She and Angus can remember each other, even though they've lived in separate centuries."

Will looked at her, amazed. "You… went to the past? For real?"

Iris smiled.

"And she remembers what you did to save her, Will."

Will whirled around to face Gray. "What *I* did? What are you talking about?"

Gray smiled. "You've been her hero for a long time, and didn't even know it. You see, a Great Tree that's been damaged will self-repair, as long as you have all the pieces. It gets tricky if the Tree has already healed. You have to remove the new growth very carefully. Iris did that, and got an ugly ax wound to the leg in the process. She showed a lot of courage. But she couldn't have done any of it if she didn't have all of the old wood. Some of it was hanging in the chapel at Rookwood."

"What does that have to do with me?" Will asked.

"Well, according to the Guardian diaries, Iris isn't the only lawbreaker in the house. Apparently, she called you from Scotland and told you she needed this thing—it was a mirror frame—and you hurled a book at it and broke the mirror so that the janitor would put it in the shed. Then you stole it and rush shipped it to her, to the tune of about a grand in postage costs."

"I did *what?*" Will laughed, incredulous. "What possessed me to do a thing like that?"

Gray shrugged. "Maybe she was very convincing. But you must have trusted her."

Will looked at Iris, a softness coming into his expression. "I could see that."

"If you hadn't done what you did," Gray continued, "Angus would still be lost, and Iris would be in jail. Will, you saved them both. Not to mention the life Angus went on to live and the children he later had. They exist because of you."

Iris leaned her head against Will's shoulder and sighed.

"How could I have done all that, and forgotten?" Will whispered.

"Because in this timeline, you never did," Jason answered. "How's that for enigmatic?"

Iris pulled out her phone and scrolled through her backlog of texts to Will, until she located the one she'd sent him on the second of January: *"How much $$ do I owe you?"* She showed it to him.

"How much… ohhh, I see," he nodded. "I thought that was an odd question. You were just trying to see if I remembered?"

She smiled again.

"I know this is a lot to take in," Jason said to Will. "But there's a teensy bit more, if you're up for it."

Will took a breath. "Alright, let's have it."

Jason nodded at Gray, who stroked his auburn beard, trying to get a fix on how to word his thoughts.

"Okay…" he said finally. "So… there's another tricky part of remembering the past when it comes to anything related to Guardians and Great Trees. Besides only keeping one timeline in their heads at a time, non-Guardians have what we call 'second-party status.' That's as far as any of this information is allowed to travel. Guardians have first-party status. We can tell anything we want to whoever we want." Gray frowned. "Whoever? *Whom*ever? Which is it?"

"I don't know, I teach physics," Jason said with a shrug.

"Whomever," Eugene and Iris said together.

"Point is," Gray went on, "a second party can only retain the information if he keeps it secret. If he tries to pass it to a third party, it gets wiped from his memory. That's why Dad cut you off from spilling the beans a while ago, Eugene. I know it's easy to forget when we're all in the same room, but if you had said a word to Will, you'd have forgotten why you were here."

"Ohhhh, right. Sorry about that," Eugene said.

"Well, I think you're doing fine, considering how strange everything must feel to you," Jason told him.

Gray turned to Will. "Iris couldn't tell you anything, Will. As much as she wanted to. If she had, she would have lost all memory of Angus, of us, and everything she'd been through. It's one of the reasons the Council of Guardians was so impressed with her in the first place. She not only survived her bout with a Great Tree, she retained it. They could only imagine what she could accomplish if she had enough support to avoid becoming an outlaw."

Will chuckled.

"She wanted the job, but it meant keeping you in the dark."

"You didn't have to," Will said to Iris. "Why didn't you just bring me here and have them explain everything, like they're doing now?"

Iris's eyes grew worried. She bit her lip.

"That's the most nerve wracking part," Gray filled him in. "You're both second parties. If she let slip even one new thing to you, she'd lose it all. And the biggest risk—it's not that she doesn't trust you, but if *you* made even one mistake and relayed something to a third person, you'd forget everything we'd told you. And because your relationship is still relatively new, you might even forget *her* completely."

Will's mouth fell open. "Forget her? How could I ever forget her?"

"We're not sure," Jason said, his expression somber. "But judging by her face, that's the part that scares her the most."

Will looked at Iris, who glanced at him only momentarily before burying her face in his shoulder. He put both arms around her.

"I would never let that happen," he said.

"Guardians *have* seen it happen, though. Memories are a tricky thing, bound up with time and imprinted in the heart as well as the brain. The energy signature of a memory is too complex for us to predict."

"Can't you guys fix it? Change the rules? I mean, she's one of you, isn't she?"

"Yes, she's one of us," Gray replied. "But the memory of Guardians has always been a birthright, not a rule. We aren't sure if just adopting her is enough to transfer it. We know marriage is, but..."

Will was quiet. Iris took a deep breath against his chest.

He finally spoke, face pensive. "So… Iris is always in danger of losing her dream. And the surest way to keep it is to… marry a Guardian?"

Gray didn't answer, but his face said it all.

"That's kind of archaic," Will huffed.

"It's a safeguard God put in place to protect our families," Jason said. "It was never meant to be issued backwards as a threat. But Iris is unique. She trusts that she's where God wants her, and so do we. We just don't understand all the details yet."

"In some cases, it's kind of a gift," Gray said gently. "Eugene, this has been tough on you. If we get you home, you could forget all of this by just telling someone else about it. Then it would be like it never happened."

"But I don't want to forget you guys," he mumbled. "And you can call me Gene."

Gray and Eugene exchanged warm smiles.

"If you get him home?" Will asked. "So… wait, he's not a Guardian either?"

"No, he's a little bit like Angus," Jason answered.

"Oh, interesting!" Will said. "So where is he from?"

Eugene began to answer. "Oh, I'm from—"

"Ah-ah-ah!" Jason cut him off again.

"I was gonna say Tucson! Sheesh!"

"Gene is from 1965," Jason filled in the rest, and winked at Eugene. "Got past a Guardian down there and studied a Tree a little too hard. Iris is tracking down the last known location of the missing piece."

"Pretty sure she found it, actually," Gray said. "She's been keeping me abreast of the situation. Gabe Iwila can meet on Thursday, so she's arranging to fly then."

"Ah, okay. Wow, you're quick, Iris!" said Jason.

She smiled at him.

"Oh, Iris, I forgot to tell you," Gray added, "I talked to someone on the Council this morning who said there's a plane in Hillsboro if you want to use it. They'll fly you to Scottsdale."

Her head came up from Will's shoulder. "Nice," she said. "I love private jets."

Will chuckled.

"So because Gray and I have to stick around here, Iris will take Eugene back to the Great Juniper, rendezvous with the Guardian down there, and the two of them will supervise Gene's return home. If all goes well, that is."

Will gazed at Eugene. "So you're… wait, how old are you?"

"Am I allowed to answer that?" Eugene asked Jason with a wry smile.

"Yeeeaaaahhh, go ahead," Jason chuckled.

"Twenty-eight."

"But you were b—"

"Born in 1937, yes."

Will shook his head in amazement. "You remember World War II, don't you?"

"Well, I was a kid. But sure."

Will kept staring at Eugene. "You're the same age as George McFly!"

"Who?"

"Uh…" Jason cut in. "We're trying to keep the anachronistic references to a minimum, for his sake."

Will nodded. "Right, sorry. My bad."

"They don't even let me read the newspaper," Eugene said with an amused smile.

"I guess that makes sense."

"So Will, how are you feeling now?" Gray asked. "I can't even describe how much better you look than when you got here."

Will let out a satisfied sigh. "Never better. Things really turned around when that guy poured a bucket of water on my head."

Everyone stared.

"What guy?" Iris asked him, growing concerned.

Will pointed at the wall. "Him!"

The group looked toward where he pointed, then back at him.

"You guys don't see him?"

Jason leaned forward on his elbows. "What's he look like?"

Will gazed across the room. "Well he's not as clear as he was at first. Now he's kinda see-through. But I don't know, he's... big. Burly. Dark hair. Has a sword."

"Extraordinary," Jason breathed. "You can see a Messenger?"

"I guess so. I see several, actually. They're all different. You guys really can't see them? I thought that was just going to be a thing now."

"Uh, no," Jason chuckled. "That's a gift that very few people possess. There must be a specific reason for it."

"How many?" Iris asked, eyes wide.

"Uhhh..." Will squinted and looked around. "Six in here. More outside. Two of them are pretty intent on you, Iris. One of 'em is really smiley."

Brennus laughed merrily.

"Oh, that made him laugh!"

The rest of the group joined in the laughter.

"Sorry, it seems weird to talk about them like this," Will said. "Feels rude somehow." He glanced around again and waved. "Hi, guys." Will smiled again. "I guess they don't mind, though."

"The reason I asked how you're doing," Gray continued, "is that I think it would be wise to finish what we've started here. You said there's still quite a bit of crazy going on back at your place, right?"

"Yeah, my gosh," Will replied. "It's a freaking mess. Iris barely got me out of there. I'm not really sure what's going to happen when I go back."

"Well, that's now illegally occupied territory." Gray's eyes became fiery. "Those dark creatures have no claim on you, or anything you own. I've had the strongest impression since yesterday that a battle was coming, so I've been preparing. I'd like to help you take back what's yours."

Will nodded. "I'd really appreciate that."

"I'll back you up," Jason said, face resolute.

"Whoa…" Will said, glancing around the room again. "Three of them just drew their swords."

Gray and Jason grinned.

"Iris, you and Gene can handle things here, right?" Gray asked.

Eugene nodded.

"Yep," she replied. "Go. I'll see you guys soon."

After the men left, Eugene and Iris cleaned the kitchen. While Iris wiped the counters, Eugene hand dried and stacked plates.

"Wow, I haven't done dishes in years," he commented.

"How come?" Iris asked. "You certainly have a knack for it."

"I don't know…" He set down the last plate and grabbed a handful of wet forks. "Eva always does it, I guess."

"She probably wouldn't mind some help," Iris chuckled.

"Yeah, she kept asking if we could get one of those portable automatic dishwashers, but we never did. Those things take up so much floor space. Plus, they're two hundred bucks. I'm not rich, y'know?"

Iris smiled. "Well you could stick *those* in the dishwasher. It's under the counter."

"What? They've got a built-in? *Now* you tell me!" he teased.

"I didn't mean buying Eva anything fancy," she continued. "I just meant doing what you're doing now. You've only been at it for fifteen minutes, and you're nearly finished. Seems like a small thing."

He sighed and leaned his hip against the counter. "Yeah, it's a small thing. You're right. There's probably a lot of small things I don't do."

"Why not?"

"Because… how do you put it nowadays? I suck?"

"Oh, Eugene, you don't suck."

"Please, it's Gene. And don't insult me. I can tell when someone sucks. I *do*. I've done nothing but find fault with that woman for the past two years."

"Well, do better, then. When you get home, you can start making things right."

His towel hung limp by his side. "What if I can't?" He looked at her, his face filled with worry. "What if I never get back?"

She sighed and leaned against the counter beside him. "I don't know."

"As it stands right now," he said, "the only lasting contribution I've made to the world is bad memories. I can't imagine leaving it like that."

"Let's not give up, okay? We'll try everything we can think of, and keep trying."

He nodded. "Thank you. And for what it's worth, I'm sorry. For… whatever. Everything. You've been really patient with me."

"It's all good." She nudged him with her shoulder. "It's not really in my nature to be patient. I think it's God doing that. Looks like He's changing both of us."

Her phone chimed. She pulled it from her pocket and swiped up. "Oh, it's an email from the junkyard owners. Let's see…" She clicked and scanned the screen for a minute. "Okay, they compared your VIN to their records and can confirm the car is there. They sent pictures from when they first got the car… oof, maybe you don't want to see these."

"That bad, huh?"

"Uh…" She clicked on another photo and grimaced. "Or maybe you *should* look, you know, so you can prepare yourself before you see it in person." She turned the phone.

His mouth fell open, then gave way to a grimace that matched hers. "Holy sh—what happened?" He shook his head. "My poor car!"

"Yeah." She looked at him sympathetically. "I'm sorry. I can't imagine seeing Daphne like that."

"Who's Daphne?"

"*My* car."

He sighed. "Well, it's like I said… nothing left of me but bad memories."

"Hey," she nudged him again. "All the more reason not to give up."

Chapter 22

Will, Gray, and Jason returned two hours later, talking and laughing like old friends. Will had showered and changed, but kept the beard.

"You guys look happy!" she greeted them.

"Yeah!" said Will. "Night and day difference over there. Went and picked up a new fire extinguisher and a picture frame, but honestly, it wasn't too bad. Between the six of us, we got it done pretty quick."

"Really?" Iris was incredulous. "Six? Oh yeah, the... Well that's amazing! Everything seemed so overwhelming there this morning."

"Smoke and mirrors," said Gray.

"It's like serving an eviction notice, really," Jason added. "It's not like they had a case."

"Granted, we had to flip some breakers," Will said, "and that last critter got a little feisty. But those Messengers kick up a pretty good breeze. And, as it turns out, the gigantic fire and pools of blood I saw last night weren't physical, so cleanup was actually pretty minimal."

Iris realized her mouth was hanging open, and closed it. "You sound like you're just describing a normal Monday!"

Will shrugged. "You know me. Life's been interesting. I guess I've just learned to accept things as they come."

"Uh, you've accepted a *lot* today."

"Yeah, well… I have a lot more perspective lately. After what I've seen and where I've been, none of the rest of it seems that crazy. Especially because I have nothing to be afraid of." He smiled and shuffled his feet. "Speaking of perspective, would it be okay if we talked? It's really nice outside. Maybe we could go to the park."

She grinned. "I'd love that."

Gray's smile was wistful. "See you guys. I've got papers to grade," he said before disappearing into the den.

Jason and Eugene exchanged knowing looks, but made a graceful exit.

Iris reached across the counter for her purse and dangled a set of keys in front of Will, grinning. "Wanna drive Daphne?"

Despite his stature, Will fit perfectly in Iris's hatchback, and managed to grind the gears only once in search of third. By the time they arrived at Iris's favorite park, a former historic army base, he was smitten.

"I've gotta get one of these," he said with a wide grin, and tossed the keys back to Iris in a perfect arc over the roof of the car.

"I can't imagine you in such a tiny car," she laughed.

"You just saw me in it! You still can't imagine it?"

She shook her head. "Nope. The truck stays. It's perfect."

He jutted his chin at her. "I see what's going on here. You just want to drive my truck again."

She took his hand as they headed down the path. "What's wrong with that?"

He squeezed her hand. "My kinda girl."

They meandered through an opening in the split rail fence and strolled toward a gazebo that boasted views of nineteenth-century army barracks and two-story officers' quarters surrounded by elegant verandas. The expansive lawn was dotted with towering oaks and evergreens. Although the skeletal branches of the smaller deciduous trees bore only tiny buds with scant blossoms and few leaves, optimistic honey bees had still come out to assess the possibilities and raid the new clover in the grass.

Iris and Will bypassed the gazebo, which, because it lacked benches, was really more of a bandstand than a place to contemplate anything. Instead, they headed toward one of Iris's favorite trees—a knobbly oak whose centuries-old trunk had split into a hollow in the center—and they sat in the warmth opposite its shadow.

Iris took a deep breath and closed her eyes, enjoying the sun. "You know," she murmured, "when I'm sitting in this place, if I ignore the cars, it's easy to imagine I'm back in another time."

Will contemplated that for several moments before answering. "What was it like… walking in the past?"

"Hmm… I guess you'd imagine it was strange, but honestly, it wasn't. Not to me. It might be partly because of where I was. I mean, St. Cyrus *has* changed since 1844, but not in ways that make it feel like somewhere else. So many of the walls, streets, fields, and buildings have been there at least that long. But it was mostly because of who I was with."

"Angus?"

"Yes. He was such a great friend." She gazed out at the swaying trees as the image of his face came into her mind. She could still see Angus growing young in front of her, white hair turning dark, blue eyes alight with exultant joy. She smiled. "Being old or young didn't change him inside. He was a great person in any century. He was… protective of me. So I guess being in a strange time didn't feel strange because he was there."

"I wish I could have met him," Will said.

"You made us doughnuts once," she replied.

"Really? What kind?"

"Scottish fudge doughnuts."

"I have *never* made those."

"I know," she sighed. "It's sad, because they were *so* good."

"Well, maybe I will again, for the first time," he chuckled. "I'm glad Angus was there for you. Sounds like a good thing he was. Gray said you hurt your leg pretty badly. Does it still bother you?"

"No more than your gunshot wound bothers you," she said. She pulled up the pant leg of her jeans, revealing a pink, perfectly healed gash along her shin. "I saw a man in a green cloak that day, after Angus prayed for me."

"Wow," he whispered. "Y'know, that's the smiley one. He wears a cloak like that."

"Really? He's been with me that long?"

"Probably longer," he replied. "I'm just glad you're okay."

"That's what I said about you," she said. She turned toward him, face earnest. "I still can't believe you're here with me. I'm still trying to get used to it. My brain has *almost* accepted it, but it's sort of like it wants to skip over the whole weekend and pretend it couldn't have happened. But I saw you get shot for me, Will. I saw you bleed out in a gutter. I watched them try to save you." Her breath caught in her throat. "And I saw you after they couldn't." She took his hand. "You were cold. And all I could think about was how I had just decided to tell you everything, and would never get to." A tear fell down her cheek.

"Come here," he said. He leaned his back against the tree, and held his arms out to her.

She turned to face him, and leaned against his chest, relishing the sound of his strong heartbeat.

"I'm glad that wasn't it," he said. "I'm glad we have today."

"Just today?"

"That's the only day I know for sure I've got."

She sighed. "I guess so. It just seems depressing to think of it that way."

"Nah." He hugged her a little tighter. "I'm starting to realize that time doesn't mean a whole lot. It's useful, but it's only meant to teach us something. We aren't supposed to let it limit us. God is always. If I'm with Him, then I'm always. Tomorrow isn't even a thing. It's not like you can live there."

She chuckled. "Well, that's true."

He sighed and kissed the top of her head. "Today, then."

Iris relaxed into his chest, listening to him breathe. "Do you think you'll be okay?" she asked.

"I'm already okay."

"I mean... do you have... bad memories of..."

"Of where I was?"

"Yeah."

"I do, and I don't," he replied. "Before, it was like a waking nightmare. There were flashbacks. Bizarre visions. Things still torturing me. I can remember it perfectly. But now I just kind of... remember it as fact. All the fear of it is gone. The voices telling me what I deserve, that I should die... those are gone. The Spirit has a different kind of voice."

"What's He sound like?"

"He sounds like safety. Love. He wants me with Him. He never wants me to hide from Him. Anything that says differently isn't Him."

"That's what He sounds like to me, too."

"Hmm, so if He's in us both, I wonder if He'll tell me what you're thinking sometimes?" Will chuckled.

"I hope that's not how it works," she laughed. "Although... I dunno, I kind of wonder..."

"What?"

"Well... oh my gosh, this is so embarrassing..."

He squeezed her. "Sheesh, just tell me. What?"

She sat up and looked into his face. "How did you know it was Grayson?"

"How did I know what was Grayson?"

"The other night! You could tell I was conflicted about something. It was partly the whole keeping secrets thing, but there was also... him. I mean, kind of." Iris stopped talking when she could feel herself blushing beyond what even she felt was reasonable.

He laughed. "I didn't know it that night. But later, it was just a combination of things. I mean, you said he was your supervisor, but you talked to him like an old friend. I was prepared to take you at your word, but then I listened to how he talked to you, and I saw the way he looked at you. It wasn't hard to figure out after that."

"Honestly, I do love Gray," she said. "But not like that. He's become like a big brother to me. I confess I was tempted for about five seconds, but it was only because he surprised me, and I was having such a hard time living a double life."

"I understand," Will said softly.

"So you don't feel threatened by him or anything, right?"

"Of course not. We're brothers now. And I don't blame him for seeing you that way. He's got great taste. I meant what I said before—he's a solid guy." He gave her a mischievous grin. "If anything, it's doing my ego a world of good. Beating him is way more satisfying than running unopposed."

She gasped and gave him a playful smack.

He laughed and pulled her into his arms again. "But seriously, I meant the other thing I said before, too."

She looked up at him, her head nestled into the crook of his elbow. "What other thing?"

"That I love you."

Iris took in the gravity of this moment before she answered. "I love you, too. So much."

He let out a big sigh and rested his cheek against her head. "I'm so glad."

"Even though my life is beyond crazy, and full of secrets?" she asked.

"Yes, even then."

"What will we do about all that?"

"We'll deal with it. That's what you do when you love someone."

"And now that you've heard everything, you're sure you wouldn't rather just forget it all and date someone normal?"

"Not a chance." He gave her a squeeze. "I don't even want to date *you*."

She sat up. "What do you mean?"

He touched her cheek. "I want to *keep* you. I want to be there for you in every possible way. I want to marry you."

She stared at him in amazement.

"I don't need an answer right now, okay? I just wanted you to know… that… I think we're better together." His expression took on a new intensity. "I don't want to live without you, Iris."

"I don't want to live without you either," she said. "Even trying it for an hour was…" She shook her head.

He held her hands in both of his. "I can give you all the time you need to think about it."

"I don't want more time."

"Are you sure?"

"Time doesn't mean a whole lot, anyway. You said it yourself."

He frowned. "Does three months feel kind of… fast to you?"

"Maybe for some people. But we've covered a lot more ground than dinner and a movie, wouldn't you say?"

"I would definitely say that."

"Does it feel fast to you?" she asked him.

"It feels like it's taken forever."

She smiled. "I want to marry you, Will."

He bowed his head, eyes closed, and let out a breath. "Thank God," he whispered. When he looked at her again, his eyes were shining.

"I want to tell you something else, because you're probably wondering," she said.

"What's that?"

"I want to kiss you."

He cradled her face in his hands as his lips curved into a soft smile. "Well that works out, since I'm keeping you."

There was no hint of shyness or hesitation when he kissed her, but she was overwhelmed by the tender innocence of it.

She let out a soft exhale of amazement, and rested her forehead against his, cherishing this newfound feeling of wholeness. It was as though she was sitting in the shelter of two strong trees—one was this man who had saved her life, the other was the mighty Creator who sustained her. Both of them had thrown themselves in front of death on her behalf, and pledged themselves to keep her. The enormity of that honor enveloped her, making her feel both small and significant, and utterly, wildly loved.

Chapter 23

I ris could barely focus at work the following day. She found herself staring off into space and grinning at the most inopportune moments. *I'm going to marry Will!*

"What's so funny?" Candace asked.

"Hmm?" Iris looked up from the room visit report she'd been failing to write for the past five minutes.

"You're over there smiling like a nut!" Candance said, eyeing her suspiciously. "Was your visit with Third Irene *that* funny?"

Iris blushed. "No, it's not that. I was just thinking about… something else."

"Care to share?"

"Uhh…" Iris smiled again. She thought of Will's parting request to her when they'd said goodnight—that she keep things between them until he'd had a chance to talk to her parents, and to Luke. *He's a class act.*

"Obviously, it's got something to do with Will," Candace teased. "Things must be going well."

"Yeah," Iris admitted. "We just had a really nice day yesterday."

"Well, good. Tell him I already miss him around here."

"I will."

"You almost finished with that report?"

Iris looked over the page. She'd written one sentence so far. "Uh, not quite…"

"Well, I just got a note from Nurse Kathy. She said Eva Thomas isn't doing so hot. I think it would be good if we spent some extra time with her this week. Everyone else on her contact list is out of town until next week. Maybe you could head in there before you leave for the day."

"What did Kathy say?"

"Well, she's got a background in hospice, you know? She's seen this so many times before. She can tell Eva probably doesn't have long."

"Oh… wow."

"Yeah. It's to be expected, I suppose," Candace sighed. "But I never get used to it." She thought for a moment. "Didn't Eva get a visit from a relative a few days ago?"

"Yeah, she did."

"Kathy seemed to think that was some kind of tipping point for Eva, like she just started to let go after that."

Iris looked up. "Oh, no… she did?"

"That may not be a bad thing," Candace said softly. "Maybe she found some sort of peace. Did that guy leave any contact info? Maybe we could let him know to come see her again, if he's still in town."

"I think I can get a hold of him."

"Please do. I think it would do her a lot of good." Candace grabbed a stack of folders and stood. "Well, I'm off to an administrative meeting. The highlight of my week, as always."

Iris chuckled. "Have fun."

"You too, smiley face. I'll see you tomorrow."

Once Candace had left, Iris pulled out her phone and sent Gray a message:

Eva is dying. Should we break it to Eugene? He might want to come see her.

He replied a minute later:

Oh no. Yes, he should know. School's out. I'll see if he's up for coming.

Iris went back to filling out her report. After that, she just had to put away the game boards in the lobby. She would save Eva's room visit for last, in case Eugene decided to come.

Thirty minutes later, Eugene walked into the lobby alone. Iris was just finishing tidying up the round cherry wood tables beside the canary cage when she saw him.

He walked slowly toward her, hands in his pockets. "Grayson dropped me off," he said, eyes downcast.

She touched his arm. "I'm glad. You sure you want to do this?"

He looked her in the face, eyes full of doubt. "No, I'm not sure at all. I've been trying so hard just to remember her the way she was. But... she's my wife. I might never get another chance to talk to her."

Iris nodded. "I can't even imagine what this feels like, Gene. But I think you're brave."

"Brave, or stupid."

"Just brave."

When Eugene stepped inside Eva's doorway, he seemed to freeze in his tracks. His face bore the same shock as it had the other day.

Eva lifted her head. "Gene," she croaked in a frail voice. "I was so afraid when you didn't come home." She reached a wrinkled hand out to him.

Iris leaned against the doorway and gave him an encouraging nod.

He took a few steps toward her.

"I've been frantic, imagining the worst! Please, Gene... are you still angry with me?" Her eyes began to water.

Pain filled his expression. "Angry? I..." He inhaled sharply, fighting for composure.

Eva's hand dropped to her lap. She closed her eyes and let out a shuddering sigh. "Are you going to leave me for good, then?"

"Why… why would you think that?"

She looked up at him, eyes full of tears. "I'm not really mad about the car," she said. "It's a beautiful car. I'm just…"

He stepped a little closer. "Just what?"

"I… I'm scared."

"What are you scared about?"

"That you never loved me at all." A few tears trickled down her cheeks. "You're gone so much, and you're so preoccupied all the time. I feel silly saying it, but I get jealous of rocks and trees!"

"You… you do?"

"Yes, you spend so much more time with them. You never show them to me anymore."

Eugene looked bewildered, but shook his head, trying to focus. "I thought that stuff bored you."

"Of course not! I just feel stupid that I don't understand half of it! Will you teach me?"

Eugene gazed at her for a long moment. He was beginning to lose the battle with his emotions. A single tear rolled down his cheek. "You're not stupid." He sat slowly on the edge of her mattress. "You're anything but stupid. You were at the top of your class, remember?"

She nodded. "Yes, I was."

"You're the smartest girl I ever met."

"Really?"

"Uh huh."

"Then how come I'm not smart enough to know how to make you happy?"

His lips trembled. He shook his head. "*I'm* not even smart enough to do that."

Eva laid her withered hand against his. "I know I've been awful. I don't mean to lose my temper. It's just because it hurts so much when you never have a kind word to say. And I know I'm not as pretty as some girls, but I'm trying!"

"Oh Eva, that was never—"

"There just never seems to be a good time to tell you," she went on.

"Tell me wh—"

"I wanted to, but you were so angry!"

"I'm sorry," he said, and laid his other hand on hers. "I'm so sorry for that. I was awful to you."

"Oh no, have you lost your wedding ring, too?" she asked, gazing down at his hands.

"No, no… I didn't lose it. It's right here," he replied, pulling it from inside his jacket. "I have it."

"You weren't wearing it," she mumbled. "Does this mean you're leaving me for good?"

"No, of course not," he said. He slipped the band back onto his finger. "I'm wearing it, see?"

She sighed contentedly. "You were always so handsome."

"What did you want to tell me?"

"About what?"

"Just a minute ago, you said there was never a good time to tell me, because I was angry. What did you want to tell me?"

She looked at him for a long time, as though she were surprised he didn't already know. "Well, about the baby."

His eyes went wide. "The… baby?"

Eva's smile was blissful as she pulled a picture frame from the shelf next to her bed. "She looks so much like you, doesn't she?" She handed him the photo.

Inside the antique oval frame lay a faded color photograph of Eva holding a toddler. They wore matching dresses. The bottom corner said "Easter '68" written in Eva's delicate handwriting. The little girl's hair was dark like his, but her lips and eyes were stunningly beautiful… like Eva's.

His hands trembled. "She's… mine?"

"Of course." She smiled peacefully. "Who else's would she be?"

He looked at Iris, tearful. "Did you know about this?"

Iris gave him a somber smile. "I knew she had a daughter. Only Eva knew the circumstances."

"She's so smart," Eva added. "Just like you. Top of her class at U of A. She's a doctor, you know."

Eugene stared at the photo, eyes swimming. "A doctor," he murmured. He touched the picture of the little girl's face with his fingertips. "You put her through college... by yourself?"

"Of course! I had to. My Jennie was too smart not to go to college."

Eugene's face took on an awed admiration. "But how did you—"

"I became a nurse!" Eva said proudly. "I only had a semester left."

Eugene shook his head. "You're incredible." He looked back at the photo. "Jennie, huh?" His face filled with heartache. "I... I missed *everything*," he whispered.

"I'm so glad you're home now," Eva murmured, and closed her eyes. "Will you take me for a ride soon?"

His tears flowed freely now. He took a deep, shaky breath and squeezed her hand. "Of course I will. You're my girl."

Twenty minutes later, Eva's breathing stilled.

Eugene sat numbly, gazing at her face. Finally, he stood. He placed the photo frame beneath her hand as it rested over her heart, and kissed her forehead. He turned his tear-stained face toward Iris.

"I'm so sorry," she whispered.

"Is she with God now?" he asked, voice breaking.

"I... I'm not sure," she admitted.

He shook his head. "I have to get home... to my family."

The following evening, Will and Iris went to the Reynolds' house for dinner. There was a sense of foreboding in the air. Iris couldn't put her finger on why—maybe because she and Eugene would fly to Arizona the following morning, and they had no idea what awaited them. Although it wasn't strictly necessary to meet, all of them—including Will—felt like the only logical place to be was here, together.

Iris and Eugene set the table. Jason, Gray, and Will huddled around the stove while Will taught them how to season, sear, and finish the most perfect medium rare steaks.

Jason shook his head in amazement and looked at Gray. "Add butter to the shopping list."

"Already?" Gray asked.

"Do not question Will!" Jason said with mock severity.

The three of them shared a laugh.

Iris came into the kitchen in search of silverware for the table, and smiled. It warmed her heart to see her worlds collide so perfectly. "Are the steaks done?" she asked.

"Yes," Will stage whispered, pointed to the cutting board. "Shh… they're resting!"

"Okay," she whispered back, tiptoeing over to see them. "How can you tell?"

"Because they're quiet," he whispered with a mischievous smile.

"No, I mean how can you tell that they're done?"

He lifted her hand to his face and pressed her fingers against his cheek. "Rare." He moved her hand to his forehead. "Well done." Then he slid her hand down to his arm and put her fingertips against his wrist, as if she were taking his pulse. "Medium." He winked, then turned back to the carrot sticks he was cutting.

She continued to stand there, cheeks pink, head not quite in the room, until she heard Jason and Gray trying to stifle throat clearing and snickering noises.

"Very handy tip, Will. Thank you," Jason said.

"Yes, I'm sure I'll never forget it," Gray added.

Iris grabbed a handful of spoons and exited, only to have to return a few seconds later, put the spoons back, and grab forks. Mercifully, none of them reacted.

Once they were seated at the table with loaded plates, Jason spoke. "Iris, I was thinking about what Gabe Iwila said to you about all the foot traffic he's been getting. Gray showed me the email. I'm wondering if you and Gene might be getting yourselves into a hornet's nest down there."

She lowered her fork. "Go on."

"The creature who attacked you knew about Eugene, and the Tree. He wanted you to fail. For some reason, they don't want Gene back where he belongs." Jason turned to Eugene. "How did you happen to find the Tree in the first place, anyway?"

Eugene shrugged. "Not on purpose. I was hiking to specific tree stands to take samples, and I suddenly had the idea to go over the next ridge, just to see what was there."

"How much time did it add to your hike?"

"About a half hour each way," he replied.

"Do you usually hike that far out of your way on a whim? Especially when you're doing research?" Jason asked.

"Actually, I've never done that. I don't know why I did it this time... I guess something told me it might be interesting."

"Something... or someone," Jason murmured.

Eugene frowned. "You think... I was led there somehow?"

"Possibly, yes."

"Why, though?"

"The whole picture looks dodgy. What would you have done with your findings?"

"Publish them and enjoy the ride to academic celebrity, most likely."

Jason sat back in his chair. "And that would've made the Tree famous, bringing people from all over the world to study it...

impressionable people, hungry for an explanation. The creatures who used you must have been trying to start something new. I guess they weren't aware that knowledge of the Trees can't spread."

Eugene sighed. "I don't really *want* to go into this, but I think it would help if I did," he said. "You remember that I was... with someone that night. A girl named Kat. I told you before that when I got back to Tucson last week, I was just trying to make sense of things... find someone, anyone, I knew. A lady at the library helped me track Kat down, and I talked to her. Remember how I told you she's changed a lot?"

Iris nodded.

"Well it's more than that. She's... not *right* anymore." His face grew troubled at the memory. "She told me that as soon as I disappeared, a dark being came and threatened her, and then she was saved by a kind being named Albion, who stayed with her for years."

"Well maybe that's a good thing," Iris suggested.

"No." Eugene shook his head. "It couldn't be. This thing taught her how to do psychic readings, and then abandoned her when she started seeing bright flashes and feeling sick during her sessions with him."

Iris noticed Will set down his water glass and slowly raise his head. His eyes followed some unseen presence behind her.

"Will, what do you see?" she asked.

"One of the Messengers looks really angry. It's one of the ones who stays with you, Iris."

"The smiley one?"

"No, the other one."

Gray spoke. "I don't think it was a coincidence that these two creatures just happened to show up as soon as you were gone, Gene. They were probably following you and Kat to see what you'd do. I think your disappearance kinda messed up their plans."

"Maybe," he mumbled, deep in thought.

"And when you reappeared, you were in Gabe's house?" Jason asked.

"Yeah, right within sight of the Tree."

"They saw you," Iris said, face grim. "They know you're back. That one who spoke to Jason called you a man out of your time."

Gray glanced at her. "And how long did Gabe say he's been getting traffic?"

"A week," she replied.

Jason leaned his elbows on the table. "They must be gathering for another attempt."

"And you guys are going to walk right into the middle of it," Gray said. "Although what the strategy is this time, I have no idea. But it has something to do with you, Gene."

Eugene blew out a breath. "I might have a clue," he said with a grimace.

They all looked at him.

"Kat seemed really intrigued when I told her I got lost right after I touched that sample. And… she said she's been planning to return to Sedona to teach. She hopes she'll find that spirit guide named Albion again."

"Okay, he is *really* mad," Will said, staring above Eugene's head. "Anytime you mention that name, he gets kind of… flashier."

Eugene stared at the table. "Man, I really screwed up this time," he moaned. "I've put you all in danger. None of this would be happening if it weren't for me."

Will looked out the window and held up his hand. "Gene, stop."

"It's true," Eugene continued. "You guys might get killed down there because of me! Having me around is like a curse. I'd be better off—"

"Gene!" Will yelled. His eyes were still on the window. "I really, *really* need you to stop talking now." He looked back at their faces, eyes wary, then faced Eugene. "There's a darkness out there. Every load of crap you say brings it closer, okay? You gotta rein it in, buddy. They like it. We don't need them in here."

"Sorry," he mumbled.

"You're not a curse," Will said more gently. "You can't be a curse and a child of God at the same time, okay? That doesn't even make sense. He's got you."

Eugene nodded.

"Maybe you should go with them tomorrow, Will," Jason suggested. "An extra pair of eyes could really help."

"That's brilliant!" Iris exclaimed, turning to Will. "Would you come?"

"Well…" He considered for a moment, and smiled at Iris. "The new job doesn't start until Sunday. I'd be happy to."

"It'll be nice to have you, Will," said Eugene. "I can't believe I'm actually saying this, but I've never had anybody yell at me because they care. It's kinda nice."

Will laughed. "Maybe it happens more than you think!"

Jason checked his watch. "Oh, interesting…" he muttered.

A second later, all of them could hear his computer chime in the other room.

"What's that?" Will asked.

"Council summons," Jason replied. "A conference call, basically."

"Oh, you guys probably want some privacy," he said. "I can start on dishes."

"Thanks, Will," Jason said. "Iris, I'll see what the nature of it is and let you know. I have a feeling it might be about you. Remember, they said they would look into your status?"

"Ohhh, right!" she said.

"I'll be back." Jason disappeared into the den while the rest of them cleared plates.

Several minutes later, Jason called for Iris and Gray to join him.

When they entered, they heard Jason say, "I'll ask Iris" to the small group of twenty or so Council members on the screen.

He turned in his chair. "Iris, the Council followed through on looking for answers for you. They went back to the earliest archives they could get their hands on. Some of them aren't even in the database yet, because they were written by original Guardians."

"Original Guardians?" Iris asked.

"Yes, the very first appointees to their particular Trees, personally taught by Messengers."

"Wow," she whispered.

"What did they find out?" Gray asked.

"The stories say that Messengers taught the first generation of Guardians before they concealed themselves in the invisible realm. But after that, many of the original Guardians ran into problems with the first Heirs."

"What kind of problems?" asked Iris.

"Doubts," Jason said simply. "Because the fathers were taught by the Messengers themselves, they had an easier time accepting that their new abilities would make them fit for their task. They could hear the life in the Trees. They could speak freely with their wives. They lived in safety as rumors failed to spread, thanks to outsiders forgetting them. But the difficulty began as they trained their sons. For the first time, new Guardians were born rather than appointed. Many of the fathers struggled to believe that their sons would be safe—that they would inherit the same abilities. Their own transformations had been sudden, but their boys were exhibiting nothing like the same experience. Believing the promise that their work would continue through their sons took a great deal of trust. Some of them really struggled with that."

"So what happened?" Gray asked.

"They were so cautious that they taught their sons to doubt their own abilities. In one case, an Heir left home because he was too afraid to stay. His father had to track him down, at great risk to their family Tree. In another case, an Heir nearly got himself killed when a band of raiders came too close. He believed he might forget everything if he warned the invaders away from the Tree, so he chose to lie to them instead, and was captured. All of this was utterly unnecessary. Those boys were full fledged Guardians. They only needed to act like it."

"But Iris is different," Gray objected. "She wasn't appointed *or* born to this."

"Wasn't she?" Jason raised his eyebrows. "Didn't we offer her the job because we believed—we all agreed—that the Spirit Himself had appointed her?"

Gray frowned, his face conflicted. "Well... yes."

Jason smiled, and looked at Iris. "Which brings me to the Council's question... Have you tested your abilities?"

"I... I didn't know I was supposed to. I mean... do I *have* any abilities? I can't even talk to anyone about this outside this group!"

"That's not strictly true," said Eugene from the doorway.

They turned to look at him.

"I'm sorry for eavesdropping," he said sheepishly. "I walked by the door and overheard a little..."

"What do you mean it isn't true?" Iris asked him.

"Well..." He shrugged. "You talked to me, and I'm not a Guardian. When I first came here, you were the one who told me everything. Don't you remember?"

Her jaw dropped.

"Oh my gosh," Gray whispered. "How could I have been so blind?"

"I didn't even think about it," she said. "I was so excited to be on board that I just plowed right in!"

"And I was so busy worrying whether I'd trained you right, making sure everything you said was correct, that it didn't even occur to me what you'd done!" Gray said, eyes wide.

Iris was stunned. "This means… I won't forget anything, ever?"

Gray's face spread into a wide grin. "Yes, that's what it means!"

Jason smiled, and turned back to the screen, where several Council members were exchanging comments and delighted murmurs. "So… yes, apparently she *has* tested her abilities and retained her memories. She just didn't realize it till now," he chuckled.

Gray leaned down to face the screen and spoke earnestly to the kind, elderly faces. "I'm sorry for failing to see clearly. I take full responsibility for the confusion and suffering Iris has gone through." He turned to Iris, eyes full of sincerity. "I'll do better, I promise."

"It's okay." She gave his arm a gentle squeeze. "This is all very new for everyone. We're not going to get everything right the first time."

Several Council members agreed with Iris, and a dozen more spoke shared sentiments, which combined and appeared in the comments: *"Grayson, your mentorship has been a success. You have trained her as a proper Heir. Be proud of her, as we are proud of you both."*

"Thank you, guys," Gray said. "That… that means a lot, coming from you."

"Here, Iris," Jason stood and offered his chair.

She sat and faced the screen. "Thank you," she said to the men watching. "I'm so grateful for everything you've done to help me."

She heard a sharp inhale behind her. Jason and Gray whispered something to each other.

After several comments were spoken, they came back translated into the same unified thought: *"You are truly one of us. We are so pleased to have you."*

"I'm glad," she said, beaming. "I can't imagine being anywhere else. This isn't just a job to me. I consider it a big part of who I am."

Jason and Gray whispered again, this time more excitedly.

Iris turned toward them, and was startled by the look of amazement on each of their faces. "What are you two on about?"

The two men looked curiously at each other, then back at her.

Gray squinted at her with a look of intense concentration. "Say it again… what you said to the Council a second ago."

Iris frowned. "I said… this isn't just a job. It's who I am."

Gray looked at his father. "Are you hearing this?"

Jason nodded and pulled out his phone. He clicked into a voice recorder and pointed it at Iris. "One more time for me."

"Jason, what are you doing?"

"Humor me."

She sighed, but spoke again with conviction. "This isn't just my job, it's who I am!"

Jason played back the recording.

The sound that came out of the speaker was definitely Iris's voice, but it wasn't English.

Iris's jaw dropped. "What *is* that?"

Grayson grinned. "It's Chaldaic!"

"But how am I doing that?" Iris squeaked.

Jason laughed. "Same way we do it! You're a Guardian!"

"But… how *can* I be?" She whirled back to the grinning faces on the conference call.

Each man spoke with great passion, all at once. When their comments appeared in the box, they melded into one unified thought:

"You guard something infinitely more precious than a Great Tree, something near the heart of the Creator: those who are helpless. He has appointed you Guardian of the Lost."

Chapter 24

Sedona, Arizona ~ Present day

A solitary figure sat on a flat expanse of red stone, eyes closed against the deepening twilight. The orange glow from a circle of flickering candles glinted off of her long, silver braid and beaded necklaces. Her lips moved in repetition as she swayed slightly, though unintentionally, to the sounds within her mind. She lifted her palms, reaching into the unseen.

The darkness above her became opaque, smudging out the cold starlight. A billowing force, inky crimson and oppressive, hovered beside her right hand.

"Bold…" Skliros whispered too softly for her to hear. "Very bold." He turned to the black shadow beside him. "This is the same female creature from before, is it not, Vroma?"

"It is," Vroma cackled. "Though she appears about to expire. Didn't her mate just traipse through here a week ago?"

"He did indeed. But now, see how she returns to my realm alone, with no Seal upon her? She conducts herself according to the scroll… yet she summons the enemy."

"No, Great One," he replied. "She summons Apateon."

"Fascinating," he breathed. "So that reckless charlatan still goes by the name of his former rival, does he?"

"Though he has spoken through other humans since, Apateon first chose to be known to this particular creature by that name.

I lingered for a time after you told him to follow her, and I heard him call himself 'Albion.'"

"Brazen," he chuckled. "I wouldn't have thought him capable of such high-minded fraud. It's almost as if he *wants* another confrontation."

"He tempts fate, for certain," said Vroma. "But his ruse has been effective. The last woman he brought back from his travels has made good on his debt of tribute to you."

"Yes," rumbled Skliros. "The scroll is…" he chuckled, "*colorfully* fulfilled, and even expanded here. I see the marks of Apateon's dramatic flair in the humans' asinine rituals. And I assign leeches to new hosts almost daily. There's a pleasing lack of general awareness toward the Enemy."

"You are truly masterful for assigning him the task, Great Ba'al."

"He's a mercurial jackass, but I did so enjoy his poem about me." Skliros grinned. "Best laugh I'd had in a century. I've not seen him in my realm in years. Where is he now, I wonder?"

"Last I heard, he was planning to lure his host across the plains to continue the same work in the distant mountains. He had really begun to relish it. Perhaps he lingers there still."

"Go and summon him. Let him know that his favorite little pet is here, longing to see him."

Vroma snickered.

"Now that her lost mate has reappeared," Skliros continued, "it's only a matter of time before he re-enters my realm in search of the Great Tree. When he does, we could empower a match that draws in real followers. The gullible travelers I've herded across Guardian land were meant as ill-timed distractions, but I think that with a little guidance, they could be much more. With enough of them, we may yet take the Tree for our own. And of course, Apateon may want to play with this female one more time before I dispose of her for trespassing."

Vancouver, Washington

Iris packed light, just as she had on her first mission. One backpack, three changes of clothes, her laptop, and bare necessities. Her mind buzzed with possibilities. *I'm a Guardian. A real one. There's nothing stopping me from telling Dad what I'm doing… maybe Mum, too. I could go out to the living room right now and tell Charlie everything!* She smiled. *Maybe I will. She believed me last time. Heck, she abetted a fugitive!*

Her phone buzzed. Finn Jacobs' picture smiled at her from the screen.

"Favorite Dad!" she answered. "It's past your bedtime, isn't it? Everything okay?"

"Aye, lass," he replied. "Of course it is. I just… well, I keep thinking about things, and I knew you'd still be putterin' about at this hour."

"You know me well," she said. "What have you been thinking about?"

"I've read it all twice now," he said bluntly, knowing she'd understand his meaning.

"And?"

"I cannae stop thinkin' on it. You say you've embraced the mystical aspects, right?"

She smiled. "I've embraced every aspect."

There was silence on the other end for a long moment.

"Dad?"

"Sorry, sweet girl. I'm just… I cannae decide how to ask you this next bit."

"Spit it out, Dad. I promise, you can't offend me."

"Arright… I guess I'm just curious if anything's happened to you lately. Since you changed your mind, I mean."

If anything's happened… She chuckled. *How to sum that up…*

"Yes, something's definitely happened," she finally answered. "I'm basically a totally different person."

Finn let out a breath.

Iris raised her eyebrows.

Finally, he spoke. "I'm so glad to hear that, my dear. Because for a second, I thought I might be off my heid."

"Dad, you sound weird."

"Sorry. I mean, something's different with me, too. I came to feel that what this book says is true. In fact, I was in desperate hope of it. So I decided to speak out loud to God one night and tell Him so. But that's gone far beyond proportions now. It's like He's sitting in my lounge!"

Iris laughed.

"I'm glad you find it so funny, cheeky thing! I'm not jokin'!"

"I'm not either!" she laughed again. "I'm just happy for you! I know exactly what you're talking about, Dad. He's in my living room, too. In my car… in my head… everywhere."

She could hear him chuckle softly. "Isn't it nice?"

"It's the most loved I've ever felt."

"Aye, we had tea today, He and I. And here, I'm supposed to be this distinguished intellectual."

"Don't you think that getting on speaking terms with your Creator is about the most intellectual thing you could do?"

"Tell that to your mother," he sighed.

"Maybe I will," she giggled. "I'm so pleased for you, Dad. I can't begin to tell you."

"Let's chat more soon, arright?"

"I want to. I'm headed out of town in the morning, just for a few days, but I'll call you when I get back. I've got so much to tell you."

"I want to hear every detail, Favorite Girl! You know I love you, right?"

She grinned at his familiar sign-off. "I love you too."

"Hey, Iris?" Charlie appeared in the open doorway of her room. "Oh, sorry…" she whispered when she saw the phone.

"No, it's okay, we just hung up. It was my dad." She plugged the phone into its charger and set it on the nightstand. "What's up?"

"I'm making popcorn… which, as we know, is a vegetable. Want some?"

"It's not a vegetable. And yes, I'd love some."

"Going on another trip, huh?" Charlie asked, eyeing her backpack.

"Yeah, a quick one."

"So, not Fiji or anyplace like that this time?"

"No," Iris chuckled. "Arizona, actually."

"Ohhh sunshine? Take me with you!" Charlie pleaded.

Iris laughed. "I wish I could! There will probably be some hiking. I know you love that."

"I'm not big on cactus, actually," she replied, blowing her blue bangs out of her eyes.

"Sedona, though… red rocks? Trees?"

"Man," Charlie sighed. "I need to reassess my career ambitions. I'm going to go cook these vegetables with extra butter now." She turned and headed into the kitchen.

Iris zipped her backpack and followed. "Sorry… if it makes you feel any better, one of the main things I'll be doing is visiting a huge junkyard. It's not going to be all that glamorous."

Charlie turned and gave her a strange look. "First old people and BINGO, then Hawaii on a private jet, now a junkyard?" She ripped the cellophane off the popcorn bag and unfolded it. "You have a weird life, you know that?"

"You just listed three of the most normal things I've had happen to me lately. You want to hear about weird?"

"I love weird!" Charlie tossed the popcorn into the microwave, shut the door, and poked the vegetable button. "Let's hear about weird!"

For the next two hours, Iris opened up her world to her oldest friend. She shared the story of a Creator who anchored the fabric of time with Great Trees scattered across the globe, each protected by a Guardian. She told her about the unfortunate day in 1844, when her friend Angus encountered a Great Hawthorn and found himself hopelessly lost. She told Charlie every detail of her part in their escape—things that Charlie couldn't remember doing. But she also couldn't deny the accuracy of Iris's detail, right down to the color of the new sleeping bags in her parents' cabin near Seattle, even though Iris supposedly hadn't been to the cabin since their senior year of high school.

Charlie asked Iris to talk louder while she went to the kitchen for two glasses of water. She ended up returning with slices of havarti cheese and fun sized Snickers to go with the popcorn while Iris told her about what she, Angus, and Will had to do to put things right again, and why none of them could remember it. She showed her the pink scar on her leg and talked about the hidden Messengers who surrounded them. She spoke of how their old science teacher, Mr. Reynolds, had come to her with a mysterious job offer, and how he and his son had shown her the clandestine world of the Council of Guardians.

Charlie listened, enraptured, as Iris continued through Eugene's story. Iris's face glowed as she savored the freedom of being real. The tiny cracks in their long friendship, caused by the strain of secrecy, were beginning to heal. And Charlie was every inch the loyal sister she'd always been—extending faith to Iris in the absence of proof, trust in the absence of logic.

Iris answered every one of Charlie's questions, backtracking and filling in details until Charlie had caught up to the present moment. When she was finished, she had only one secret left— the one between herself and Will—but it felt wonderful to hold on to that one.

Charlie leaned back against the sofa cushions, staring at the ceiling. "Whew. Well, I was right," she said.

Iris sipped her water, realizing her throat had gone dry after so much talking. "Right about what?"

"You have a really weird life."

Their eyes met, and they burst into laughter.

"I can't imagine how hard it's been for you, keeping all that locked up inside," Charlie said. "Kudos for maintaining a functional level of mental health."

"Thanks. I'm glad I don't have to live like that anymore. It was hard enough when I was just trying to hold onto my memories of Angus. But once I took the job, it was becoming impossible."

Charlie gazed at Iris with a thoughtful expression, then frowned. "I feel kind of bad, now."

Iris frowned back. "Why in the world would you feel bad? I was the one keeping all the secrets!"

"Not really."

"Is that a fact?"

Charlie gave her a sad smile. "We've known each other since third grade. You're my best friend. And yet… this is the first time we've ever talked seriously about what we believe. The kind of faith you've just found? I've had that since I was a kid. When we were eight, you kind of talked about it for a little while, so I just assumed you and God were fine. But… I never actually asked you. I'm sorry I never did. I should have."

"Wait… you love God, too?"

Charlie nodded. "See what I mean? It shouldn't be so hard to tell! But I don't know… I guess I've always kept my faith private because I didn't want anyone to feel like I was trying to shove it in their face."

"I wouldn't have thought that," Iris said softly.

"I know." Charlie pursed her lips. "I guess the longer I kept quiet, the easier it was to stay quiet. But I just watched you talk about it like it was the most natural, beautiful thing in the world. I haven't felt that way in forever. My faith isn't like yours. It's more like… wallpaper."

Iris gave her a compassionate smile. She was about to say, "it's okay," but something stopped her. She thought for another moment until the right words came.

"I don't think either one of us can afford to have it be wallpaper. Not considering what we're actually dealing with."

"I guess it's easy to forget that," Charlie admitted. "Apparently, I've been underestimating a lot of things. I mean, Will actually... died?"

Iris nodded, a pained expression crossing her features at the memory of it.

They sat in silence for a moment.

"It shouldn't seem beyond the realm of possibility to me that he's back," Charlie said at last. "It's not like it's never been done. But I just... didn't think stuff like that ever happened anymore!"

"Well it sure caught *me* off guard!" Iris said. "And Gray acted like it was the most logical thing in the world. So I guess you and I both have things to learn."

"For sure," she agreed. "So... obviously Will knows everything, too?"

"Yeah. In fact, he's been a huge help with Eugene. Actually, with... all of it."

Charlie glanced at her with a knowing grin. "He's smitten with you. I can see it."

"That's fortunate, because I'm smitten with him, too!" Iris laughed.

"You're openly admitting it now!" Charlie gasped. "Progress!"

Iris sighed happily. "I'm glad you like Will, because he's definitely going to be around."

"Good. You two seem great together."

Iris yawned. "I'm sorry I've kept you up so late."

"Nah, it's fine. I have tomorrow off."

"Well I don't..." Iris said, checking her watch. *One in the morning. Yikes.* "I should shuffle. But I'll give you Jason's number, okay? In case you need anything and can't get a hold of me, or...

I dunno, if you want to ask them anything. He and Gray are awesome about that." Iris pulled out her phone and forwarded Jason's contact info to Charlie's number.

"I don't know if I could call Mr. Reynolds 'Jason,' though."

Iris smiled. "I thought the same thing at first, but he makes it so easy. He and Gray are both really easy to talk to."

"Hmm." Charlie nodded, staring at the ceiling again. She only seemed to be half listening. Suddenly, she smiled.

"What?"

Charlie looked back at Iris. "What what?"

"What are you smiling about?"

"Ha. Um…" She smiled again. "Did you ever put in a good word for me?"

"With Grayson? Oh, I kind of… thought you might be kidding about that," Iris replied.

Charlie gave her a look that suggested very much otherwise.

"Sorry, I didn't," Iris said with an apologetic smile. "But I have acquired some intelligence."

"Spill."

"He and I had a discussion the other day. He kind of… liked someone, but she wasn't interested. I don't know for sure, but he might need some time to get over it."

"Poor guy!" Charlie said. "Who in the world would be insane enough to turn down someone like him?"

Iris smiled. *So maybe I have more than one secret left.* "A total idiot, clearly," she replied. "But maybe he'll be up for meeting someone amazing soon. I was thinking about introducing him to Candace."

"Now *that's* just mean!"

Iris laughed. "We'll get together soon, I promise. Will's been wanting to, anyway." She yawned again. "Arright, seriously. Bed for me." She leaned in and hugged Charlie. "I'm so glad you're in my life."

"I'm glad, too," Charlie said, giving Iris's hair a playful tug. "More than ever."

At the small airport in Hillsboro, Iris walked out to a Gulfstream jet, followed by Will and a wide-eyed Eugene.

"Hi, guys!" An elderly man, deeply wrinkled by years of smiling, waved at them from the plane's open door. He had silvery salt and pepper hair, bronze skin, and dark, narrow eyes that twinkled when he spoke.

"Are you Mr. Kellutuq?" Iris asked him.

He trudged down the small flight of steps to meet them. "Pretty much. Try saying 'kesh-YU-tuke' if you want to get a little closer. But I'm just Ed." He grinned and extended his hand. "You must be Iris."

"I am! So nice to meet you!" Iris replied, shaking his hand. "This is Gene, and this is Will. Thanks so much for letting us borrow your plane."

Ed waved his hand casually. "It's my pleasure. Our little mining operation isn't real busy this time of year, so my wife and I like to come down where it's warm and spend a few weeks."

"You think Oregon is warm?" Eugene asked incredulously.

"Compared to Alaska right now?" Ed chuckled. "Yes."

"Oh, so you're an Eskimo," Eugene said.

"Gene, that's not really…" Iris began, but then shrugged and turned to Ed. "Sorry, he's a little bit… old school."

Ed laughed. "I'm Yup'ik, actually," he said to Eugene. "But you don't have to be politically correct for me! I was born in thirty-seven, so I've been called a lot of things!"

"Hey, that's the same year I was born!" Eugene grinned.

Ed clapped him on the shoulder. "It only gets better, my friend. Eighty is the new thirty." He turned toward the plane. "Well, my two guys are on board, ready to go. I don't have a cabin crew, but I keep a lot of good snacks in the back. Help yourselves to whatever's there."

"Thanks so much," Iris said. "When do you need it back?"

"Take your time," Ed replied. "We're down here for a couple weeks yet. My guys aren't mad at the idea of a few days in Arizona. Just give 'em a call when you're ready to head back."

About two hours later, they made a smooth touchdown in Scottsdale, where it was eighty degrees and sunny.

When Eugene stepped into the sunshine, he stretched and turned his face toward the light. "That is *so* much better," he murmured. "I can already feel myself thawing out."

"Ha, ha," Iris smirked. "Washington isn't *that* bad."

"Said the Scottish girl," Will laughed.

"All right, you two," she huffed, shouldering her backpack. "Let's see if we can find Gabe."

The moment they stepped onto the sidewalk outside the terminal, a late 1960s turquoise Bronco rumbled to the curb. Iris could hear the muffled sounds of U2 right before the grinning driver cut the engine.

Will smiled. "If that's him, I like him already."

A tan, dark haired man with a striking goatee hopped out and bounded toward them. "Iris!" he said, beaming at her. "You made it, girl! And Will and Eugene, I presume." He fist bumped each of them. Though he couldn't have been taller than five foot six, his presence was enormous. His energy seemed to bubble up from his toes.

"Nice to see you, Gabe," she giggled. "I hope this airport wasn't too far out of the way."

"Nah, the trip from my house to this airport is literally the same as getting to Sky Harbor. Maybe one minute's difference. Oh my gosh, Danny wanted me to let him out of school for this *so* bad, but I had to play the Serious Dad card today. You guys hungry? I know *the* best tamale place close to here."

"What's a tamale?" Iris asked.

The three men erupted in simultaneous protests of disbelief. Most shocked among them was Will.

"Yes, let's get her some tamales," Will laughed. "Because that's just sad!"

"I have a feeling I'm about to become more cultured!" Iris chuckled.

"Heck yes, tamales and a junkyard!" said Gabe. "That's cultured, all right!"

Once Iris had enjoyed a proper education in Mexican cuisine, they set off in Gabe's Bronco for the half hour drive to the scrap yard. Iris understood from her research that the place encompassed acres of cars, but her brain had still not grasped the scope of it until she stood in the gravel, staring down aisles and aisles of rusted bodies, open hoods, dingy glass, crumpled fenders, and staring headlights.

"My car's out there somewhere?" Eugene mumbled. "I'd only made one payment on it!"

Will patted his shoulder. "Sorry, man."

He let out a breath. "Let's get on with it. How do we narrow it down?"

"Can I help you?" asked a voice behind them. They turned to see a man standing in dusty cargo shorts, a tattered baseball cap, and a smudged t-shirt printed with the company logo.

Iris held out her hand. "I'm Iris Jacobs. I emailed you guys a while ago about a sixty-five Mustang convertible."

The man shook her hand. "Yeah, yeah I remember that. Nice to see you. I'm Brian. Well, I know for sure we've got 'er, paperwork wise, but as you can see, she ain't exactly gonna be right on top. I can take you to the Mustang corral and give you a general idea where to look, but after that, you'll just have to see what you see."

"That's fair," Iris replied. "We'd appreciate any help you can give us."

"Follow me," he said, and began walking. "You looking to buy back an old friend? Or…"

"No," said Eugene. "Just looking for something I left in the car."

"Oh." Brian stopped. "Well anything that was in the car would've been bagged and held for ninety days. After that, we woulda sold it. Whatcha lookin' for?"

Eugene's shoulders slumped. "Just an old tool. Sort of looks like a long drill. I doubt there would be much demand for something like that."

"Any idea if you guys would have seen that?" Iris asked. "Would've been around maybe 2016?"

"Oh, that long ago?" Brian shook his head. "No way it's still around, whatever it is."

Iris and Eugene exchanged grim looks. Eugene stared at the gravel.

"Hey," Will said. "No stone unturned, right?"

"Exactly," agreed Gabe. "We've gotten all the way here. Let's just see the car."

Brian shrugged and continued walking. "Suit yourselves. The cars get cleaned out pretty good, though."

After a minute's walk, they arrived in an area littered with old Fords, mostly Mustangs, stacked in twos.

"This is most of 'em, although there's prolly a few others around," Brian said. "Anyway, good luck. I'm supposed to be looking for a hood for a GTO right now. But let someone down at the office know if you need anything else, okay?" He disappeared down a dusty aisle.

"Well?" Will said, hands on hips. "Where do we start? Should we split up?"

"Actually, that's not a bad idea," Gabe replied. "Iris, I heard a rumor that you've come into some interesting abilities lately. That true?"

She smiled. "Yeah. Actually, it's possible they've been there since I took the job, and I just didn't realize it."

"Happened to me, too," Gabe said. "My dad had such strong abilities, I kind of wondered if I'd ever grow into his shoes. But that kind of thinking dulled my hearing. I had to believe I was made for this. When I did, it turned out I was even better at it than he was!" He grinned. "So I propose we each take an aisle. You and Will go that way, Gene and I will go this way. Use your ears, Iris."

"Use my ears? For such a tiny piece of Tree?"

Gabe raised an eyebrow. "What'd I say, girl? Doubts make you deaf! Close your eyes for a sec."

Iris obeyed.

"Okay, remember the loudest sound you've ever heard from a Tree."

She immediately recalled the deafening racket produced by the Great Hawthorn trying to heal itself before its new growth was chopped away. "Got it."

"Now think of the quietest sound you've heard a tree make."

She reached farther back into her memories, until she could recall the whispering hum above her, the day she woke up in the woods in 1844. She nodded.

Gabe's voice was soft. "Guardian ears are a thousand times more sensitive to it, so it'll be somewhere in between those when you hear it. Just focusing like this will help."

She opened her eyes and smiled. "Let's do this."

He fist bumped her. "Shout when you find it."

The group split off. Eugene followed Gabe. He felt strangely sad, searching the stacks of ruined vehicles for a car he'd driven brand new less than two weeks ago.

"Dude, it sounds like it was a pretty sweet little 'stang. You'll have to send me a picture of you next to it when you get back home."

"If I get home, I'll be sure and do that. And... by the way, I wanted to say thanks. Y'know, for trying to make sure I was okay before. I was pretty rude to you."

"All's forgiven," Gabe said. "I'm glad you're back."

"Me too."

"Hey, Gene! Gabe!" Iris shouted from eight stacks over. "I think this might be it!"

They hurried to join her and Will in front of a rusted, somewhat flattened Mustang convertible with the remains of a white fastback on top of it. Its hood, passenger door, headlights, rearview mirrors, and wheels were gone.

"Ugh, I can't believe this," Eugene moaned. "It's even worse than the photos!"

"Sorry, Gene," Iris said, her face sympathetic.

He sighed. "No, y'know what? I'm glad I'm seeing this. Nobody gets a chance like this, to see the final outcome of their decisions. I have a wife. I have... a daughter. They're still around. Nothing matters more than that."

"That's right, man," Gabe said. "Family. One of God's greatest gifts."

"So this is for sure the right car?" Will asked.

"Sure looks like it," Eugene replied. "That's the right upholstery color. But who knows?"

"Okay..." Gabe said, fingers on lips.

Everyone was still.

Iris and Gabe drew closer, listening. They looked at each other and smiled as they heard the faintest little high pitched hum coming from somewhere within the car.

"Tell me you can hear that," he whispered.

She nodded.

Eugene and Will exchanged looks and shrugged.

"I think it's under the seat!" Iris whispered and pointed.

"Right where I left it!" Eugene said excitedly.

Iris knelt and peered beneath the seat, but saw nothing but clumps of dried grass mixed with shredded upholstery and stuffing from the gutted seat. "Well, no wonder it's still here. Must have gotten stuck behind this packrat nest, or whatever this is." The sound grew louder as she pulled away bits of debris.

At last, she saw a corner of a ruined leather strap, and tugged it out from under the seat, bringing with it the remains of a crusty leather satchel. As soon as she did, she began to hear another strange sound, almost like a buzz.

"Iris, back up!" Gabe shouted.

Before she could move, a mottled green and brown rattlesnake slithered out from under the seat on the driver's side, coiled itself beneath the steering wheel, and stared at her, rattling its tail in a blur of motion.

Iris froze, barely able to catch her breath, heart pounding, as she watched the creature.

"Oh geez, that's a mojave," Gabe murmured, just loud enough to be heard. "Not good. Iris, you gotta back away very, *very* slowly, okay?"

Slowly, centimeter by centimeter, Iris released the strap from her hand and took a partial step back.

"That's right, nice and easy..." Gabe whispered.

The snake tensed its neck into a tight "S" shape and rattled more loudly.

Iris kept her eyes on it, and moved to take another half step. She set her foot on an uneven clump of earth, causing her to tilt crazily to one side and throw an arm out to catch herself. In a flash of motion, the rattlesnake crossed the three foot gap between them and sank its fangs into her forearm. She gasped in pain.

Chapter 25

Phoenix, Arizona ~ Present day

A plume of black streaked into the sky over the graveyard of metal and glass. He let out a jubilant cackle. Finally, something was going right. Things had been difficult enough ever since his host had been marked by the Enemy, sending him into near banishment. He'd had to watch from a distance, waiting for the opportunity to reclaim him.

He pointed his eyes northward. The male creature out of his time was journeying back to the Tree anyway. May as well get a head start on him. He didn't relish the idea of another conversation with the arrogant crimson lord of the red stone castle, but the thought of that beast's ire—though it did nothing to inspire his loyalty, was enough to force his cooperation. Besides, there was now a morsel of gossip so delectable that it might please even that pompous blowhard.

As he approached, he sensed a growing thickness in the atmosphere, a delicious brooding and churning below. He circled to get the feel of his surroundings. There was a murky cloud above a distant clearing, where a ring of vehicles surrounded a campsite. In the center, beside a black fire pit, stood an old female, speaking to a group of a few dozen creatures. He shifted his eyes to the north and spotted Skliros, who was trying as ever to appear larger and louder, flanked by Vroma, his sycophantic lackey, and none other than Apateon.

"Well now," he said as he settled above the ground beside them. "That's an interesting gathering over there."

"Thelo!" Apateon greeted him. "You seem to have lost someone."

"Oh, I know precisely where he is," Thelo retorted. "I merely come to report to lord Skliros that he is within hours of returning to these lands."

"Have you done something right, for a change?" Skliros let out a satisfied grumble. "Your creature is late to the party, but we can still make use of him. His mate leads that ridiculous gathering in the clearing. Apateon has created quite the little disciple. She follows the scroll handed down from the princes as if her life depended on it. And she longs for him, *begs* for him to return, even after all these years. Does yours even realize you left?"

Thelo ignored the dig, eager to avoid prolonging the conversation. "I have other news," he said.

"Do tell," Skliros drawled.

"Surely, you know of the female Guardian who stands watch over those out of their time?"

"Of course. She is spectacularly annoying. I've tried twice to dispose of her since she began meddling with my property."

Thelo scoffed. "No need to concern yourself further with her. She is as good as dead."

A deep, echoing laugh rumbled from within the crimson fog. "Is that so?"

Iris stood in shock, unsure what to do with the four foot long creature that dangled from her arm by its fangs. Gabe, Eugene, and Will seemed temporarily immobilized by the sight. But seconds later, Iris came to her senses and gave her arm a little shake, allowing gravity to release the rattlesnake's grip. It left two trails of blood tinged with gooey streaks of pale yellow venom across Iris's arm as it fell away, landing in the dust with a thud and slithering out of sight between two piles of rusted cars across the aisle.

Will was the first to move. "Iris! Oh my gosh…" He ran to her side. "Gabe, what do we do? I don't know anything about snakes!"

"Iris, you gotta sit down and try not to move, okay?" Gabe said, his face pained with worry. "Keep your arm low, below your heart. I'll call an ambulance." He pulled out his phone.

Iris sat in the shade beside the gutted Mustang. "Actually, I think I might be okay…" she said, but rested her arm at her side anyway.

Will knelt beside her, an indecipherable expression on his face.

Iris met his eyes. *Is that worry? Anger?* She touched his cheek with her other hand. "Will, it's okay. I'm fine."

Eugene's face was somber. "Iris, I don't want to scare you, but there's no way you're fine. Mojaves have neurotoxic venom—it does damage for days. We have to get you to a hospital."

"Well, how fast does it work?" she asked. "Because—"

"Fast," Gabe said. "And it's hemotoxic as well. The ones in this area have been cross-breeding for a couple of decades." He frowned at his phone. "Gah, I can't get a good signal here. I'm going to run back to the office. Stay still, okay?" He bolted away.

Iris looked at Eugene. "You know about snakes?"

He nodded, his lips pressed into a grim line. "I've lived in Tucson my whole life, and half my work is outdoors. I've learned everything I can. Y'know, to be on the safe side."

"So what happens now?" she asked.

"Let's not get into all that," he replied. "Just stay calm, okay?"

"I just…" She let out a big sigh and glanced down at her arm. "I can't really feel anything."

"Numbness can be part of the symptoms," he said.

"No, I mean…" she sighed again, and looked at Will as something occurred to her. "Do you see anything happening?"

"Anything happening?" Will repeated.

"Yeah, like… things I can't see?"

"Oh," he said absently, looking around. "No."

Iris frowned. "Just… no? They're not here?"

"They're here," he finally said. He searched her face with a look of desperation. "But they're not doing anything. They're just… waiting."

"Oh."

Within minutes, an ambulance bumped down the gravel aisle toward them and parked. Three EMTs hopped out and surrounded Iris. Gabe and two of the yard employees caught up on foot several seconds later.

Iris sat silently, somewhat befuddled, listening to the conversation of the eight worried people around her. They took her blood pressure, examined her arm, and peered into her eyes with a flashlight. Someone swabbed her arm for a venom sample. What did the snake look like? Where was it now? How long ago was she bitten? Was she experiencing any trouble breathing? Pain? Sleepiness? Paralysis? Swelling? Blurred vision?

In frustration, she finally spoke over the din: "You guys, I'm *fine*!"

The conversation died down as they all gazed at her, bewildered.

"It's been over ten minutes!" she went on. "Shouldn't I be feeling *something* by now?"

One EMT, a woman in her early forties with short brown hair and a kind face, knelt in the dirt beside Iris. "Hi, Iris. I'm Michelle."

"Hi." Iris smiled.

"Well," Michelle said, "your blood pressure's normal. Pulse ox reading is ninety-eight. You're clearly not in any kind of distress." She tilted her head. "Nothing goin' on, huh, kid? No pain whatsoever?"

Iris shook her head. "Other than the initial bite, no."

She took Iris's wrist in her hand and gently lifted her injured arm. She felt Iris's fingers and checked both sides of her hand. "Make a fist for me."

Iris obeyed.

"Excellent perfusion. No edema." She looked up at the others. "I got nothin.'"

Will frowned. "Iris, are you positive? You're not dizzy or in pain, or anything?"

"I feel totally normal!"

"Maybe it was a dry bite?" Another EMT commented.

Michelle gave him a look akin to a mother scolding a teenager. "Gimme a break." She held up Iris's arm. "There was venom oozing out of there when we got here. You swabbed it yourself. Given the total lack of symptoms, that substance couldn't have been white blood cells."

He pursed his lips and frowned.

Michelle squinted at Iris with a knowing look. "You must be up to something important."

Iris met her gaze and nodded, a slight smile crossing her face.

"Well, I guess that's it for us, then," she said. She stood and pulled her purple gloves off with a snap.

"What?" said both of the other EMTs at the same time.

"We should at least take her for observation," one of them protested.

Michelle shrugged. "She said she's fine."

"But a rattlesnake bite—"

"Would have caused symptoms by now if it was going to," she finished. She looked at her watch. "We're going on closer to fifteen minutes, actually. Look at her. She should be writhing in pain and struggling to breathe. Her arm should have doubled in size by now. Looks like she's got someone looking out for her."

"I believe her," Gabe said. "It's not like there isn't a precedent for this."

Will and Eugene both stared at him, dumbfounded.

The other EMT shook his head. "I don't know what precedent you're referring to, unless you're saying she's got superpowers."

"Hm, maybe she does!" Gabe winked at Iris.

She smiled and shook her head, and stood up.

Everyone watched her suspiciously, as if they expected her to topple over at any moment.

She raised her eyebrows, looked around at their befuddled faces, and gave them an awkward smile. "Could I maybe just have a Band-Aid?"

Michelle chuckled and opened her supplies. "Pick a color."

"Purple!"

The EMTs had decided to stick around for fifteen more minutes "just to chat," but really to see if Iris developed any delayed symptoms. She finally convinced them to go, and got a laugh out of Michelle, by promising to get to a hospital immediately if she developed even the slightest case of hiccups.

Once the ambulance had left, Iris, Will, Eugene, and Gabe climbed back into the Bronco. Gabe cranked the air conditioning to full blast, then turned his body to face Eugene in the passenger seat and Will and Iris in the back seat.

"Well, that was an adventure!" he said.

Will and Eugene just stared at Iris in exhausted disbelief.

"What did you mean when you said there's a precedent for this?" Will asked.

"Oh, it's happened before," Gabe said simply. "There's one example in the Histories where a guy got a venomous bite to the hand. Everyone expected him to swell up and die, but nothing happened at all. God protected him."

Will looked at Iris's purple bandage and back at Gabe. "The Messengers sure weren't doing much about it."

Gabe gave him a contemplative look. "It's amazing that you can see those guys," he said. "And it's amazing that they're on our side, and we get to partner with them. But they're just Messengers, y'know?"

Will frowned, deep in thought.

"We're privileged," Gabe went on, "because God works with us personally. Sometimes the answer to the problem is something He's already put inside you. His Spirit in you is far more powerful than any being outside of you. The Messengers move at His command. When they hold back, it doesn't mean He's holding back. In fact, it often means He's about to do something even more powerful, because He's doing it with His own hands."

Will gazed at the floor. "I guess I can't see everything. I can't even see the most important things."

"Hey, it's okay. None of us can see everything... *yet.* Don't be discouraged, though. This is brand new stuff to you. The longer you walk with God, the more you'll know. But we can be sure He never stops working, even when we don't see it."

Will nodded.

"The question is," Iris said, "was it all worth it?" She turned to Eugene and smiled. "I think we got what we came for. I can hear it."

He grinned and pulled the crusty leather bag from the floor to his lap. "This is it, all right. I can't believe it was still there."

"I can," Will said. "There was a guard posted beside it. He's gone now."

Eugene shook his head. "And I also can't believe the kinds of statements I consider to be normal now. Of course there was a guard. Why not?" He rolled his eyes and smiled, and lifted the bag's flap. "Ugh..." He grimaced when he saw the water damaged journals, maps, and notebooks, blackened with mold and disintegrated. But along the side lay the pieces of his increment borer. He gasped. "Whoa… that's totally wicked."

"What?" Iris asked.

"The handle and extractor are completely wrecked, and most of the shaft is covered in rust. But look at this…" He pulled a long, thin piece of metal from the bag. The last three inches of it were still shiny, untouched. "Look at the auger bit!"

"Is that where the wood is stuck?" Will asked.

Eugene nodded. "It looks like it hasn't aged a day!" He turned the bit and peered into the hollow end with one eye. "Yeah, it's clogged alright. There's even still some sawdust in the threads. Now I'm glad I didn't clean it!"

"Procrastination pays off!" Gabe chuckled. "Let's get back to Sedona, y'all!"

The ninety minute drive up I-17 flew by in a flow of easy conversation and laughter. Iris made up her mind to stay in the moment and just enjoy the camaraderie. She refused to think about what the rest of the day might bring, or what uncertainty threatened the next part of Eugene's journey. This would be her third time witnessing a Tree repair. Although each one so far had brought a few unexpected twists, she wanted to focus on what could go right. As Angus had said, she could trust a God whose specialty was the impossible.

She also didn't want to take for granted the living, breathing miracle on the seat beside her. She used to believe that Will's greatest gifts were his creative talent in the kitchen and the fact that he was a good listener and fierce protector. In reality, she hadn't had the slightest clue how beautifully he would fit into her supernatural world. He was already incredibly perceptive, but now, his ability to see into the spirit realm was beyond anything she'd imagined. The possibility of him forgetting everything they'd done together, even if it was only a remote chance, was intolerable. *If I'm a Guardian, then I could protect his memory by marrying him.* She felt tiny butterflies. *But what's that going to look like to everyone else?*

She frowned. In the whole scope of things, she hadn't been immersed in this world very long. But it had been long enough to solidify this way of seeing reality. Sometimes, finding a person stuck in the wrong time was just a fact of life. Occasionally, dark creatures tried to kill you. Death wasn't always fixed. The Histories were true. Oh, and sometimes people completely forgot you if they weren't careful. This was her life now.

Another fact? She had never loved another human being more than she loved Will. What could be more logical than to marry him as soon as possible so that things could stay as they were?

It was easy to forget that most people, like her mother, didn't even have a grid for understanding time travel, supernatural beings, or what it was like to have someone take a bullet for you. All Heather would see was a couple of starry-eyed twenty-three year olds who met three months ago and were about to rush into what could be the biggest mistake of their lives. But in the end, who cared what anyone else thought? Wasn't it Will who mattered more?

But that's what stopped Iris from dismissing public opinion so easily. Will had a brilliant career ahead of him, and he had her. What he lacked was family. Besides his little brother, he was alone. The thought of Luke and Will seated at the table with her, Finn, and Heather… and even Granny Cora and Granddad Liam, filled her heart with an irresistible warmth. She would never want to place an obstacle between Will and her family. He deserved their total acceptance, but he'd never have it—especially not from her mother—if they thought he'd started out by doing something rash. *I'll just have to be patient.*

She looked at him, and realized he'd been watching her for some time in utter, dimpled amusement.

Geez, will I ever quit blushing around him?

"Thinking hard again, huh?" he murmured in her ear.

She smiled and leaned her head against his. "Was I moving my lips again, too?"

"It's cute," he whispered. "Besides, a healthy inner monologue is a sign of genius."

"Or psychosis."

"Be nice to my fiancé," he breathed. "I'm very protective, y'know."

"I have noticed a pattern there, yes." Iris was suddenly warm from head to toe, and no longer cared how ridiculous her smile looked.

"Okay, here we go!" Gabe announced as he turned off the dirt road they'd been traveling for several minutes onto what appeared to be no road at all. Two minutes later, they pulled up beside a modest house made of red stone that matched the rock formations.

They piled out of the Bronco, stretching and yawning.

"So let me guess," Iris said as she gazed appreciatively at the house, "your family has lived in this building for four thousand years?"

"What? Of course not!" Gabe laughed. "Who does that?"

"Oh, I guess I thought—"

"I'm just messin' with ya!" he laughed again. "We've been on the land almost that long. This place is only about six hundred years old, though. When the rest of the Wipuk migrated to the plateaus, I guess my ancestors decided it wasn't such a big deal if their house matched the neighbors' anymore. So they put this bad boy up. Stays a lot cooler, that's for sure. C'mon in and meet the fam!"

A waft of air conditioned, chili-scented air hit their faces as they came through the front door.

"Oh my gosh, tell me that's dinner!" Gabe called toward the kitchen.

A little boy with a dark, curly ponytail ran out of the kitchen bellowing a battle cry. He ran straight up to Gabe and slugged him in the ribs. Gabe doubled over in dramatic fashion and died a glorious death on the rug. The boy sat on his defeated foe with a satisfied grin.

"This is Danny," Gabe gasped from beneath him.

"Wow," Danny whispered. "Are you really Iris?"

"Yes I am," she chuckled. "These are my friends, Will and Gene."

"Nice to meet you!" Danny said. He hopped off of Gabe to give each of them fist bumps. When he got to Eugene, he smiled. "I remember you. You're that funny, grumpy dude."

Eugene laughed. "That's me! Don't worry, I'm nicer today."

"Danny, don't be rude," said a woman who emerged from the hallway. She was petite, with bright blue eyes and long, brown curls. "Sorry about that."

"At least he said I was funny," Eugene laughed.

Gabe stood and put his arm around her. "Guys, this is Brittany, the love of my life. Britt, this is Iris and Will... and of course, I'm sure you remember Gene."

"Uh, definitely," she chuckled, and waved at everyone.

"Sorry about the wonderful first impression," Eugene mumbled with a sheepish smile.

"It wasn't so much that," she replied softly. "I've just never had anyone suddenly appear in my living room while I'm folding socks. It's a little startling!"

The group shared a laugh.

"What is that delicious smell?" Will asked. "Poblanos?"

"Very good," Brittany answered, looking impressed. "Ben's making his famous albondigas al chipotle con arroz, y rajas de chile poblano con crema."

"Geez," Eugene said in wonder.

"Wh... what's he making?" Iris asked.

Gabe laughed. "Meatballs and rice with chipotle sauce, and roasted creamy peppers."

"Okay, but the other thing you said sounded good, too!" Iris chuckled.

"I'm glad!" Brittany laughed. "It took me awhile to learn how to say all that!"

"Do you think he'd mind if I watched?" Will asked Gabe.

"C'mon," Gabe tilted his head.

Will, Iris, and Eugene followed and introduced themselves to Ben, the retired Guardian who had been a teenage boy in this house the last time Eugene had seen 1965. He greeted Eugene kindly. Although Ben had only met Kat that night, he had heard his father speak of the scientist who had come to study the Tree. Later, Ben had been the one to take pictures of the weeping wound Eugene had left behind. But he said nothing about that now. Instead, he offered Will an apron and Eugene a cola.

"I thought poblano peppers were the hot ones," Eugene said after dinner, "but those were so good, Ben."

"Thank you," Ben replied. "Nah, poblanos are pretty mild. On a scale of one to crazy, I'd give 'em maybe a two."

"I love it when Ben cooks," Brittany said. "It's why I married Gabe."

Gabe feigned shock. "You said it was for my dashing good looks!"

"That too," she said, and winked at him as she rose from the table. "C'mon, Danny, we're on dishes."

"Aww, I want to listen!" he objected.

"Not this time, dude," Gabe said. "Listen to Mom."

Danny stood and stacked all seven dinner plates from the table and grinned at Iris as he hefted them into the kitchen. She gave him a little wave as he left.

"He's a cool kid," she chuckled.

"Thanks! I think he's pretty awesome, too," Gabe said. "I can't decide what to do about him tonight, though. I was thinking maybe I'd have Britt take him out for ice cream and then over to watch movies at my dad's, so they're not around here. Y'know, in case things get crazy."

"So you want to get right into it, huh?" Eugene asked him. "I wasn't sure, since we're going to lose the light pretty soon."

"Well, I thought you'd want to get straight home," Gabe replied. "Don't you?"

Eugene sighed. "I think so." He looked around the table. "I'm not used to this feeling, though. I kind of like it."

"What feeling?" Iris asked.

"Having people actually like me," he said. "And liking them back. I'm used to having colleagues, but I don't really have many... friends."

Iris and Will smiled.

"Well, we *are* your friends, Gene," she said. "So you'd better stay in touch!"

"Of course!" He grinned. "But Gabe, you're right. I should get home. I'm not looking forward to that first night. I'll be walking straight into a tangled mess, but it's my mess. I have to clean it up."

Gabe nodded. "Iris, any idea what we should expect?"

Iris thought for a moment. "Not totally. I mean, this cut is unique. I've only ever dealt with branches, never a trunk. Theoretically, the repair process should be basically the same, but I guess we'll have to see. The real trick is going to be removing the new growth. That's the part that's got me a little nervous, if I'm being honest. Taking off a branch that shouldn't be there takes precision too, but at least it's straightforward. Taking out a core sample is... well, let's just say we might as well wear blindfolds."

"Don't you just start in the same place?" Will asked.

"I doubt it," Eugene replied. "It's probably moved a little since 1965. It's a twisted trunk. It could be not only higher, but also at a completely different angle than before. And if my angle of entry is off by even half a degree, it won't be the same spot at all."

"Oh, no," Iris said, staring at Eugene. "We're forgetting something else."

"What?" Will asked.

Iris looked at him. "The borer is almost completely wrecked. We're going to have to find a new one!"

Gabe and Ben exchanged looks.

"You wanna tell him, Dad?" Gabe asked him.

Ben pushed himself up from the table. "I have gifts!" he announced, and disappeared into the other room for a moment. He emerged carrying two boxes—both narrow, but one smaller. He set them both in front of Eugene.

"What are these?" he asked.

"Open 'em!" Ben said, eyes twinkling.

Eugene obeyed. Inside of one was his core sample—the one he'd taken from the tree and carefully examined under the lamp light before he'd been stained by its inky sap and found himself in the next room. It was still tucked halfway inside its little paper straw, and emitted a faint, tiny hum, not unlike the sound of a fly's wings.

Inside the other box was a brand new increment borer, still in its original packaging.

"Wh—this is beautiful! How did you…"

Ben shrugged. His smile was playful. "I knew you'd be back. I read the diaries about Iris's famous first case. The MacCranns had to fetch an ax in a hurry or risk losing their entire Tree. I knew the same thing could happen to us, and I wanted to be prepared. We would need a way to make the same cut as before, so I learned what the heck it was you used, and got the same tool."

"You're a genius!" Eugene exclaimed. "This is absolutely perfect!"

"That just leaves us one last problem," Gabe said.

"What problem?" Iris asked.

"I don't know what we're going to do about that crowd out there. You remember I told you about all the hikers and campers coming around the past couple weeks?"

"Yeah…"

"Well they've kind of banded together now. There's one huge campsite just east of our land. Every day, it seems like they either get bigger or closer. There must be almost fifty of them now."

"Can't you tell them to leave?" Will asked. "They're trespassing, right?"

"It's federal land," Ben said, face grim. "Technically, they're allowed to be there. As long as they move their campsite every couple weeks, they can pretty much live there."

"What are they doing?" Iris asked.

"They just… hang out, pretty much," Gabe replied. "They listen to a woman teach."

Eugene's head jerked up. "What woman?"

Ben shrugged. "Long hair, long skirt. Old. I met her once, when I was a kid. The night you came. She was a blonde back then."

"Oh, no," Eugene moaned. He rested his forehead on his hand.

"What's wrong, Gene?" Iris asked him.

His face was bleak. "That's Kat. It has to be."

"No way," Will said.

Ben nodded. "I think he's right, actually."

Will frowned. "Why would she come here now?"

"It's my fault," Eugene said, just above a whisper. "Last time I saw her, I was just trying to explain to her where I'd been, you know? I didn't know anything about the Tree then. All I said was that I'd touched it. That's it!"

"Why didn't he lose his memory?" Will asked Gabe.

"Because that was firsthand knowledge," Gabe replied. "He was telling his own experience, not something he learned from a Guardian."

Iris sat back in her chair with a pensive look, processing that information.

"Thankfully," Gabe went on, "there isn't much you can learn just by looking. And people rarely get close enough to hear or touch. Those who do, get pretty short answers."

Ben smiled. "My father was a master at that."

"I agree," Eugene said, half smiling. His face grew serious again. "I'm so sorry. If it weren't for me, Kat wouldn't even know where you are. I led her here. And when she found out I was back, she must have wanted answers."

"But what's she doing out there with fifty people if all she wants is answers?" Will asked.

"She told me she was a teacher," Eugene replied. "Yoga, meditation, that kind of thing. She said she's been wanting to live here. I guess... she moved up her plans?"

Iris shook her head. "This is such horrible timing. The last two times I saw Trees repair themselves, it was pretty darn loud at first. It would be enough to draw a curious crowd. I wouldn't want anyone to get too close... just in case."

"It shouldn't matter though, right?" Will asked. "I mean, once the Tree is back to normal, the timeline disappears. So anyone who happened to see it won't remember."

"That's true," Gabe said, "as long as they don't get close enough to interfere with the process."

"What happens then?" Eugene wondered.

"They get trapped in the energy field and drawn backwards in time," Iris answered. "That's how I ended up in 1844. It was only for a day, but I knew not to mess with anything. Imagine fifty people running around in 1965 for a day!"

Will whistled.

"Man." Eugene let out a breath. "Well, she was really nice to me last time we spoke. I mean… a little angry, but… she talked about just wanting good karma and balance back in the universe. Maybe I could persuade her to take everyone somewhere else for a little while."

"Uh…" Will frowned. "I don't think that's such a good idea, Gene."

"Why not?"

"Because it was pretty dark over there. You might not be dealing with the same Kat."

"You don't have to go out there, Gene," Gabe said. "Dad and I can probably keep them away while you and Iris deal with the Tree. Will can help us."

Will nodded.

"Three against fifty?" Eugene objected. "And what if I still don't have it all? What if I try the repair and nothing happens? Then I'm sticking out like a sore thumb, and you've still got fifty curious people on your doorstep."

Gabe eyed him doubtfully.

"Gabe, please. It's my fault they're here. I want to help get them a safer distance away. Just… let me go out and talk to her. It's the least I can do."

Gabe glanced at Ben. "Dad, what do you think?"

Ben considered for a moment. "Not sure. That woman was pretty tricky last time I saw her. She faked a broken ankle."

Eugene bowed his head, then looked up at Ben. "Actually, I put her up to that," he confessed.

Gabe sighed. "Okay, I guess… if you're set on this idea, it might not be terrible to at least try. Maybe she'll listen. But take Iris and Will with you, okay? They can back you up. Worst case scenario, she hates your guts and refuses to go anywhere. We'll be no worse off, and we'll go back to Plan A. Everybody good with that?"

Iris, Will, and Eugene nodded.

Chapter 26

The sun was low on the horizon when Iris, Will, and Eugene edged their way along the east side of Gabe's land, taking a circuitous route toward the group campsite.

Brennus, Aimsir, Varick, and Elias walked in formation around them, swords drawn. Their objective was to conceal their charges from sight until the opportune moment.

"Has word reached Albion?" Brennus asked.

"Days ago," Aimsir replied. "He is delayed."

"But he has met this foe in battle before?" Elias wondered.

"Yes, in the realm across the ocean," Aimsir answered. "Apateon used to lead ritual sacrifices with a band of oak-men in what he taught them was a sacred grove. Albion's battalion drove him out, but he returned four centuries ago as a superstition. He had somehow convinced an entire village that he was a witch living inside one of the same oaks. They lived in fear of him, even as they promised him their loyalty. It was sickening. He had to be routed again."

"I'm surprised to see him all the way over here," Brennus commented. "I thought he preferred Britannia."

Aimsir's face was stern. "He only seems to prefer dramatic rituals and having plenty of space to work, regardless of the continent."

Varick gripped his sword more tightly as he walked beside Will. "He will pay sevenfold for his treachery. I wish I could strike a blow myself."

"As do I," Aimsir agreed. "But for the love of the Master, we will stand our ground. He is sending a special detachment."

"Name theft *is* an extraordinary offense," said Elias, shaking his head.

Aimsir's eyes flashed. "The Master is all too familiar with the feeling. He has decreed that Albion will answer personally."

"We have our four guards around us," Will whispered as they stood behind the first vehicle parked in the ring surrounding the campsite. He turned to Eugene. "But it's pretty thick over there. I still think it might be good if you hang back for a minute until Iris and I get a feel for what's going on."

"I'm sure it's going to be fine," Eugene whispered back. "That's definitely Kat."

"All the same…" Iris said, looking doubtful.

Eugene nodded and stood aside while Iris and Will assumed casual postures and wandered into the group. A few people smiled and welcomed them, but most took no notice. Will took Iris's hand and gave it a reassuring squeeze as they found a spot to stand near the outer edge of the crowd.

An elegant woman in her seventies stepped front and center, behind the glowing fire pit. The warm, flickering light danced across her wavy silver hair and beaded necklace.

"Friends," she began with a beatific smile. "This has been an extraordinary season of growth and joy for all of us!"

There was scattered applause.

"There is a vortex of supreme life force in this place. I believe we are merely at the edge of it, but we draw ever closer to its eye. I have taught you the deep knowledge of Father Sun and the divine consciousness of the earth goddess. As she evolves, so do we!"

The crowd applauded more loudly this time, and a few heads nodded.

"But now, I am gratified to share with you that Albion, the great teacher, has returned. I was his instrument many years ago. He, too, can sense the rare beauty of this place and the divine importance of this moment, because he has agreed to speak to you himself."

The crowd murmured appreciatively.

Kat's friendly face underwent a bizarre shift, as if her eyes had grown wider and her skin had stretched into a gruesome smile.

"As Time ascends from its nadir to its zenith," she continued, "the earth ushers in a Golden Age of harmony and unprecedented awakening." Her voice had deepened, and she'd begun to speak in a strange British accent.

Will and Iris exchanged befuddled looks.

"We do not wish to deceive you… with that great awakening must also come a sacrificial purging." She paused and swept the crowd with her gaze. "There are those who live in blindness. They cling to ancient ideas embraced by those less evolved—those who would be foolish enough to see an anthropomorphic Creator Being as literal and all-powerful. Thus has it ever been. In ancient times, the Brotherhood of Light taught of this Creator Being as a metaphor, and so it is—a metaphor for the divine consciousness which has brought forth all life. It lies in three perfect coils inside each of us, ready to awaken, ascend within, and empower those who are worthy to travel to higher planes. The ancient people of this land understood this teaching, as do we!"

Iris looked at the faces of the crowd around her. Most were smiling and nodding. Some had blissfully closed their eyes.

"How long will the earth goddess tolerate the blindness of the stubborn masses who crawl on her back? How long will she allow their negative auras to poison her faithful children who embrace the divine oneness of all life kingdoms? I assure you, it will not be much longer."

Several people began to match Iris and Will's expressions, glancing uncomfortably around.

Kat squinted through the crowd and pointed at Iris. "And who is this, but an example of everything that's wrong with this world?" she asked. "*You* stand in defiance of nature, child."

Iris felt her heart leap. "Are you talking to me?" she asked, as the people closest to her began stepping awkwardly away from her.

Kat's voice took on a deeper, menacing tone. "That *is* a serpent's bite, is it not?"

Iris glanced down at her bandage, but didn't reply.

"Lesson one," Kat called out to the group. She strode up to Iris, snatched her wrist, and stripped away the purple Band-Aid with a sharp yank.

Iris gasped in shock. She tried to free herself, but Kat held her wrist with an unearthly strength and lifted Iris's arm to the astonished onlookers.

"Fang marks!" she yelled.

The crowd murmured.

"The kundalini is awakening within you, but you refuse to see it. This is what happens when you fight it." She released Iris's wrist and turned to the people. "The serpent is a harbinger of awakening and renewal, shedding away the old self and seizing the healing of enlightenment. The goddess has reminded this child not to resist her own evolution! Her life is proof of progress toward supernatural ascension, yet she stubbornly clings to antiquated notions by staking her hope in One divine Being."

"The one true God *did* save me!" Iris said boldly.

Kat whirled to face her. "Ah, you are partly right! God saved you… because God *is* you. I know this god well, because *I am*." She grinned. "And who's this?" She pointed at Will. "Another freak of nature! Marked for death by the Dark Brotherhood, yet standing before us, unscathed. Now the Brotherhood of Light demand answers of you. What are you doing with your newfound sixth-ray enlightenment? Regaining your oneness with the earth? Teaching others how you escaped death, as one who has progressed through such a profound initiation should?"

"I'd be happy to tell you how I escaped death," Will replied.

"No, we'd rather you didn't." Kat sneered. "We know precisely what you'd say, and it would be a waste of breath, because your experience was also a waste. You'd tell us there's only one escape from death, but you would name the very Name that closes the chakras. So instead of gaining true knowledge, you've surrendered your third eye to delusion and resigned yourself to hanging around this female creature. Almost like a watchdog... or perhaps a pet?"

Will tilted his head, undeterred. "Female creature? You mean a woman? You speak as if you weren't one, too."

Kat scoffed. "I am neither male nor female. I have ascended to a spiritual plane beyond that of being a mere creature. It should be patently obvious to someone like you—who has journeyed beyond the physical plane—that I am one with the divine. Yet you do not see it. Let this be a second lesson to all of you!" she called out to her followers. "Experience does not guarantee knowledge!" She turned back to Will. "You are such a tall human being, yet you have such tiny vision."

Will smiled as words appeared in the air above her head, then blew away like mist. "Oh, I can see you just fine... Apateon. Or is that... Deceiver?" Will asked serenely.

Kat released an eerie snarl.

"That's enough," said a voice at the back of the crowd. Bodies parted to allow Eugene passage to the front, where he stood in front of Kat. "I'm the one you're mad at. Quit picking on my friends."

She let out a derisive laugh. "Well now, look who's decided to show his face. Someone I thought I got rid of." She slinked toward him with slow, deliberate steps, but he planted his feet. "You don't *have* any friends," she whispered. "Everyone you love becomes your enemy." Her withered face, only a foot away, now appeared skeletal, like a death mask. She reached around him and lifted his wallet from his back pocket, just as she'd done as a teenager.

He jumped. "What are you doing?"

Her grin was daunting. "Lesson number three!" she shouted to the crowd, lifting Eugene's wallet in the air. She flipped it open and yanked his driver's license from its sleeve and held it aloft. "This is Eugene Allen Thomas, age twenty-eight! Anybody want to guess his birthdate?"

People whispered to one another.

"You," Kat said, pointing to a man in the front.

"Me?" he asked timidly.

She strode up to him and put Eugene's license in front of his face. "Does that look like him?"

He perused the black and white photo, then looked at Eugene and nodded. "Yeah, that's him."

"Read the date of birth out loud for me."

"N-November sixteenth."

"Year? Nice and loud, please."

The man cleared his throat. "Nineteen thirty-seven."

The crowd murmured loudly.

"Nineteen thirty-seven? My goodness, that's an old man right there!" Kat flicked the card at the next person and chucked Eugene's wallet back at him. "Go ahead, take a look. Pass it around. Maybe it's fake." She paced in front of the gathering. "But why on earth would someone carry a fake driver's license with a date *that* far off?" She sidled up to one woman and nodded at Eugene. "Does he look older than me?"

The woman squinted at Eugene. "No."

"Well he is!" Kat cackled. "We know this, because our instrument, this human goddess who speaks to you now, knew him when she was eighteen years old. And that," she leveled an accusing finger at Eugene, "is exactly how he looked then… when he abandoned her."

"Are you serious?" asked the woman.

Kat fixed her with a malevolent stare. "Have I ever deceived you?"

She quickly shook her head.

Someone in front of Iris perused Eugene's license and murmured something to his neighbor before shaking his head and passing the card to Iris. She slipped it into her pocket without even a second glance.

"The sick pervert didn't bother to mention that he had a wife, though," Kat continued.

Eugene didn't move, though tears had gathered in the corners of his eyes.

Iris and Will exchanged alarmed looks.

"I'm sorry, Kat. I was wrong," Eugene said softly.

Iris began to speak, but Kat interrupted.

"See, everyone? He admits it! But that's not the part that bothers me now!" she growled. "What's *really* twisted is that he knows the secret to eternal youth, and he's keeping it all for himself!"

"No!" Eugene said, shaking his head. "I don't know anything about that!"

Kat stared at him for a moment before letting out a deep, deranged sing-song laugh. She turned to her disciples. "Does it *look* like he knows something about that?"

She received several shouts in the affirmative.

"We're getting nowhere with this," Iris whispered to Will. "It's not even her anymore. We should go." She tilted her head at Eugene, who nodded.

"Oh, but we know exactly where you're going!" Kat laughed. "To the cute little stone house where the cute little Indians live? We wanna go, too! That Ben Iwila thought we were hot, back in the day. Should we go see him? Maybe he's still a fresh-faced baby, too!"

"Leave them alone," Iris said. "They have nothing to do with this."

Kat narrowed her eyes. "Yes, they do. Let's make sure these kiddos don't try to leave without us, shall we?" she said to the group, and snapped her fingers. Six of the largest men in the group stepped forward, blocking their exit. Each man took one of their arms and held fast.

"Let go!" Eugene yelled.

The men didn't move.

"Will, tell them to let us go," he whispered.

Will's eyes were wide. He looked at Iris, and back to Eugene. "It won't do any good," he whispered back. "They're just people. They're doing it on their own."

Kat tsked. "Gene, Gene, Gene," she said and shook her head. "You've been a big, fat liar since we met. And that's your big, fat problem. It's keeping you from seeeeeeeing. Plus, you run with mentally blocked nitwits! They're going to get you nowhere, do you understand? That one," she pointed to Iris, "*might* have potential. Surviving a snake bite is pretty significant. We'd give her fifty-fifty odds of becoming someone, given time and proper instruction. *That* oaf, however…" she pointed at Will, "is beyond stupid if he can't even see his own divinity after facing death. He's worthless!" She put her hands on her hips and faced Eugene. "But you! You don't need them. You carry the biggest gift of all. And it's not just for you… it's for the universe. It's right inside you! We can see the energy of it ascending through your chakras… life force! Life itself, a spring of eternity awakened, and held down only by your own lying mind!"

Eugene struggled against the two men who held his arms. "Kat, there's nothing there for you. I promise. It's not what you think."

She pursed her lips. "No, there definitely is. Because you said it had something to do with that giant tree. The one Joseph and Ben Iwila wanted us to stay away from!"

"Well I was wrong!" Eugene shot back with a look of panic.

"Lying agaaaiiin!" Kat sang. "We've been getting closer and closer to that tree for a couple weeks now, and we are *definitely* onto something." She grinned. "Shouldn't he share his secret with the rest of us?" she shouted to the crowd.

They voiced their agreement.

"Let's go hiking!" she giggled. "We remember how much you like to hike. C'mon, beautiful people!"

Kat turned westward and walked, followed by the six men who half carried, half shoved Iris, Will, and Eugene. The rest of the group trailed behind them.

In the time they'd spent trying to get Kat to see reason, hulking clouds had begun to gather over the red painted rocks, choking out the last rays of the sun. Thundering storm cells billowed upward into blue towers in the sky, crackling with flashes of static against the deepening evening.

Vancouver, Washington

Grayson sighed and shifted in his armchair by the fireplace. He pursed his lips, reading an answer that a student had written on her lab worksheet. He chuckled to himself and began to write a comment in the margin.

"What's so funny over there?" Jason asked him. He sat in the opposite armchair with a stack of lined notebook sheets and a thick textbook on his lap.

Gray shook his head. "Oh, nothing. It just cracks me up that there's always at least one kid in every biology class who thinks that their opinion has some bearing on lab results. This semester I have three like that, and they all sit together. I think they're hoping to reform photosynthesis into a democratic process."

Jason laughed. "That's why I prefer physics… there are opinions flying right and left!"

Gray smiled at his father and continued writing. He shook his pen. "Ugh, stupid thing…"

"Here," Jason said, offering him a spare red pen.

"Nah, thanks anyway. I prefer to use green," he said. "Makes me seem less critical."

Jason raised an eyebrow. "Does that actually work?

"Well…" Gray stood and stretched. "I don't have a bar graph to show you, but I've noticed I get fewer arguments."

"Cool, I might have to try that."

"Want anything while I'm up?"

"Root beer?"

Gray nodded and wandered toward the kitchen, when he heard a sharp knock at the front door. He frowned and changed direction.

When he opened the door, he saw a small woman standing on the doorstep. She wore tattered jeans, a pink polka dot top, and a black leather jacket. The dying rays of the sunset lit up her blue hair from behind.

"Hey," Gray said. "It's… Charlie, isn't it?"

"Yeah," she said, suddenly looking sheepish. "Hi again. Um, I'm really sorry to just… intrude like this. I remembered where your house was, and… I was actually trying to get a hold of Mr. Reynolds. Y'know, Jason. I mean your dad."

Gray smiled. "Well, all three of them are home. Come on in."

"Thanks."

"Dad? You have a visitor!"

"Really?" Jason stood. "Oh, hello Charlie! Gosh, it's been a while! Love the hair!"

"Ha, thanks. Hi, Mr. Reynolds. Sorry to just come over here unannounced. Iris gave me your number and I tried texting you, but uh…"

"Please, call me Jason." He patted his pockets. "Dang it…"

"Dad, you left your phone in the bathroom again, didn't you?"

Jason chuckled. "You can always count on your kids to say the perfect thing. Is everything okay, Charlie?"

She frowned. "I'm not sure."

"Well come on in, have a seat. Gray was just about to get you a root beer."

She smiled and took a seat on the sofa.

Gray rolled his eyes and disappeared into the kitchen.

"I gotta admit, I feel a little silly right now," Charlie began. "But something strange happened to me a little while ago, and for some reason, I couldn't get the idea out of my head that I should talk to you about it."

"I'm good with both silly and strange," Jason said. "I'm glad you came."

She smiled. "Iris said you were easy to talk to."

Jason smiled back.

Gray returned with three cans of root beer and passed them around.

"Charlie was just about to tell us something strange," Jason told him.

"Sweet," he replied. "We love that sort of thing. Go ahead."

She cracked open her can and took a sip before forging ahead. "Okay. Well you should know that I understand what you guys are. And what Iris does. She told me everything. This is going to sound odd, but I actually wasn't surprised by any of it. If that makes sense."

"So…" Gray hedged, "all that information didn't… challenge your worldview at all?"

Charlie gave him a faint smile. "You mean, do I love God and trust His Son? Yes, I do."

Both men's faces lit with delight.

"Straight to the point," Gray said. "I like that."

"If anything, my worldview is much clearer after talking to Iris. But that's where it gets weird. I believed everything she said happened to her. I trust her. She's never been one to joke about things like that. But the more I heard, the more I realized I didn't believe before. Now, it's like..." She looked up, searching for words. "It's like a switch got flipped inside my head. Ever since she left town, I just see dark clouds when I think about her."

"Dark clouds? Like literal ones?" Jason asked.

"Maybe," she replied. "I don't know. Sometimes they look like storms. Other times, they look like black fog. I've been trying to blow this off as just my silly imagination. I've never had something like this happen to me before. But just a little while ago, I felt like I had to pray for her because I saw lightning, and then I saw some crazy old lady!"

Gray leaned in. "What'd she look like?"

"Hard to tell. She had long hair, but I didn't see a lot of detail. It was more her presence. She was so... creepy."

Jason and Gray looked at each other with disturbed expressions.

"Anyway," Charlie continued, "it's probably nothing. But I couldn't get it out of my head, like I said. And the only thing I could think of was to talk to you. Iris isn't picking up her phone."

"Charlie, I'm really glad you came," Jason said. "You were right to come. Warning visions are actually not uncommon, and should never be taken lightly. We happen to know of one woman who could be a factor in what Iris is dealing with. Her name is Kat. It might be her that you saw."

"Let's try some more numbers, shall we?" Gray suggested, pulling out his phone. One by one, he dialed Iris, Will, Gabe, Brittany, and Ben. Each call went straight to voicemail. He frowned. "How can *all* of their phones be off?" He squinted, deep in thought. "Hm, let me see something..." He opened another app on his phone and tapped through a few menus. He turned the screen toward Jason and Charlie. It was a weather radar map of Arizona. It bore an angry red and orange blob right in the center.

Charlie's jaw dropped.

"Time to pray," Gray said.

Jason stood. "I'll alert the Council to back us up."

Sedona, Arizona

It was only a five minute walk from the group campsite to the edge of the Iwilas' land. Kat didn't even pause. She strode right up to the front door of the little red house where Gabe stood guard, arms crossed.

"So which Indian are you?" Kat asked him. "Has old Joseph gone backwards? Is sweet little Ben all grown up, but still too young? Or are you a new one?"

Gabe arched an eyebrow. "That's one of the weirdest questions anyone's ever asked me."

"Yet you know the answer!"

"I have no idea what you're talking about, ma'am," he replied casually. "There's no old Joseph or little Ben living here. You must have the wrong house."

"Don't give me that," she snapped. "You look just like them!"

"Well, I've heard that my people all look alike."

Kat narrowed her eyes. "Tell us your name."

"Let's hear yours first." He glanced behind her. "And while you're at it, I'd love to know why you're on my land, and why you seem to have… prisoners."

"Oh, don't you know these people?" she asked, eyes wide in mock surprise. "They wanted to visit you, so we just tagged along." She strolled casually past him, toward a distant cluster of scrub oak that surrounded a giant juniper. She turned to face him. "You see, we're all super interested in gardening. You've done such a great job here. Tell us your secrets!"

Gabe shrugged. "Oh, y'know us Indians. Rain dances and what not. I mean, my mom's side is Mexican, so I've added a little salsa, too. Gotta keep it real, am I right?"

Kat let out a mocking laugh. "Clearly, it's time this land had better management. It's doubtful that *your* kind will survive the coming purge anyway."

Gabe's eyes narrowed. He kept his arms crossed, but Iris could tell by his clenched biceps that he was struggling to maintain his casual attitude. He took a deep breath through his nose, and let it out slowly. He closed his eyes for a few seconds, and began to chuckle. He glanced at Will, Iris, and Eugene, who wore bewildered expressions.

"Oh, you got me, lady!" he laughed at Kat. "I thought for a second that I was dealing with a normal, sane person. I'm really glad I'm not. You brought a little friend! Now it makes sense why you're so rude. And ugly!"

Kat's face twisted with fury, but before she could speak, Gabe continued.

"Okay, whoever you are. I don't mind wasting your time, but I'd rather not waste mine. So tell me what the goal is, here."

"You will tell us how to access the divine energy of the Great Tree."

"Nope."

She grinned and pointed at Eugene. "Then *he* will."

Lightning crackled across the sky, leaving a static charge in the air. Almost instantaneous thunder echoed off of the distant rocky ridge. Iris felt goosebumps as the hair on her arms stood on end.

Gabe gave Eugene a split second smile of reassurance before addressing Kat. "I think you tried asking him already, didn't you? I mean, I assume that's how these supervillain plots work. First you interrogate him. Then, when he refuses to talk, you do the whole hostage thing and raise the stakes. Aren't we on step three right now? Seems silly to go backwards."

"Oh, we haven't gone backwards!" Kat chuckled. She walked calmly up to the crowd and approached one of the men who was decked out in camping attire. "May I?" she asked. Without waiting for an answer, she pulled a camp knife from the holster on his belt.

The crowd murmured in confusion as she examined the jagged six-inch blade.

Gabe reached for his phone. "How about instead, I call you some help? Hm? Some nice men in white coats who can help you with your anger issues?"

"How about not?" Kat said in a deep, menacing voice. She gestured at the phone. The battery symbol flashed zero percent for a second before the screen went black.

Gabe glanced up at her in shock.

The crowd murmured again.

"Don't worry, beautiful people!" she called out to the onlookers in a soothing tone. "Manifestations of the ascended masters can sometimes kill a battery, but that's a small price we pay to stand in their presence! This is exactly what we've been teaching you this whole time!" She sidled up to Eugene and stroked his cheek with her free hand. "This man is divine. We have believed so ever since we met him. Deep within him is the knowledge to take us all to a higher consciousness. But he must be initiated, mustn't he?"

The people nodded.

"Ascension is found in truth," she said to him, giving his chin a little tweak at the same time. "Therefore, we will give you another chance. Perhaps... it's been too long since you saw your beloved Tree. Shall we get a little closer?"

"No, I don't want to get closer!" Eugene shouted.

"Is that so?" Kat raised her eyebrows.

"Don't you get it? I didn't gain anything! I lost everything!"

Another ripple of lightning and thunder cracked the sky open above them, sending a cascade of static charged air across their faces.

"In that case, you require liberation," she said, her expression stony. "Ascension is found in truth. Truth is found in liberation. Your potential is locked away in your mind, like a butterfly in a chrysalis. You will not realize your truth until you shed your pitiful existence in this physical form. Then, you will ascend to greater awakening and return to benefit your fellow earth-kind, as the great teachers before you have done."

"Shed my physical form?" Eugene cried. "What the heck are you talking about?"

Horrified, Iris struggled against the hands that held her arms. She looked at Will, who was trying to do the same and gaining nothing but reddened skin.

"You can't let her do this!" she said to one of the men.

"Do what?" he scoffed. "She hasn't done anything. She's just being persuasive."

"Yeah, he'll talk pretty soon," said the man next to him.

"You're in pain, living this way. I can see that." Kat ran her fingers through Eugene's hair. "This is the most compassionate thing I could possibly do," she said in a silky tone. "Since you lack the courage to be free."

Gabe's eyes widened. He took several steps toward where Kat stood with her back to him.

She grabbed a handful of Eugene's hair and yanked his head to one side, exposing his neck. "When you return," she whispered, "you can use my body." She lifted the knife to his throat.

She saw Gabe out of the corner of her eye as he leaped toward her.

Chapter 27

With almost serpentlike precision, Kat's knife hand swung in an arc behind her at the same moment that Gabe's body collided with its path. She snarled as he used his momentum to seize her by the waist and yank her away from Eugene. They both rolled into the red dust.

After a moment, it was Kat who stood, bloodied blade still in hand, and glowered at the gasping man curled up on the ground in front of her.

"Gabe!" Iris shrieked.

"At last, we learn his name!" Kat chuckled. "That wasn't so hard, was it?"

Iris struggled against the men holding her, and suddenly found that they'd loosened their grip at last. The six of them stood dumbfounded, staring first at the red sliver trickling down Eugene's neck, then at the almost-black pool spreading beneath the man on the ground. Wide-eyed, they began to back away.

Panicked conversations erupted in the crowd of Kat's followers.

Will, Iris, and Eugene knelt beside Gabe, speechless with worry.

He looked up at them, his face drawn with agony. "Tell Britt…" he gasped, "and Danny…"

"Gabe, you're going to be okay," Iris whispered.

The next moment, the air around them grew so thick that every sound was dampened almost to silence, before a massive pressure wave hit the atmosphere, generating an unearthly, echoing boom. Iris could feel it hit her back, pressing her down for a few seconds.

She, Will, and Eugene put their arms across each others' shoulders and huddled together to shield Gabe from the blast of wind created by the shockwave. Around her, hats flew off, trees bowed, and terror-stricken people stumbled toward the ground, bending at the waist under the gale.

As the wind died down, Iris looked around her. Kat had fallen to her knees and was staring at the sky in disbelief. Iris followed her gaze, but saw nothing except churning thunderstorms against the deepening dusk.

"Will, what's happening?" Iris whispered. "What's she looking at?"

"It's an army," he murmured in awe. "There's gotta be five thousand at least. The leader is bright white and huge!"

A faint blue shimmer began to appear everywhere she looked. The tops of every tree and shrub, the tips of every cactus spine, the peak of Gabe's roof, came alive with spires of neon sapphire flame. Eugene held up his arm, feeling the static charge in the dense air. Iris could see goosebumps across his skin as the hairs stood on end and tiny pointed flames danced at the tips of his fingers.

Gabe made a small choking sound. Iris stroked his hair and prayed over him, not sure what else to do. Her phone was dead, and she had nothing she could use to stop the bleeding.

"Albion?" Kat gasped in fear and began to crawl backwards in the dust.

"Something really dark is standing inside Kat," Will whispered. "The leader of the army is pointing his sword at it."

"Fine!!" Kat shrieked in an unearthly voice. "Albion is *your* name, not mine!"

"Whoa..." Will whispered.

A sudden whoosh of air kicked up dust around them, as a whirlwind whipped through Iris's hair and swept across the landscape. The blue flames disappeared.

"All the dark ones just flew away and the army is chasing them," Will said, looking into the sky, his face full of astonishment. He looked back at Iris. "They're all gone! Except a few around us."

Gabe took a ragged breath.

Iris kept praying.

After a moment, Gabe smiled. "I can see Him," he wheezed, staring vacantly beyond their faces. "I... I don't want to leave my family... but... I ain't mad at the view." He let out one last cough, and grew still.

Iris, Will, and Eugene stared at each other in disbelief.

Iris shook her head, fighting tears. "We have to fix this. *Now*."

Eugene stood, jaw clenched in fury. He whirled to face Kat, who still sat trembling in the dust. "Are you happy now?" he snapped.

She drew back, cowering in fear, then scrambled to her feet and hurried away in the same direction as her followers.

Eugene turned to her group of disciples, who had been looking on in speechless terror, gradually backing away. "How's that for enlightenment?" he shouted at them. "That man has a family! Is this the kind of world peace you want? My God would never treat you like that!" The crowd began to scatter, some hurrying, some flat out sprinting away.

Eugene turned back to Iris. "Let's get this done."

"I'll stay with Gabe," Will said, a tear rolling down his cheek.

Iris nodded, catching his tear with her thumb. "Thank you," she whispered.

Eugene dashed into the house, and tried to flip on a light, to no avail. He felt around the kitchen table and finally collected his old tree sample and both increment borers. He joined Iris outside and they sprinted toward the Tree.

They stopped within twenty feet of the circle of scrub oak. Eugene knelt down and placed the boxes on a rock. "I think I should probably get that stuck piece out of the old auger first," he said.

"Good thinking," Iris puffed, pacing beside him. "But maybe we should leave the old wood back here for a little bit. If we have it all, it's going to try to reattach, and the new growth will repel it. *Big* problems. Learned that the hard way the first time."

"You're the expert." He pulled the long, thin extractor from the new borer and used one end of it to gently prod the bits of wood out of the old auger and into the lid of the box. Then he gave the shaft several sharp taps to release the sawdust from the threads. Finally, he opened the second little box Ben had given him, which contained the core sample. He removed the paper straws and tipped the stray pieces he'd collected from the borer into the box with the larger piece, before carefully sliding the lid into place.

"There," he said. "That's all I've got. I sure hope it's enough." He assembled the new borer and stood, sliding the extractor into his back pocket as he usually did.

They peered through the trees.

"Whew," Iris said. "This might be harder than I thought, Gene. It's… *really* dark in there now."

"I could go look for a flashlight," he said.

She looked doubtful. "If none of our phones survived that power drain, I seriously doubt that anything with double-A batteries fared much better."

"We can't wait for morning," Eugene said quietly. "I'm not leaving Gabe like that."

Iris touched his slumped shoulder. "We can't rush this, either. Making a mistake right now won't help Gabe *or* you." She sighed and looked back into the trees. "I guess we could at least get a closer look and see if there's some way to tell what we're doing."

They stepped carefully through the hedge of scrub oak, which Eugene saw was noticeably taller than last time he'd been here. When they reached the Tree, it was emitting the same familiar hum as before, though Iris thought it seemed louder than usual.

"Where were you standing last time?" she asked.

Eugene stepped gingerly toward the trunk. "I guess right about here."

"And where did you drill?"

He pointed to a spot exactly at chest height.

"Okay…" Iris drew closer. They both squinted at the spot in the darkness. She let out an exasperated sigh. "Yeah, I can't see a thing." She put her hands on her hips. "And if the scar is in a different place now, where do you estimate it would be?"

"Well…" He looked the trunk up and down. "It's hard to tell. I mean, I don't know how fast growing it is, since it's not actually a juniper. It doesn't have rings, so I could never guess its age…" He shook his head.

"I'm sorry, Gene," she said softly. "This might be a pointless exercise until morning. We need light."

The air around them crackled as another lightning bolt shot across the sky, partially illuminating the shaggy bark.

Iris gasped. The tiny glowing blue points returned, illuminating the tips of each frond and berry on the Tree, and even the end of the extractor protruding from Eugene's pocket.

"This is such crazy weather," Eugene murmured, watching the static dance on his fingers again.

"I know," she whispered back. "I used to be scared of lightning storms, but this is so different."

"Yeah, it isn't lightning, thank goodness."

"No, but it does give me an idea."

She bowed her head, searching her memories for a specific moment. She had been standing beside Angus and Ré MacCrann near the Great Hawthorn. It was a night as dark as this one. They had watched the cracks of the healing branch glowing like embers as they sealed themselves off.

Iris had assumed that this glow only occurred during the healing process, once all the right pieces were back together. *But what if that isn't true? I've only ever tried a repair in daylight!* She thought of the two fallen branches that she and Angus had chopped away and left on the forest floor. They had burned to a cinder and fallen to ash. *Don't burning things glow? Maybe...*

"Iris, what are we doing?"

She glanced at him. "Gene, I might have been wrong about how to do this!" she said excitedly. "I thought the pieces of old wood might give us fits, but what if they're the answer? I mean, they *will* give us fits, but that just means you'll have to work a little faster!"

"Okay... what?"

She grinned. "We need light! Displaced pieces of Great Trees glow when they're near the source. If we bring that sample over here, the old hole might just light up like a laser pointer!"

"You think?"

"There's a decent chance! But you'll have to get that hole drilled as fast as you possibly can so the core sample has somewhere to go, and you don't end up with it sticking out of your back instead."

"Geez."

"We can try it this way, or wait till morning."

Eugene didn't hesitate. "Let's do it."

They stepped back through the scrub oak to retrieve the little box of wood they'd left behind. Twenty feet away, near the rock where Eugene had set the box, an old woman hunched over, reaching down. A flash of lightning illuminated her stringy silver hair and pale, bony hand.

"No!" Eugene shouted, and bolted toward her. He skidded to a stop when she straightened to face him, the box in one hand and a knife in the other.

"You are unbelievable!" he said. "I'm trying to make all this right, don't you see?"

"You've ruined everything!" she screamed. "How can you possibly make anything right?"

"I ruined everything? I'm not the one who just killed a guy!"

Iris caught up and stood beside him. "Gene," she murmured, "I don't think it's a good idea to yell at her."

Kat clutched the box and began to sob. "I don't know what all of this is about. I just want to go back to when I was happy!"

"I do too," Eugene replied, his voice softening. "That's what I'm trying to do."

"Kat," Iris said gently, as thought she were speaking to someone at Rookwood. "You helped Eugene get close to a Time Tree. You're holding the pieces he cut away from it. Those caused a time disruption. None of this was supposed to happen. If he puts the pieces back together, you'll be eighteen again. Wouldn't you like that?"

She sniffed and nodded.

"You'll need to let us have the box then, okay?"

She hesitated. "Everyone lies to me," she whispered into the dark.

Iris looked at her with compassion. "You've had some real whoppers thrown at you, that's for sure," she agreed. "But it was your choice how to respond. It's still your choice."

Kat stood still for a long moment before holding the box out to Eugene with a shaking hand. "You humiliated me," she whispered.

He gingerly accepted the box, then caught her hand. "You're right. I was selfish and thoughtless. You were just a kid. You deserved to be protected, and I hurt you instead. Please forgive me."

She sniffed again. "It's too late for that." She squeezed his hand and released it, then turned and walked away. A few steps later, they saw the knife fall from her hand and land in the dust left behind by her footsteps.

They watched her retreating form until she was a tiny speck in the darkness. Iris wanted to make sure she didn't change her mind and circle back. Once they began this process, there would be no convenient time for interruptions.

Iris heard another sound coming from the direction of the house. It was Gabe's Bronco.

"Oh, no," she muttered. "We have to go, Gene. Let's move."

They covered the twenty feet back to the grove of trees as quickly as possible, but not in time to miss the grief-stricken screams of a woman and child who had just discovered that their beloved leader and protector had fallen.

Iris batted away the tears that tried to cloud her vision and focused on the job at hand.

"I think..." she sniffed and let out a shuddering breath. "I think the best way to do this is to open the box for several seconds and get the pieces to attract..." She inhaled, trying to control her breathing.

"Hey," Eugene said gently. "We can fix this. He's got us."

She nodded and closed her eyes, ignoring the stinging tears. She took another breath, imagining God's Son standing beside her. When she opened her eyes, her mind was clear.

"Okay..." she began again. "I can't be too close to this process, or I'll end up coming back with you to 1965. It's a lot easier if I don't. But I want to help you as much as I can, so I'm going to try something a little different. I'm going to open the box for a little while and let the Tree start attracting the pieces. That should show you where to cut. Once they start to lift out of the box, I'm going to see if I can keep them contained long enough for you to make a hole without them making a hole in you."

"Sounds like the best plan we've got," he said.

"Ready?"

He took the borer in his hand and nodded. "Ready."

Iris stood close to the tree, held the box near the spot where Eugene had pointed earlier, and lifted the lid.

A mixture of chaotic piping and humming emerged from the box as the little pieces began to tremble.

"Is it working?" Eugene asked.

"I think so," Iris replied. "Hear that?"

"Sort of."

Iris could feel the box begin to vibrate in her hand as the disorganized sounds grew in volume. She stared at the tree trunk. "C'mon," she muttered. "Where's the spot?"

The smallest pieces of sawdust began to luminesce, taking on the faintest golden shimmer. The chips from inside the auger soon followed.

"Wow," Eugene whispered, watching the glow begin to light the inside of the box.

"Gene, watch the Tree!" Iris reminded him.

"Sorry." He scanned the trunk. "Still nothing."

Iris shook her head. "This better work, or it's going to get really dangerous in a minute."

The largest piece of core sample began to shimmer. Within half a minute, Iris could feel heat radiating through the bottom of the box onto her hand.

"Anything?" she called out.

Eugene shook his head. "No, there's..." He let out a frustrated grunt.

The pieces began to float up from the bottom of the box, just millimeters from its surface.

"Oh my gosh, I'm such an idiot!" he yelled. "The hole was in a furrow, I remember now! It's moved up *and* sideways. It's right inside this crack, I can see it! It's glowing!"

"Go!" Iris cried.

He placed the teeth of the auger directly over the glowing spot on the Tree and gave it a hard turn. Unlike last time, the threads seated themselves perfectly and dug in with very little pressure. "Weird, it's like drilling through chalk!"

"The pieces are getting away from me, I've gotta close the box!" she said over the noise.

"Do it," he said. "I think I'm okay here." He spun the handle as fast as he dared, sinking the borer's shaft farther into the trunk with every turn.

Iris moved to shut the lid of the box, but the pieces of wood had created an energy field around themselves that not only allowed them to levitate, but to repel the lid. "Well there goes that idea," she said. "They got away, Gene. You'll have to hurry."

"That's what I'm doing," he said, feverishly turning the handle. The glowing bits of wood had floated toward him and began bumping into his hands and the bark of the Tree. "That isn't so bad," he said.

"Yet," Iris said. "Okay, this is where I step back. You're doing great, okay?" She retreated about a dozen steps away and stopped near the scrub oak.

"Great," he mumbled, and kept turning. Ten seconds later, the borer stopped. He'd hit the end of the chalky wood. He yanked the extractor from his pocket and slid it carefully into the shaft, gave the handle two counterclockwise turns, and felt a slight give. He slid the extractor partway out of the shaft.

"Whatever comes out of the Tree, don't touch it," Iris called to him.

"Gotcha!" He pulled the newly cut core the rest of the way out, and gasped. It was glowing like a dying ember. The extractor suddenly grew so hot to the touch that he snatched his hands back, sending the metal and wood flying into the nearby grass. He briefly considered checking to make sure it didn't start a brush fire, but right then, a glowing chip of wood flew by and hit him in the face with a sharp sting.

He flinched as more pieces came toward him. They seemed to be rotating in a pattern. First they'd move toward the Tree in an upward motion, then bump into the bark before floating upward and away, then back again. They started to catch him in the face and hands with every pass, growing louder and moving faster each time. He spun the handle of the borer counterclockwise as fast as his arms would allow, while leaning away from the path of the moving wood as much as possible. The largest fragment collided with his knuckle as it flew by, removing a few layers of skin. He ducked as another one whizzed past his face, but kept turning the handle.

After another minute, the borer fell free of the Tree, sending Eugene sprawling backward. The glowing shards of trunk stopped mid air and quieted. As they arranged themselves into a thin, perfect cylinder, their dissonant pitches settled into a harmonious chord. The pieces solidified into one, then shot straight into the hole like an arrow. The Tree let out a final deep groan as its branches shivered. The desert was quiet.

Eugene stood and turned to look at Iris. She could still see him in the faint glow that radiated from the healing scar on the Tree. He began to fade from view. She held up a hand and waved. "Stay in touch, okay?" she called out.

He waved back, but she couldn't hear his reply. He was gone.

As Iris walked back toward the house, she experienced a strange mixture of relief and dread. Getting Eugene home had been a long haul. She was eager to hear how things had gone for him since 1965. He had changed so much in just the short time she'd known him. He was bound to have untold impact. Perhaps he'd written them a letter, as Angus had been fond of doing. *Or maybe we won't hear from him at all. Maybe he chose to forget.*

She turned her thoughts toward the little stone house, and the anguish she'd felt walking away from Will as he'd kept vigil over their dead brother. What would she find when she got back? How long would it take to erase the timeline?

As she approached the house, she got her first answer. The porch lights were on. Apparently, they had entered the version of reality where the power hadn't gone out. She pulled her phone from her pocket. Yep. The battery was at 43%. As she covered the last fifty feet, it began to rain. The threatening thunderstorm had finally decided to express itself. She sighed as water soaked her hair and ran into her eyes.

She trudged past the clean soil, which in this reality, had never soaked up blood. It was then that she spotted Gabe sitting on the porch, barely visible in the shadows. He was staring out at the desert, elbows propped on his knees, with rain dripping from his jet black hair. She lowered herself to the cement slab beside him. She felt just as he looked—weary.

"It went well, I take it," he commented with hollow enthusiasm.

She shrugged. "It wasn't without difficulty, but it's done now. The Tree is healing."

He nodded and continued to gaze into the distance.

She looked at him. "I wasn't sure what I'd see when I came back here."

"Not dead," he said simply, and rested his forehead on his arm.

"You okay?"

He let out a hoarse laugh. "Uhhh…" He faced her, his usually joyful brown eyes full of confusion. "Yeah, I'm okay, if we define that term loosely. I think I'm supposed to be happy to be here, right? I'm trying to be."

Iris let out a sigh of realization. "You were with God… Oh Gabe, I can't imagine."

His expression was pained. "No, you can't. It was… breathtaking. He's so beautiful. So loving. Nobody else knows what I saw. Britt doesn't remember what happened because she only spent a few minutes near the fluctuation, so she kept the other timeline instead. And Danny didn't see much. I guess I'm glad they were spared that. But I suddenly feel like a traitor, y'know?" He let out a shaky breath. "Because I couldn't stand to leave that place. I used to kiss my wife and play with my son and feel like that was the happiest I'd ever been. Now, it's like…" He shook his head, fighting tears.

"Please don't go through this alone," Iris said earnestly. "Tell Brittany. She needs to know."

"I should." He sighed and thought for a long moment. "He told me something, though."

"God did?"

Gabe nodded. "Yeah. He said that… He wants to hear me speak up more. Every time we were in danger today, I was too scared to speak against it. And I could have. I'm pretty good with Guardian stuff, but I always feel out of my depth around darkness. And there's really no good reason for that. But… you want to hear the best part?"

"What was it?"

He struggled to steady his voice. "He said He wasn't disappointed in me."

Iris smiled.

They sat quietly, soaking in the rain, until the shower passed through on its way north. Iris could see a few stars as the wispy edges of the clouds swirled aside.

The front door opened and Will stuck his head out. "Oh, Iris, you're back! I'm so relieved. Things must've… Hey, are you guys okay? You're soaked." He stepped onto the porch and sat beside Iris. "What happened?"

Iris touched Gabe's arm. "Is it okay if I tell him?"

Gabe nodded.

She turned to Will. "Gabe's working on being okay. He's just… dealing with memories from the other timeline, y'know? When he was, um… killed."

Will nodded in sober recognition. "Right. Guardians remember both timelines. Oh my gosh." He sighed, and paused for several moments before turning to Gabe. "Was it scary?"

"Maybe for a minute. That's not really the part I mind. It's now."

"Ohhh…" Will digested that for a while.

A coyote howled far in the distance.

Finally, Will spoke again. "Can I tell you something?"

"Sure."

"I was killed once, too."

"Seriously?" Gabe's eyes went wide. "How can you stand to be back? I feel like I'm going to live the rest of my life wishing I was somewhere else!"

"Well…" Will smiled sadly. "I like it a whole lot better, actually. Because I was nowhere near God when I left. I had rejected Him. Talk about wishing you were somewhere else."

"Oh… dang." Gabe was somber.

"I'm not saying that what you're going through isn't real," Will went on. "I can't even imagine what it's like right now, being back. But if I were you, I'd want to hang onto every detail I could remember. Cherish those things. What a gift that must've been, to see that place for yourself."

Gabe nodded again. "You're right."

"I think your experience is going to bring people real hope. And you'll get back there someday. In the meantime, you still have a chance to fight for your family and do some good."

"Thanks, man." He held up his fist to Will and they bumped knuckles. "It was just such a shock to the system to feel so alive and at peace, then be back in this body all of a sudden. But you're right. I'm not done here." He sighed and looked at Will. "You holding up okay?"

"Yeah, I'm good." Will shrugged. "It's been such a weird day. One minute we were fighting this crazy lady and a group of hippies outside, then I'm sitting beside you in the dirt, and the next minute I'm inside with your family and Danny's telling me I owe him hundreds of dollars in Boardwalk rent. *With* hotels. It was bizarre. And they couldn't remember anything I'd just seen. I mean… we *did* come here with a guy named Gene, right?"

Iris nodded. "Yeah, we did. He's safe and sound in 1965 now. At least I hope so."

"Okay, so I'm not going nuts."

"Nope. It all happened." Iris said. "Can you remember anything from the other timeline?"

"Not really," Will replied. "I could tell when we switched, but don't ask me what I supposedly did all day. I remember everything the three of us and Gene did together, and I remember what happened to Gabe. I was sitting beside his body when Brittany and Danny got home. She started screaming, so I was trying to help her shield Danny, and suddenly we were all around the table playing a game. Everyone was happy, and I was just a visitor. Danny asked me if his dad was okay, and I said yes. Brittany told him that you guys were out running an errand, and he accepted that. So I guess that's the official version now?"

"Yeah," Gabe replied. "Weird, right?"

"I wish I could remember both," Will said sullenly.

"At least you and I remember the same version this time," Iris said.

"True."

Gabe turned toward Will. "You… stayed with me?"

"Of course, man. I couldn't leave you like that."

"I appreciate it."

Will nodded.

They sat in peace for a few more minutes, listening to the sounds of the desert. As the clouds rolled away, the night turned chilly. Iris shivered.

"We should get you into some dry clothes," Will said.

She sighed. "Yeah, probably."

"Me too." Gabe stood. "I've got logs to do at some point. But first, there's a story I should tell my family."

Will stood and helped Iris up.

"Want some company?" Iris asked.

Gabe smiled. "I'd love that."

Chapter 28

Sedona, Arizona ~ 1965

Eugene raised his hand to wave at Iris. Her outline rippled like a heat wave, fading from view. "We'll talk soon, I promise!" he shouted. She was gone.

He turned back to the Tree. Within a fissure in the bark, a tiny, pulsing orange glow radiated through the dusk. He looked down and realized he was holding an increment borer—his old one—still gleaming and sharp. *Am I back?*

He glanced around him, squinting in the dim light. *It's not as dark out... if I'm back, then it's March. Longer days.* There was his bag, still on the ground where he'd left it. He felt his pocket. The extractor was there. He quickly disassembled the borer, tucked the extractor back into the shaft, and stuffed the pieces into the bag next to his beautiful maps and still perfect notebooks full of research. He slung the strap over his shoulder and marched out of the trees with long, hurried strides.

As he came within view of the little stone house, Eugene could see Joseph Iwila and fifteen year old Ben rush out the door and run straight toward him. In the distance, he saw young, blonde Kat sneak off in the other direction and scurry away into the desert.

When Joseph and Ben caught sight of him, they slowed to a stop, their faces bewildered.

Eugene had no idea where to begin. "Hi," he said lamely.

Joseph crossed his arms. "You decided not to make a hole in the Tree after all?"

"No, I definitely made a hole in the Tree."

Joseph frowned. "That would have created a separate timeline. Yet you are still here."

"Well, I'm not *still* here," Eugene said sheepishly. "I'm actually *back*. I had help from a couple of Guardians to fix the Tree." He shuffled his feet. "I'm really sorry about all that."

"Which Guardians?"

"Um… your grandson. And someone named Iris."

Ben's face lit up. "Iris Jacobs?"

Eugene looked at him, astonished. "Yeah… how do you know her name? She hasn't even been born yet!"

"I know, but we've had records of her since the eighteen hundreds."

"Well, she's amazing. And so is Gabe."

Ben tilted his head. "Who's Gabe?"

Eugene smiled. "Gabe is your son. And he's a hero."

Ben grinned in amazement. "That's totally wicked!"

"How does the Tree look?" Joseph asked.

"Good," Eugene replied. "Back to normal, except the glowing part that's still healing up."

Joseph nodded. "We are not likely to remember what happened until the healing is complete."

"Something to look forward to, I guess," Eugene said, kicking the dirt. "I seem to have a knack for giving people bad memories."

"No need to berate yourself," Joseph said. "You seem to have learned from your mistake. But you may want to find that young girl. She's been a bit of a troublemaker."

"I'm headed there next," Eugene sighed. "She's not really a troublemaker. She's just had some bad influence." He looked at their faces. "I guess I have a lot of things to make right."

"You are well on your way," Joseph said softly. "I see change in you already. Do not lose heart."

"Thanks," he replied, and reached out to shake their hands.

Ben cleared his throat. "I suppose my uh… son… probably explained to you that you can forget all of this. That is, if you want to."

Eugene shook his head and smiled. "Never."

He turned and walked into the fading sunset.

When Eugene arrived at his little campsite, he was astonished by the scene that greeted him, though he couldn't understand why. It was the same girl he'd brought, leaning against the same brand new burgundy Mustang he'd driven here. Such simple things. The car was perfect, with its top down and its sleek lines gleaming in the light. And Kat was like the cover of a magazine. Together, they looked like the picture of what he had thought would make his life perfect.

But seeing them now filled him with a different kind of feeling. It was nothing like the excitement of coming here—the pride of vanity, or the thrill of an illicit ego boost from the attention of an attractive woman. This was something else. It was hope. It was love that protected. It was the awe of being given another chance.

"That was so much fun!" Kat giggled when she saw him. "We're a regular Bonnie and Clyde!" Her bright blue eyes danced in the warm twilight. "Did you get it?"

He smiled back at her and set his bag on the seat of the car. "No, I'm afraid I didn't."

"What! Darn it!" She pouted. "Didn't I buy you enough time?"

He sighed and looked into her eyes. "I had all the time I needed. I just decided to do better."

Her brow furrowed. "What do you mean, do better?"

He walked over and leaned against the car beside her. "I need to do better by *you*." He smiled sadly. "I haven't done that so far."

She shook her head. "Gene, you're not making sense."

"I know. But hang in there with me. In fact, let's sit for a minute."

"Okay…" She got into the passenger seat of the car and turned to face the driver's side as he sat.

"You're beautiful," he said bluntly.

She grinned. "Okay, so why do you say it like you just gave me bad news?"

"I think it's made you scared."

"Wh… what?"

"Has anyone ever told you that you're good at caring for people? Or that you have a mind so brilliant that it borders on scary?"

She gaped at him. "Well… no."

"Don't ask me how I know. I just do. But I think that being pretty has made you afraid to trust those other things. People see your looks first, and think they know all about you. But they don't. I made the same mistake. I saw you, and didn't wonder who you were inside… at all."

Her eyes began to tear. "Why are you telling me this?"

"Because you deserve to know. You don't have to let other people tell you who to be. You're *so* smart, Kat. And you have a great big heart. Look at how you've loved and trusted me so far. And I don't deserve your love, *or* your trust."

A tear slipped down her cheek. "Why not?"

"Because the night we met, I was just helping out a fellow human being. You were a kid who dropped her stuff. That's where it should have ended. Every time I saw you after that, I knew better, but I didn't do better… because I was messed up inside. In ways that had nothing to do with you."

"So you're saying… you don't really love me?"

He gazed warmly at her. "I *do* now, actually for the first time. But the love I'm talking about means honesty, and doing what's best for you no matter how much it hurts. I wasn't loving you before. I was only thinking of myself. I knew my selfishness would cause you pain, and I didn't care. I can't do that to you anymore."

She sniffed. "So… are we breaking up?"

"We never should have been together in the first place," he replied, his eyes full of sincerity. "It's hard for me to tell you all this, because you have so much fire and potential inside you. Even if you forget everything else I say, please hang onto this: God wants you to know Him firsthand so the two of you can take the world by storm."

She crossed her arms. "Really?"

"Yes, really. I don't want you to miss out on that because a selfish idiot you randomly met on campus one day betrayed your trust, thinking you could solve all his insecurities. The selfish idiot is me, by the way."

She chuckled, despite her tears. "Selfish idiot, huh?"

"Definitely. You could also add egotistical."

"But I just don't get why you've changed your mind all of a sudden."

"It's actually not all that sudden." Inhaling some courage, he leaned over, reached into the glove box, and put his wedding ring back on.

"Oh." She squeezed her eyes shut and sighed. "I kinda figured that."

"You did?"

She gazed at him, and suddenly appeared weary. "Yeah, I suspected. I just didn't *want* to see it. I was hoping for recently divorced or something." She gave him a sad smile. "I should trust my gut more."

"I'm so sorry," he whispered.

"I know," she sighed. "Does she make you happy, at least?"

"That's not her job. I'm starting to realize that nobody can make you happy if you can't even make yourself happy."

"Didn't I make you happy?" she asked quietly.

He frowned. "Getting away with something isn't the same as being happy. But that's on me. It has nothing to do with you. I think you're going to meet someone really amazing someday. I don't want this experience to make you afraid to love. Promise me you'll do whatever it takes to forget me, okay?"

She nodded. "It won't be easy, but I guess I can try." She gave him an odd look. "It doesn't have to be weird between us though, does it? If I ever run into you on campus, I mean."

He chuckled. "No, it doesn't have to be weird. I might have to smile at you at least, because you're a great person."

"I might even smile back."

"Thank you. I know it doesn't feel like it now, but this is the most I've ever loved you, because I'm finally telling you the truth. Make sure you don't fall for another weasel like me, okay? Go for someone close to God. You'll be a lot safer."

She exhaled and frowned. "And you really think God is interested in *me*, huh?"

"Without a doubt," he replied.

"My parents keep saying that lately, but… that's *their* thing, y'know?"

"I've recently made it my thing. I hope you will, too."

"I'll think about it."

"Please do. The world shouldn't miss out on you, being who you were made to be."

She crossed her arms and leaned back in the seat. "Thank you… for saying all that. It's strange… You're the first person who's ever seen me as smart. I've never had anybody tell me I should try to be anything except a fashion model or an actress."

"Is that what you want?"

She shrugged. "I don't know. I mean, I enjoy acting in plays. But… when I was a kid, I wanted to be a…" She squinted. "Promise you won't laugh?"

"I promise."

"A surgeon."

Eugene sat forward, brows raised, and grinned. "Do it, Kat! You'd be amazing!"

"You think so?"

"Yes! You should go for it!"

She looked down at her hands. "People won't take me seriously."

"Then you'll just graduate at the top of your class anyway, and *make* them take you seriously."

She smiled. "Imagine me, cutting somebody open!"

His eyes widened. "Actually, it's surprisingly easy to imagine."

Eugene rolled up to his and Eva's little rented house in Tucson just after eleven. It had taken very little time to throw the rest of his gear back into the car and leave Sedona just after sunset.

Kat had spent the first hour of the drive in quiet contemplation, occasionally fiddling with the radio. But her newly sparked imagination wouldn't allow her to stay quiet for long. By the third hour, they were chatting like old friends, and by the time he'd dropped her by her dorm, she was plotting to change her major, travel the world, and become the chief surgeon at a prestigious hospital, give or take a Nobel prize.

It even occurred to him that she hadn't smoked a single cigarette the whole way home. *Was she only smoking to impress me?* He shook his head. *I'm glad she doesn't feel the need to anymore.* He said a prayer of thanks that he'd finally gotten something right. Kat was going to be okay. They had parted as friends and agreed to wave at each other if the occasion ever arose.

He opened the glove box and crumpled up his last pack of Marlboros. *I don't feel the need to impress anyone either.* He thought of Jason on the day he'd last smoked.

"Your body is free of those... Probably shouldn't try that again if you want to keep your breakfast."

He chuckled to himself. He'd have to wait a long time to see that guy again. *Is he even born yet?*

Eugene looked at the house. No lights on inside. No blue Beetle in the driveway. He didn't even know what day it was, or how long it had been since he'd seen his wife. He wracked his brain. This had to be Sunday, the same day he'd left. He hadn't seen Eva since their big fight Wednesday night. He began to feel a crushing weight of sorrow on his chest. Four days. Four full days since she'd been home, and he hadn't even called around to find her. He hadn't even been curious! He hung his head.

"She should leave me and never look back," he muttered.

Then a memory drifted into his mind. It was Will, staring out the window of Jason's dining room and yelling at him to stop talking.

"There's a darkness out there. Every load of crap you say brings it closer, okay? You gotta rein it in, buddy. They like it."

He thought of Eva, the last time he'd seen her at the nursing home.

"I'm scared that you never loved me at all..."

"Okay, I take it back," he said softly. "She loves me. I know she does. Please... just show me how to reach her."

He got out of the car, closed the door, and leaned against it, trying to decide what to do with himself. He could go inside and call Eva's sister. Better yet, he could drive over. It was only ten miles. Then he could just see if her car was there without waking anyone up. But then what? Throw pebbles at the window? His shoulders drooped. I should just let her sleep.

Just then, the characteristic puttering sound of a Volkswagen made its way up the street. Eugene's heart leaped when he saw that it was Eva's. She pulled up to the curb behind his Mustang and looked at him. She seemed to hesitate. Though he was so relieved to see her and so worried about what to say that he almost felt like he'd vomit, he tried instead to offer her a calm, reassuring smile.

His smile may not have appeared as calm as he'd hoped, because she gave him a strange look. But she turned off the engine anyway, and opened her door. He walked around the car and offered his hand. She looked at it as though she'd never seen a hand before. When she raised her eyes to his, he could see pain and confusion.

His heart filled with sorrow, but he held his emotions in check and kept his hand steady. He would not for one second make whatever happened next be about him. He bent every ounce of his focus on her.

At last, she sighed, grasped his hand, and stood. Her fingers were cool and soft. He tried to remember the last time he'd even touched her like this. Months. He gazed at her face in the glow of the streetlights, and realized it had been even longer since he'd *really* looked at her. Maybe years. And she was exquisite. Her hair was the color of milk chocolate. Her eyes were like amber. Her lips were full and soft, dark pink even without lipstick, and her skin was a creamy ivory with girlish freckles across her nose. He felt his skin grow warm. How could he have forgotten what it felt like to be near her?

She let go of his hand. "I thought you were gone."

He nodded, trying to refocus. "I was. I just got back."

"Aren't you supposed to be out doing research all week?"

"Yes…" He hesitated. There was so much to say, and all of it seemed important, but Eva looked like a frightened deer, about to bolt. "Will you… come inside and talk?"

She looked back at her car, then up at him.

"I guess for a minute. I just came to get a few things."

He went up the front walk, unlocked the door, and held it open for her.

She cast him a suspicious look as she went inside. She pulled the chain under the shade of the floor lamp and sat on the sofa.

He sat beside her, but gave her plenty of space.

"So… suddenly you want to talk to me?" she asked, her expression stony.

"It probably feels sudden to you, but I've been thinking about you a lot since the last time we talked."

She stared at the shag carpet. "That was a *talk*?"

He hung his head. "No… that wasn't a talk. It was a horrific display of selfishness on my part."

She jerked her head up at his admission.

"I lashed out at you every chance I got," he continued. "I made you feel worthless. I cursed at you. And I made you afraid."

She shook her head in disbelief, as if he had just borrowed every word in her mind. Tears formed in her eyes.

"And while I'm at it," he went on, "I could also mention that I've been a terrible excuse for a husband. I've done nothing but find fault with you for a very long time. When you left, I… I should have come after you. I regret every moment that I didn't. I had no right to make you feel so alone."

Tears dashed down Eva's cheeks, though she seemed determined to ignore them. "Where is all this coming from?" she demanded. "What happened to 'Go be happy somewhere else'?"

His face filled with shame. "I *did* say that. And at the time, I thought I meant it. I've been a very unhappy person for awhile now, and I blamed it on you, because you were the closest. But it wasn't your fault. It was mine."

"You're telling me you're unhappy? What am I supposed to do?"

"I don't want you to do anything. It's not a wife's job to make her husband happy, no matter what anyone says. And…" He half smiled. "I'm not unhappy anymore. It turns out, I wasn't just unhappy, I was totally lost. Nothing in my life meant anything to me, because everything I did was selfish. I was at the bottom of a pit. Eva, you could have been a perfect human being and it wouldn't have helped."

"And now?"

He met her gaze, eyes full of sincerity. "Things are very different for me. I'll tell you all about it sometime, but right now, I just need you to know that I love you. I don't want you to go."

She laughed bitterly. "You want me to believe you've had some kind of epiphany, and now everything can go back to the way it was?"

"Not at all," Eugene said fervently. "I *never* want to go back to how things were. Things were terrible! I've needed to do better for a long time. And I don't blame you for not trusting me right now. I wouldn't either. I've let you down, over and over." He searched her sweet face, which he knew would only grow more elegant with age. "And though it's really going to shoot my case in the foot, and maybe even get me kicked out of here, I'm going to come clean to you about something else…"

A look of fear crossed her face.

"I… went out with someone last week. I was a complete idiot to do it. I thought it would make me happy. But instead, all it did was prove to me that… *nobody* holds a candle to you."

Fear was still frozen on Eva's face. "Did… did you sleep with her?"

He shook his head. "No. I'm glad to say I didn't. In fact, I ended up telling her I was married and that I wanted her to forget all about me. And I'm confident that at one point, she seriously wanted to murder me."

Eva looked down. "Was she pretty?"

"Well…" he said, and reached across the sofa to caress her cheek with his hand. "Frankly, it's hard to remember when I'm looking at you. Right now, all I can think about is that this gorgeous woman, right here, has the same last name as me…

447

because she wanted to be my wife." He took her left hand in both of his and tenderly kissed it. "What an honor that is. You've given me everything. I can't take that for granted anymore. I need to give *you* everything. So that's what I'm doing. I don't expect you to come running back to me if you're not ready… I'm just asking for a chance."

She squeezed his hand, flooding him with hope. It was the first positive sign she'd given him. Slowly, she shifted on the cushion and leaned against him. When he put his arms around her, such a warmth and relief filled him that he couldn't hold back tears any longer.

When she heard his sharp inhale, she lifted her head and looked at his face, startled. Her expression softened, and she laid her head back against his chest. The sweet, familiar scent of her filled his mind with memories of her laughter, her witty humor… her kisses. Suddenly, almost like a movie reel, images of Eva over the past month flashed through his brain, forming a picture in his mind. *It was so obvious that only an idiot could've missed it.* He could barely speak.

"I've missed you," he said softly. "I've missed you, and I've missed *out on* you. And it's my own fault." His voice choked with emotion, but he pressed ahead. "Everything I want is right here, and I haven't been paying attention. I should have seen it."

She sat up and looked at him. "What do you mean?"

"You wanted me to quit smoking because you care about me. You're worried about money because you want to be in a safer neighborhood. And you've been working so hard to keep things up around here… but you've had to slow down and sleep more lately, because… you don't feel very good, do you?"

A light of relief shone in her eyes. "No, I don't."

"How could I have missed that you're carrying my baby?"

She let out a sound that was a perfect mixture of a laugh and a sob. "I've wanted to tell you!"

"You mean you wanted to tell that guy you lived with last Wednesday?" he scoffed. "He was a selfish moron. No wonder you couldn't find the right moment."

Eva laugh-sobbed again. "I'm starting to think there's hope for him!"

"Forget him," Eugene said with a little smile. "Marry *me* instead."

She nodded through her tears. "I sure didn't want to do this alone."

"You certainly could have pulled it off. You're amazing. But you won't have to. I don't want to miss another second of our life together."

"So… you're happy about this? I wasn't sure what you'd think."

"Happy?" He laughed. "The love of my life is going to make me a father! I can't think of anything better! I want to go outside and yell it to the whole neighborhood!"

She gasped in delight. "I'm so glad! Well maybe not that last part… I think people already wonder about us. But… I've just… I've been so scared, Gene. I thought maybe…"

"That I never loved you at all, and I was going to leave you for good?"

Her eyes widened. "Actually, yeah."

He cradled her face with both hands and kissed her lips, reveling in their softness. "I'm not going anywhere. I will love you until you're old and adorably wrinkly. And if you lose your marbles, I'll be there to help you look for them."

She giggled.

He kissed her again, finding this time that she responded. It made him dizzy.

She pulled back a few inches. " I can tell you haven't been smoking."

"That's because I don't smoke."

"You quit?!"

"Uhh… it's more like they quit me," he chuckled. "But I'm never looking back. I want to live a long time so I can be there for you. And for her, too. Every day that I can be."

"Her?"

"Our baby girl."

"You think it's a girl?"

"Not only that, but I think she's going to be magnificent. Smart and dazzlingly beautiful, like her mother."

Eva shook her head in amazement. "I've never seen you like this."

"Meeting God will do that to a person."

"This, I need to hear about!"

He grinned. "Want to go for a drive?"

Chapter 29

Vancouver, Washington ~ Present Day

Charlie set two bags of groceries on the kitchen counter. Her feet ached. She'd had to do three wash-and-sets for elderly ladies who came to the salon every Friday, because their usual stylist was out sick today. That was three more than she'd wanted to do, but at least she'd also gotten to do two really interesting colors and a shaggy bob. It hadn't been a completely boring day.

Her phone buzzed. It was a text from Iris:

Landed safely. Home in about an hour.

Charlie tried to remember what Iris had told her about this trip. She'd gone to Arizona for *something*... hiking? Research? She shrugged and sent a quick wink next to a thumbs up. Regardless, it was nice of Iris to let her know. She was a considerate roommate.

Charlie contemplated the bags of groceries and decided against putting them away. Her feet were complaining that she'd already moved each of those items five times in the process of getting them here. None of it was perishable. Her feet were, though. She reached into one bag and snatched a box of cheese crackers and a bottle of iced tea—the kind that Iris found reprehensible—and headed for the sofa. There were comfy cushions and a brand new D.M. Hawthorne novel beckoning her.

She had no sooner kicked off her shoes and sat down than someone knocked at the door.

"Seriously?" she muttered, and stood grumpily. "This better be someone with cookies."

She swung the door open. Her jaw dropped.

Grayson Reynolds stood in the sunlight, his wavy auburn hair and beard looking almost golden. He had his hands stuffed into the pockets of his jeans. His blue-green eyes were gazing at her with an almost shy expression.

"Hi," he said.

She felt her face go pink. "Hi... Gray, right?"

"Yeah..." A quizzical frown crossed his face.

"Iris isn't home yet. I can tell her you stopped by, though."

"Oh, uh... well, it's actually you I came to see."

Charlie looked mystified. "Really? Um... okay, do you want to... come in for a minute?"

"Sure." He stepped awkwardly inside as she turned toward the sofa and plopped down.

"Have a seat!" She offered him her cracker box.

He smiled and shook his head, but sat at the other end of the sofa. "Sorry to drop in on you like this. I was just going past... and I thought I'd stop by and tell you that you were totally right before. We just heard from Iris, and everything you saw was spot on."

"Everything... I saw?"

"Yeah! The clouds, the crazy lady, all of it. But Iris and Will are completely fine. And Gene is home."

Charlie began to laugh.

Gray frowned.

"I'm sorry..." she said, still laughing, "but... *what*? Who's Jean? And what clouds and crazy lady?"

"Oh..." Gray studied her, unable to decide what to say next. Charlie's smile faded. "You're serious?"

"Yeah, I mean... you were so worried when you came over last night. I just thought you'd want to know the outcome of..."

Charlie leaned forward, brows furrowed in bewilderment.

"...your vision," he finished lamely.

"Vision?"

"Yes."

"I came over last night... to your house? But... I don't even know where you live!"

"Across from the school."

"Oh, that's right. You live with your dad. Iris did tell me that." A sudden look of astonishment crossed her face. "Ohhh my gosh, wait a second... is this that trippy forgetting thing that Iris told me about?"

"Shoot." Gray let out a sigh. "I think we should probably back up."

Charlie laughed. "I think that would be wise!"

He squinted at her with deep concentration. "We've met before, right?"

"Just once, on Iris's birthday. You brought some stuff over." Charlie blushed, remembering how she had felt the first time she'd seen him.

"So this makes the second time for you?"

"Yep."

"But you know who I am? I mean... did Iris tell you..."

"That you and your dad are Guardians? Yes. And she is too, now. And she told me about Angus, and the Tree in your yard-slash-cemetery. And the Council. Pretty much all of it."

"Okay. *Good*," he breathed with relief. "That makes things so much simpler. I think Eugene must be the missing piece, here."

"Eugene?"

"Yeah, that makes sense," he mumbled, staring at the carpet.

"Wanna clue me in?"

"Uh, sorry. So, this whole time, while you were talking to Iris about Guardians and Trees, we've been on a timeline that included a man named Eugene. He was lost like Angus was. Iris just helped him get home. That means that officially, he was never here in the first place. Anything about him gets wiped from peoples' memories."

"But you guys and Iris can remember?"

"Right. Only Guardians can retain two different versions of the same time period simultaneously. She probably did tell you about him, actually. She also ran into some trouble down in Arizona and needed some backup. That's where you came in."

Charlie leaned in. "What did I do this time?"

"You were given a vision of what she was facing. It troubled you so much that you came looking for my dad, and the three of us prayed most of the evening. Then you went home."

Charlie sat for a moment in astonishment. "This is so trippy! It's just like when Iris told me I gave Angus a haircut and loaned her my car! I don't remember doing any of that!"

Gray chuckled. "Well, you did. It's a matter of record."

"Dang, man. I feel like this is some kind of Guardian humor, where you guys have a contest to see who can get people to believe they did the craziest things. So far, you're in the lead."

He let out a hearty laugh.

"You're seriously not punking me?"

"I am seriously not punking you."

She gazed at him, still befuddled. "Am I going to remember you coming here today, or am I going to be like Dory the fish with a bad case of amnesia every time you walk up to me?"

He laughed again. "That only happens when a traveler creates a separate timeline and then it gets erased. It's really rare, and there aren't any around right now. You're safe. You'll remember everything about me sitting awkwardly on your couch, as long as you keep it between us and other Guardians."

"Right, no third parties. I do remember that."

He gave her an awkward smile. "I'm a little sad you don't remember last night. I was really looking forward to talking to you about it. And... I dunno, just... talking to you again, in general."

"Really?"

"Yeah, I mean… Iris has told me all about how much faith you've shown her. You've been willing to accept some pretty crazy things—true things—but they would sound unbelievable to most people. I'm not sure you realize how rare that is, to find that in a person. Iris is lucky to have you."

Charlie looked down, afraid if she looked too long at his face, she'd forget what she was saying. "Well I guess it makes up for all the times I harass her, or leave the kitchen a mess."

"I would say so. I mean, I haven't seen what kind of mess we're talking about, but yeah. A friend like you is hard to find."

She smiled shyly. "Thanks."

"I've enjoyed getting to know you, too. Even though you don't remember it."

"I'm sure I enjoyed it, too. In fact, I'm a little mad that I can't remember it!"

"Well, I could tell you all about it. We could grab dinner."

"I'd like that."

"I must warn you," he said with a serious expression, "it could involve glowing commentary about you. I hope you're not squeamish about that kind of thing."

"Please, I'm a hair stylist. I eat glowing commentary for breakfast."

"And you should also know straight up that I'm asking because I want to go out with you. I'm terrible at being smooth. Ask anyone."

"I'm not smooth either. You probably noticed I've been blushing since you got here, because I want to go out with you too."

"Thanks for confirming that."

"You're welcome!" She grinned. "Fessing up to it just made it worse!"

"I can see that!"

She laughed. "Did we just skip all the boring parts of this conversation?"

He grinned. "Life's too short to have boring conversations."

"Oh my gosh, take me to dinner. Right now. Because this just got *so* interesting!"

He laughed. "Didn't you say that Iris is on her way home? You don't want to—"

"Iris who?"

Iris dashed along the cherry-paneled corridor at Rookwood Senior Home, eager to reach the Activities Office before Candace left for the day. She rounded the corner just in time to see Candace rummaging through her massive striped canvas bag for her keys.

"Hey!" Iris puffed, out of breath.

"Hey girl! Right on time, as usual. How was your trip down south?"

"Rainy."

"Really?"

"Yeah, they get some pretty freaky thunderstorms down there. But the trip was a success. I definitely got what I went for. Thanks again for being so flexible about my hours."

"Of course." She stopped rummaging and looked up. "As much as I feel like we can't do without you around here, I know you need to have other stuff going on in your life. You're such a bright girl. I wish we could keep you forever, but I'd be kidding myself to think that's ever gonna happen!"

"What? I love it here!"

"Pfft. I know you do, but that's not the point. You need adventures. And without Will's pastries here anymore, what's really the point of *any* of it?" Candace winked. "So I figure the best way to keep you around longer is to make sure you get to zip off and do crazy things now and then." She took a long sip from her water bottle. "Besides, I had the loveliest visit from your boss while you were gone. He explained how these little excursions sometimes pop up without a lot of prior notice. He made it seem like they can't do without you either!"

"My… boss? He came here to see you?"

"Such a nice man. Anyway, I'm really glad you could make it this afternoon. I have an appointment I can't cancel, and you *know* how I feel about art therapy."

Iris laughed. "Yes, you've told me."

"I mean, it's bad enough at BINGO with the ink daubers."

"Don't worry, Candace. I got it."

"Bless you."

Iris headed toward the door, a thoughtful look on her face. "I'm surprised Gray would come all the way here to talk to you."

"He said his name was Jason. Rather attractive gentleman, I must say."

"Ohhh…"

"He's not… single, by any chance, is he?"

Although Iris actually did enjoy leading group art therapy, she could feel her brain and body beginning to disconnect. Yesterday had been long and stressful, followed by a short night of sleep and another flight. Just realizing that when she'd woken up yesterday, Eugene was still here and they hadn't even found his car yet boggled her mind. She felt like she'd packed a week's worth of events into one day… and she wasn't even the one doing the time traveling!

She'd had just enough time to complete the logs for her trip before rushing over. She hadn't even laid eyes on Charlie since she got back. *I think I'm ready for a nap.*

Iris stared at the art supplies. *What would make for a shorter cleanup today?*

No paint. Would they be happy with just markers? She thought of Betty. *Okay, markers and glitter glue. And baby wipes. Lots of those.*

She set out the supplies and hit the hallways to gather participants. By now, experience had shown her which residents had enough cognitive ability to get something out of art therapy, and which of them considered it a giant nuisance. She hit the back corridors looking for Fred, Doris, Walter, and Betty. She could almost count on First Irene to cover the lobby for her, waving her calendar and calling out the time.

As she passed by a familiar doorway, she half expected to hear the same little voice she always did, calling out for help to locate her missing wedding ring. But no one called out. Iris paused and peeked inside the door. Everything in the room looked different. She checked the name on the door. *Lily Evans? Who's Lily Evans?* Then a realization hit her. Eugene had sat beside Eva in her last moments. Maybe… she had passed away in this timeline, too.

Nurse Kathy walked by.

"Kathy?"

"Yeah, hon?"

"Where's Eva?"

Kathy tilted her head. "Eva who?"

"Eva Thomas?"

"We've never had an Eva Thomas."

"Oh. Okay, sorry. My mistake."

Kathy walked on.

Suddenly, a little woman, no taller than four foot six, came out of the restroom, gleefully flinging water off of her fingers. "Hello, Iris!" she called out. "Have you come to take me to art?"

Without warning, a torrential rush of thoughts came into Iris's mind. Pictures, conversations, and new memories flew by her mind's eye too quickly to register. She gripped the handrail to steady herself. For about ten seconds, she was genuinely afraid she might pass out.

Finally, the pictures stopped. Iris gasped. *What just happened to me?*

"Hello?" The little woman shuffled up to her and took her hand.

Iris looked into her twinkling eyes and took in the sight of her. This was brand new, and familiar at the same time. Lily. Of course! She'd taken Lily to art therapy several times. How could she have forgotten? This had always been Lily's room. There had never been an Eva Thomas living at Rookwood. Just like there had never been an Angus Armstrong here. And yet, there had been.

When they reached the Activity Room, Lily took her usual place at the table and reached for a handful of markers. The people that Iris had already brought were busy rendering their impressions of landscapes, weather, and fried chicken. Several other participants trickled in and sat down. Iris put on some big band music and told them to draw whatever they felt like today. Now, all she had to do was avert chaos for the next hour, catch any marker caps that Betty threw into the air, and remind Walter that nude art was strictly off limits. After that, it was a matter of making sure everyone had a constant supply of clean paper so they didn't switch to tattoos. Cleanup should be quick... she'd brought two full packs of wipes this time, having learned her lesson from last week. Then she'd be home free.

"You're bald, Iris!" Lily cackled.

"Whaddya mean, I'm bald?" Iris teased. "Look at me!"

"No, no. I mean your picture! I need orange."

Iris came and stood behind Lily. On the left side of her page, there were two large blobs of gold glitter. Between them stood a stick figure with only a circle for a head, but it was wearing a crude rendering of blue jeans and a green top, just like she was wearing. On the right side of the page was an enormous tree, covered in red splotches. Iris handed her an orange marker. Lily began to draw long, wavy hair around the circle.

"That's a picture of me?"

Lily smiled up at her. "Yes. You're taking care of this big tree!"

"I am? Well that's a beautiful tree, Lily. I can see why someone would want to take care of it."

"Yes, because someone hurt it!"

Iris felt a stirring in her soul. Something was happening here that she couldn't name.

Lily scribbled more orange hair onto the stick figure, until it appeared to have a wicked case of bedhead. "There."

"Very pretty. I look great! And I love all the glitter in the clouds!"

"Oh, those aren't clouds," Lily corrected her. She pointed with a shaky finger. "This is Brennus." She moved her finger to the other blob of glitter. "This is… I'm-sure."

Iris felt butterflies. "Brennus… and who did you say?"

Lily chuckled. "It's hard to say. He has an accent. It sounds like I'm-sure, or Ahm-sure… something like that. Yes, it's more like Ahm-sure." She lifted the page. "Do you have a refrigerator?"

"Um, yes."

"Stick that on it!" she giggled.

Iris hugged her, overcome with a strange, warm feeling. "Thank you, Lily. It's beautiful."

Behind Iris, Brennus and Aimsir exchanged amused looks. Aimsir winked at Lily, who waved back at him. Brennus laughed.

Iris clocked out and trudged to her little hatchback, already fantasizing about the pillows on her bed. The late February afternoon looked warmer than it felt, but Iris was still glad for the sunshine, knowing that it had made the inside of her car nice and toasty.

As she approached her parking space, she realized that someone was watching her. He was leaning against the door of a burgundy Mustang convertible with its top down. He wore classic jeans and a black Harrington jacket. His silver hair was slicked to one side.

"Still driving that little toy, huh?" he said with a wide grin.

She grinned back. "Y'know, you only rode in it about a week ago, right?"

He chuckled and held his arms out.

She embraced him. "Hi, Gene."

"It's good to see you." He held her at arms' length. "I've had this day marked on the calendar in my head since March of sixty-five. Jason told me not to try to come before now. And I know better than to argue with a Guardian." He winked.

"I'm glad to hear it!" she laughed. "So how was the long way around?"

"It's been a real trip!" he replied. "Wrote twelve books. Had three kids, seven grandkids, two great-grands. One in the oven." He sighed. "Life is good."

"Wow, three kids. Did you name the first one Jennie?"

"Of course. That was Eva's idea. Jennie became a doctor. She's retiring this year. When she moved up here, we came too. Didn't want the grandkids so far away, y'know? So we actually live pretty close to here. Never thought I'd say it, but Tucson's too hot. Our two boys are both up here now too."

"Sounds like you raised a beautiful family, Gene."

"Well…" He smiled. "Eva did most of the work."

"I was just wondering about her today, actually," Iris said. "I noticed we've never had her living here."

"Nope, she's never needed any kind of professional care. She and I, we take care of each other. We go for walks. We're part of a bowling team, and a Mustang club. She went back and finished her nursing degree in sixty-eight… still volunteers at the hospital. She's probably sharper than I am!"

"That's amazing," Iris said.

"Oh, it doesn't really surprise me. Y'know what the research says… being married to someone who loves you helps you keep your marbles!"

"Good to know!" she laughed. "I like my marbles where they are."

"So what about you? Have you married Will yet?"

"Gene!" Iris gasped.

"What?" he laughed. "I'm old. I'm allowed to be blunt!"

"I know it feels like years to you, but I got engaged four days ago. He hasn't even talked to my parents yet!"

"Well, don't wait too long. I can see how great you two are… and you're even better together."

She smiled. "That's what he says, too."

"Smart man."

"We'll work on it. It's just been a busy few days. Had to fix a Tree yesterday, y'know?" She winked at him.

"Man, I can't believe that was yesterday for you. But I still remember it like it was yesterday. And I just…" He lifted his wrinkled face. "I just want to thank you. I'll never forget what you did for me, as long as I live. Probably even longer than that."

She smiled. "I'm happy I could be there to help."

He embraced her again. "Bless you, dear girl." He touched her cheek, and then turned to open his car door. "Oh, wait… could you help me with one more thing?"

"Sure, what's up?"

"Could you use your telephone to send a picture of me to Gabe Iwila over the interwebs? That day we found this car in a scrap heap, I promised him that if I ever got home, I'd send him a photograph of me standing next to it. I want to keep that promise."

She chuckled and pulled out her phone. She took several steps back. "Smile!"

She attached the picture to an email and sent it off within twenty seconds.

"What's it doing?" he asked, leaning over to see her screen.

"It's traveling across the interwebs," she giggled.

Her phone buzzed.

"Oh, it's Gabe! He says… 'No way! Lookin' good, Gene!'"

"I sure like that Indian," Eugene said wryly.

Iris gaped. "Gene, wh—"

"I'm kidding! I never say that anymore! I'm just yanking your chain."

Iris laughed.

"Well, listen. I'd say I'm in the book, but nobody has phone books anymore. So I left my number at the front desk in there for ya. Don't be a stranger."

"Oh, I'll be in touch. You can count on it."

Iris came home to find a sticky note from Charlie on the bathroom mirror:

Out with Gray.
On a DATE.
😃 *WHAT!!*

"Interesting!" she said aloud, then giggled. *I was only gone a day and a half! Clearly, I have some catching up to do.*

Chapter 30

I ris dabbed on some clear lipgloss and then gave herself a final check in the mirror. She turned her cheeks from side to side, making sure there were no telltale signs of cheese powder leftover from the snack she'd just had with Charlie. Whenever she and Charlie were in the same room with snacks, it inevitably turned into a game where they tried to launch whatever it was into the other person's mouth. M&M's had been off-limits since the unfortunate dental debacle of 2010. But thankfully, cheese puffs were soft. The game had made a lot more sense when they were eight. Why they were still doing it fifteen years later, no one but the two of them understood. Will and Grayson would just have to adapt, since they both seemed determined to stick around.

Iris flicked one last crumb out of her hair and straightened. She was wearing a new aqua green cotton dress she'd found on sale. She didn't actually need to shop sale racks anymore, but she found it far more satisfying. And this dress was classic and whimsical. She'd also added her crown pendant with the three irises on it that Angus had designed and her father had given her. Tonight required whatever confidence boost she could muster… she was going to dinner with her parents. Her mother had hinted on the phone that she had a promising lead for her. *Ugh. I already have a promising lead!*

It had been a month since she had returned from Arizona. After the February she'd just had, Iris was grateful that March had been quiet. She'd had a chance to go over her logs and fill in more detail, to the delight of the Council. She had even tackled a few of the missing persons cases in her queue and solved two of them just by doing research in her pajamas—no travel required. One of the travelers was deceased. The other, a twenty year old woman, had been purposely living under the radar. Although she'd been born in 1672 and was now stuck in current day Massachusetts, she had gladly accepted the change, and even become rather tech savvy. When Iris had tracked her down, she'd made a strong case to stay where she was. The Council agreed with Iris that it was better not to interfere.

Will had started his new job at the upscale restaurant by the waterfront. After just three weeks, they'd decided to put him in charge of all desserts and one special entree every weekend, besides his regular duties. He was ecstatic, but he'd had to start going to bed earlier. Even so, he spent as much time as he could with Iris.

And that had been the best part about this month for her— the quiet days she'd been able to spend with Will. She was at peace with the way things were going. After all, they'd gotten off to such a crazy start, and they had conflicting memories about a sizeable chunk of it from when Angus's timeline had been erased. They'd been through death and worse together, and were more in love than ever. But they needed to survive the mundane for a while, too. So as the days grew warmer, full of blossoms and birdsong, they hiked, went to concerts in the park, talked about the Histories, and just enjoyed being alive.

She heard a knock at the door.

"I got it!" Charlie called out.

Iris emerged from her bedroom just as Charlie opened the door.

"Oh, hey Mr. J.!"

"Hello, Charlie. Nice to see you," Finn said cordially. He smiled at Iris with admiration. "There's m'wee bonnie lass. You look like a queen!"

"Thank you." Iris grinned. She never got tired of her father's familiar banter. He'd called her the same set of nicknames since she was a toddler, and it always made her feel loved.

"Ready?"

"Yep!" Iris grabbed her purse and sweater, when she noticed a stray cheese puff lying on the counter. She picked it up and launched it. "Heads up, Charlie!"

Charlie's reaction time was impeccable. She caught it with a crunch and wiggled her eyebrows.

"You two are crazy," Finn chuckled.

They walked out to the car, and Finn opened her door for her.

"Hi, Mum," Iris greeted Heather, who sat primly in the front seat. She wore a pale pink cardigan and pearl earrings.

"Hello, dear. Glad to see you at last!"

Normally, Iris would have felt slight irritation at a dig like that. But today, she just smiled. For a change, Iris could sense the love beneath the comment.

"I've missed you too, Mum."

A look of surprise crossed Heather's face, which morphed into a subtle smile.

"So where are we headed?" Iris asked.

"Newer place down by the river," Finn answered. "Thought we'd give it a go. It's been getting great reviews lately."

"Sounds good." Iris leaned back and crossed her arms, intrigued, but said nothing else. There were dozens of restaurants along the river. Her father could have been referring to any of them.

When they pulled into a parking space along the curb, Iris almost laughed out loud. It *was* the same place Will was working. In fact, he was off work in about an hour.

This ought to be good.

The hostess seated them near a window that had great views in all directions. On one side lay the panoramic scenery of the waterfront; on the other, the elegant dining room and bar, plus a direct line of sight to every person cooking in the kitchen. Iris caught sight of Will's messy-on-purpose brown hair, since it stood a few inches above everyone else's. He was putting something on a part of the stove with a lot of tall flames. She smiled.

"So, uh… any particular reason why you chose this place?" she asked her parents.

"I came here last week with my book club," Heather replied. "Such a lovely spot."

"And… that's the only reason?"

Heather raised her eyebrows innocently. "Why else?"

"Arright." Iris shrugged. "It *is* a nice place." She opened her menu.

"You know my friend Loretta, though…" Heather went on. "She's such a foodie. Watches all the cooking shows. Well, she tried the sticky toffee pudding cake, and she just raved. The chef came out and thanked her personally, so of course she was over the moon about that."

Iris chuckled. "I see."

"Such a well-spoken young man. And I have to say, his lavender honey cake is superb."

"Is it, now?"

"Well that's a very technical thing to make, according to Loretta!"

"I'll have to try it, then!" Iris agreed, enjoying the look on her mother's face.

"My dear," Finn said to Heather, "it's obvious there's something on your mind, so why don't you come out with it?"

"Nothing at all!" Heather said. "I just thought he was a nice, intelligent man, and Iris might enjoy the desserts. And if we happen to see him again…"

"The lass has told us she's arready seein' someone."

"There's no harm in saying hello. Iris likes chefs!"

"Mum, I've dated *two*. And one of them barely counted." Iris looked back at her menu, scanning the dessert section. She smiled. With only one exception, she'd tasted every one of them. She'd been present when three of them were invented. Suddenly, she decided to play along. She looked back at her mother.

"Actually, you're right, Mum. I love chefs. I just think it'd be nice to marry a man who can cook, y'know?"

Heather gaped at her for a few seconds. "Did you just say 'marry'? I thought you were all about career these days."

Iris shook her head. "A girl has to think about the future."

Finn raised an eyebrow at her sudden change of rhetoric. She gave him an impish smile.

He suppressed a chuckle and raised his menu high enough to shield his face from view.

"That's sensible, I must say," Heather said. "And that man from work you were dating… you never did plan a time to bring him round. Are you even seein' him anymore?"

"Well… y'know… I wanted to give it more time… find out if he was a keeper. But I'm certainly interested in seeing who *you* think would be suitable!"

Heather eyed her with a doubtful expression. "Since when?"

"I've always known you've had my best interests at heart, Mum," Iris said sincerely.

"That's very true. I'm glad you can see that."

"Absolutely." Iris nodded. "And if you think this guy is so fabulous after only meeting him once, it seems like I should at least take a look, right?"

"My goodness, now you're making me sound like I'm trying to get you into an arranged marriage or something."

"Nope," Iris chuckled. "I just trust my mother's good taste. That's all."

Finn's menu was shaking slightly with his poor attempt to conceal his pent up giggles.

"Well for heaven's sake, let's not get carried away," Heather said, straightening her shoulders and returning to her menu. "We're just going to say hello, after all."

They enjoyed a surprisingly pleasant conversation over dinner. Iris's concession seemed to have softened her mother, inspiring her to offer less "constructive feedback" and ask more questions about her daughter than Iris could remember her doing in a long time.

All three of them had ordered tonight's special, which bore the telltale title of "Angels with Bagpipes." It was a twist on classic haggis and root vegetables. But instead of the traditional recipe, whose ingredients Will had been disgruntled to learn aren't even legal to purchase in the U.S., this was made of lamb and spiced oats, and served with a delicious buttery sauce over the creamiest pureed neeps and tatties she'd ever tasted. Halfway into that, it hardly mattered to any of them what the conversation was about.

But after a dessert of sticky toffee pudding cake, Heather had also made good on her promise to pass her sincerest compliments to the chef. True to form, the tall, handsome chef came around the bar into the dining room five minutes later. Will had taken off his stained apron and left behind the towel he always kept on his left shoulder, leaving a perfectly crisp, white chef jacket with the sleeves rolled up to the elbows.

Iris saw him pause about ten feet from their table, taking in the scene. She gave him a shrug and a wry smile, answering the question he'd asked her on the phone earlier this afternoon: "So where are your parents taking you to dinner?" She could see him laugh a little, then straighten. He didn't hesitate for long.

"So my server tells me there are some true Scottish natives here tonight!" he said. "I hope you enjoyed your meal."

"Aye, it was brilliant!" Finn replied. "Tasted just like home."

"Thank you," Will said. "I hope you paired it with one of our Scotch whiskies. Really makes it pop."

"That I did!" He lifted his glass. "At my daughter's suggestion."

Will nodded to Iris. "She has excellent taste."

"So that was your recipe as well?" Heather asked him. "Because I'd heard you were more the dessert person."

"Both, yes," he replied. "It's nice to see you again. I remember you from last week. Heather, isn't it?"

"Yes. You have an excellent memory!" Heather grinned and fiddled with her pearl necklace.

"And you must be Finn," Will said, offering his hand. "Iris has told me so much about you both."

Finn shook Will's hand with a look of astonishment, while Heather froze, wide-eyed.

Iris burst out laughing. "Mum and Dad, this is Will Donovan."

"Is he now?" Heather breathed, eyes wide.

"*Very* pleased to meet you, young man," Finn chuckled.

"You both as well," Will replied warmly. "Well, I'm just about at the end of my shift, so I have some things to wrap up. But I'd love to meet with both of you very soon. I think it's time we got to know each other, since I'm in love with your daughter."

Finn and Heather both stared at Will, speechless.

Iris went pink in the face, but smiled proudly at him.

Finn was the first to find his voice. "We're free the rest of the evening, if you'd care to stop by."

"I'd love that," Will agreed. "In fact, I'll give Iris a ride, if I may. That way she can give me directions."

"You may indeed!" Finn laughed.

Will smiled, then stooped down to kiss Iris on the cheek. "See you in ten minutes."

Heather watched him walk back into the kitchen, then turned to Iris, her face full of awe.

Iris smiled. "Do you like him?"

Heather beamed. "Well done, you!"

Iris and Will climbed into his truck and looked at each other before bursting into laughter.

"That was insane," he chuckled. "Of all the ways to meet your parents…"

"Yeah, I really didn't see that one coming. But y'know, I don't think there could have been a better way! You had them totally impressed before they even laid eyes on you!"

"Whew," he sighed. "First big moment, and it went well. Let's see how long I can skate by on a great first impression."

"I'd say indefinitely. After all, you made a great first impression on me, and it's still having quite the effect."

He smiled and kissed her hand. Then he let out a big breath. "Okay. Evening with your parents. I can do this." He turned to face her. "I think we should make a quick stop at my place first. I smell like haggis."

"How is that a bad thing?"

He laughed. "I'll just change clothes real fast. And there's something I want to get."

"Arright. My mom won't mind, anyway. If we get there too quickly, she'll automatically assume you were either speeding or trying to avoid being alone with me."

"We can't have that."

"Not at all."

The drive to Will's place was quick, with little traffic. Will wondered aloud what Finn and Heather would want to talk about, and Iris reminded him that the anticipation was always worse than the actual torture.

She sat on his sofa, flipping through a recipe-centric magazine for five minutes while he changed.

He emerged with a look of uncertainty. "Does this shirt say 'I'm cool' or does it say 'I'm trying too hard'?"

She smiled. "Neither. It says, 'I'm Will, and I don't need my shirt to say things.'"

"That works for me." He came and sat beside her.

"Hmm," she said. "Actually, you do smell better now."

"Told you," he laughed. "So you really think they liked me, huh?"

"Heck, yes."

"I was thinking I should ask for their blessing."

"That's very traditional of you, but I think their blessing is now a foregone conclusion."

"In that case, I have something for you." He opened the drawer on the coffee table and pulled out a small box. "I ordered it a month ago, but it just arrived. I wanted to give it to you for my birthday."

"For *your* birthday?" Iris looked at him with a quizzical smile. "Your birthday isn't until July eighteenth. Oh my gosh, I just realized that you and Angus have the same birthday!"

He smiled.

"Sorry, not the point," she giggled. "So you want me to open it early?"

"I really think you'll want to."

"Okay…" She opened the box, and gasped. Inside lay the most breathtaking piece of artwork she'd ever seen—a heart shaped diamond set into a band of rose gold vines and leaves twisted into elegant Celtic trinity knots, one on each side. Nestled above it was a thinner band which placed a perfect crown on top of the heart.

"Will," she breathed. "It's… perfect!"

"I'm so glad you like it," he said. "I actually designed it myself. I wanted it to be one of a kind, like you."

She admired the fiery points of brilliance that danced in the lamplight before meeting his eyes. "I can't imagine anything more perfect."

"Neither can I," he said, gazing at her. He knelt in front of her. "Are you busy on July eighteenth? Because if you're free that day, I'd love to marry you."

She rested her hands on the back of his neck, and stroked his hair. "I wish today was July seventeenth," she murmured. "Because I can't wait to marry you."

His kiss was gentle and lingering, full of tenderness.

"Do you want to wait until I talk to your parents before you put this ring on?"

She smiled. "Definitely not."

The End

Epilogue

Iris sat on her bed, bathed in the blue glow of her laptop screen, logging the final details of her conversations with Eliza, the stranded traveler who had decided to make a new life for herself in Massachusetts. Iris copied and pasted the Council's final recommendation and Eliza's written response at the bottom of the page, just to complete the record.

She sighed. *Time for bed.*

She gazed down at her hand, admiring the sparkle of the exquisite ring she was still getting used to, and relishing the warmth that came over her soul when she thought of the man who had designed it for her.

An email notification flashed on her screen. It was marked "urgent." She poked the screen and read the message that popped up. Her brow furrowed.

What was that again?

She scanned through it three more times, just to make sure she'd read it correctly. For the most part, it was a pretty typical sounding email from a Guardian many time zones away. He'd found someone out of his time and was requesting her involvement. Not a problem. However, it was the last part of the email that had her stumped:

> "He won't be in the database as missing, because he hasn't been born yet. The day he damaged the Tree is still in the future… Any idea how to proceed?"

To be continued...

Note to the Reader

I'm honored that you've traveled with me this far! It's my hope that these stories are opening your imagination and helping you think think BIG about God and His kingdom. I want all of us to have a renewed fire within us to find out who God is, how amazing He is, and how complex His world is, both the seen and unseen aspects of it. His word says some pretty crazy things, but let's not shy away from that. Instead, I pray that those truths inform how you step out into the world and walk with the people around you. It's so crucial that we not waste a single moment of our lives being anything other than God's poetry, whom He joined to Himself and destined for great things, even before we were born (Ephesians 2:10)! If you have not yet experienced the mind-blowing love that God wants to lavish on you, I urge you to boldly see for yourself what He has to say in His word. Start with the book of John—it's one of my favorites!

Lisa Rae Morris

P.S. While the characters in this story are fictitious, every single miracle and supernatural manifestation in this novel is based on real, documented occurrences… yep, every single one. But let's not be surprised by that…

> *"I tell you this timeless truth: The person who follows me in faith, believing in me, will do the same mighty miracles that I do—even greater miracles than these, because I go to be with my Father."* —Jesus (John 14:12 - TPT)

In God's kingdom, reality is so much better than fiction.

Acknowledgments

The Three—Yahweh the Father; His Son, Yeshua the Anointed One; and the Promised Holy Spirit. May the eyes of our hearts be flooded with light, so that we can be ever more aware of your heartbeat, the majesty of your love, and the transfiguring power of your presence.

Raymond—My favorite human. Thank you for making this book possible. I love you. I said it last time, and it's even truer now! I love that you get mad when I blurt out spoilers. Best compliment EVER.

My wonderful kiddos—Thank you for your endless enthusiasm for this story. Reading this book to you chapter by chapter during its creation was nothing short of magical. I'll never forget that special time with you. Be fearless faith warriors—you're rolling with some big guns!

Mutzer—You're my favorite research and editing buddy! Seriously, I didn't want to wash Sedona out of my coat.

Dear friends—Thank you for sharing this journey with me by contributing your time, influence, support, critique, and encouragement (and in some cases, inspiring a character):
Gabe & Brittany Moreno, Daniel Fusco, Evie Poythress, Hannah Rothwell, Kathy Hanson, Thomas Hanson, Michelle "Smelly" Johnson, Rachel & Tyler Reinhardt, Denise Long, Angela Swingle, Ronda Butterfield, Kerry Keast, Lauren Glasgow, Rhonda Bolling, Judy Coleman, Faye Bryant, Missy Maxwell Worton, Martyn Wood, and Kary Oberbrunner.

Time Tree Chronicles Facebook Group—You guys are amazing! Thank you for helping me shape this book into something even better than I could have imagined!

Brian Orme — For inspiring the character Jason Reynolds, and for your faithfulness to God's word. You've helped me take the Scriptures as logically and fearlessly as I should have from the very beginning. Everyone go see him at www.iborme.com!

Want
More?

**Follow Iris
on Instagram:
thatirisjacobs**

Join the Time Tree
Chronicles  Group
for discussions &
giveaways. Contribute your
ideas to future books!

Visit
LisaRaeMorris.com

for updates and
extra goodies!

Made in United States
North Haven, CT
14 March 2023

34014230R00296